BONE OF MY BONES

It was a cold day [...]
the trees and blew the [...]
tiny drifts. A small [...]
through the forest. [...]
ice tumbled over the [...]
lung majestically on [...]
the atmosphere an a[...]

But all was not [...]
of nature. A young [...]
a moss-covered roc[...]
the shallow depth [...]
Her face was glum, [...]
worn, and her tired [...]
hard work was grad[...]
youth. To see her ey[...]

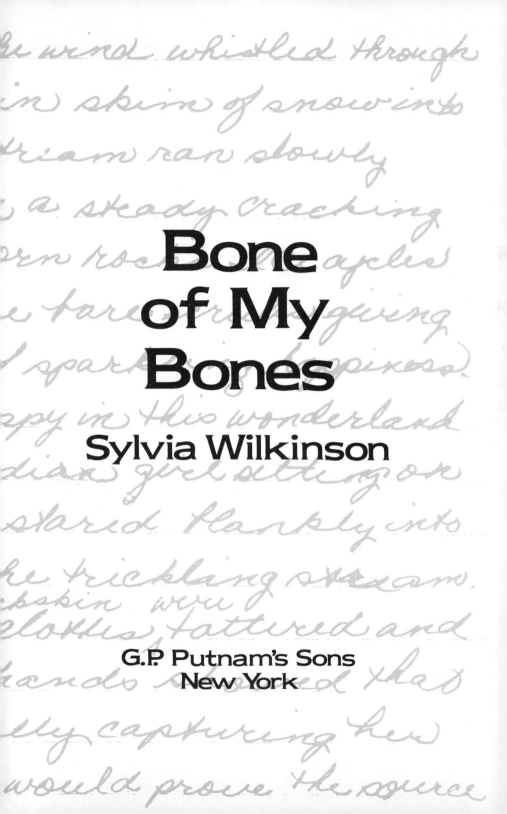

Bone
of My
Bones

Sylvia Wilkinson

G.P. Putnam's Sons
New York

The text of this book is set in 10 point Times Roman
and 10 point Melior.

Library of Congress Cataloging in Publication Data

Wilkinson, Sylvia, date.
Bone of my bones.
I. Title.
PS3573.I4426B6   1982   813'.54   81-12053
ISBN 0-399-12628-7   AACR2

PRINTED IN THE UNITED STATES OF AMERICA

I wish to express my gratitude to
the John Simon Guggenheim Memorial Foundation.

And the man said, *This is now bone of my bones, and flesh of my flesh: she shall be called Woman, because she was taken out of Man.*

—Genesis 2:23

The tribe was in danger of invaa[...]
[...]at its chief was dead. Little Star's
[t]welve year old brother was suppose[...]
[t]he next chief. Realizing this the[y]
were trying to think of a solution to [it].
[L]ittle Star was [afraid] they were goin[g]
[...]r, her mother, [her brother], and her
[...]nd choose one of their strongest [...]
[ta]ke his place. This would probably
[...] the tribe, but from the start it
[w]as disliked. Nothing could be do[ne]
[...]hen her husband was chief, but
[...]hat he was dead they would ha[ve]
[...]nd a home elsewhere. They ha[d]
[...] go and no one to turn to. Her moth[er]
[...]mily was killed when the Apach[e]
[at]tacked the wagon train, and [her]
[...]ther's parents had died leaving
[a] brother who was killed in the s[...]
[He]r life had been hard and frie[...]

I built the box real careful with scraps out of the kindling pile. I didn't have any way to miter the corners so I covered the outside with tar paper and the inside with velvet I got out of Mama's quilt scraps. It looked like a square casket about big enough for a baby. I made it to be a time capsule. In it I put a three-cent stamp and a postmarked airmail, a penny and a nickel, a tiny glass horse statue from Japan, a deck of Old Maid cards, three folded-up horse drawings—one with colored pencils—and a headline from the newspaper Mama saved since the war ended: HITLER DEAD. BLOWN UP WITH WIFE OF ONE DAY. I put in three Red Hots and a Mary Jane which I went back in and took out because I was afraid ants would get in after them and mess up the other stuff. When we studied about Hitler in school, I took all the stamps with his head on them out of my stamp book because I couldn't stand to look at him, but I put them in the box. And I put in a Blue Horse notebook, my favorite kind to write in. My notebook was the most important thing that I had made the box to fit.

My name is Ella Ruth Higgins and it is 1950 the year I will be ten years old. I live in Summit, North Carolina and at the time I am burying this time capsule, the country is called the United States of America. We do not have much money (money is what you buy things with—the two round metal things in here) so there isn't much I can put in this box for you except the glass horse my big brother got me at the fair (glass is made from hot sand I think), an extra pack of Old Maid cards I got for Christmas (a game that has one old ugly lady that you are if you lose), and some Red Hots which is what we kids like but they almost hurt more than they taste good, and a Mary Jane that gets stuck in your teeth and pulls out your fillings if you have them (fillings are metal stuck in holes in your teeth where rotten places used to be). I hope they don't make bugs get in this box. If the candy isn't here, you can betcha that is what happened to it. It might not be fit to eat by the time you find this anyway, but I heard there were seeds in the Pyramids that would grow. I put in some stamps from the United States (the good country in the war) and from Germany (one of the bad countries). The man whose picture is on them is dead, thank goodness. I hope you can understand me. This is pretty hard to do not knowing how much I need to explain. But by the time you find this my bones will be dust and my childrens childrens childrens might be too.

The real reason I am writing this is to tell you the story of Little Star. She is a Croatan Indian, and the white people are very cruel to her. The Indians were here in the United States first, before me and before you and whoever might come to take over from you. Except for the Lone Ranger and Red Ryder who have friends called Tonto and Little Beaver, the cowboys all kill Indians that are called savage redskins. Its like if you decided to build your house right in my backyard and acted like it was yours first. I would get mad and do things to try to make you move away. At least thats the way I see it.

Starrie hid in the woods when the white man made her tribe march west. She is cripple but not so bad she can't get around, and just so you would notice it and maybe make fun if you were mean. This is one of her stories, how she got cripple. I am still just thinking about that one because there are a lot of ways it could have happened and I can't decide. Everyday when I imagine I ride my horse and every night when I get in bed, I think of new stories for Starrie and I am putting them in here. Her horse is named Blaze and her dog is Fang. Starrie is pretty in a wild sort of way. She wears a buckskin dress and goes barefoot in summer and wears moccasins in winter. Her hair is inky black and was never cut. She can sit on it. Mama took me in for a trim and before I could tell the lady she was mixed up, I saw pieces of it eight inches long hit the floor. I was too shamefaced to tell her, you want the truth. Daddy said I deserved to have my head shaved, not speaking up for myself. Then I let her burn blisters on my head with these pad things putting in curls that turned to frizz and made my short ugly hair stand out like an awning. Maybe Daddy is right about me. I will almost wet my pants before I will get the nerve to ask where the bathroom is. But I want to stay on Starries story. I won't mark out what I wrote because you might be interested to know how different we are.

I showed my teacher one of my stories where Starrie is listening to her grandmas stories and the old woman is picking ticks off her dog while the dog licks the sores on her legs. The old woman and the dog look alike, you know how people do sometimes look like their dogs. They both have crooked legs and jaws that hang. My teacher said that was disgusting about the ticks and the sores and I told her that the old lady was getting the ones the dog couldn't reach and that my grandma said if you let a dog lick your sores, they would not get infected and get well quicker. Anyway my teacher

14

tore that story up right in front of me and said for me to write what she told me to write which is why I am putting these stories in here.

The main thing I remember when I was five years old was when I told Mrs. Albright that the President was dead. I didn't know anything about the President except Daddy and my big brother, Matthew, who doesn't live with us, got in a fight over him. Daddy said, "Don't you think for a minute that S.O.B. didn't know the Japs were coming. He just turned his back and let them blow our ships to kingdom come, then come out saying they were the ones who started it."

"They did start it, Daddy," Matthew argued. Then Daddy slammed his fist on the table.

"The goddamn President sold us out," he yelled.

"Out of what?" I asked.

"Shut up, Ella Ruth," Matthew said. I was glad he didn't live with us, thinking he could boss me around.

I didn't think Daddy cared for the President one way or the other, but as soon as he heard he was dead, he slammed his fist on the radio to make it quit buzzing and made me go to tell Mrs. Albright. She had a blue car with back windows that had turned yellow and crackled all over like sugar candy. The back fender had a dent like a basketball that needed air. I saw her do that when she hit the milk truck and broke his bottles. Mama wouldn't let me go out of the yard without shoes because she didn't get up all the glass. Mama didn't know, but I saw Daddy give Mrs. Albright the gas stamps out of my ration book in trade for her likker stamps.

Mrs. Albright was in her greenhouse. I didn't knock because I didn't think a greenhouse was the same as a house. I cracked the door.

"Mrs. Albright?"

She was fussing over some tomato plants. They were overloaded with red pear-shaped tomatoes.

"Think they were poison. I heard about a man kept tomatoes with him and ate them just to frighten people."

She pointed her finger at me. "Did you know that 'bout maters? That folks once believed them to be pisen?" She changed to the country way of saying things to talk to me like I didn't have enough sense to know what she meant when she said it right. Acted like I was white trash or a colored person and she could only talk right when she was talking to herself.

"No ma'am, I didn't."

It felt like summer inside the glass house.

15

"Well, John Bleems acts just like them old fools. Close the door behind you."

She began throwing the tomatoes into a basket. I saw a fat one split open, big red lips saying oh-h-h-h and drooling.

"Just because these are *pear-shaped*, not *round*." Her eyes became very round. "He thinks that people won't eat them in the restaurant. Oh, I could kick myself for not planting the regular seeds. Buy them because of a fancy picture on the package."

She kicked the basket of tomatoes. I felt bad they were getting such rough treatment. I didn't like her at all.

"So I have to make juice, or soup, or throw them in my succotash and eat tomatoes till they run out my ears . . ."

I stared at her and imagined red juice pouring out of her ears and splashing down her skinny arms. I must have made a face. She stopped talking and her round eyes turned to slits.

"Your mama know you're over here bothering me?"

"Yes, ma'am."

I don't know why I didn't tell her right then what I'd come to say. She grunted, then went back to tearing the tomatoes off the plants. She slapped three of them in my hands and said, "Here, get on back home and take these to your mama. And go straight home and don't lay them down someplace and forget them. Git!"

I looked at the tomatoes nobody wanted.

"Mrs. Albright," I blurted.

"What!" Her head jerked up.

"The President is dead."

"What! What?" She grabbed my shoulders. I felt like a pear-shaped tomato.

"The President is dead, dead, dead."

I don't know why, but I said it like the preacher. I shouldn't have because she slapped me. It wasn't a solid hit since she lost her balance. I turned and ran home, not shutting the door behind me, forgetting to look both ways, but I was lucky because a car didn't hit me. I dropped all three tomatoes in the street. I ran into the house and when I was stopped inside, I was crying.

"Honey, what is it?"

It was Mama. Daddy was still bent over the radio, hitting it when it whistled. I put my head in Mama's lap that smelled like the potatoes she'd been peeling. I could barely feel the place Mrs. Albright had hit me. I rubbed it with my fist to make it red.

"She hit me, Mama."

"What? That old fool hit you? Maynard, that damned old fool hit Ella Ruth. Why did she hit you, honey? I'll break her scrawny old neck."

16

"Because I told her the President was dead."

Mama whispered, "Idiot," and held me tighter. "Maynard, you go give that old fool a piece of my mind. You never should have sent this child over to a crazy person's house."

I thought a minute, not sure if I would say it. I decided to because Daddy wasn't listening.

"Why did she hit me, Mama? I didn't kill him."

Mama squeezed me tighter. I was getting hot because too much of her body was touching me.

"You never killed one living thing. He was just an old beat up cripple man had no business still trying to be President. And he just died, that's all. Patricia Albright will join him soon enough."

Mama rocked me for a while like I was a baby. I watched out the door until all three tomatoes got run over, then I climbed down. At that point in my life, so far as I knew, it was true: I had never killed one living thing.

Next I want to tell about what happened to my duck and my doll. I was seven years old when I got my doll. Her whole name was Saint Nicholas. Her head was hard like a ball that wouldn't bounce and her arms dangled. I could mash her stomach in with my thumb. It was her arms that weren't like they were supposed to be in real life. They were like the ones on old Rubus down at the feed store. Saint Nick and Rubus could turn their arms around backward. Except Rubus had one good arm that looked like he got the arm from somebody else. He bent it and made a muscle and told me he stole it off Joe Louis. Sometimes I thought of Saint Nick as a poor little cripple child that God wanted me to look after. If I laid on top of her, she got almost as warm as alive.

I wished I hadn't spilled my milk on her because she smelled like baby throwup. Daddy painted her a new face where the old one rubbed off. He tried hard. He painted show cards down at Simon's and he was real good at putting sparkles on the letters. But Saint Nick's face didn't come out so good since he said he didn't have anything to go by. After that she looked scared all the time. Mama told me I better make a lot over him because he painted the new face.

I thought it might be her eyebrows curved too much so I scratched them off and he got so mad I thought he was going crazy. He shook me back and forth till I felt like a rag in a dog's mouth. Then I fell down in the truck when we were driving to Grandma Higgins's and split her head wide open.

I took Saint Nick in my arms and jumped off the bed in my room and pretended: *I am Tarzan, King of the Apes. I sail through the tops of trees to escape the evil hunters who are trying to capture Nkima. They'll put her in a cage in a zoo. She is happy in her jungle home with her friends and doesn't want human beings staring at her and laughing. When she was just a little baby, she fell from a treetop and cracked her skull, but I saved her and she is my friend for life.*

Daddy said don't ask him to glue the damn thing up. My feelings were real hurt. I told him I'd just ask Santa Claus for a new one. And he said, "You just do that," real ugly. I felt bad after I said that because you don't just break a Saint Nick and ask for a new one. Anything else I got I could, but not her.

Not long after that, Christmas came and I got Baby Ruth. I asked for new clothes for Saint Nick, but I didn't get them. Daddy saw Baby Ruth in Simon's and played with her workings until the lady who waited on you frowned at him.

When I saw Baby Ruth Christmas morning, I knew there was no Santa Claus. Only my daddy would have picked a doll baby like that for me, with a key in her stomach that made her say: "My name is Baby Ruth—Please pick me up—bar-r-r-k."

"Wind it up," he kept saying, after I was tired of hearing it. So he wound it up and she talked. She never seemed like a doll baby, just a windup talking thing put in a doll's body. I didn't like being told that had to be her name. I had a good name on my mind, Little Star. Even if I put on her dress, that key stuck up in her middle.

I don't remember when I did it, but I took it apart, good and apart, long after my daddy had lost interest in it and after the voice had got so scratchy you had to know ahead what she was saying, like the radio at night. The whole middle was a little record player. I made it work for a while outside before it broke for good. And there was ugly Baby Ruth, with a hole in her stomach. I was glad I didn't use up Little Star on her.

But it all led to Oscar Roscoe. He was my Easter duck, a white one when he grew up. When he was a yeller baby, he would cry his heart out every time I left him. Daddy told me ducks think the first thing they see is their mama.

I couldn't tiptoe away without him squawking. He was happiest of all sitting on my stomach. Sometimes he forgot where he was and doodooed on me and I had to stretch out my undershirt under the outside spigot. There got to be times when I had to be away from him. That's when I thought of Baby Ruth and made Oscar Roscoe a nest in her stomach. He would sleep all night in there without a peep if I left him with Mama's Baby Ben wound up to have a heart beating. Even after he had all his white feathers, he still slept on her and plastered her face with duck do-do.

Once I made Oscar Roscoe eat about twenty corn worms. I admit

18

I didn't know about ducks. Ducks don't eat worms. Unless you make them. I had about two hundred fresh ears of corn to shuck for Mama. The sticky worms were wedged in the ears where they had eaten out the grains. I kept calling my duck stupid and cramming them in his mouth, rubbing his neck until he swallowed them, telling him he shouldn't pass up such a treat because it wasn't every day he'd get such fat corn worms. Come winter he'd want a fat juicy worm as much as I'd want a fat juicy ear of corn. Now that I know better, I can lie awake at night and make my stomach flip thinking of my insides filling up with worms. Then I learned my last lesson about ducks.

He had a bad foot. I was looking so forward to setting him on the pond where he could swim with that foot down under the water and not stumble. He could bob along good in the commode till he got too big. Floating on the water he looked normal.

"That was a real stupid thing, setting him out on that pond," Daddy told me, pointing his skinny finger in my face. "You oughta known animals don't put up with weakness. Mother bird has a messed up baby, she kicks it out of the nest. That's why animals and bugs have so many extra babies so just the tough ones make it. It takes human beings to waste their time and money on cripples."

Then he took out one of his newspaper clippings from his cardboard box and made me listen to him read.

"Dr. Gustav Schuebbe, head of the Nazi Annihilation Institute at Kiev, Germany, said this: 'I still maintain that, just as one prunes a tree—by removing old, undesirable branches in the spring—so for its own interest a certain hygienical supervision of the body of a people is necessary from time to time.'"

I said I thought a prune was a black thing you ate, chewy if it was raw, mushy if it was cooked with a seed to suck on. He said I was too old to be so ignorant. I was eight.

"Hitler just got his ideas crossed, see," Daddy went on. "He should have put them Jews to work like we did the niggers. Too much trouble to kill them all. Although I can see his point, killing them off before there's so many of them. Should have sent them in the ovens with a nigger under each arm." Then he giggled and looked at me funny. "You want to know what prune means?"

I said no.

"Dr. Schuebbe killed 21,000 human beings in nine months. Do you understand that? Killed. Pruning means removing something, like your Mama cut the dead limbs off the apple tree."

I had helped her. I painted the sores with tar so the tree wouldn't bleed and so bugs wouldn't get in. Mama would look at each sore, frowning when she saw some green in the brown wood.

"That one might have made it." She shook her head. "It had a

19

little life left." Mama didn't even like pruning off half dead tree limbs.

Mama shook her head and made a sad humming sound. "A doctor," she said. "The shame of it being a doctor supposed to take care of folks."

Mama said folks and Daddy said human beings.

"He took care of them," Daddy laughed. Then he got serious and said, "He picked out the ones worth saving and took care of all the puny, cripple morons that drain a society. Survival of the fittest. One rotten apple'll spoil the barrel. Saving all the weak born weakens a whole race of people."

Mama would straighten and prop a puny tomato plant and Daddy would walk behind her and pull it up.

Finally when he stopped to catch his breath, Mama threw words against him that left him wobbling like the scarecrow in Mrs. Albright's garden.

"Didn't *you* have rheumatic fever as a child, Maynard?"

When I went down to Dr. Horace Sanders's pond with Oscar Roscoe, a lot of white ducks were already there because everybody's Easter ducks had grown up. He saw them and started wiggling and squawking and they squawked back at him. The whole group turned and moved towards us, as perfectly together as the ducks in a shooting gallery. Oscar Roscoe jumped out of my arms and went paddling out to make friends.

Suddenly they all came at him and jumped on him. I screamed for him to come back. It was hard to tell which was him in all the white feathers and yellow beaks.

Me and Oscar Roscoe both almost drowned before I got him out. It was October and I got a rotten cold from getting wet. One of the big ducks came at me and beat on me with his beak like a stick. He pecked the blood out of my arm, then he chased me until I ran across the street into the woods. I carried Oscar Roscoe who felt ten times as heavy. I laid on the ground for a long time and Oscar Roscoe kept trying to squirm away. I told him the bad guys weren't still after him, but you can't talk to a dumb duck.

While I was sick, Daddy told me he gave Oscar Roscoe to a lady to cook. He said he was too big and nasty to stay in the house in the winter. While I had my fever, I dreamed a dog took me in his mouth and shook me back and forth. I would cough so hard I would fall out of my bed, and Mama and Daddy would lift me back in. I scratched at the floor because the wood felt cool under my body. Anyway, when I got well, my duck was gone. Sanders's pond froze and the other white ducks went away one by one. Mama said foxes got them.

At first I hoped that big mean one got picked to the bones. Then I saw a pile of bones and white feathers that the fox had left by the water. The beak and feet looked like rubber parts from a toy.

When I was crying about my duck, Mama sat on my bed and patted me. "Don't worry, Ella Ruth, honey. Come Easter and I'll get you a brand new pretty little yeller duck."

Last summer when I was still eight, I got three things I'm going to keep the rest of my life. I put the ring in my time capsule and the gun under my bed. The third thing was a round white scar in the back of my leg that Mama thought I got when I fell down in the woods. She said what she always says: "It'll get well before you get married."

Me and Al and Stevie went to the picture show together every Saturday. All they ever talked about was cowboys, cowboys, cowboys. When we got back to my yard, I got a book and acted like they weren't there because I was so mad I could spit. What I was burned up about was that stupid Olive Oyl. Popeye and Olive Oyl and Brutus are lost in the desert. They crawl in the hot sand, Sweet Pea wiggling along in his footie nightshirt like a slug. They are hot and sweaty and their tongues are hanging out. Olive Oyl's hair comes out of the bun and is stringing across her face.

I can't understand why Popeye and Brutus would fight for her. She is so ugly. She looks like the lady on the Old Maid card that doesn't have one in the pack to match it.

Brutus sees a palm tree with a pool beside it.

"An oasis," he grunts.

He runs to it and it disappears. A mirage.

But Brutus's mirage left a glass of water. The glass of water is real.

Popeye snatches it to keep Brutus from drinking it all himself. The two men are arguing about dividing it up when they hear singing. They turn around and Olive Oyl is washing her hair with the glass of water.

That was just so dumb. You know a boy was the one who made that up. If Al and Stevie say one word about look what the dumb girl did, I'm going to kill them. Just let them try to get me to be Olive Oyl when we play Popeye. I couldn't even look at the rest when Popeye sucked the spinach through his pipe. You don't find a stupid can of spinach in the desert. I hate spinach. I hate Olive Oyl even worse.

"Johnny Mack Brown is a fairy."

"Is not."

Al and Stevie started arguing while I was trying to make out a word in my Little Golden Book. There was a fairy and she had a stick that made sparkles like bubble stuff. Fairy Godmother. Mama brought me bubble stuff every time she went to town.

"Is too. Takes him three bounces in the stirrup to get on his horse. And it ain't even the same horse. It's an old half dead one that'll stand still. Then this guy puts on Johnny Mack Brown clothes and that dumb egghead hat and gets on a real horse and makes like he's him."

"That don't make him a fairy."

When I got a new bottle of bubble stuff, Mama would pour part of it into another jar so in case I turned it over, I wouldn't spill it all. Once I turned around and saw my whole bottle full was a slick place in the grass.

"He's a pussy fairy. He gets in a fight. Pow! Pow! And his hat don't even fall off. Hit him for real and his glass jaw'll bust like a light bub."

Sometimes when the wind was still, a bubble would hang in front of my face and get so full of holes that it would go away without popping.

"None of them really gets hit, you dumbhead. Don't make him a pussy fairy because his hat don't fall off."

"The hell he ain't. He's so high pockets he gets his money out with his tongue." Al Sawyer stuck out his tongue and pretended to reach toward his pocket. I closed my book and put it on the steps.

"Hit a bump with his horse and stick his tallywack up his nose."

That was Stevie Green who never talked much. They giggled. Stevie's tallywack was the first one I saw, even before my daddy's, because he was always peeing on things. One day he tried to write his name on a sheet of tin in Mrs. Albright's backyard. Tinkling like the wind hitting a wet limb over the roof. He ran out on the first *E*. The man who wrote Coca-Cola in the sky over the playground never got done with the Cola before the Coca blew away.

I had an imaginary mouse who flew a little airplane. Not Mighty Mouse. He was too much of a goodie-goodie. My mouse didn't mind stealing things for me. He could write *Coca-Cola hits the spot*, perfect. It was a mouse instead of a little person in my airplane. I didn't believe there could be little people. The man could have done it Co-cola and we would have known what he meant.

"Horses don't hit bumps, you dumb ass," Al teased. "They ain't got fucking wheels."

Al made me pitch to him. I couldn't throw overhand because it hit ground before it got there and he cussed me. Then I threw underhand and he made me get closer and closer and he hit one with all of his might, but I just heard the crack. It had hardly left my hand before it hit my chest. I went over like the milk bottle Matthew hit at the fair. It made a lump on my left side. I hid in the bushes and cried, not making noise. I was there a long time because I peeped twice. The lump felt hard. When I looked at it, I saw I had a tittie on one side. My flat nipple got big as a quarter. I looked at the other one. A dime. It went away, but for a long time it was blue, then yellow, like when Stevie painted me with Indian war paint.

"Johnny Mack Brown's hat looks like a nipple."

They giggled again. I wasn't sure if they meant a real one like Stevie's mother who pulled it out in public for Baby Marvin. Or the one on his bottle. The hat looked more like the one on the bottle to me, but that didn't go with their laugh. The one on Stevie's mother was brown, not white, with hair around it in a circle. I giggled because if you climbed up and looked from behind her, it looked like Baby Marvin had whiskers.

"Johnny Mack Brown jumped off a roof to his horse and busted his balls."

Al busted a persimmon against a tree and the insides hung on the bark like guts. Stevie made himself burp.

Stevie and Al giggled more when I giggled. They liked for me to laugh when they talked dirty though usually I didn't. Stevie buckled his gun belt around his chest and tried to draw his gun with his armpit. He got it out of the holster, but dropped it. A piece broke off.

"Shit." He threw the broken-off piece into the trees.

Stevie had a temper. He loved to have an excuse to get really fighting mad. I could tell he was trying to think of something else to fuss about.

"My old man said no Hadacol. He said it wont nothing but liquid shit." He threw a rock where he'd thrown the piece of his gun. I heard it crack through the leaves like a bullet. I figured someday something would jump out and get us for all the things we threw in Dr. Horace Sanders's woods. "Mama said Hadacol would do him more good than the rot gut he got at Parson's."

Hadacol was giving a cartoon show at the Carolina Theater the next week and to get in, you had to have a box top. Al stole his in Simon's right off the box before old man Simon heard about the show and put them in the glass case behind the counter. Al said it wont like stealing because he didn't get the juice.

"Daddy said he heard it would lock you up," Stevie said.

"Lock you up in what?" I asked.

"Your bowels, dummy." They laughed and I felt dumb, but tried to look snooty.

"Niggers love that stuff," Al added. "Check the garbage on Haiti Alley."

"You dumb as Ella Ruth is. Niggers go to the show."

23

They had their own picture show, but the movie never changed. It was always *The Red Shoes*. There was a poster with a red toeshoe out front. My daddy said, "Red shoes, my ass. White pussy." Mama shut him up for saying ass in front of me.

From the colored balcony in the Carolina Theater, the popcorn boxes made black spots on the screen as they sailed through the light beam. When the screen flashed with bombs on the newsreel, you could see their eyes and teeth up there like stars. We tried to throw things back, only most of it fell back on us.

One Saturday, something wet hit Al on top of his head. Stevie told him a nigger peed on him, and after the show they fought behind Parson's until they got tired. Al said it was a drink, but Stevie said a nigger wouldn't waste a drink.

I had some trouble thinking about when there were cowboys and Indians. At the show it seemed like those things were happening right now. Were they on the same place I'm on right now, right here in Summit? Or were they in another world somewhere? I figured they had to be inside our ball with us or else we wouldn't know about them. When Buster Crabbe went in his spaceship to the other worlds, I wondered how he got out of our ball, if there was a hole in it somewhere for him to fly through like an invisible door and why our air didn't go out that hole.

Mama has a picture on the mantel that she says is me as a baby. I have to believe her, but it is hard. I don't see how those little hands and feet can be the same ones I got now. and how I got in that little washtub on the back porch. But I'll be big as Mama is someday. Buster Crabbe said something about a star being a million times bigger than the world. I know I heard him right because I saw the movie four times. I got to ask Miss Mims because I don't see how they can fit inside our ball if they are that big. I told Stevie and he said I was dumb, that they looked little because they were a long way off. I knew they were a long way off. There are countries on the other side of the ocean and you can look as far as you can see and not see a one of them.

Stevie went home. Later that afternoon me and Al busted bottles at the sawdust pile and were heading home.

"Start running," he said.

"What for?"

"Start running for cover," Al screamed.

I ran, zigzagging back and forth across the road. Something made a tingle inside my chest, like doing something wrong, but my mind wouldn't tell me what it was.

Stevie and Al got a tingle. No, a tickle. They said they would go to the playground and hang from the monkey bars and get a tickle.

24

Then they laughed the dirty laugh, the one when they were talking with words I couldn't understand. Tickle is something dirty, that's for sure.

I heard a shot. It was Al's rifle. He wasn't supposed to really shoot. After the bang I heard the bullet hit the leaves, starting high and going by me, then getting low and thump. It had hit a tree. It was an old rusty gun of his brother's that didn't shoot good.

I stopped and turned around. He was small down the road, but I could see he was putting in another bullet.

"Hey," I yelled. "You weren't supposed to *really* shoot."

I was mad. I wished Stevie was there because he knew better and Al didn't. He was lifting the gun. Then I did stupid. I should have run into the bushes. Stevie would have known to do that, but I just took off down the road, right there in the open. I heard the crack, just like the ball hitting Al's bat, but it hurt at the same time. Hit me like a big rock, and knocked me flat. I skint my elbows when I landed, but it was stinging like a bee bite. I bent my leg around and right in my calf it sat like a bee only the bee was almost all the way in my skin like he had a drill on his head.

I got real mad.

"You dumb fucking asshole bastard, Al."

He came running up and he was scared. He knew I was mad because I wouldn't cuss unless I was. I didn't do it to be cute like he did.

"You bitch bastard fuckhead, Al. You shot me."

"I didn't mean to."

"Horse hockey, you didn't mean to. You didn't mean to shoot nobody fucking else."

"I didn't mean to hit you."

"Don't you know the difference between a real gun and a toy one? First time you ever hit the broad side of a barn and it's my fucking leg."

I didn't mean to cuss my own leg. I could get real tough with Al when Stevie wasn't there.

Me and Al picked at it awhile, trying to get the bullet out. He started crying when blood came around the bullet. I tried to get up and walk like they did in the cowboy movies, but it hurt so bad when I touched my foot down, I couldn't stand it. I had hurt myself a lot worse before, like when I caught my britches leg in my bike chain on Umstead Street Hill, but I had to admit it hurt pretty bad for such a little hole.

Al was crying real hard now and I started to get worried he might go running off. I'd have to crawl twenty miles in the desert sun like Red Ryder and get home with my skin all burned with my clothes ragged and lose a lot of blood. I don't think I'd lost more than about five drops so far, but I had smeared them around to make Al feel bad. I decided not to make him any more scared because I'd never catch him if he took off.

"Tell you what, Al. You go back to the trash pile."

"OK," he sobbed. "Where we busted the bottles."

"Yeah. Now watch out for the glass." Made him feel bad acting like I cared if *he* got hurt. "And watch out for black widows. Take your gun or a stick or something and turn over some boards and find me a wad of spider webs. Get about enough to make a marble. Not a shooter, a regular."

"You keep the gun. I don't want the old thing." He threw it beside me.

While he was gone, I pressed around the bullet like you do a splinter and it came right out and fell on the ground. The leg didn't hurt anymore, but it started bleeding like a son of a bitch. I was cleaning the bullet on my shorts and getting ready to plug the hole back up with it when Al came back.

"Is this enough?"

He could hardly talk he had run so hard. His fingers were twisted with gray webs. I slid over next to the ditch and washed the hole off with my hands. It really stung then, and when I cried out, Al cried louder than me. I saw tadpoles in the water before my blood dirtied it.

I pulled the webs off Al's hands. His hands were hot as fire. I stuck the webs down in the hole and pretty soon it stopped bleeding. Al was a mess, filthy from the trash pile, his face streaked from crying. He had a big scratch on his leg that made my other leg hurt a little in the same place. My shot leg had started to sting again and throb like my heart was where the hole was.

"Does it hurt?"

"Does a bear shit in the woods?"

"I'll give you my Phantom ring."

I couldn't believe it.

"When?"

"When we get up to the house."

"Uh-uh. I want it now."

"Ain't got it."

"Lie like a rug. I seen it when you put your mark in Albright's cement."

He took the ring out of his pocket. The skull still had some cement caught between the crossbones so I washed it out in the blood water.

"Catch them tadpoles out and put them over in that other puddle," I ordered.

26

I watched him take the tadpoles who curled into black dots in his hands.

"Got three that time."

He was starting to feel better as he fished for the tadpoles so I decided to quit being so hard on him.

"Move the eggs, too."

I watched him lift the slimy eggs, their black dotted jelly sliding between his fingers as he crawled to the other pool.

"That OK?" he asked. I nodded. "Does it still hurt much?"

"Yeah, but I'll tell Mama I fell back on a sharp stick."

We walked back to the house. I walked like I was faking a limp, but I couldn't put my weight on my foot. I carried the rusty rifle because Al was going to leave it. He said he was mad at it for what it did. I wore the Phantom ring and *I was a slick gray man on a white horse with a coon mask on my eyes. My body looked smooth and rubberlike. I looked like a shark. The Lone Ranger has silver bullets, but when the Phantom slugs you, he leaves the mark of the skull.* I wouldn't pretend I was Olive Oyl if hell froze over and pigs could fly and chickens had lips.

I loved my Mama and Daddy, but sometimes when I studied them, I knew I must have been left in a basket on the doorstep. Anybody who knew my mama would know I never could ask her about that because her feelings were so easy to hurt. It hurt her feelings real bad that Matthew hardly ever came to see her. He sent her photos of his two children and she said, "Might as well cut these out of a magazine. Can't bounce a picture on my knee." Matthew drove a big, shiny car Daddy said he couldn't afford. I didn't love him much.

When I was ten we had the windiest March I could remember. As the kites began to appear over Summit, Mama's was always the highest at the end of a knotted string from a winter's supply of cord saved off meat wrappers. The field beside the outhouse was where the best kite straws grew, the hollow ones that were strong enough to hold the butcher paper and flour glue that Mama and I put together every spring. When Mama's hands tied the kite straw corners, her fingertips moved like a lifted-up turtle kicking under his shell.

"We beat 'em all, Ella Ruth. Elizabeth Sawyer's ain't even with the smoke stacks yet and it's already starting to fall."

I saw her heavy body in the field beside our house, as much a part of things on the ground as the trees and rocks.

Mama gave me the string and I felt the kite tug like a bird. When I got dizzy following it with my eyes, I laid on my back and tied the string to my wrist. I watched Al and Stevie's kites, darting blind as bats. Suddenly they fell out of the sky as though they were shot. I smiled a hateful smile; I should have known better. My kite dropped too, let go by the same dead wind, and before I was on my feet to pull it in to safety, it sucked around the phone wire across the street.

Mama came out of the house, panting behind me and before I could get a tear in my eye, she said, "We'll make a better one. Sam Parson's saved me the prettiest pink paper you ever seen. You go round the outhouse and get the straws."

She snapped the string from my trapped kite, winding it around a stick for the next kite, giving up on it like it was no more than a cake she made to get eaten at Sunday dinner. I watched those fingers making rosebuds on a cake, tying strings on a kite, never believing Mama could expect it all to go away. I always felt a hurt when I lost something, even as little as my cat's-eye marble that rolled down the storm drain. Mama gave up like it was the only right thing to do.

I wandered through the outhouse straw garden, looking for straight dry sticks, seeing the ones I turned down for my first kite. The reason we still had an outhouse was because Daddy said the bathroom in the house bound him up. He called it his library and he would read the newspaper in a place where most people couldn't even see. I could barely stand to go inside, even for hide and seek.

"Says here in the paper," Mama had told Daddy, "that black widows are bad this year. Two reported already, one bit the mailman over on Star Route and one got a person in an outhouse."

"I don't put my ass down till I seen one ain't built over the hole," he answered. Daddy would pull a kite straw on the way to the outhouse and bang it around in the hole to break the web.

"Don't say that was where it bit him," Mama said.

"Well, it was," Daddy answered.

"Don't even say it was a him," Mama added.

I had a nightmare of being locked up in there, but the outhouse in the dream had no door. Vines were coming through the cracks and filling up the inside with red and black spiders growing on the runners like flowers. The only way to escape was to jump down the hole, but I woke up before I had to. When I was awake, I decided that you thought crazy when you were dreaming because I would have been much worse off down the hole than facing up to those spiders. They might not even have been the poisonous kind.

"Man's got to be where he feels safe when he's got his britches down," Daddy said.

He told this story again and again.

"It's private business. Ever seen an Indian man take a leak? He squats down and hides like a woman. Animals are different from people. Two alley cats can be tearing each other's balls off, but they call time out when one's attending to his business."

28

He always started out saying it was private, but he was making public things that nice people never talked about.

"I don't like them public toilets and I'll tell you why."

I thought if I had counted it would have been fifty times, because I heard him tell it to new people. Everybody who met my daddy got to form their impression of him from that story. I guess it wasn't the wrong impression.

"I was in one of the booths down at the bus station, before they put them locks on you had to put a nickel in to open, though I can be sure that wouldn't have stopped them two . . ."

He carried a lot of cash money and let people know it. When Mama called it bragging and a little man trying to feel big, he would bounce around the kitchen like a featherweight boxer, sinking his fists into her soft body. Sometimes she farted; sometimes air came out her mouth. He always stopped when she hollered like the game was over.

"These hands come under the door, four of them grabbing at my loose britches, trying to get hold of my wallet, you see. Then 'fore I could move, two of them hands buckled my belt 'round my legs. And I saw one of them other hands slide out my wallet."

Just as his listener was starting to feel sorry for him, they found out he grabbed the hand that had his wallet, pulling half his body under the door and stomping his face in with both his legs still strapped together.

"When the fellow knew I had my money back, and all he was out to get was the worst licking of his life, he slid out on his belly like a snake." Then Daddy laughed, "But I could have done him one worse, him with his face in the floor in front of me on that toilet, interrupting me before I'd finished my business, you know?"

They knew, everybody knew. But if he was a little drunk they got the description of what he could have done added to what he did do.

So what did my daddy do after that experience? Did he quit carrying so much cash and flashing it? No, he quit using public toilets and sat in his rotten outhouse every morning with his pistol beside him.

I saw my kite on the phone wire, flipping over in the wind. I waited, hoping it might come loose, but soon the bones began to break. I started gathering my new straws for Mama to make me another one.

When I snapped the straws close to the outhouse, I called out, "Daddy, it's just me, Ella Ruth. Don't shoot, please don't shoot me," even when I was almost certain he was not even at home. I heard my voice as thin as the sound of the sticks rubbing together in my hand.

29

Daddy said Mama was limited. All the Akins girls were, but since she got to be the prettiest, she was the most limited. While she was young, people were always telling her she was prettier than Hedy Lamarr. When she was fifteen, she left to go to Hollywood and got as far as Greensboro which is fifty miles west of Summit.

In her pictures her hair was frizzy, her eyebrows a thin line and her lips so dark they looked black. I tried to imagine all the actresses and Mama, made up like they'd be now and not so old-fashioned looking. I was trying to tell if they really were pretty or not.

I never knew Mama pretty. Her chin had enough white bristles to be on an old man. Her features were lost in too much flesh, her nose much too tiny for her face. Her plucked brows were loose hairs, grown together across her forehead. I tried to imagine which hairs I would leave if I pulled them out to have a new moon left over each eye. Only her eyeballs, clear blue and round as marbles had kept their shape. I never knew Mama thin, either. Big as a barrel, Daddy called her.

I never thought Mama was limited, because I saw all the things she could do better than other women. She canned tomatoes and succotash and string beans, filling the jars with a scoop. I liked the rows of glass jars, prettier to see than the pictures on the cans at the grocery store. We sat in the front room and listened for the pop of the jars sealing, Mama counting each sound.

"There goes the last one," she smiled. Then we carried them to the basement shelves, some of them still warm against my stomach. In the winter she'd send me down for the snap beans or the pole beans or the late beans, telling me exactly which shelf to go to for the right jar. I would carry the cold jar up to the kitchen and listen for it to hiss when she pried the lid and let the fresh smell out.

When the time was up and a jar hadn't sealed, Mama would frown: "Guess we're having succotash for supper whether we like it or not."

She'd spin off the screw rims, find the still open jar with the loose flat lid and put it in the refrigerator. My Grandma Higgins was always missing open jars. Mama would walk through the rotten smell in Grandma's basement, find the spoiled jar and take a spade and bury the insides. She would run her finger around the rim, feeling for the chip. If she felt it, the jar went in the garbage. Grandma Higgins would fish it out and call her wasteful. Mama would shake her head and tell me, "Wasteful is throwing out your hard work. She'll get it mixed right back in with the good jars and do it over again, mark my words." I thought my daddy was wrong about which woman was limited.

I was Mama's second family. Matthew got married and moved to Raleigh before I knew him good. I remember when I was nine, I saw "Dear Mama," and wondered why he thought he had the right to call my mama, Mama. Daddy said I was the one who broke her down. She was soft and already too chubby, but it wasn't till me that all her veins squeezed out to the surface and broke, and her jaw took a dip like her face had knobs on it. I used to hear the word "breaking," that so and so was starting to break. I thought it meant they were getting cracks and were going to fall into a million pieces like the shepherd boy on Grandpa Higgins's grave that Daddy got gypped into buying. Nothing left but the lamb and a stump. I didn't weigh but five and a half pounds and couldn't see how I could have done all that. But a tiny wasp felled my Grandpa Higgins. The wasp stung him on the neck and his throat swelled up so tight it cut off his windpipe. He suffocated on the ground in the hog lot.

"Six feet, four inches tall and it felled him," Daddy said.

I imagined Grandpa, six feet four, falling like the dead persimmon tree, hitting the ground stiff and sending up a dust cloud. In his hair was a robin's nest like the tree in the poem that only God could make. Even his shepherd boy got felled. I wished I could see Grandpa upright, walking along as straight as a pine. I asked Mama.

"A fine figure of a man," she smiled. "Your own daddy just likes to talk about the ruin of folks. I think I loved his daddy first. I had to tell myself he belonged to Maynard's mama and I couldn't have him. I settled for Maynard. That's like getting the last biscuit on the plate. Somebody has to make you take it because it ain't good manners to take the last one, but the reason it's there is it's the least one. People pretend they been just reaching out and getting a biscuit, but they been picking and choosing all along. Then you take that last one and it's hard and cold. Hard and cold and you wish you'd left it be and done without."

I knew that a fine figure of a man was what my daddy wasn't. He was like a joke, only you had to be careful when you laughed at him. Bugs of all kinds seemed to go after him. His skinny arms were always flapping like a windmill. After he said he was sick and tired of being stung by Mrs. Albright's honeybees, he bought a beekeeper suit at surplus. I saw him out in the garden yelling because three bees were inside the veil on his coolie hat, circling his head in a bee race. Mama and I were scared for him till he took off all his clothes and ran in the house naked, his tallywack wiggling like a worm coming out of an apple. He got a leech on his balls when he was cutting cattails in Sanders's pond and came out of the water like a rocket ship. After we picked blackberries, Mama had to paint his bellybut-

31

ton with her red nailpolish to smother the chiggers. It was funny that all the bugs in the world bit him, skinny, rag-bag Daddy, and his strong daddy was the one who got felled.

He talked about the Germans and their pruning. He would have been the first skinny limb to go plunk on the ground. Didn't need a saw to prune him, just Mama's sewing scissors would snip him off, if you were to compare my daddy to a limb. But when I thought of him I thought of what he said, not what he looked like. My daddy would have made sure he was the one with the saw.

"And where does beef come from?"

"Cows."

"Correct. And where do we get pork?"

"Porcupine!"

Al Sawyer said that. Miss Ketchen, who was our sixth-grade teacher, couldn't help but laugh. She was no good at being mean. I was the same way. Like I knew I was supposed to ignore boys when they talked dirty, but sometimes what they said was really funny. There weren't any girls on my block anyway, to be on my side.

On the way to school one morning, Al took up for me. My lunch box opened by accident and my jam and peanut butter biscuit, my chess pie and my apple fell out on the ground. They weren't hurt though because they were wrapped in wax paper. I was stooping to get the pie when Raymond Linton took a giant step out of his way just to step on it. And before I could get over to my biscuit, he stepped on it too. Ruined my lunch. I threw my smashed biscuit at him and missed a country mile, I was so mad.

Al Sawyer told him that was a son of a bitch thing to do.

They didn't fight, just kept walking. Mama would have packed me another one and brought it over to school had she known.

All I had for lunch was a carrot he didn't like I got from Stevie and my apple I found where it rolled under a car. It had a soft brown spot, but I ate it anyway, spot and all, I was so hungry.

I saw Raymond Linton at the water fountain. I saw myself in my mind pushing his head down and busting out his teeth on the metal spout. If I was a foot taller, I could have done it. They sent you to the principal for pushing people's faces into the water fountain.

Miss Ketchen called me up before lunch. I thought it might be about my lunch or what I planned to do to Raymond Linton. She would sometimes give people money for their milk when they said they forgot it.

"Ella, I have a little note here that I would like for you to take home to your mother."

32

I didn't know what to say. I must have looked scared.

"Don't worry, dear. Don't look so frightened. You haven't *knowingly* done anything wrong."

Knowingly. I walked home with my stomach growling, the note in the pocket of my corduroy pants where Miss Ketchen had stuck it. I had to pee so bad, I almost wet my pants before Mama could get to the door and I couldn't use the bushes because Stevie and Al were bouncing a basketball in the street. While I was on the commode, I told Mama about my biscuit and pie. She made me another biscuit with extra jam and had two pies, a regular and a lemon chess for me by the time I got to the kitchen.

"What a fine thing to do, ruining a child's lunch and making her go hungry. Your daddy ought to jerk a knot in him. None of the Lintons have ever turned out any good. You got enough, honey?"

I loved the fuss she made because it was just what I knew she'd do. I figured my daddy wouldn't jerk a knot in Raymond Linton or anybody. He looked like somebody had jerked one in him and forgot to undo it.

When I finished my milk, I remembered the note. I handed it to Mama.

"What's this?" She looked at it like she was scared.

"From my teacher to you."

"What does it say?"

"Didn't read it. It wont to me."

"Read it to me." When Mama read she pointed at each word with her finger, real slow. I opened the note and saw the big round letters Miss Ketchen wrote on the blackboard with.

" 'Dear Mrs. Higgins,' " I read, " 'I am writing you this now to avoid . . . embarrassment in the future. Ella must start dressing as a girl should. They will not even *allow* pants in the junior high.' Not allow pants, Mama! I'm not dressing like Sunday School to go to school."

I saw that Mama was already embarrassed. Her eyes were watery and pink around the edges like she was holding back a cry. Mama would get on her knees before we left for church and polish my patent leather shoes with a biscuit when I didn't give a hoot. "Your teacher doesn't think my little girl is a little lady."

"She wants me to have to wear those dumb leggings under a skirt and have to come in early from playground to get them off, Mama. With all the boys trying to look up you. I can't stand a dress at play period. Might as well not go outside. I'll just quit school, Mama. Dumbest thing I ever heard of."

Mama never heard me though I kept rattling on about turning

33

cartwheels and how the boys talked about getting their picture took with Mildred's Brownie because she didn't know how to sit with her dress tucked under.

For the next month I heard Mama sewing every spare minute. It was like she thought the note said I had to dress like a princess. She sewed on braid and lace and embroidered and crocheted trim and made matching hair ribbons.

"Act the fool," my daddy said. "Act the fool over a little criticism." I never knew what he meant and she didn't seem to, either.

From the moment when I gave her the note that made her so unhappy at first, she became another person. She smiled and hummed while she worked. She looked at pictures of clothes for little girls in magazines and said things like: "There's a pretty little lady." She said the word lady like it tasted like candy and smelled like flowers. It was as if the doctor just told her she had a girl and it was what she always wanted.

I went to my room and stared at Pandy. I did that when I wanted to stay mad. Pandy couldn't stare back because Daddy took out his eyes after my brother Matthew wrote that his daughter, Becka, swallowed one of the eyes out of hers. It was the kind with the prong and she had to have an operation. I had enough sense not to take out his eyes and swallow them. It was like being accused of something you didn't do.

When I was nine and a half, I decided to ask Mama and Daddy if they knew where babies came from. Mama acted like she was scared she didn't know the answer. Daddy tried to explain it to me.

"This is how it goes, Ella Ruth. The man, he takes his pecker, see? And he makes it stiff, like, uh, like a broom handle. And the woman, she's got this tunnel thing way up to her box . . ."

"Maynard!"

". . . up to the place where the baby grows inside her. And the man, he squirts a baby seed up there and sometimes it takes root and grows. Sometimes, if he's lucky, it don't."

"How come some kids look like their mamas?"

"Shot who?" Daddy would say that sometimes when he thought what you asked didn't make sense.

"OK, I mean, if it's the daddy's seed," I explained, "the mama's just a bucket of dirt, right, for it to grow in? That means . . ."

"Naw, naw, that's not right. See, you left something out, Ella Ruth. See, she's got this egg . . ."

"People don't lay eggs."

"It's a soft one without a shell so this man seed, see, can get in it."

34

"Where's the tunnel?"

"Down there. Between your legs."

"Not between my legs, it isn't. I don't have any tunnel."

"Maynard!"

"Yeah, you do. It's just real little now and it's got this little door over the end that damn well better stay there . . ."

"Maynard!"

"Shut up, Maxine. I know my goddamn name."

"Did you put a seed in Mama's tunnel?"

"Ella Ruth. Maynard. Go eat your dinner."

"It ain't dinnertime," he said.

"Well, go outside then." That's what she always said to me when I was bothering her.

Daddy got up and walked into the kitchen. He started opening the cabinets.

Mama whispered to me. "Ella Ruth, Jesus brings little babies."

"Jesus does?"

"Yes. He brings them at night. To the hospital. People who want them go there to pick them up."

"That's nice, Mama."

I went back to my room. I had gotten a real good book on babies at the Public Library, but I decided not to show it to them. As Grandma Higgins would say: "What they don't know, won't hurt them."

Mama had big fears at night. She was scared of things that weren't even there and she would fret and toss until Daddy got another bed to sleep in. One for screwing, one for sleeping, he said, because he was tired of the covers being yanked from around him. Mama did hog the bed. When she got under the covers, they hiked up around the bed like a skirt that had gotten too short.

One night Daddy hit her to make her sleep. I thought he should have been sorrier than he was, making her nose bleed when she couldn't put up a hand to stop him. But to steal sleep from him was worse than to steal his money. He could fight a man for stealing his money, but Mr. Albright, who left for work an hour earlier than Daddy wanted to wake up, was worse than Caleb Green, who never brought back his best hoe.

"Grating that gravel with his tires," Daddy growled. "Now why don't he park it where he can slide away without waking up the neighborhood? 'Cause he don't give a rat's ass about other people, that's why."

Mama had bad dreams that you had to tell her you believed in too. If you told her she was crazy like Daddy did, she sobbed until she strangled. One night she was screaming that spiders were dropping from the ceiling. I crawled all over the bed, killing each one she pointed out to me, smashing it with her shoe. My daddy was laughing and cussing, a little drunk I think, but I was after those spiders for Mama and never laughed once. Not because I thought they were there, but because she did. I still think maybe a little one did fall off the ceiling and her dream made it big. I heard that if a gnat bit you you could dream it was a mad dog.

Mama thought all her problems could be solved by love magazines. She kept cutting out coupons and ordering things in plain brown wrappers. There were coupons for getting rid of fat and facial hair and headaches, stretch marks, baggy chins and blackheads. After that you could send in coupons for long lashes and fingernails, wigs and stuff to grow long hair fast, and black lace underpants with no crotch. I saw a coupon to order live seahorses and when I asked Mama if I could, she looked at me like I was crazy.

"Ella Ruth, what in the world would anybody want with live seahorses?"

She always asked me to fill out her coupons, saying she couldn't write in small spaces.

"Shaking like a nigger writing a check," Daddy teased as she struggled over the tiny coupon with a blunt pencil in her left hand.

"Here, Ella Ruth, honey. You finish it for me," and I erased her oversized letters and started over. Then I ordered three seahorses. One of them came dead and the other two died in a week, but Mama had to admit they were pretty cute while they lasted.

One day I saw Mama in her regular chair, but I stopped and stared because she looked different. The skin around her neck was splotched pink and white like cotton candy. I imagined poking my finger in her neck and having her stick to me. That must have been near the time when my big brother, Matthew, came to visit and took me to the fair again and got me cotton candy. I got it stuck in my hair. It was too sweet and made me so sick to my stomach that I threw up after I rode the Wild Mouse. I think that's why I had a bad thought about Mama. She looked like she was about to explode.

"Mama, how come you look so feverish? It's not hot in here."

She answered me, her words puffing out like air from a pump.

"Marvelous—molder—figure—holder." She wiggled in her seat and turned redder. "Said it was so comfortable you'd forget you had it on. Bull hockey!"

"Bullshit!" Daddy shouted and giggled from his chair, his bones jutting in every direction. He never understood her problem because it wasn't his problem. He ate as much as she did and stayed the same. Mama thought he had a tapeworm and hoped she would catch it. He told her when she walked her butt looked like two little niggers fighting under a blanket.

"See, I'll tell you how it works," he snorted. "You finally get your ass up outa that chair and make it to the table and every time you try to dish up a plateful, it snaps your arms back."

He pretended, jerking his arms back, and the loose skin on his bare arms fell into place like ripply cardboard.

"Guar—ran—teed, or your money back."

"You could do with a little body building yourself, Mr. Charles Atlas." Mama's eyes bulged like a toad frog. "Put on your trunks and strut down Myrtle Beach and see how many times you get sand kicked in your ugly face."

He did look like the drawing of the ninety-seven pound weakling when he wore his baggy polka-dot swim trunks.

"Asshole!" Mama shouted. Mama was like me. When she cussed, I knew she was really mad.

"Mama," I asked softly, "maybe you should have got a larger size."

"One size fits all," Daddy put in.

"It ain't a girdle, Ella Ruth, honey. It's to work off inches while you move around."

"In that case," Daddy broke in, winking at me, "why don't you chase me around the house? Be skinny as a rail by sundown."

Mama saw his wink. "No, I wouldn't get skinny, you scrawny little asshole runt, because I would have hit you upside the head with a brickbat by noon and be back in my chair resting."

There were times when I was growing up that I felt older than my parents.

When I was eleven years old, I got accused of stealing a lot of money from this dead lady, but I didn't do it.

I had watched her in her house where there were so many plants that their breathing fogged her windows from inside. Even though she was almost as big as Mama, she looked like a fish shadow in the water at Horace Sanders's pond. I couldn't tell her back from her front.

One day she came to the window like a fish coming to the top for a bug. At first I was afraid she knew I was spying on her, but her face wasn't angry. It wasn't not angry either. Her lips moved, letting out imaginary air bubbles but making no sounds. Then she was gone and I was left staring at an empty greenish square, too far away to see my own reflection. She made chill bumps on my arms.

We rode home on the same bus every day. She got on at Peachtree and Main. She always sat in the same seat, up front behind the

37

driver, except one day a kid who didn't usually ride our bus got in her seat. She stood up, wobbling with the overhead strap in her hand, glaring at him, though there were plenty more places she could have sat.

We got off at the same stop. I always let her get off first, though I think she would have whether I let her or not. I walked behind her until she turned up her walkway, walking slower than I would have if she wasn't there. She always carried a giant purse that bent her over sideways as much as carrying a suitcase. I wondered why a woman who didn't use lipstick and powder needed such a big purse. Then one day, her not looking any way different than I could remember, she fell in a heap so fast I almost fell on top of her.

She went forward on her face with the big purse almost completely under her. I bent over and tried to talk to her.

"Hey, get up. Hey, can I help you? Hey, lady!"

She didn't move at all. A horsefly lighted on her back, moving his legs like he was going to doodoo on her.

I started running. For a few seconds I was just running away from her, then I turned down a walkway because I saw a lady on the porch doing some sewing. I had seen her before and she always smiled and waved when I came home from school. She looked startled that I was running up her walk.

"Ma'am! Ma'am, there is a big lady who fell down on the side-walk."

I pointed and she squinted, but we were too far from the lady for her to see anything but a dark mound.

"Did she hurt herself, child? Is that what you're trying to say?"

"No, ma'am. I mean, I don't know. She isn't moving at all. And she wouldn't answer me."

"I'll call an ambulance."

She didn't rush into the house. She walked to the edge of her yard. I saw what she was doing. She was checking to see if the mound really was a lady. I could see her head, face down like a giant dark turtle from where we stood, not moving at all.

"You go wait with her, dear, in case she wakes up. I'll call the ambulance."

I walked back to the lady and stood beside her anyway. I looked at the big purse and thought about pulling it from under her because she was mashing it. I didn't see anybody coming so I tugged it twice, but it was hung on something.

The ambulance got there and two men ran up to her. They rolled her over and one of them pulled her fingers off the purse.

"Here, you hang onto this," he said to me, so I took it. It felt hot. I wondered if the hottest side had been the one against her. It must have been because I had to brush sand off the other side. Dead people got cold. She must not be a dead person. Until right then I hadn't even considered that she might be dead.

They put a thing over her face. I thought it would be hard to breathe with that thing covering her nose.

"Where does your mother live?"

"Up the street."

"What can you tell me about her?"

At first I thought he meant *my* mama. He meant the lady on the sidewalk. I was glad I caught on before I said something dumb.

"She just fell down. I don't know nothing." Anything. I knew better than to say that except at home.

"I mean do you know anything about her health? Any history of heart trouble? How old is she? Who's her family doctor?"

I looked around. I had never heard such hard questions. There was nobody to ask. The lady who had called the ambulance was at the end of her walkway, her face just a white dot.

He nodded at the purse I was holding. "Look in the purse." I unsnapped it and looked inside. I felt funny going into a stranger's purse. I would never have done it with people around if he hadn't told me to. There was a pocketbook between some other things. I opened it up. It had a lot of dollars in it. There was a card with the dollars. The other man took it and read it out loud.

"La—vo. La—vo—ni—a Pitts. Appointment at 4:30 Thursday." I never heard of anybody named Lavonia before.

"Appointment with who?" he asked. "A doctor?"

"Dr. Albert Dennis."

"Dr. Quack. Fucking bonebeater. She's probably had a pain in her shoulder for a week and that fucking quack told her it was rheumatism."

I didn't know that doctors talked like my daddy. While they worked over her, her fat body spread on the sidewalk, her tits hanging out the front of her dress, unbuttoned where they pressed on her chest. I saw one whole tittie with a brown nipple that looked like a hat on a fat head. The men worked one after the other until one got tired and the other took over. Her skirt came up and her garter belt showed. Her panties pulled away from her crotch and I saw she had black curly hair on her biscuit. I never would have thought a woman like her would wear lacy panties. Maybe big baggy drawers. I pulled her skirt back down, but they didn't notice me. I touched her leg by accident. It was colder than my hand.

They lifted her to a stretcher. She had fallen out of her shoes.

When I picked them up, one of the men led me by the arm to the ambulance. I started to pull away when one of them said, "You have to go with us."

"Mama told me never to ride with strangers."

I rode looking at the dashboard. We were going faster than I had ever moved. The man not driving reached up and made a siren noise each time we crossed a street. I felt like a big rock rolling down the street when I saw all the cars move out of our way.

When we went into the hospital, I left her shoes in the ambulance. I didn't like the way they smelled. I still had her heavy purse. I couldn't remember where I left my booksack. I finally found all the things the nurse needed to fill out a form in compartments in her pocketbook: her whole name—Lula Lavonia Pitts—her house number and the name of my street. I found a card with her age on it: fifty-nine. All the while this was going on, Lula Lavonia Pitts was gone to the back room. I never saw her again.

I sat down on a plastic seat after the form was done. I was still looking, trying to find next of kin. There was a box of jewelry, the kind that makes your skin turn green. I found a recipe book, each recipe with a name: Sarah's lemon cake, Myrtle's vanilla pudding, Gertrude's heavenly hash. She must have had friends I didn't know about. There were cigarettes with matches held to them with a rubber band though I had never seen her smoke. It wasn't allowed on the bus.

I tried to remember her fingers, if they had cigarette stains like my daddy's. I could picture her hands on her purse, white as snow.

There were letters to her, some of them two or three years old by the postmark. They just came from Mebane, which wasn't far away. then I found something very strange. There was a picture in a frame with a cracked glass, I guess from her falling on it. It was of a young boy. Only he was a colored boy, very dark and shiny with big white teeth. On the bottom of the picture I made out the writing, "To Aunt Lavonia, Love from Mason." I didn't know why there was a colored boy calling her aunt. I thought of her lying on the sidewalk, her white skin on the big tittie that fell out of her dress, her biscuit with white skin showing through the black hair.

I started counting the money. I counted it down inside the plastic purse because I didn't want the people in the waiting room to know I had it. I got to one hundred and thirty and quit because I lost count. I had never touched so much money before. Then I found a piece of paper between the money: "In case of accident contact Sula Smith, sister. In case of death I want to be buried in Mebane." That was when I remembered I better get the nurse to call my number. Mama

40

put a card in my booksack like that. The nurse dialed the number and handed the phone to me.

"Mama?"

"Honey, are you all right? I've been worried sick. I heard the ambulance and called the hospital. A lady brought me your booksack she found on the sidewalk. I thought sure some sorry old man . . . I thought sure you'd been run over by them crazy . . ."

"Mama! I am at the hospital, Mama. You won't let me get a word in edgewise."

"Oh." She sounded a long way off.

"But not for me, Mama. Don't worry. For this lady I saw fall down."

"What lady?"

"Lula Lavonia Pitts."

"I don't know any such person."

"She lives in the plant house, you know. The one who don't talk."

"The crazy lady?"

"She had a coronary."

I didn't know if Mama knew that word. I heard one of the men say it.

"A heart attack."

"No, a coronary." I thought I said it right.

"Why don't you come on home?"

"They said I have to stay here."

"Well, you come on home."

Mama didn't understand. Sometimes I wished I could tell her things easier because she got so mixed up. When I hung up, the nurse said, "There's been some mistake?"

"I called my Mama," I said.

I told the nurse about Sula Smith and she called both of the numbers on the paper. The second one was at the mill. After about twenty minutes, Sula Smith got there. I didn't know it was her. I saw a colored lady come in and I went back to looking through the big purse when I heard her say to the nurse, "I'm Sula Smith. I understand my sister is here."

I didn't understand. How could one sister be colored and the other one be white? I tried to see if the nurse acted surprised, but she didn't. She just took out the form and started asking questions, trying to fill in the rest of the squares.

Sula Smith sat down on one of the plastic seats. I looked at her and had a funny thought: if I should ask her if she would go and water the plants in her sister's house. She looked mad.

41

"How much longer till I know something? I had to take off work."

The nurse picked up a phone.

"Mrs. Smith?" I called.

She glared at me. "Mrs. Smith. This here's your sister's purse."

She looked at me a second and then jumped and pulled it away from me like I was starting to run off with it.

"What you doing with it?"

"I found your sister on the sidewalk."

"What you mean on the sidewalk? She drunk?"

"No ma'am, she had a coronary."

"Heart attack!"

That's when I realized they must be the same thing.

"There is a lot of money in there," I said. I didn't know why I said that. The colored woman began to scramble through the purse.

"Did you see her savings book? I know she had a savings," she mumbled.

"I don't think she has a savings book in there. It says she wants to be buried in Mebane."

"Buried! She ain't dead!" Her eyes were big.

"I don't know." My voice cracked. I was scared of this woman. I had never had a colored person talk so forward with me.

The woman kept scrambling through the purse. She pulled out the pocketbook with the dollars and stared at me, her eyes like slits.

A doctor came in and saved me from her. I guess he thought I was the big woman's child. He took my hand.

"She's passed," he said softly.

Passed what, I thought, then the sister screamed so loud I jerked my hand away from the doctor. It was like someone had burned her, stuck a hot poker up her ass, my daddy would have said. She kept screaming out and bouncing on the seat, but no one in the room looked at her.

"She's her sister," I said to the doctor.

He didn't act shocked either. He turned to her and said the same thing, "She's passed."

Why didn't anyone act surprised that a white lady had a colored sister? They didn't tell her to get quiet either. My daddy would have popped me good if I'd acted like that.

I thought of the money in the big purse and the picture of the colored boy. The money smelled older than the three-year-old letters.

"Mebane is fifty miles away. I know her. She thinks her daddy's folks would let her in their plot. That bones is bones. Blood is still blood."

I jumped when I heard the voice. It was Sula, calm again, but babbling now.

"Why can't she just go under right here in Summit?"

She was talking to me, but I couldn't answer her question.

The doctor walked out. As soon as he moved, she started screaming again. A nurse came in with a paper sack.

"Who is next of kin to Miss Pitts?" she asked, looking at me.

"I'm next of kin," the sister butted in, proud-sounding.

"Here are her clothes and her brooch."

The nurse gave Sula Smith the sack, then held up a plastic container like goes in the refrigerator. "Her teeth are in here."

I didn't know her teeth weren't real. I saw the brooch twisted at her neck while the man pumped her chest. I thought of her naked now, not able to cover herself.

That's when I was sure she was dead, when they gave away her clothes and her teeth because she wouldn't need them anymore.

"You wait," Sula snapped when I got up to go.

"I got to go home."

"You got her savings book?"

"I ain't got nothing of hers."

I don't know why, but I ran outside. After I got around the corner, I looked back but she hadn't chased me. I was a long way from home and I had already used up my bus token. I walked down the street. I couldn't help but start to cry. It was getting dark. I wanted to be at my home with my mama and not all these mean and dead people. Suddenly I heard a familiar hiss and felt light come around me. I looked and saw a bus. It was my regular driver.

"What you doing clean over here, Ella Ruth?" His bus was almost empty.

"I'm going home. I don't have another token."

"You can pay me tomorrow."

I got on and felt good as soon as I got in the seat I always got in at the front by the door. I looked at Lula Lavonia Pitts's empty seat.

"Thank you very much," I remembered to say. I liked him, Mr. Evans. He used to get out and walk across the street with me when I was in the first grade.

He nodded and smiled. "You still didn't tell me how you got so far from home with it getting dark. Your mama will be worried to death."

"You remember that lady," I asked, "the big one with the plastic purse who always got off at my stop? The one who sat right there behind you?"

"You mean Mrs. Pitts? Yeah, she worked near Main and Peachtree somewhere. Never said a word. Don't know if it was Mrs. or

Miss. Reason I know her name is she used to clean down at the station."

"She's dead."

He looked shocked. "She died right after she got off your bus. Today. That's why I'm over here. I went to the hospital with her. But I'm thinking she was dead as a doornail soon as she hit the ground."

"No kidding. Didn't look a bit sick. Just dropped dead?"

"Heart attack," I said.

"Can take them quick. Especially when they get too fat." Then he paused. "And her folks didn't have the common decency to take you home?"

"She didn't have no folks. Just a sister."

"Well, she could have given you bus money. Some folks lose their heads in an emergency."

When we passed through town, I thought of all the money again. I could still smell it. Why did I keep thinking of the money? It wasn't mine. She could have given me enough to ride the bus for a month and not even missed it.

"She was a colored person," I said.

"Naw."

"Yessir, she was. And there was a picture of a colored boy inside her purse who said aunt to her on his picture."

"Well, no wonder. No wonder she was such a tight lip. She could pass all right."

"The doctor said she passed."

I was about to ask him what that meant, when he laughed and pulled up to a stop.

"Here's your street. Now you run home and I'll watch you as far as I can see."

I hadn't even recognized my own street at night. I took off running. I passed her house without turning my head. I thought her sister would get a key and go water the plants. She had the key in the purse. Everything was in the purse. The savings book must be there somewhere. I didn't take one single thing.

I heard the bus door hiss as I ran out of the street light. I stopped and turned and saw it pull away. I started running again. Mama had the porch light on for me and I could see her face at the window.

When I got in my bed, I thought of taking all the money from Lula Lavonia Pitts's purse to the bank and having it turned into pennies. Then I decided nickels because it would look better silver. I would have to use Daddy's truck and carry it in bushel baskets. And I'd put it all in a pile in my room and do like Uncle Scrooge McDuck

44

and sit on top of it and throw it into the air. There was a big house on the hill behind our house where Dr. Horace Sanders lived. I always imagined he looked like Uncle Scrooge McDuck until Mama pointed him out to me. Though I knew better, I expected him to be a duck in a black suit.

I shut my eyes and thought of the tinkling sound when my money hit—tink, tink, tink. It would be cold on the back of my legs when I first sat down like Grandma Higgins's toilet seat because she didn't heat the bathroom. If I sat still the nickels would press into my skin, making pictures of buffaloes on my heinie. When I was just about asleep, I could get the money smell in my mind again. Mama said money was dirty because there was no telling who had handled it and I should never put it in my mouth. I laid back in the money and it was cold like a new place in the bed when I was trying to get away from the heat in the summer.

I wondered if Lula Lavonia Pitts ever read a Scrooge McDuck comic. She kept it all in dollars so she could carry it in that big purse. She might have a room in that house full of nickels and maybe quarters and fifty-cent pieces. If I had saved her life, she might have given some of it to me. Sula Smith will shovel it in bags and take it with her because she is next of kin. She thought I took some of that money. I could have, easy as pie.

Sometimes Scrooge McDuck threw his money up and let it hit him on the head. He burrowed through it like a mole, dived into it like a porpoise. He took a bulldozer right inside his house and pushed his money into piles.

I remembered a bulldozer. Daddy showed me the picture. It was pushing people into piles, naked people, white and stiff as china dolls, and the man driving had on a mask with a long snout like a wart hog. Lula Lavonia Pitts was naked, her clothes in that paper sack, and her teeth in an icebox container. I wondered if they took those teeth out, looking for the gold.

The next night, Mama let me go ahead and start eating because Daddy was so late to dinner. He walked in as I was starting on my dessert, raspberry cobbler. He stuck his face in mine and said, "I see you waited for me like two dogs." He smelled so much like likker and his nose and cheeks looked so much like raspberries, I lost my appetite. I hated to hurt Mama's feelings about the cobbler so I decided to wait and see if my appetite came back.

"I'm ashamed to death of you, Maynard, if you want to know the truth." Mama had tears in her eyes.

Daddy laughed real loud. Too long, though. He was just making like he thought what she said was funny.

"Go on, laugh your fool head off. You probably got enough laughs down at the Rebel to think you're ready for the stage." Her face was twitching. Mama was really mad at him.

"Look at your mama shake, Ella Ruth. Shaking like a dog shitting bottle caps."

"Shut up, Maynard."

They both got quiet and Daddy started eating. I decided to eat my cobbler. Mama's temper was like a fire going out, a coal would flare up now and then, but soon she'd go out for good and by morning, her ashes were cold. She had a funny idea of shame too. She would carry Daddy's likker bottles in grocery bags and put them in one of the cans in the alley behind the Rebel Bar or the 5 & 10. She didn't want our garbage man to know how much Daddy was drinking, but the neighbors could see him come home every day, clutching a bag twisted around a bottle of High Heaven.

"Albert Albright told me what you said, Maynard, if you want to know."

"Albert Albright can kiss my sweet ass."

"Where do you think we're going to get the money, Maynard, if one of them decides to take you up on it? Baltimore! You couldn't buy a ticket to Raleigh for your own child to go visit her brother and you offer to buy any colored person in town a one way ticket to Baltimore. Do you know how many colored people are in this town? Cyrus Solomon couldn't make such an offer."

Cyrus Solomon was the name everybody used to talk about more money than they could imagine because he owned the hosiery mill and almost all the colored houses in Haiti Alley. Sonavabitch Solomon. I called him that once and Mama popped me. I didn't know it was a cuss word then. I thought it was his first name. I messed up another name. Joker Summers. I called him Mr. Casummers because I was too little to call a grown man Joe. Daddy was there. They all laughed, but I didn't get popped.

"I'd buy that sonavabitch Solomon a ticket too. I ain't partial to niggers over Jews."

"It wont your idea no way. Old man Riggs come up with it. I heard him say it after prayer meeting. Only you know good and well he meant it in a Christian way."

"Another sin in the name of Christianity," Daddy sputtered.

"He did. It was because we couldn't keep them up. We had more than we could use and he thought they'd have a better chance of getting work in a city."

It took me a long time to realize what my daddy had said. He would offer any colored person in town a one-way ticket to Baltimore if they would leave. Daddy got up and crawled face down on

46

the couch. He wheezed, then mumbled, "This house is hotter than a pair of jumper cables at a nigger funeral." I heard a muffled giggle as he laughed at himself.

"I just hope to gracious there wont one of them in there sweeping to hear you and let that get out. You get likkered up and you ain't got a lick of sense. Won't be a bit surprised someday to hear you traded the house and furniture for a lame racehorse."

Daddy was almost asleep. "Just might get me a racehorse."

"Get your sorry self off my settee if you're planning on passing out."

She pushed him with the broom handle until he got up, jabbing him each time he stopped until he was through the door. When he called her ugly names, she poked harder so he shut up. I heard the springs jingle as he hit the bed.

After Daddy went to sleep, I decided to tell Mama about Mrs. Pitts. I heard his snoring when we were scraping the dishes. It had been three days since I saw her die and I hadn't said much of anything about it. Mama found her name in the paper and that she lived on our street.

"Mama, have you ever known a colored lady that had white skin?"

"For goodness sake, Ella, how can she be white if she's colored?"

Mama sighed and sat down on the kitchen stool when she remembered it was Daddy that she was mad at, not me.

"I'm sorry, honey. Would you say that again real slow?"

"That lady, Lula Lavonia Pitts. She was supposed to be a colored lady. I mean do they ever get born with white skin so you can't tell?"

"I seen a high yeller once. Had blue eyes. Lot of colored people got mixed blood. Down near the ocean you see them near about white. Lotta crossing over the line."

She stopped talking for a minute. I started washing the glasses.

"What do you mean Lula Lavonia Pitts? She lived on our street, Ella Ruth," Mama said, like that was all the answering my question needed.

"I know, Mama. But in her purse there was a picture of a colored boy who was calling her aunt and when her sister came to be next of kin, she was a colored lady."

Mama stared at me quite a while. She had that look on her face she got when she was trying to figure out something hard.

"Don't tell your daddy. Don't you breathe a word of it to him. He'll make us move. You're sure of that, that her kinfolks was colored?"

I nodded. Mama didn't start drying and the draintray was filling

47

up. She talked scared. Mama didn't hate colored people like Daddy did. He hit a dog in Haiti Alley once and didn't stop because he said it was just a nigger dog. I know it died too because we passed it and it had been rained on and no one buried it. Finally I had to ask my mama to start drying the dishes. She did it like she was in a daze, almost as if she was as drunk as Daddy was.

As it happened I didn't have to tell my daddy about Mrs. Pitts. He found out by himself. In a few days a lot of colored people started coming to her house. I had gone over after she died and looked in all the windows, up closer because I knew she wasn't in there. The fog had left the inside of the glass. I figured that she must have made it with her breathing and not the plants. It was hard to tell anything about her house with it so dark inside. The plant that was growing in the window had started to get limp and the runners were hanging down like strings. I wished I could go in and water it.

Al Sawyer came up behind me and said "Boo!"

"Goddamn you, Al, you almost gave me a coronary."

I fell off the loose brick I was balancing on and skinned one of my elbows. I hadn't even told Al she was a colored lady. He had a big mouth. For the next two weeks people started coming to the house and carrying out things. They were all colored people, not one of them with the white skin of Lula Lavonia Pitts. I hid in the bushes when I saw the sister, Sula Smith. I wondered if she found the savings book. She came out of the house several times and busted the dirt out of flower pots and put the pots in the back of the old pickup she drove. She had let all the plants die. She must not have liked them like her sister did.

After my daddy found out, all he could talk about was Mrs. Pitts and her relatives. It took him a long time before he sat down to eat. Mama told me not to start eating until he did because he was already in a bad mood.

"Niggers. We had a nigger living right here on our street, right between Sam and Edna's and old lady Ferguson's house and didn't even know it. Didn't even have the right to protect our property."

He was pacing around in the living room.

"This street ain't worth a tinker's damn now. I wish to hell I had got wind of it one day before that old coon bitch decided to drop dead. I'd of unloaded it lock, stock and barrel on the first sucker I seen. Couldn't give it to a white person now."

"Maynard, for goodness sake. The lady's dead. Come eat your dinner."

"She ain't a lady. She's a nigger passing for white."

I heard that word "passing" again. The bus driver and the doctor had said it.

48

"She ain't living on our street now, Maynard. She's dead. So just forget about it and don't let your food get cold."

"Forget about it! Who you think owns that house now? How many white people you seen toting out stuff? I bet you money that house will have a dozen jungle bunnies living in it before the month's up. Ferguson's already got a FOR SALE sign on hers and she'll sell it to the first nigger who offers her a dime."

"Dinner won't be fit to eat."

"And shut up talking about stuffing your fat face."

I was so hungry I couldn't stand it any longer. I started eating and waited for both of them to fuss at me, but they didn't even take notice. I carried my plate to the kitchen before they started eating. They didn't say another word about Mrs. Pitts that night.

Not long after that I started getting phone calls from Sula Smith. For a while she called once a day, twice one day because she talked to Mama while I was at school. Mama was afraid of her. She made Mama cry. Daddy said, "Let that nigger call when I'm home and we'll put a stop to her."

"I want to know when you're going to give me the savings book you stole," Sula Smith would say.

I could hear her words over and over in my head, then they would cut off when I put the phone down. Once I dropped the receiver and ran to the other side of the room. I could hear a noise coming from it like a hornet's nest until Mama put it back on the hook.

Sometimes Sula Smith would start out by saying, "Listen, you white bitch. Don't you hang up . . . " And I would hang up. She never made me cry because I knew all I had to do was hang up the phone, then leave it off the hook for a while. Daddy told us she would never have the nerve to come to our house.

Finally the calls stopped coming. That was after she called late one evening. All three of us had gone to bed and Daddy answered the phone. I heard part of what he said.

"You tired of living, nigger? One more call from you to this house and we'll see how much you like waking up in the morning. I would kill you, nigger, without . . ."

His voice was slurred because he was part drunk and part sleepy. I knew that time that Sula Smith hung up since Daddy quit in the middle of a sentence.

I truthfully didn't know what happened to Mrs. Pitts's savings book. Daddy asked me if I took it. Mama got mad at him and said, "Maynard, land sakes, that child never told a lie or took anything that didn't belong to her in her life." That wasn't true, but I didn't say anything. Daddy grunted and looked at me and nodded.

"I ain't got it, Daddy."

49

I used bad English at home sometimes. I thought it made me sound more honest. I quit being afraid to answer the phone soon because I knew my daddy would protect me from Sula Smith. Being drunk didn't seem to matter with the telephone.

I had a dream. In it I didn't notice the man when he came in. He had been milling around a place that looked like Parson's Store. As soon as I saw what he had in mind, my first thought was, Why is he picking on me? I was counting out bubblegum and he made me look up. In his hand was a black stick. It seemed too thin to have been a gun, but I guess it was or I wouldn't have been so frightened. I wished I hadn't let him get my attention and I had never seen it. Then maybe he would have tried someone else. I was sorry right away that I had the money from my glass bank in my purse. I had fished it out with a knife to count it, but this time I hadn't put it back in. I wondered if by some lucky chance I might have left my purse somewhere else, or stuck it in a drawer so I could say I didn't have it with me. I couldn't look and see. I had all these thoughts before I had the big one. It all must have taken just a few seconds to scoot through my mind. The big thought was that he might do something to hurt me and it might be very bad because a man who would do what he was doing wasn't like anybody I had ever known.

I wanted to wake up from my dream so I did. I yelled for my daddy, but Mama came instead.

"I want my daddy."

"He's asleep, honey. Don't wake him up. Mama's right here."

I got mad and pulled away from her. I said I wanted my daddy again. She sat there awhile before she got up and went back to their room. She thought I was asleep. I didn't go to sleep until it was daylight and I heard my daddy get up. It wasn't until then that I knew I was safe from the man with the gun. Then I wrote down my dream so I could put it in my story box.

Starrie, the half breed—One day a terrible tragedy came to pass. It was a cold day, the wind whistled through the trees and blew the thin skim of snow into tiny drifts. A small stream ran slowly through the forest. With a steady cracking ice tumbled over the worn rocks. Ice cycles hung majestically on the bare scrubs giving the atmosphere an air of sparkling happiness.

But all was not happy in this wonderland of nature. A young Indian girl sitting on a moss-covered rock stared blankly into the shallow depth of the trickling stream. Her face was glum, her buckskin clothes were tattered and worn, and her tired hands showed that hard work was gradually capturing her youth. To see her eyes would prove the source of her unhappiness and loneliness.

50

They were sky blue, clear as a mountain pool, showing the world she was a half breed. Beside her set her dog who also was a half breed, but different from the girl; he was respected by his kind because of his supreme strength resulting from his wolf father. He, who loved his mistress dearly, would be her faithful companion for the rest of his life.

Sometimes, Starrie tried to hide from people that she was part Croatan Indian. Croatan was carved on a tree where the Lost Colony was supposed to be. Starrie's great great grandmother might have been Virginia Dare so she might have been a half breed before her mama married a white man. Once a girl at school asked her if she died her hair because it was so inky black. The girl said real mean like that regular white people never had hair that black naturally. Starrie told her maybe I am part colored person and that shut her up for good. Starrie knew for sure she was half Croatan because her mama had been one hundred percent.

Starrie came home to their log cabin and to her surprise and horror found her mama had fallen in the floor in a big lump. Her mama was very fat and heavy so she couldn't help her up. She called the ambulance to come help, but they wouldn't come because she was a Indian and didn't have any money. They said maybe later, but they had white people to take care of first. She waited through the night and the doctor never came. After that Starrie hated white people very much. She had loved her mama and now she was all alone.

I think I better go back and change that story. I don't mind making bad people die in my stories, but making good people die makes me too sad. I don't know what makes me do it.

The year I was in fifth grade, Daddy made us move to town.

"I ain't liking it here, Ella Ruth. I declare I can reach out and shake Mr. Simon's hand out my window." Before we moved, Mama always talked about Dr. Sanders's beautiful white house on the hill behind our house: "Horace Sanders's house up there on that hill looks like heaven to me." She didn't mind being "towered over," but she hated being "hemmed in," Mama called it.

Mama never reached out that window to shake Mr. Simon's hand. She hardly even opened it. She didn't like the noises: people walking around on the sidewalk below, cars honking and passing under our window. She didn't like hearing other families. And, most of all, she didn't like for Daddy to be so close to the Rebel Bar.

Mama said that wasn't the way life was meant to be, for houses to be so close that people knew other people's business. Mama thought everything in the whole world was supposed to be just the way she was used to and if it wasn't, it was wrong. Every time I would tell her about something I saw in a store or want to show her something pretty growing in the park, she would turn her head like a mule with blinders on.

"I guess it's all right," she would say, "if you got any use for such as that. Me, I got none. None a'tall."

It was getting close to time to plant a garden. Mama had fears we would starve to death when we used up the food she had canned. Since she wouldn't go outdoors anymore, I had to take my wagon and go get groceries. She told me to go all the way back to Parson's Store where we used to live. I did once, but it took me half of Saturday afternoon, so next time I just went to the one around the block. Actually we didn't live in town but two months before we had to load all our stuff in Daddy's pickup and move right back home. That was after Lula Lavonia Pitts's house got sold to a white person. When Daddy drove over to make sure, he saw two blond children on the front steps.

Mama sang the whole time she was packing our things back up. When we got it all loaded, she asked Daddy to stop for a box of sodie crackers. Daddy got grumpy because he wanted to hurry up, but he didn't know what Mama was thinking and I did. She told me about her papa coming home after he had sold the tobacco, hearing him coming and knowing when he'd had a good day, telling by his whistle. When he had a real good day there would be a box of sodie crackers under his arm for them. He would tease her with them, giving her one at a time. When Mama ate a sodie cracker, it wasn't like eating anything else. She made that little square go as many as ten bites, when I'd seen her take a cookie that size and put the whole thing in her mouth at one time.

Then she told me when things had gone bad for her papa, the summer when the government man came in and cut down his tobacco because he had planted over his allotment. They didn't get sodie crackers that year. They didn't even get enough to eat. The government man didn't cut down the spindly plants that got drowned out by the road. Mama said he went right in with the stalk cutter and sliced down stalks so juicy you could hear them squeal when he went through.

"It was a crime against the Lord, Ella Ruth, to waste a growing thing so green and healthy. Though I never had a taste for tobacco myself."

After a hailstorm, when what they had left got cut to lace and the worms took over, her papa knew his load was going to weigh light. The mule was pulling the wagon too easily.

That's why Mama said she made so much food on Sunday. Because they went hungry that year. And she never knew when Matthew might show up with his family. To my knowledge, Matthew never went hungry a day of his life.

Every Sunday I watched Mama in the kitchen that smelled of greens and cornbread, covering all the big bowls with plates. Then at dark she would say, "Guess I can put the food away. Don't look like they're coming." I would see Mama in the kitchen eating the cold food out of the big bowls. She would tell me, "Don't want it to go to waste." And Mama filled her body with all the food for the hungry people who never came.

The day we moved back to our old house, Mama sat in the pickup, her body shoving me against the gear shift with Daddy grumbling at me to move each time he had to change gears. I didn't have anywhere to move to. The pickup drooped on Mama's side and stayed drooped even after she got out. She had her box of sodie crackers in her lap that Daddy stopped and bought. She was nibbling at the squares like a mouse. She gave me one and told me: "Put the whole thing in your mouth and whistle me a little tune." I wasn't about dumb enough to fall for that old trick.

A big smile came on Mama's face as we turned into our old driveway. The grass was a foot high and there were rotten newspapers on the walk. Daddy's outhouse had fallen over.

"Home again, jiggedy-jig!" Mama giggled.

A short time after we moved back home, Daddy said we were going to get a horse. He wanted one to plow the garden in our vacant lot, but I figured that during the winter when there was no work to do, it would be for me. I got a little peeved at Mama because she tried to talk him out of it. I would have guessed she would have wanted one because for sure we could never move back to the apartment in town if we had a horse.

"Maynard, a horse, for goodness sake. You get some crazy ideas. No more garden than we got, why do we need a horse?"

"Because I'm damn tired of pushing that plow, that's why."

"Why don't you get a little tractor with a motor, like the one Gerald Mason has."

"Because I don't want a little tractor with a motor like Gerald Mason has," he mocked. Daddy had trouble using anything with a motor attached to it: lawnmowers, spray-paint guns, drills. He even made fun of Mama's electric mixer. "I could break an anvil with a wooden spoon," he said.

"One more thing for me to look after," Mama complained.

"I'll do it," I said quickly. "I'll look after it every day. Please, Mama."

That was when she stopped bucking Daddy. "You two done chose

53

sides against me," she said. He smiled at me because he knew he got his way because it was my way too.

I had her name all picked out—Blaze. Except none of the horses we looked at had a blaze. We got her near my twelfth birthday so I pretended she was a present. Daddy and I weren't looking for the same thing. He wanted something big and muscular and I wanted something lean and spirited. We settled on Maudie. She fit his idea. I couldn't be disappointed with anything long though, because anything was better than what I already had. Dr. Horace Sanders said we could keep her in his barn on the hill behind our house if Daddy would row up his garden every spring.

One day in June we were working in our garden. I got down on my knees to pull the wild grass out of the bunch beans. Daddy plowed with Maudie. I kept feeling something bumping me on my back and figured it was Stevie and Al throwing clods at me from somewhere. Only I couldn't tell where they were, just kept feeling that bumping that would sting for a while. On the next hit, I decided to spin around as fast as I could and catch sight of them before they had time to jump back to cover. That's when I got the scare of my life.

I spun around, looking across the street for a glimpse of them. Then I saw what it was that bumped me, right in front of my bare feet. A snake. A snake with a wide face spread out like a fan, puffed up mad at me. I screamed and held my legs still as posts. Daddy came running. When he saw the snake, he started laughing at me. The snake turned its face to him and rared back.

"Just an old hognose," Daddy said. "You ain't never seen a hognose, Ella Ruth?"

I never saw anything like that even in a nightmare. I stepped back and the snake looked at me again. I got where it couldn't reach.

"That's a puffing adder. All bark and no bite."

Daddy threw a clod at the snake and it wheeled to face him, swelling up even more.

"Go on, bust your gut wide open," he jeered at the snake. The snake clumsily squirmed into the grass where I hadn't weeded and with a hissing like a tire going down, it disappeared. I looked at the grass where it went. No way I was going to stick my hands in there.

Then that afternoon, a strange thing happened. Daddy started feeling things hitting on him too, just like me, and when he turned, nothing was there. Only he was getting hit up high on his back. The snake couldn't have reached that far. I was still getting out wild grass, shaking all the dirt off the roots so the sun would kill it, only this time I was working with a hoe so I would have a long handle between me and that snake. I had my back to Daddy when I heard Maudie squeal. I ran through the corn and saw her start throwing her head up and down. She yanked the reins out of Daddy's hands and when he went reaching over to get them, he stumbled and fell onto the plow. Maudie squealed again and before I could get to them, she bolted out of the garden. Daddy got wedged in the plow when it fell over on its side and Maudie pulled him behind her, ripping through all the rows of corn until I could see daylight through the garden. I ran through the hole and caught up to them, but it seemed forever before I could get her to stop. Even when she did, she kept kicking at the plow and my trapped daddy.

"Stop it. Maudie, stop it. You're killing him!"

She didn't kill him, but she messed him up bad. He had never been like that in front of me before. I had seen him drunk and throwing up on himself, but he got drunk on purpose. By then Mama was in the garden and I made her hold Maudie by the bridle. Mama was scared silly of horses and Maudie knew it so she kept biting at her and shoving her with her head.

"Dammit, Mama, hold her still. I can't undo him if you keep letting her jerk the straps out of my hands."

"I'm trying, Ella Ruth. I can't help it. Oh stop! Make her stop!"

I was really irritated with Mama because I was having enough trouble trying to get Daddy untangled without her acting like one of those prissy girls at school who started squealing if a bee buzzed around her head. Daddy was the one who was hurt.

"If you aren't going to help me, Mama, get on back in the house. You're just making it worse." She didn't leave, but she didn't say any more about the horse either.

When I got the straps off Daddy, he pushed me away and finished getting himself out. He was mad like I knew he would be, but he was hurt too and that made him different. Every time I would see a new hurt on him, I'd hurt in the same spot. He kept turning around his arms and legs to look at new places because everywhere he felt a sting there was a scrape or cut that was filled with blood and dirt.

I took the horse from Mama. As soon as I did, she ran up to Daddy.

"Maynard, honey. Come on inside and let me doctor you up."

He didn't answer. Too dumb to be a doctor, I thought. She led him toward the house. He leaned on her as they walked. I was the one who saved his life. He didn't even thank me.

For a minute I couldn't do anything. I watched Mama and Daddy until she helped him up the steps and through the door before I unhitched Maudie. While I undid the harness buckles, my hands shook. Maudie was calm now, though there was a cut on her leg where the plow hit her. I heard Daddy yelling from the bathroom as Mama washed out the cuts and her talking sweet to him, but I couldn't hear what she was saying, just like when I heard them in their room at night. He wouldn't let me be a big baby like he was being. I patted Maudie. I wasn't mad at her. Right then I didn't care if both of them went away and I got to live by myself.

After I got Maudie to her stall, I washed out her cut and rubbed in some pine tar and lard. I held the pine tar can under my nose to clear my head as I looked out the window of her stall. Just as I stuck my head out, something hit the side of the stall and this time I saw them: Stevie and Al with their popgun pistols. Then I did something that didn't make a lick of sense. I got my hoe and went looking for that snake. If I found him, I was going to chop him into a million pieces.

I didn't feel like myself, wanting to hurt something. If I'd seen my reflection in something, I wonder if that mad person would have even looked like Ella Ruth Higgins? Her face would have puffed up and looked back and said, "What are you looking for? You're the snake in the grass that ruined everything."

Everything Mama and I made was supposed to look exactly alike, which made our work harder than it ought to be. I spent a whole day painting cookies, which was my favorite thing to help Mama. The day before I had made cream cheese and parsley rolls, and then in the afternoon, I had dusted ladyfinger cookies with powdered sugar. If one was too large or too small, Mama took it out for us to eat because the ones we sold had to be perfect. I made tart crusts by the dozen for Mama since she couldn't make them at all. Her fingers were so large they wouldn't fit inside the grooves in the pans. I had been making them since I was five years old and Mama paid me five cents a dozen. It never seemed like work because the pie tins were miniature, like playing dolls. But that's where I was wrong; it just didn't seem like work to me.

Mama would work into the night, sampling each batch she took from the oven. During the Christmas season she was always fatter than ever, not because she had fun when she ate a lot like most people, but because she was afraid to let a single batch of tarts or cookies leave the house without eating one herself. I watched her bite the leg off a gingerbread man with a painful look on her face and heard her mumble, "Not sweet enough, I declare, but it'll have to do." She said I was no good as a taster because I liked everything. I ate the rest of the gingerbread man and he tasted fine to me. Also I

56

ate as many of our odd-sized failures as Mama did, but stayed my spindly self.

"Sure as anything, you take after your daddy," Mama said when she wrapped her fat fingers around my arm. "Blow away in a high wind."

I would watch Mama start to tire, her face sweating over the hot stove, her dress dark in spots from her sweat. When she passed me, drops landed on me like rain. She dipped batter on a branding iron shaped like a star. It exploded into shape when it hit the hot grease and like magic, a hollow, fluffy star appeared. Between each cookie she lifted her apron to wipe the sweat from her face, then placed her hand at the base of her spine as she walked to the counter to put the cookie out to drain. I would take the cookie after it cooled and dust it with powdered sugar. After Mama got tired, she didn't talk to me any more than the pot of hot grease. She would start to make grunting and groaning sounds, sometimes wheezing in a way that sounded almost like words.

Soon the top part of her body would bend forward, the hand at the end of her backbone no longer enough to brace the hinge, her breasts hanging like heavy sacks. I thought if she could empty those sacks, her back would go straight again. Then she would go to her broom closet and take down her back brace.

"Hook me in my corset, honey," she said softly. I strapped Mama in the brace on top of her clothes if no one was coming for a while. I felt bad because she would cry out each time I hooked a buckle. I thought of Maudie when I tightened the saddle, but if I let Maudie hold her breath, then me and the saddle would fall off. Daddy showed me how to knee Maudie in the stomach and pull the strap before she sucked up air again. He came in our kitchen drunk one night, ate a tart out of a perfect dozen and then told me to knee Mama like Maudie. When he laughed at himself, I wished I was strong enough to push him into the oven and shut the door and cut it on full blast. I hated him then, when we had to hurry out another batch just to fill in that one tart.

When I fastened the last hook on the corset, Mama was straight again and moved around the kitchen as stiff as a wind-up soldier. Her eyes, clear as blue beads when the day started, took on a glaze like hard candy dipped in cream. They would stay like that till she made me go to bed.

One day I painted thirty-two gingerbread men for a birthday party. They were for Marcel Sanders, who lived in the white house on the hill. I had to cut out eighteen girls and fourteen boys and paint them with skirts and pants. I used silver balls for their eyes that

57

looked like metal and not something you should eat. I always took the eyes out of my men because I didn't like crunching down on them like bones.

I was given a guest list to write the name of each person on their man, blue for the boys, pink for the girls. Some of them had long names, Christopher and Danielle Jane, and I could barely fit it all on. I saw the guests in my mind, around a table scrambling for the one with their name. I imagined a story about a little girl named Julie who thought she had been invited to the party, but couldn't find the cookie with her name. One version of my story had a little boy named Gerald who couldn't find one with his name either. Julie and Gerald snuck out together and played in the fields and watched, from the hill behind the house, as the other boys and girls in their party clothes played silly games. And they were glad they weren't at the party and could play with the birds and rabbits. Another version didn't have Gerald, just Julie. Julie, whose feelings were hurt, ran out of the house and was killed by a car. There had been a mistake on the guest list and her name was accidentally left off. I checked the names over and over to be sure I didn't miss a name. I counted the men five times to be sure. There were two Nancys and two Bills and a Billy. What if one Bill grabbed one and hid one? I thought awhile before I went to sleep of how bad I would feel if I had been the one who had caused the little girl to get hit by the car. I didn't know how to do that kind of story, where the person who made the cookies messed up, a person who didn't mean anybody any harm like my Mama. I could just do the kind where a snobby rich lady made the mistake. When I gave one of my made-up stories a sad ending, it bothered me so much it seemed real.

The next morning I counted them one more time before Mrs. Sanders came to pick them up. She came in the kitchen and looked at me and said, "Aren't you lucky to be Mrs. Higgins's daughter? You get to have a party every day."

A dream for my story box: I had a terrible dream about my daddy. He was driving a black car. We don't even have a car, just the old pickup he carries his paint stuff in. He came home and told Mama that he had hit an old lady.

"I know I hit her, Maxine. There's a place on the hood where her body is pressed into the metal."

I ran out in the driveway and saw the place he was talking about. I thought that he meant it was going to be like a footprint you make in the mud. It wasn't. She was cut out of something black as though she had been made by a giant cookie cutter. Only there was no decoration on her. Her eyes weren't shiny pearls and there was no dress drawn on. I wasn't even sure if she was out of anything eatable.

Mama was rocking in her chair and moaning. "Help me, Ella Ruth. Help me think of a way to hide her from the police."

"He didn't mean to do it, Mama."

"I know, honey, but this is the second one. He killed one last week and they let him get out of it. Now he's killed another one. Two times they will never believe was by accident."

My daddy was crying so I knew he didn't mean to do it. I had seen him cry only a few times before, only when he was drunk. In the dream he was crying because he was sad to be himself.

I felt so sorry for him. I knew the police were coming so I started eating the black lady. I wasn't one bit hungry. She tasted like licorice. She was so big I wanted to get Stevie and Al and all my friends to help me, but it couldn't be done.

"Mama, let me ask the ones who didn't get invited to the gingerbread man party to help me."

"No," she said. "They would find out."

That left it up to me and Mama because Daddy couldn't stand licorice, no matter how much trouble he was in.

I woke up with a terrible stomach ache.

I thought I liked being by myself as good as I liked having people around, but the day Mama and I went to the doctor the first time, I got so lonesome I could barely stand it.

I got out of school early to go with her. Mama made me take an excuse to my teacher that it was me who had to go. She was embarrassed for my teacher to know a grownup was afraid to go to the doctor by herself.

Mama said, "Ella Ruth, will you go to the doctor tomorrow?"

I wondered how Mama knew I had hurt myself. It had happened the day before when I was riding down Umstead Street Hill on my bike. I was going the fastest I had ever gone. Umstead Street Hill was where Stevie went under a car with his sled last winter and split his head open and had seventeen stitches. It was where me and Al and Stevie, all stacked on one sled, had to swerve and hit a fire hydrant because stupid old Mrs. Albright was sliding back down the hill in her car and ran us off. I had on so many clothes that time it didn't break the skin. Yesterday I got to the bottom and was going a hundred miles an hour, and I hit these wet leaves and slid off into the ditch. I have a boy's bike and I hit the bar in front of the seat which made me bleed between my legs. I had to lie on the ground for a long time before it stopped hurting enough to move. I thought if there had been wolves around, they would have smelled my blood and eaten me alive and I wouldn't have been able to do a thing to stop them. I felt my crotch get sticky. Finally the hurt let up so I went into the woods to pull down my pants and see if it was blood. I didn't tell Mama. I washed the blood out of my underpants and hung them to dry in my closet. My biscuit was still so sore last night I had to sit sideways on the kitchen stool.

"Why do I have to go to the doctor, Mama?" Before I could say it would get well on its own, Mama answered: "Please honey, go with me. I'm scared to go by myself."

"You're sick, Mama?"

"I don't know, Ella Ruth. I'm something." She went into the pantry and started banging pans which meant she didn't want to talk about it. I printed an excuse for me to get out of school and she signed it.

When I got home from school she was sitting in the living room chair. Her black plastic purse was in her lap and she wore a thin dress. She put it on over her long underwear top with long sleeves and her dress had short sleeves. Sometimes when Mama dressed poorly, she said, "It doesn't matter. I won't take off my coat." But she knew the doctor would see under the coat and the dress and the long underwear. I never saw my Mama's naked body, but Daddy peed with the door open.

When we walked to the bus stop, she pinched at my arm, then let go, making sure I was still there as if she was blind. Her legs were bent, curving under the weight she kept adding on top of them. Her shoes spread on the sides, opening and closing against the side of her foot with each step like a mouth gasping for air. Her coat had two moth holes in the back. She must not have seen them because the ones in front were mended. I was trying to remember if Mama ever cared how she dressed. I think maybe she thought she looked good.

We sat on the couch in the waiting room. The room was overheated and soon my legs stuck to the vinyl. My biscuit was starting to itch. Mama would say that meant it was getting well. I was waiting for her to want to take off her coat. Then everyone there would see the short-sleeved dress and the long-sleeved underwear.

"Hot as a firecracker," she said finally, so I tried to slip the coat from her shoulders so the people in the room wouldn't look up. When Mama rose to her feet so I could pull it from under her, her legs and feet made popping sounds. Mama beat at her sides a few times like she was fluffing up a pillow. The lady across from us looked up. When I folded the coat in my lap, I felt a chill from the sweat at the back of my legs. Mama could be so bold sometimes, then she'd turn around and be too shamefaced to ask for a bathroom.

60

Now she's sick and I got no idea in the world what she's got or whether she's hurting in her head or her heart or her stomach or all over because she won't tell me. The lady across from us smiled at me and looked back at her magazine.

Suddenly the door from outside swung open and banged against the wall, rattling the thick glass that held Dr. Samuel's name. The glass was already cracked in one corner. Mama's mouth dropped open.

It was a large family. The kids came in and went quickly for seats, wedging between the people there like the room was getting ready to move and they had to sit down fast. Their parents walked slowly to the nurse. The mother could barely walk. Her legs were tied with stained rags. The man, bent almost double, put his hand behind her waist. It was hard to tell who was the sickest one, but he must have been helping her.

"Ella Ruth," Mama whispered, her head turned sharply because one of the dirty children had sat beside her. "Worst-looking bunch of folks I've ever seen."

The mother wore a sweater, its sleeves rolled until they hung open and stretched. Her hair was matted and was just on her head, not fixed. I watched Mama. She looked at me with clouded eyes flecked with yellow like bits of egg. Mama's hair was parted straight and stretched smoothly into a bun. Her long hair was a lot of trouble to comb and dry, but it was the prettiest thing about her. Her undershirt was buttoned tight and had been neatly patched around the neck. She looked so elegant, so fine, my mama.

"Remember that lady that Daddy told us about, Mama? The one who came out of the restroom and prissed across the waiting room in the doctor's office with the back of her dress tucked in her underpants?" I giggled and Mama said, "Sh-h-h-h." That story made her laugh at home.

When the nurse called her name, Mama put her purse in my lap. It made me have a bad thought I wished I hadn't had. Mama's purse was smaller, real light. I didn't look inside because I knew what was there: her wallet, a Kleenex, and a pack of Life Savers, one of which she would give me on the way home, slipping it to me so no one else would see and she wouldn't have to offer them one. I felt my eyes get hot when I thought of Lula Lavonia Pitts going through that door flat on the rolling stretcher and not coming back again except a paper bag with her clothes and an icebox container with her teeth. Mama had false teeth too. If Mama died, her teeth would come back, but her long black hair would go with her. I hated the thoughts I was having. I was making up things like my dreamed-up stories with the sad endings. Only my mama was one of the characters.

61

After she had walked across the room, the poor family staring after her, I rubbed the fingerprints off her purse. Her skirt pulled away from her wet legs and dropped over her knees as she walked, covering the garter rolls of her cotton stockings. On her left hand was the wedding band that she couldn't get off. They couldn't bring me that ring. Unless dying shrank you up. There was a special tree in our yard that Mama showed me. A honeysuckle had wrapped it when it was young and it had a twisted groove all the way to the top. In the center Mama's clothesline was grown into the flesh.

"That little tree is bound and determined not to be messed with. Like you as a youngun, Ella Ruth. You'd throw off every stitch I put on you till you were four years old. You walked in when the preacher was visiting, naked as a jaybird." I didn't remember but it made my face burn when she told me. I couldn't stand to think of taking my clothes off in front of people now. I was getting so lonesome for Mama I felt like running through those doors.

After Mama was gone, I noticed a smell. It was the little boy who had been beside her. I could see the lice in the back of his hair. It was then that I knew Mama had taken her soap smell with her, Ivory soap. She took it into the doctor's office. Maybe he would notice that my mama smelled good, not like that family. Maybe he would see her and care enough to want to make her live.

Sam + Sallie make up
Dance
Arrival of Julie (19 year old
Harrie out riding catches ru
changing brands of five hole
Draws gun, Jan walks up that
she is thrown in rapids, Jo
Rustler believes her to be dead
son - He [illegible] and said he [illegible]
of her dead [illegible] Rustler finds
she to took from gun tells
trail - Harrie appears
[illegible] crook - [illegible] shot - lies [illegible]
Jan [illegible] to see [illegible]
her brother in town - not su
its him and he's not sure w
Talks to him behind store

1954

"Mama, you ever heard of Chester Alan Arthur?"

She stopped rolling dough a moment and wheezed. Then she picked up her dish towel and wiped the sweat off her face, like my question was the same as calling time out at a ballgame.

"Chester Arthur. Now let me see. Does he go to our church? Seems like I heard the name."

"Naw, Mama." I guess I sounded irritated, but sometimes she could be so dumb. "He was a President."

"President of what?"

"Of America."

She started rolling her dough again.

"If you knew, why'd you ask me?"

Mama answered me like she did Daddy. He liked to make her look stupid and it made her mad. I tried not to, but it was hard sometimes, especially in front of people.

"I've got to do my notebook on him. Of all the Presidents I got to get one nobody ever heard of."

"You'll do just fine in school, Ella Ruth. You always do. Your teacher told me at PTA that you were a real smart little girl when you applied yourself."

Mama smiled as she pounded the dough. It looked strange, that sweet smile and those fists hitting the dough hard enough to kill a baby. I wished I'd known Mama young and pretty before that body grew under her head. Her face isn't much to look at, but she does have some nice expressions. When I heard her wheeze, I thought of her heart struggling to pump through her veins that the doctor said were clogging up. She told me what he said on the way home on the bus when I was eating a green Life Saver. Green was my favorite back then, but I don't like them anymore. Mama took her medicine awhile, then decided it was too expensive for something that she couldn't eat or keep on her whatnot shelf. Daddy told her to take a spoonful of Drano. He said she was like the plumbing at Grandma Higgins's, too much grease and garbage had gone down the drain. When I heard Mama cough, I thought of turning on the spigot in Grandma Higgins's bathtub and watching the water spatter brown and burp up chunks of rust.

65

"Al Sawyer got Theodore Roosevelt, Mama, and there must have been twenty books in the Public Library on him."

Mama's face brightened. "Now I know *him*. He was President when I was a little girl. Sad, sad man. His mama and his wife died on the very same day."

"How did you know that?"

"I've not got the foggiest why I remember such things. His mama said the most curious thing. I believe it was his mama. Teddy goes to a wedding, she says, and wants to be the bride. He goes to a burying, he wants to be the dead person. Ain't that the funniest thing? Ain't it strange I recollect such a thing after all these years?"

It didn't exactly seem she was asking me those questions. "That's just plain weird, Mama."

"Now you think on it, Ella Ruth. Who gets paid the most attention to at a wedding? Not the man, I can guarantee. The pretty girl in her white dress with her bunch of flowers. Everybody's waiting for the bride to come down the aisle. That's the most important moment in her whole life when everybody's turning to see her, oohing and aahing when they play 'Here comes the bride.' And her husband just beaming."

"Did you have a wedding in a church?"

"Naw. We got married with the preacher's maid as one of the witnesses. I worried myself for weeks it might not be legal not having a white person. My papa wont alive to give me away."

"Why'd he want to be dead?" I asked.

She looked confused.

"Theodore Roosevelt, I mean."

"Same thing, I'm figuring. Just like the bride. Center of attention. Everybody starts thinking of every good thing about a person he can, when he knows he's dead. You'll remember till the day you die the very last thing a person says to you. I hated it terrible what I did to my papa. He asked me to get him a breath of spring branch he could see from his bed. 'Maxine' "—Mama imitated his weak voice—" 'I want that there pretty limb in here in my glass.' He pointed with his bony finger so I went right out and pulled him the wrong one. He got in such a fret I left the room to get away from him and forgot clean about it. Then Mama told me that very afternoon he'd passed. Wouldn't have taken me ten seconds to do that one little thing for him. But, I declare, he had run me ragged getting him this and that and nothing pleasing him."

Tears came to Mama's eyes. She was quiet a moment, then she spoke in a strange voice. "He talked real high and squeaky like this." Mama made her voice like a bird.

"Grandpa Akins did?"

"Naw, not Grandpa Akins. Teddy Roosevelt."

I laughed and thought she would go on, but she didn't. "I don't remember nothing else about it."

"Aw, come on. Try."

She took down the orange juice can she used to cut out pie crusts. When Mama's brain ran out of facts, it cut off.

"Al Sawyer says President Roosevelt used to go out and run around the Washington Monument."

Mama slid me the pie tins, bumping them against my hand. She acted like a dog who wanted to be petted. Instead of asking you to do something, she would nudge you till you noticed her.

"Now ain't that the silliest thing for somebody to tell on a person. You know good and well that's made up."

"No more made up than a man wanting to be a bride, for crissake, unless he was a pansy or something." I don't know why I slipped like that sometimes and forgot I wasn't with Al and Stevie when I was with Mama.

"Ella Ruth! Such talk for a lady."

"Lady?"

"Don't you sneer."

"Who wants to be a lady?"

Mama's mouth snapped shut. I'd said the wrong thing and I knew it before I said it. I had to have done it just for meanness, I guess. I don't know what made me be mean to Mama because I hated Daddy when he was. Sometimes I teased her just to get her goat. When she went on and on about being a lady, I couldn't say my feelings because Daddy was always laughing so hateful that I didn't want him to think I was taking his side.

Mama doesn't think Mrs. Albright is a lady because she wears pants like a man and swears at people and talks with a cigarette hanging out of her mouth. One morning Mrs. Albright ran out of gas after she took Mr. Albright to work. Because Daddy passed her standing by the road in her bathrobe and curlers, Mama thinks she should be shamed for life though more of her body was covered than when she wears a dress.

"Let that be a lesson to you, Ella Ruth," Mama had said. "Don't ever go out of the house without clean underwear. Think how shamed you would be if you had an accident and they took you to the hospital and saw your dirty raggedy underbritches."

"I think I'd be more upset over what they had to take me to the hospital for," I told her, but she didn't understand me one bit.

"You don't have to be the most beautiful creature on this earth," Mama had said. I figured she was saying that because it was getting to be pretty certain I wasn't going to be. "You don't have to have a million dollars. But people can always say, 'Ella Ruth Higgins? Why for certain, Ella Ruth Higgins is a lady.' "

"Maxine Anne Akins?" Daddy snorted. "Why for certain, Maxine Anne Akins is the fat *lady* in the circus."

"You shut up, Maynard Higgins. I was the prettiest lady in Summit when you married me."

Daddy grunted and said, "Yeah, only back then I just intended to be throwing my wild oats in the air. I didn't count on one of them taking root. That was your brother, Matthew, and the lady in question, Ella Ruth, was your mama." He laughed his mean laugh.

Mama cried that day and I saw her hands were still. I hardly ever saw her hands not doing something. Her blue eyes were rimmed in red and stared as though someone held a mirror in front of her face and forced her to look. But Daddy was already gone, stumbling through the kitchen, opening cabinets, then running into the doors, looking for his bottle. She didn't move. I closed all the doors he left open. I never said my feelings but I knew I was madder at Mama than I was at him. How could Mama have let her beauty go away, turn to something so ugly that nobody on the street would know she was ever anything else? If I could have been lucky enough to have been born beautiful, I would take such good care of it, it would stay that way forever.

"You taste it. I can't tell no more," Mama said, interrupting my thinking.

She pushed the lemon pie batter toward me, dipping her finger in one more time on the way and licking it with a frown. I could tell her feelings were still hurt.

I tasted it. "Good."

"I'm counting on you, honey." She smiled like you do when you get a shot and are trying not to cry. When she began to pour the little crusts full, I realized I had no idea what the filling had tasted like. I just stuck my finger in, then in my mouth and said "Good."

It shouldn't be so easy not to tell my mama the truth.

When I was in the ninth grade, I got my worker's permit so I could clerk at Simon's Department Store. It wasn't that I wanted to be a clerk for the rest of my life. I just thought it was something I could learn to do without much trouble. What I really learned was to make sure I did good enough in school so I never had to clerk in a store again.

"Aw, come on, Ella. Be a sport and try them on," Hazel said. She was head of jewelry.

"Leave me alone. I don't like that junk pinching my ears." The other clerks teased me when we were unpacking the new spring jewelry. When the floor walker wasn't around, they turned the customer mirrors backward and tried on every new earring.

"You've got to grow up sometime," Hazel sneered.

I never liked her. She was always talking about how my clothes weren't grown-up enough for fifteen. I was the only one working who still went to school. I knew who Hazel's daughter was at Summit Junior High. She bleached her hair in a streak and she wore one of those pointy padded bras that got pushed in when she carried her books against her chest. Hazel asked me if I had enough to wear a bra and I ignored her. I was wearing a Honeylane undershirt.

Hazel took out the bracelets that we were to mark two dollars.

"Looks just like real opals. I know. My grandma had one she promised to leave to me and my bitch aunt Sadie stole it with her in her deathbed," Hazel said. The opal bracelets had safety chains to make them look expensive, but their cloudy glass was backed with paper to fake the opal colors. "That burned me up, her knowing how much I love jewelry and how well I wear it. She probably took it to Greenberg's before poor old Granny was cold."

If I could have chosen my department, I think hats and jewelry would have been last on my list. I figured you could throw all the hats and jewelry departments in the world in the ocean and nobody would be any worse off.

When I worked on Saturday, it cost more than an hour's work—sixty-five cents—to eat at the store lunch counter. I did only once when I had to leave for work before Mama could get my lunch packed. I felt guilty paying that much for a sandwich and slice of pie I could have at home for nothing. Daddy said I was a tightwad, always saving, but Mama called me the little red hen. I knew one thing the little red hen wasn't going to let Daddy have money to buy—a bottle of High Heaven.

The workers' lounge was large, but everyone sat against the wall. When someone new came in they walked to the center, sighed and looked for a spot between the sprawled women. They headed for the vacant seat, turned around and fell back into it. I didn't know any of their names, except the ones from the hats and jewelry department. Maybe the women there felt sad because they had to eat out of paper bags like kids at school who didn't have money for lunch.

That didn't bother me because I never knew what Mama had packed and it was a nice surprise to see what was at the bottom. I knew it would be cookies or tarts, maybe a cupcake that wasn't perfect enough to sell. I did notice that most of them ate sandwiches with soggy spots on the bread. I was the only one who had a caterer pack her lunch.

The women emptied their change purses where everyone could see to count bus fare or to get a Co-cola out of the machine. Their legs had swollen purple veins with knots that came from standing behind a counter all day; their fingernails had notches from pulling price-tag pins. They pressed their fingers against their foreheads. They had the kind of tired that they didn't get over by going to sleep at night.

I was glad I knew I could walk up to the floorwalker and say "I quit" and I would still have food and a warm house tomorrow. I couldn't have stood that job if I hadn't believed I was different from everybody else there.

One day I took a cup and saucer from the dime store. It cost thirty-nine cents. I was going to give it to Mama for her whatnot shelf but when I imagined how excited she would be, I couldn't stand to know it was stolen.

She would say, "Ella Ruth, that's the prettiest thing I've ever seen, but it cost so much. You had to work forty-five minutes to buy this little thing for me." I was much more nervous putting it back than when I took it. I couldn't see spending that much for it. I went back the next Saturday and bought her one for a quarter that she liked just as good.

Hazel wore jewelry home every night. She said it was good advertisement to wear it while you worked, but she never brought it back. One of the young girls who worked with me borrowed jewelry—I saw her wearing it to church—and put it back on Monday.

As I rode the bus home through the colored end of Peachtree, I saw that people were dressed in their Wednesday prayer meeting clothes, clean and starched, sitting under single light bulbs on their porches. Moths swarmed around them. I saw colored women wearing the hats I sold at Simon's where the manager made me ask them to try them on with tissue paper over their hair.

"How I gon tell what it becomes me or not with all that paper plopped on my head?" they said. I hated handing them the paper. The floorwalker saw the blackened bands inside the hats that sat on the rack like giant blossoms of Queen Anne's lace and said, "Don't ever let niggers put these flat on their hair, you hear," so loud that everyone in the store could hear. I hated breaking the twenty-dollar bills they took out of brown envelopes too. One dollar and thirteen cents, ten cents luxury tax I had to explain, for plastic flowers that sealed against the sides of their faces like starfish, and pinched their lobes. The law said to cover your ears was a luxury, your head, a necessity, I explained. Didn't make sense to me either. I got along good with the colored women; they asked for the little girl with the horse's tail.

"Leave the clips open when you take them off," I told them, "to loosen the tension."

"You ain't got no screw-on ear bobs?"

"No, not in the new styles."

Sometimes I would run a nail file under the spring to ease the latch. They would try them on again and smile at me like I'd taken a thorn out of their paws.

I saw one of my plastic ear flowers in the gutter. I flipped it over with my toe and saw that the latch was gone, as useless as a blossom snapped off its stem. I got a chill thinking of the woman's anger at me when she looked in her mirror and saw her empty ear. I hoped she came back so I could slip her another one.

I looked around me in the bus. I didn't know anyone. I put my transfer ticket in my mouth and started putting my change in my purse, pretending I had a paralyzed left hand.

"Can I help you, honey?"

That was the lady beside me. She was almost as fat as Mama and had a mustache and a dark spot on the side of her face that had hair as thick as her head. I took my transfer out of my mouth with my good hand so I could talk.

"No, ma'am, but thank you anyway. I like to try to take care of things myself."

She nodded so I went on. "I used to be able to. I wasn't always like this, just since I had polio in 1950."

"You do real well," she offered.

"Thank you. I did what you were supposed to back then, stayed away from crowds. I didn't go to the swimming pool at all. Before they closed it for good that summer, I was already in the iron lung at Duke Hospital."

She just grunted. I guess she wasn't interested in my story. I was going to tell her I was part Indian, but I was afraid she'd say you don't look it. She pulled the cord for the driver to stop. That was dumb because he always stopped at Mangum and Hillsborough. We got off and transferred to different buses. I didn't see anyone from my old bus get on my new one, but I did see one person I recognized. Old lady Brentwood. She had blue hair and a fur coat on that looked like it ought to be on an Eskimo. And she had on blue tennis shoes and white wool sweat socks. She was the richest lady in Summit, but she stole. One of the new girls at Simon's got fired for catching her filling her purse with leather gloves. I didn't think it was fair to fire her because nobody told her what we were supposed to do was make a list of everything she took and give it to the floorwalker. They would send a bill to her son and he either paid for the stuff or had it sent back.

71

Mrs. Brentwood sat down beside me and put her purse in her lap. She was in the store today, but she didn't know I was the clerk who was watching her. I knew she had three pairs of white plastic flower earrings in that purse.

"Dear, would you do me a favor?"

"I beg your pardon." I pointed at my ear. "I'm hard of hearing. I had an ear infection as an infant."

"Dear!" she almost screamed. "Would you do me a favor and see if there are any nigras in the back? I have a stiff neck."

I peeked over the seat, scared of what I'd see. I wished I hadn't made her talk so loud with my ear-infection story. The back was empty. "No, ma'am."

"Thank you, darling. I have five nigra maids and I bought them a little present."

She opened the purse and started taking out the earrings I had watched her steal. I couldn't believe it. She had gotten two more pairs than I had listed and she had the rhinestone pair that we only had one of, the ones that looked like what Elizabeth Taylor wore on the cover of *Silver Screen* last month and that I was saving to buy. I didn't know how she got them because we kept anything over five dollars inside the case. She spread her loot out in my lap and asked me which one would look best on Geraldine and which one best on Maddie.

"I think fat women can wear the big ones better," I explained, just like she was a customer. "And ones with skinny faces shouldn't wear the danglers."

Her eyes sparkled. "You're a bright little girl." I guess no one had ever taken up so much time with her.

"Some colored women have short necks," I went on, "and don't like the drop flowers because they get caught on their shoulders."

"You got Maxine's number."

"What?" I thought of my mother and her short fat neck.

"You hit my Maxine right on the head." She pulled her head down into the fur coat. "Got a neck like a turtle," she mumbled from under the fur.

"Mrs. Brentwood?" It was the driver. He had stopped and opened the door. Mrs. Brentwood stood up and walked to him, dumping her purse in the aisle.

"Yes, young man." He had gray hair.

"This is your stop."

She turned slowly and looked out the open door. I started gathering up her things and putting them back in her purse. I saw the sparkling rhinestones and pecked them up like a crow.

"You're right, young man."

She started to get off.

"Mrs. Brentwood," I called. "Don't forget your purse. And your presents."

I met her in the aisle and hooked her purse over her outstretched arm. I filled her hands with the plastic flower earrings which she stuffed in the pockets of the giant fur coat.

"Such a fine little lady, you are. Let her ride compliments of me, driver. As soon as my new house is done over on McMannon, both of you will come to dinner. I have my smoked salmon flown in from Denmark."

McMannon was the street where all the old mansions in Summit were falling apart. They had long ago been taken over by colored families.

Mrs. Brentwood climbed down the steps and the door shut. I saw the pink gravel at the foot of her driveway and splotches of her pink mansion through the trees. I felt a tap on my back. It was the driver, handing me a token.

"Compliments of Mrs. Brentwood," he chuckled.

I took the token and went back to my seat. I felt in my coat pocket and my fingers touched the cold stones of the rhinestone earrings.

That night I looked in the mirror in my room, wound up the one long strand of hair that came to the center of my back and stuffed it under my cap. My face seemed so plain without hair. I looked like the flaky-faced nuns at the Catholic school. I tied a scarf around my chest to make a strapless dress. Then I took the rhinestone earrings and clipped them on. The triangles hung heavy on my ears, stretching my lobes. One of them fell off.

"What did you break, Ella Ruth?" Mama called from the kitchen.

"Nothing, Mama." I looked around the top of my dresser. "Just dropped my key chain."

I know the ones I saw her wearing on the cover of *Silver Screen* were real diamonds. I wondered if diamonds were heavier than rhinestones. I couldn't keep looking at myself like Hazel did at the store, ugly wrinkled Hazel with her bleached hair and painted eyebrows. Hazel could fluff her hair and look at herself forever. I couldn't look at me and see anything but what was there.

Her face had a diamond shape and her lashes were thick and black. I read in *Movie Star* that she used no mascara and her eyes were violet. I had never seen anyone with violet eyes. I thought about trying some makeup, but then I saw a picture of her playing a half-breed without a speck of makeup and she was still perfect. I wouldn't mind if they got her to play Starrie instead of me. My nose had a bump it didn't used to have. I couldn't remember being the person in the little washtub in the photo on the mantel, but I remembered being the one in the sailor collar in "School Days, 1947." I was prettier then. When I went under my sheet at night, my body used to feel slick as an otter. Sometimes I felt myself under the covers and thought that it wasn't me, that the real me had died. Like Teddy Roosevelt. I was in my casket looking up at the people who came to see me before they shut the lid. I made all those people sad because I had died before my time.

Like my permanent teeth, I knew the nose with the bump was the last nose I'd get. There was a space between my front teeth and Daddy just laughed at me when I asked for braces. If I opened the front door and Michael Anthony was standing there with a million dollars, braces would be the first thing I'd buy and a new stove and refrigerator for Mama and I'd never tell anyone where I got the money. I was homeroom queen all the way through grade school, but now I didn't want anyone to look at me. I sat in school with my fist against my face to mash up my cheekbones and press in the nose bump. I thought, What if I could have an accident and mess up my face. Then I'll get a plastic surgeon to make me another one. Sandy Fletcher got scalded when she was a baby and one side of her face looks like a dried up peach. I don't know why in the world she doesn't get it fixed. I could change my name even if I couldn't change my face. I hated Ella Higgins. Ella Ruth Higgins. I sounded like a cow. I changed it in my mind to Starrie Dawn. I wrote it with my fingernail on a leaf and slipped it in the cement when Daddy poured the steps so it would be permanent.

She was perfect. She rode the horse in *National Velvet* and they pulled off her cap and saw she was a girl and her beautiful black curly hair tumbled down. I pulled off my cap and my hair fell brown and limp, as straight as Maudie's mane. It had taken a long time for it to grow back out again. I looked away from the mirror and out the window. I had watched my tears when I made them come. I didn't like watching them when I tried to blink and stop them and they came anyway. I could remember crying when I had hurt myself, but I never did that anymore. I just washed the cut out or put witch hazel on the bruise myself instead of crying so Mama would do it. Now I cried because I didn't like me and what I looked like and because of who I was going to be. And what my life was going to be like. I wasn't able to daydream that I might grow up to be beautiful like I used to because I was getting too old to change much.

How could Hazel spend so much time painting her face? Witch Hazel. She had a hooked nose and her eyes were too close together. She did things to draw attention to herself. Daddy knew her; he said she was ugly as homemade sin. If I looked like Hazel, I'd just give up. Daddy said she ought to wear a bag over her head. But Hazel looked in the mirror with an expression that made you think she saw Elizabeth Taylor's reflection. Grandma Higgins made me so mad. She said Elizabeth Taylor had no right to be so proud, because she didn't have a thing to do with being beautiful.

"God made her face and it belongs to Him. Don't praise her for it," she said. "She'll get old and wrinkly and won't look a bit better than Michelle Sue." Michelle Sue had something wrong with her because Grandma Higgins had her too late in life. "She come in this world with nothing and she'll leave with the same. If she has taken the Lord Jesus Christ as her personal savior, she'll take a soul to heaven and leave that face for the worms."

I don't know where Grandma Higgins thought she got the right to talk about Elizabeth Taylor like that.

Maudie was looking at my window. I couldn't tell if she saw me. Sometimes I made like she could talk to me like Francis the Talking Mule. When I tapped the glass, she tossed her head and whinnied. I liked to make her nicker because she just did it for me and it made people think she loved me. I didn't know if she did. Animals may just love you because you feed them, but if Maudie loves any person in the world, it's me.

Bluegrass of Kentucky. I saw the movie. I didn't know if the horse really died, if it was a real story. Bluegrass wanted to run and win. The jockey held it back because bad men paid him to, but it ran hard anyway, fighting the bit in its mouth and it won. But its heart burst. I cried so hard when it died, I didn't want them to cut on the light in the movie theater. When they did, nobody looked at each other because they were all crying and were as ashamed as I was. I redid the movie in my mind before I went to sleep. I heard what the jockey was going to do so I locked him in the tack room and disguised myself in his satin suit. I put my hair under his hat just like Elizabeth Taylor did. We won the race. In the real movie they buried the horse with the bursted heart at the racetrack. I guessed a dead horse would be hard to move very far. Daddy said they sell them to glue and dogfood factories. Sallie's Food Store got caught selling horsemeat for hamburger. I would have gone to see that movie again and again if Bluegrass had won the race like in my version.

I tried to imagine my heart bursting, exploding like a dropped jar and splattering. I wondered what it would be like if there were ropes around my legs and I couldn't run, like in a bad dream when you can't get away from an evil person. When my heart beat hard, it felt like it could split through my chest, even through my eyes, all over my head. I imagined if someone tied me up and held me back like Bluegrass, I would die, my heart running out inside of me and not making a puddle on the ground. I remember the first time I heard my heart, booming in my ear on my pillow, and I ran to Mama and asked her to make the noise stop. I was too little to know that meant I would die.

I decided to take the rhinestone earrings back the next day and slip them back in the case. Hazel never knew they had been gone. She had never tried them on. She didn't care about anything but moonstones and phony opals that Liz Taylor wouldn't wear to a dog fight.

Last Sunday after I told Grandma Higgins my teacher said the first people looked like apes, she sent me to look in *Genesis*. She said a man in Tennessee had to go to prison for talking that monkey business. She told me I should quit school and go to work. I told her I already was working at Simon's Department Store, every day after school and during vacations, that I had to say my family was a hardship case to get a worker's permit so young. She tut-tutted me like I was lying. Then she said, "You ought to be helping your mama." My mama replied that I did help her, every night when she had orders to fill. Then Grandma Higgins said, "You ought not go off riding that horse all the time and start acting like a lady." I just quit answering her. I rode before school every day, which was the only fun I was having and I wouldn't be having that if I was asleep then like everyone else I knew. I got tired of talking to Grandma Higgins real fast. She already had her mind made up before I said anything.

"Apes. Apes! How can you let such foolishness in your head when it says right there in the Bible that God made Adam and Eve as the first people on this earth and he didn't make them to look like no hairy ape."

"Because scientists found the bones of the first people and they could make them out to look like apes and monkeys, that's why. One day they started walking on two feet instead of four when they were on the way to being people."

"Sheer, unadulterated malarkey. If they found ape bones, they were ape bones. Or niggers'." Then her mouth snapped shut like a mousetrap. I couldn't stand talking to her.

When I was in fourth grade, I wrote the Starrie story about the dog licking the sores on her grandma's legs to soothe them and make them heal. I told Grandma Higgins my teacher said that was an old wives' tale.

"Tell your teacher her shame is she don't know her Bible." She threw the Bible open in my lap. "Luke 16, verse 19: 'There was a certain rich man, which was clothed in purple and fine linen, and fared sumptuously every day: And there was a certain beggar named

Lazarus, which was laid at his gate, full of sores, and desiring to be fed with the crumbs which fell from the rich man's table: moreover the dogs came and licked his sores.' Licked his sores!" she shouted, "And Lazarus died and went to heaven and the rich man didn't."

"But it doesn't say here the sores got well. I think it means the dogs came to eat scraps and so did Lazarus and he was worse than a dog because they licked his sores."

She snatched the Bible back out of my lap and looked at the passage again. "Then it says it somewhere else." And she closed it and put it back on her bedside table.

I remember when I learned something at school that I had been thinking about wrong for a long time. I knew that Columbus discovered America and that the people in Spain thought he would fall off if he sailed too far out into the ocean. But I had it pictured all wrong in my head, I mean almost as wrong as the people in Spain. I knew the earth was a ball, but I thought we were *inside* it like a fish bowl instead of sitting on the outside. I thought the sky was like a roof and up there was Heaven and the golden city sat on a cloud. I blame Sunday School for getting me so messed up. I started having some trouble in my thinking. What happened when you went to the edge of the land? You ought to fall off that the same as the ocean. What was the ball made out of, some kind of glass? Could you fly an airplane all the way up and hit the top? What did the heavenly city sit on days when there were no clouds? When I asked my first-grade teacher, Miss Mims, she went in her closet and got out a globe. That was the most wonderful thing I had ever seen. I told her when I got rich, I was going to have my own globe. It made so much more sense the way she explained it for the people to be on the outside.

Then I asked her where was the end of space? And what was after the end? She showed me about planets and stars and the sun. Those other worlds could have different kinds of people, ones that weren't bothered by being too hot or too cold, depending on where they were situated. It made me dizzy to think there was something as big as space. She said there was no end to it.

When I told Grandma Higgins, she screwed up her face and said, "World without end, Amen, Amen."

I hated her. I was ten years old when I told her, "You think all you have to learn is what is in one book," I said. "My school has a whole library full of books and you never read a single one. There's a bunch of stuff you don't know about hiding in those books."

"The word of the devil," she snapped.

"Then the devil must have had a whole lot more to say than God and Jesus," I told her. She made me stay in the closet all afternoon. Mama didn't like her doing that to me one bit, but said we had to do

77

what Grandma Higgins said when we were in her house. My daddy never said anything to his own mama; he just walked in her house and found a place to sleep when we went visiting.

Last Sunday when I asked him about the ape people, he said the living proof was right over in Haiti Alley, that God just made white people.

When I got home I looked in *Genesis* again:

" 'This is now bone of my bones, and flesh of my flesh: she shall be called Woman, because she was taken out of Man.' Do you believe that, Mama?" I asked her. "That business about the girl coming from the man's rib bone?"

"It's in the Bible, Ella Ruth."

"There's lots of stuff in the Bible you can't go by, Mama. There is. Quit acting so scared like I'm going to make lightning come down and get you just saying so. There's a bunch of stuff in there about fighting and killing people and paying them back. And even Jesus, who's supposed to be such a goodie-goodie, he killed a fig tree just for meanness proving he was big stuff in front of his friends. Just because he wanted figs and it wasn't even the time of year for figs and he gets mad at the poor tree. And he sure didn't treat his mother very nice."

"I don't know about that," Mama said softly. She had a way of acting stupid when she didn't want to know so much about something it would confuse her. Like when somebody started saying ugly things about a person she liked, she would close her ears by saying, "I don't know about that." What she meant was, I don't *want* to know about that.

"Why couldn't God just make a woman separate? Why did he have to take her from the man? Anybody who could make a person up from scratch could just as easy make another one. I don't believe that, you know. I just think some man wrote it that way."

"But the woman was there to make the man do bad, Ella Ruth. She made him eat the apple off the Tree of Knowledge. She let that snake talk her into doing what God didn't want her to do."

"Yeah, I know. And because of her we have to wear clothes. Well, I like wearing clothes. I'm glad she did it. I would have done it too. Nobody can tell me that all these apple trees are OK, but you leave that one alone when they all look just the same."

"It wasn't a person, Ella Ruth. It was the Lord."

"Well, that makes me think that there's something mighty special about that apple tree and He was keeping it all for Himself. Besides, Adam was just a big crybaby. He stands right there and lets her eat the apple when he was plenty big enough to slap it out of her hand. God comes and he doesn't admit he ate the apple too. He says *she*

78

made me do it. Big tattletale. He didn't have to do it. Nobody makes you eat an apple. It's not a little pill you can poke in somebody's mouth. It takes a lot of bites to eat an apple. Adam just wanted somebody to blame it on."

"I think you miss the point, Ella Ruth."

"Maybe I do. But it looks like to me that God just decided on making people a certain way so he could sit back and watch them do wrong. He made real sure they couldn't do the things He could do. He didn't make them so stupid they didn't have any curiosity. It's like you put a cat in a box of biddies. You shouldn't spank the cat because he gobbles up one of them. You're the one who ought to be spanked for putting him in there in the first place."

"It's just to tell a story, Ella Ruth. You shouldn't take it so serious."

"It is serious! I got Grandma Higgins telling me today I can't put a hem in my Sunday dress when it's bagging out on one side and I have to go to church looking like that and Aunt Inez telling me we have to stay up late Saturday night doing the cooking so we don't work on Sunday. Telling me I have to go to church every Sunday and prayer meeting Wednesday night or I'll go to hell."

"You're a good girl. You won't go to hell."

"Grandma Higgins said I'd be in hell hurting so bad I couldn't stand it, but God wouldn't let me die." My mama shivered. "What if I told you I didn't believe in God? Would you say I was going to hell?"

Mama was quiet. I had hurt her feelings. I always went too far arguing with Mama. I should have known better. Mama could even get her feelings hurt when those Jehovah's Witnesses came to the door and started making her feel bad because they said they loved God more than she did.

"I'm sorry, Mama. I just want to figure out things for myself, I suppose. Did Adam and Eve have belly buttons?"

She smiled again, faintly, then she was herself.

"You know, Ella Ruth, I declare I don't know. I don't reckon it would be hard to make a belly button if you could make a whole person out of a rib, but if you were scratching up people out of the clay instead of letting them be born, they wouldn't have a belly button naturally since they wouldn't be hooked onto a mama. Maybe God made them belly buttons so they'd look like everybody else."

Mama's words came out one at a time like steam out of her pressure cooker, her brain puffing to put thoughts together. Confusing thoughts went over Mama's mind like a breeze over water, stirring up a few ripples that lapped at the bank, but soon there was only the clear stillness of a mirror as if the breeze had never passed. I was completely different. I couldn't keep confusing things from working at my mind even if I'd rather forget them. Sometimes I felt bothered and didn't even know what was bothering me.

"How would Cain and Abel find anyone to marry unless they married their sisters?"

Mama laughed. "You ask your Sunday School teacher. Goodness gracious, your poor old mama can't answer questions like that."

Mama picked up a sock from her sewing box and started darning it. It was still the Sabbath.

I could imagine Grandma Higgins whining, "Putting stitches in her soul," if she knew Mama was sewing.

I didn't believe for a minute that God would do anything bad to my mama.

For Christmas, Grandma Higgins gave me a little white statue of an angel praying. I was polite and acted like I liked it, but I would rather have smashed it against the side of her house.

"What a dumb present, Mama," I said on the way home. "Looks like something that oughta go in the church."

"Shoulda give you a bucket of coal and a bundle of switches." That was Daddy, who was three sheets to the wind since before we got there.

"Does seem a trifling thing to waste your money on with you needing underwear so bad," Mama said, "And I even told her you wore size five."

That night when I got into bed, a strange thing happened. I cut my bed light out and was lying there thinking how sad it felt, that tomorrow Christmas was over and wasn't there to look forward to for another whole year. On the other side of my room where I had left my presents I saw something glowing. I got out of bed and when I got closer, I saw a little angel praying. I picked it up out of the dark presents and held it in my hand. It was cold, but it burned with a green-white light.

I called Mama and she came running.

"Ella Ruth, honey, what's . . ." She saw it. "Oh, Lord Jesus! An angel." Mama started whispering. I think she was saying the Lord's Prayer.

"Mama, Grandma Higgins didn't know it could do this."

"Oh Lord in heaven above, it's a sign. It's an angel of the Lord, come to take one of us."

"Oh, Mama, it is not. It could just as well have been a monkey. Or a baseball player. It would glow just the same."

Mama walked closer to it like she was afraid it would jump up and get her. She was afraid to touch it.

"I don't think I want that thing in my house."

"Don't be silly. It's just got some kind of stuff on it. Like what's on lightning bugs maybe." I rubbed my finger on it, but it didn't come off. When I held it close to my hand, I could see the grooves in my skin.

"You can just put it in your closet where it don't show, Ella Ruth. I won't mind a bit and I promise not to tell Grandma Higgins."

Mama patted me and left my room. I didn't want to put it where I couldn't see it. I put it on the table beside my bed. I intended to ask Grandma Higgins if she knew it glowed, but she got so she didn't have good sense before I got around to it.

"You remember the prayer girl you gave me for Christmas last year?"

"No such thing."

"I mean the angel statue. Did you know it would shine in the dark?"

"Pshaw!" She screwed up her face. "Look me straight in the eye and tell me a bald-faced lie."

That made me feel better. Every night I looked at it before I fell asleep like it was magic. I squinted and made it a fairy or a leprechaun instead of an angel. Now that I knew Grandma Higgins didn't know it glowed, I didn't have to feel bad about liking it.

The day before yesterday when I was putting up Maudie, I saw Al and Stevie and two of their friends coming out of Dr. Sanders's old packhouse that he didn't use anymore. I had heard them in there before playing cards. They asked me to play once, but I said no because they played for money.

Al Sawyer called me over.

"I don't want to play, Al."

I was afraid they'd gang up and cheat me out of my money. I did kind of want to play. I had this daydream of acting dumb, then winning all their money.

"Naw, not that. Come'ere. I want you to show these guys something."

"Like what?"

He was acting real proud of something.

"Show them where I shot you."

I looked at Stevie. Tiger and Ernie were behind him.

"Full of shit as a Christmas turkey, right, Ella Ruth?" Stevie said and winked. Stevie got on my nerves. He was always trying to hunch his shoulders and sneer like Elvis. I think he thought he looked sexy or something.

"No, it's true," I said. "He shot me." I made it sound real matter of fact. I liked shocking Stevie and knocking that cocky look off his face.

"How come he didn't go to prison, then?"

"Because I didn't call the cops, that's why." My daddy had called the cops after they shot Maudie with BBs and the juvenile officer gave them a talking to.

"I don't believe you," Stevie said.

I walked over to him and turned around, pulling up the leg of my jeans. My socks were all bunched up with beggar-lice from the woods. The bullet hole was in the back of my calf, a circle smaller than a pencil with the skin stretched over the hole like plastic. They all stooped down and looked at it, even Al, until I started feeling silly.

Then that damn Stevie let out a wolf whistle and said, "When are you going to start shaving your legs, Ella Ruth? You look like the Piltdown woman." They all started laughing like he was some kind of comedian.

Al was more interested in bragging about how he didn't go to jail than my hairy leg.

"See, I told you I shot her. Got her on the run." He pretended to shoot a rifle at something that was moving. He was starting to make me mad.

"I'm not a goddamn rabbit, you know? You tell them what *I* got, Al Sawyer. I got your rifle and your Phantom ring for not telling."

"Hey, hey. Sawyer is going steady," Stevie started kidding. "Got your ring, Sawyer. Sawyer's the caveman type see. He spots a woman he wants, pow, he drops her on the run. Got him a Piltdown woman."

I would like to have put the mark of the skull right between that damn Stevie's eyes. I could still hear them teasing Al while I went down the hill to my house. Al Sawyer could pick up that crummy Stevie and break him in two if he wanted to. Al ended up being the strongest guy in our neighborhood. For a long time he was so skinny, it didn't look like he'd ever fill out. Then people started calling him wiry because, even though he looked like a beanpole, he never lost a fight.

That's why I was so shocked yesterday when I saw him down at Sanders's pond and he'd been crying. He was throwing this gig thing at the bullfrogs, but they were pretty safe unless he hit one accidentally. Something must have made him mad enough to cry and he needed to be doing something mean. He figured if he hurt a frog, he'd feel better. For a while he went after the spear when he threw it, then it went in too far to reach without getting wet so he started throwing rocks.

He heard me coming up, not because I was making noise, but every step closer to him I got, another frog jumped into the pond: chirp—plop, chirp—plop. I would never have walked up on him like that if I'd known ahead that he was crying. I couldn't pretend like I didn't notice it. He whimpered like a little kid does when he's trying to stop crying and can't. I sat down beside him and looked at the pond, trying to think of the right thing to say. He threw two more rocks and the ripple circles ran together.

"I guess you know," he said finally.

"Naw, I don't know." I thought a car must have hit his dog.

"I figured they'd all be talking about it by now."

"Who'd all be talking about what?"

"Stevie. Ernie." He sounded disgusted with me for no good reason. Then his voice changed. "Tiger is going to kill me."

"What the hell for?" I didn't even have to do it on purpose now. I started using cuss words whenever I talked with the guys.

He was quiet a long time. "That motherfucking Miss Whitmore."

Miss Whitmore was the homeroom teacher in the other ninth grade. I didn't like her either. At the ballgame Mr. Sawyer said, "How's my kid doing?" and she said real snotty, "I beg your pardon, sir, a kid is a baby goat." She knew good and well what he meant. I figured Miss Whitmore could kick Al out of school or even get him thrown off the baseball team, you name almost anything, but a teacher couldn't make him cry.

"What'd Miss Whitmore do?"

I started to answer my own question with something cute like "take your dirty pictures away?" but decided I better be serious. I remembered when Al and Stevie got their first naked woman pictures they stood by the side of the road and held them up to the cars that passed. They thought they were pretty cute till the preacher drove by and then called up their mothers.

"She made me hold Tiger."

"Hold Tiger how?"

"Hold him while she beat the shit out of him with a frigging book."

"That little piss ant beat Tiger?"

"Beat the holy Christmas shit out of him. Everytime she hit him, his dick hit the blackboard tray. Almost ruined him," Al's voice broke and went up high on the "ruined." He sounded mad, but I knew it wasn't at me. Not yet, anyway.

83

"What'd he do?"

"Mouthed off at her when she told him to go to the office."

"Big deal."

"So maybe she was on the rag or something, I don't know."

It made me mad as hell when they said that, like they're so damn blessed they aren't ever on the rag and the only reason is they were born boys. Another thing that made me mad as fire was the radio calling the hurricanes by girls' names. Even if I could stand Hazel at work, I wouldn't like her because her name made me think of the time I saw all the pear trees get pulled up in the backyard and my poor old chinaberry tree that was my favorite of all get torn to pieces. Hazel tore down all the best rides at Carolina Beach. If Ella ever comes through, I hope she blows all the boys in a hole full of cow shit.

"How could that short, fat little bitch hurt a guy as big as Tiger?" I asked.

That was the wrong question to ask.

"I told you. Because I was *holding* the cocksucker for her."

"How could she make you hold him?" I should have shut up two questions ago. He must have asked himself the same thing after it was over with.

Al said real quietly, "She asked me and I did it. Just like that. Like she asked me to carry a stack of books or something. And it was to help her half kill my best friend. He looked at me and tried to pull away and I shut my eyes and held on. I don't know what the fuck was the matter with me, Ella Ruth."

Al put his face in his hands. He had been calling me just Ella lately. But he never asked me to go to the movies or anything with just him. It was always with Stevie and Ernie and Tiger and I felt dumb with all of them.

"Maybe it was like she was a grownup, Al, like your mama or something. I mean, if it had been Mr. Armour, you'd have said fight your own battles, you hear, dipshit? But because it was a woman. Maybe that's why, Al."

He didn't say anything or look up, but I got the feeling he'd rather I kept on talking now. I knew those bastards, Stevie and Ernie and Tiger, were making him feel like he was a criminal.

"Did you hear what Jigger did to Mr. Armadillo?" I asked.

No answer.

"Jigger got Hubbard to take a shit in this paper sack and put it on Armadillo's porch."

Al looked up. I saw a twinkle in his eye.

"Yeah?"

"Yeah, and then he set it on fire and old Armadillo came running out and started stomping it with his foot."

Al laughed, "No shit."

"Naw. A lot of shit. All over his black and white wingtips."

Al's cheeks and neck got flushed when he laughed so now his eyes didn't look so red. Then he got quiet. He was thinking.

"I don't know, Ella. Old lady Whitmore would just pour water on it or something. She'd never let her precious little tootsies get close to a fire. She really swung that book at Tiger though. The history book, like a ball bat. I didn't know she was that strong."

"Yeah. Let's think of something else. Wouldn't want to copy that asshole Jigger anyway."

"Yeah, thinks he's hot shit on a stick with his Carolina jacket." Al thought a minute. "I could fill up a rubber with water and bomb her when she comes in to school."

"Might miss."

"Yeah. Could poison her cat."

"Al!"

"Just kidding."

"You better be." I kept thinking. "Al, how about the water tank?"

"What about it?"

"I mean something in big letters."

I could tell by his face that I had hit home. He sat there with a big grin on his face, then he stood up without a word. He held up one finger.

"Tonight," he whispered. Then he got up and walked away.

My rear end started to feel wet from sitting on the ground. I saw little sets of pop eyes start to appear around the edge of the water. Dumb frogs thought they were safe. Like Al Sawyer could have hit the broad side of a barn anyway, if it wasn't with a baseball.

The next morning going into school I passed Al, Tiger, Ernie and Stevie. Stevie had his arm across Al's shoulder and they were laughing the dirty laugh. They didn't speak to me, but they never did unless they were by themselves.

I walked down to the football field where I could get a good look at the water tank. I looked without looking so nobody would think I did it. It was in giant red letters.

I guess I was disappointed. He hadn't put much thought into it. I thought Al Sawyer was more original than that. I think he ran out of room and didn't get the "s" on dicks. Or maybe he ran out of red paint. Or he heard somebody and got scared. Or maybe he just is that ignorant.

By afternoon the tank had a new coat of silver paint on one side. I wondered if they got a white man or a colored man to do it. I bet not one person in Summit, white or colored, didn't see it but my mama who hardly ever left the yard.

Miss Whitmore's class had a substitute for three days. When she came back, kids were still talking about it. She looked like she'd been awake the whole three days. Although they painted over it completely, I can still see it just as clear as if it was still there: MISS WHITMORE SUCKS NIGGER DICK.

I met Gretchen McKensie at school. She caught me by surprise and pushed me down the bank over the playground. I rolled all the way down, skinning both my elbows before I stopped. I got mad as fire when I saw grass stain on my white monogram blouse Mama gave me for Christmas. Stevie and Al were pointing at me from the baseball diamond. Stevie hollered, "I seen all the way to the Promised Land." I didn't see how he could have seen up my skirt from that far, especially since it was pleated and hardly over my knees when I hit bottom. I pretended I didn't hear him, then I got up and climbed back up the bank.

"You sugar-coated hunka shit. We don't shoot in the back around here," I told her.

I grabbed her arm and got her in a half nelson. She had on a shirtwaist and it ripped away from the sash when I threw her to her knees.

I was too mad to quit even when I knew Miss Brown was coming. I hooked my foot around her ankle and threw her flat on her back, but she stung me good on my arm before she went down. A bunch of boys came and watched because they loved to see girls fight. Al said I didn't fight like a girl which was why I was winning. But that was also why I got all scratched up, because guys don't use fingernails.

"I'm glad you think I won, Al Sawyer. I feel like I came out on the short end of a cat fight."

My arms were stinging like they were scalded. I felt a bloody ridge on my cheek. I would have to tell Mama that came from getting hit with a branch on Maudie. Gretchen McKensie crawled back up the bank I had thrown her down. I tensed back up again in case she came back for more, but she saw Miss Brown, who must have scared her a whole lot more than I did.

We had to stay in after school. Miss Brown gave us a long lecture on how, for young ladies, fighting was disgraceful. It was a little embarrassing when she said we acted like we should still be in the grammar school, not the ninth grade. I wondered what she was going to do since this was the first time I ever got into a fight on the school playground. Al and Stevie said they got taken to the principal and he whipped them with his belt. I was pretty nervous about what was going to happen and so was Gretchen, but we found out that girls just get talked to and have to stay in after school for a week. I only had to stay fifteen minutes anyway because I had to be at work.

We got to know each other, staying in after school. When Miss Brown would leave we would talk. We would never have known each other since our neighborhoods weren't close. Gretchen had gone to grade school on the other side of town. She was real impressed with how I could fight. She thought sure she could have beaten me or she wouldn't have started it. I told her I was a good fighter because all my friends were boys. After we got to be friends, I didn't hang around with the boys anymore.

I was better than Gretchen at fighting, but she was better than me at a lot of things, especially at riding horses. She had her own horse that stayed at Grassy Knob Stables. I got real tickled at her sometimes because, for a tomboy, she could be real prissy. We had to pee one day when we were riding and Gretchen was going to ride all the way back just to use the toilet. The first time she did it, she peed on her foot. I showed her how to pick a downhill place.

"All those boys always afraid somebody's going to hit them in the dingaling," I told her. "Now you know one thing it's good for." She got real tickled and blushed when I talked about dirty things like she'd never talked out loud about them before.

One night before we went home from the stable where she kept her horse, we heard some men unloading a new horse. It was an albino stallion.

Gretchen and I went over to see it. The horse didn't act like any I'd ever seen. It acted crazy, its eyes as pink as people's eyes in a flashbulb photo. She explained it was brought in to breed palominos, that its ghostlike coloring would make blond babies come from brown mares.

The horse squealed as it ran up and down against the fence, rattling the wood as it slapped its body against the barrier. Suddenly it reared and came down on top the fence rail. It struggled to pull its front legs back, but each time its body lifted, it came back down on top the fence with a terrible splintering sound. The two grooms who unloaded it rushed to rescue it. One tied a rag over its pink eyes while the other snapped handcuffs on its front legs. The gardener and another man I didn't know ran to the corral. The four men got under the stallion's chest and lifted him to the ground.

When the horse's legs were at last still, I saw something moving under its belly. Gretchen saw it too: his pecker was long and stiff. He trembled and jabbed his back legs toward the fence he could no longer see. His pecker spewed white stuff that broke from a long string and rolled into balls on the ground.

Gretchen and I slipped away quietly so the men wouldn't know we'd been watching. We moved up close to the barn so we could get all the way out to the front of the stable to wait for her mother without being seen. Gretchen's cheeks were flushed and she looked down. I wanted to talk about what we'd seen when we got out of earshot, but she didn't.

The next day we looked for the stallion, but it was gone. Gretchen asked one of the grooms, who said, "Crazy as a loon. First mare we put him with cut loose and kicked him in the shoulder. Drew blood. She was right ready to be bred, but wouldn't have no part of that crazy fool."

We walked over to the empty pen, disappointed that he was gone. Gretchen touched the gashes his hooves had cut on top the fence.

"Have you ever seen a horse get bred?" I asked her.

She shook her head.

"Me neither."

It had rained the night before and the spots on the ground had washed away.

I guess I should have thought about it before I did it, but it just seemed the natural thing to do. Gretchen's parents were going to be gone overnight to a convention in Raleigh so I asked her to spend the night. I didn't think to ask my daddy to be different than he usually was since we had company that wasn't family. He could be strict with me at the dinner table and I couldn't be with him which wasn't fair. If I broke wind or turned my milk over he made me eat in the kitchen. I can still see his plate the night I hit my milk glass when I reached for a biscuit.

"See where your boardinghouse reach gets you," he screamed and jumped up before it ran into his lap. I looked at his plate and saw his English peas floating in white. Mama and I cleaned it up and she gave him a new dish of food, but before she got it heated up he was in the living room with his bottle of High Heaven.

The night when Gretchen came as we sat down to supper, I noticed Mama was very happy. She loved cooking and she never got to cook for other people except the ones who paid her. Since we got to be best friends, she called Gretchen her other daughter. Mama gave us paddles to lick, one each, when she was making a chocolate cake. Mama sewed our school letters on our windbreakers when we made the basketball team. I quit my job until summer so I could practice and made my money helping Mama. Sometimes it seemed that Gretchen didn't have a mother. When we wanted to feel comfortable making scrapbooks or anything messy, we went to my house. Gretchen's room was like one in a magazine. She wasn't allowed to put pictures on the walls unless they had frames. I had only been in houses like Gretchen's when I delivered Mama's cooking to rich people. Mama said she would love to sleep in a rich person's bed and she didn't see how I slept a wink in mine at home because I had a life-sized poster of Ricky Nelson on the ceiling. Mama didn't complain even though I stood on the bed and put it up with thumb tacks into the pink paint that she had done herself.

The night Gretchen came to my house, for some reason Daddy started telling jokes. Maybe he was showing off. Mama and I had heard them so we knew what was coming.

"Did you hear the one about the Scotsman?"

Gretchen said no, and Mama gasped.

"He was too cheap to buy toys for his boy so he cut holes in his pockets." Daddy laughed by himself, then asked, "Don't you get it?"

Gretchen got it, but didn't say anything. She looked down at her plate and pretended he wasn't talking to her. I wished she'd said, "Yeah, I got it."

"He cut holes in his pockets so he could play with himself."

"She got it, Daddy," I said.

"Think you know it all, do you?" he snapped. Daddy was saying opposite things these days. He would say, "You're grown up now," then turn around and say, "Think you're grown up, do you?" depending on whether it was convenient to have me grown up or a little kid.

Mama had gone back to the kitchen for more biscuits when he said in a loud whisper. "Hear the one about the fat lady who got caught in the bathtub?"

"We heard it, Daddy," I answered quickly, but it didn't stop him. Once he started a joke, he was like a toilet that already had the lever pulled.

"Her husband called these guys to get her out, see?" He spit on himself on the "see" and I smelled enough alcohol to set the room on fire. "Then she started hollering about how she was naked and didn't want them to see her. So her husband says, 'Here, cover your . . . cover your *thing* up with my hat.'" He said "thing" in such an ugly voice, he might as well have gone on and said it. "So she did, see? She put his hat down there."

He pushed out his chair and pointed to his crotch. I don't know why but I looked at the front of his paint-spattered overalls when he pointed like there was something to see. Gretchen giggled and looked at me. Her face was bright red. "See, the fellows got there who was going to rescue her, and they come in the bathroom and one of them says to the other one, 'I think we can get her out, mister, but I'm afraid the fellow underneath her is a goner.' "

Daddy started laughing and almost immediately got strangled. Mama had come through the door on the punchline.

"Maynard Higgins, you are a shameful sight."

Daddy didn't answer because he was still choking. He was trying to say "water," I thought.

"Go on and choke your sorry self to death. See if I care. That's the devil in you."

Mama was furious. She wasn't going to get him a glass of water. He kept pointing his skinny finger at the kitchen sink and banging his empty tea glass on the table. I remembered the other times he told that joke. Once she said, "Why is it that fat ladies are always the butt of your jokes?" Once she just smiled and shook her finger at him and said, "Maynard, for shame," real easy-like.

Daddy got up and stumbled into the bathroom, still strangling. The sound muffled as he shut the door. I think he was throwing up. Mama started sobbing.

"Oh, Gretchen. Oh, Gretchen, dear."

He hadn't done anything but tell a dirty joke. Mama was making it a bigger deal than it was.

"It's OK," Gretchen said. "My daddy tells dirty jokes all the time, Mrs. Higgins. I'd already heard it."

Mama stopped crying when Gretchen said that. I was amazed at how she could always think of the right thing to say.

Gretchen's room, like mine, was filled with things she had outgrown. Yet I knew how different our lives had been when I saw what she had: a collection of tiny dolls—miniature women, not a real-sized baby like mine—dressed in costumes from different countries and different times: a Dutch girl, a bride, an old-fashioned lady with a bustle. They were dolls that you put on a shelf and looked at, not ones you held or changed clothes on or gave names to even.

She had a stamp collection with beautiful unpostmarked stamps from foreign countries, stamps you had to buy from approval companies. Her parents gave her an allowance. My collection I soaked off envelopes I found in Grandma Higgins's attic or off the ones the secretary at the church saved me from the missionaries. We were working on our collections together one day when Gretchen saw a set of butterfly stamps from Angola that I had taken out of her book and hidden under the cover of mine. I bet she would never have missed them. She wouldn't have found them either if she hadn't been checking in my book to see if my Chinese stamps had any glue on them.

We both laughed when she found them, but it bothered me the rest of the day. I decided never to steal anything from Gretchen again. It's hard to be honest, even with your best friend.

Once I spent the night at Gretchen's. It was the first time I'd ever been away from home overnight when my parents weren't there except at Grandma Higgins's. Gretchen had matching twin beds in her room. When she stayed at my house, I slept on a cot Mama kept in the attic and Gretchen got my bed. She had expensive sheets because they felt like wearing a silk slip instead of crawling into bed. I wondered if the sheets at my house had bothered her. Mama had washed them fresh, but they never felt like Gretchen's. I forgot my toothbrush so she gave me a new one and told me to keep it. I guess nobody would want it after I used it, but now I had to explain to Mama how I got it because she would feel beholden.

At breakfast I felt like a person in a movie. They had a glass-top table and white iron chairs out on a porch that smelled like boxwoods. The smell of boxwoods always made me think of money because I smelled them when I went up the walkways at the houses of Mama's rich customers. There was a section of cantaloupe on a china dish. I had a fork, a regular spoon, a sharp pointed spoon and a knife. I didn't know which things they wanted me to eat it with. Mama always cut off the rind and chopped it into squares for me. She called it mushmelon. I never had it for breakfast before.

"You don't like cantaloupe?" Gretchen asked and picked up the spoon with the sharp end.

"I like it fine." I picked up my sharp spoon. She giggled. I think she saw straight through me.

Gretchen's mother came out and sat down. I felt nervous, that we did the wrong thing starting without her. I was already down to the rind, but so was Gretchen. Her mother poured a cup of coffee from a silver pot and put in a square of sugar. Gretchen always brought sugar like that to give to the horses. I was wondering if all I was going to get for breakfast was a piece of cantaloupe when the colored woman who let us in the house after school brought in a plate of bacon and eggs for me and Gretchen. Mrs. McKensie didn't have to cook it. That was why she could come so dressed up to breakfast. Her nails were painted and she wore lots of diamonds, not just her wedding ring.

"Are you spending the day at the stable, dear?"

"Yes ma'am," Gretchen answered.

They talked, saying a few more things, but it seemed funny. Like they were strangers talking. They asked each other things, but didn't care about the answers. I ate a round piece of toast. I had never seen a round loaf of bread. I wanted some jelly but said no thank you when Mrs. McKensie offered because I didn't know how to take it out of the little silver container properly. Gretchen piled hers high and I was sorry I hadn't taken it when I watched her eat the orange marmalade, my favorite kind. We always ate stuff out of what it came in, jelly out of jelly glasses with pictures of cartoon characters on them, mustard out of a mustard jar, and pepper out of a pepper can. Everything at Gretchen's had been switched to fancy containers. I guess I thought that was kind of nice.

While we were eating, I got a feeling. Mrs. McKensie was being nice to me, polite I should say. But I started thinking she didn't like me. I don't know why I felt it, but I thought a fancy lady like that couldn't like Ella Ruth Higgins, daughter of Maynard and Maxine Higgins. Maybe she had asked me over just to get a closer look at me, not because Gretchen had come to my house. But Gretchen liked me. I was her best friend.

A chipmunk ran out on the flagstones and looked at Gretchen. She pinched off some bread and threw it to him. He grabbed it and ran. It was as if they were friends already.

"Gretchen, how many times have I told you not to do that."

Her mother frowned and her face that I thought was pretty before wrinkled all over. When it relaxed I saw lines I hadn't noticed. She had frowned a lot of times before.

"They'll be all over the table and we'll have to eat inside."

Gretchen ignored her and kept on eating. I was proud of Gretchen. I decided Mrs. McKensie didn't like Ella Ruth Higgins and the feeling was mutual.

Gretchen's father came in. He had on a coat and tie. I remembered Gretchen telling Mama that her daddy told dirty jokes too. I think Gretchen told Mama a lie. That man would never tell a dirty joke in front of women. After he arrived, everyone seemed stranger still. No one said anything with any feeling in their voice. It seemed like a movie, but like all the people were bad actors who had memorized their lines and weren't saying them with any expression.

The next day when I was at home I took the grape jam and piled my square toast high to make up for the day I missed.

Mama said, "Seems a shame to waste good money on jam when I could make it if we had the grapes. Maynard, you ought to get around to stringing up that grape arbor."

Daddy said, "Have a little bread with your jam, Ella Ruth." It was like every little thing I did got paid attention to. I took a giant bite out of my toast.

"It's my glass when it's empty." Pluto was on it and the one I had now had three red pigs, but it had so many chips I could only drink from one spot.

I ate my scrambled eggs. Mine were yellow and white because Mama broke them straight in the pan and didn't whip them up like the colored woman had at Gretchen's.

"Wipe your mustache," Daddy said. I wiped the milk off my mouth on the sleeve of my flannel shirt.

"Do you know Mr. McKensie, Daddy?"

"Yeah, I know the asshole."

"Maynard!"

"How rich is he, Daddy?"

"Rich as two feet up a bull's ass."

Mama said softly, "I think that Gretchen is a mighty sweet little girl, rich or not. Her mama puts on the dog a little though, setting out front beeping the horn when it ain't ten feet to walk up to the door. Give me the knife, Ella Ruth."

I handed the knife to Mama. We all used the same one. I watched Mama cut the butter. She had made it with her mold that had the acorn on top. When she cut it, I could see white drops of milk on the yellow, just like her two-tone eggs. I thought of Mrs. McKensie with her tiny knife spreading a piece of toast that looked about like a cracker. Mrs. McKensie sat up straight and her navy blue suit was buttoned at the waist. One square of sugar, ploop, in her coffee and Mama held her spoon over her cup and poured it out of a sack with three times as much going around the spoon as caught in it. Mrs. McKensie's suit coat wouldn't go around one of my Mama's legs.

I couldn't help it but I just kept watching Mama and that butter, thinking all that fat that went on her body and clogged her veins up she had made herself, stuffing too much food into her mouth. It got easy to see how because Mrs. McKensie didn't. Men would turn and look at Gretchen's mother and say, "Nice-looking woman for her age." They would laugh at my mama and call her "Fatty, fatty, two-by-four, couldn't get through the bathroom door."

"Where are you going with your lip out so far I can sit on it?"

I stopped at the door. That was Mama. Mama sitting on my lip. Mama sitting on a lip that was a yard wide even.

"I'm going to ride Maudie."

"Well, pardon me for asking."

I knew it wasn't fair, to be mad at Mama when she hadn't knowingly done a thing. But how could she have let it happen? I was never going to get fat if I had to starve myself the rest of my life.

In the hall at Gretchen's house were two small frames with

"McKensie" in one and "Powers" in the other. Above the fancy writing were shields, one blue and silver, one red and gold. I asked Gretchen and she said they were her family coats of arms.

"My great-great grandfather McKensie was a general in the Civil War. His plantation was on the James River in Virginia." She showed me some of his things, an old gun and a sword. On a shelf in the den was a blue cup and saucer. "That was all that was left of his house when he came home from the war." I looked around at the cabinets full of silver and china dishes. In less than a hundred years, the McKensies had collected a lot more stuff than they needed.

"Mama," I asked that night when we were getting dinner, "does the Higgins family have a coat of arms?"

"A what? Coat of arms? Now let me see. Naw, I don't believe so, Ella Ruth. I don't believe people in this country had much use of them. It was just King Arthur who used them over in England, I think."

I had to think on that awhile till I figured out Mama thought I meant a suit of armor.

"Do you remember your Grandpa Akin?" I asked her.

"Never knew him. Knew my grandma for a while. Not a beauty by a long shot. Her and her eldest daughter had a knockdown dragout fight and she had a nervous breakdown, they say. All I remember of her is her biscuits, three pans a day for the folks and two pans for the livestock. Till she went down for good I seen her out back every morning, a biscuit crumbling out of her little fist and the guinea hens shoving the chickens out of the way to get it. Day she went away she was still talking on her biscuits, fretting there wont enough. Poor old soul didn't know the reason all them folks was gathered was because she was going. There she was, thinking on her woman's duty to fix extra for company. If there's no flour and lard in heaven, I don't know what Grandma's finding to do."

Mama poured a hill of flour in her wooden bowl and made a cavern in the top which she filled up with milk. Then she scooped out a fistful of lard and started squeezing everything through her fingers.

"This here was her bowl."

I was surprised. Mama had never told me that before.

"I got her iron wash pot rusting away in the basement and her butter mold. My sisters made off with the rest."

I thought of the blue cup and saucer at Gretchen's, all that was left after the Yankees came through. Maybe it was better not to have been so rich.

"Did your grandma tell you about the Yankees coming through?"

"Lord, yes. It was hard to tell the winners from the losers, she reckoned, they was all so rag-bag and poor-looking. After a war there ain't no laws far as people's concerned. Everything folks had was theirs for the picking. My grandma and her sisters hid out in the barn, hoping the Yankees wouldn't know they was there, but there was their wash on the line, big as day. Might as well a hung up a sign saying there was women there somewhere. Grandma watched a Yankee knot up the legs of her best pantaloons and fill them up with taters like they wont no more than a gunny sack. Took all their store of food for the winter and left them starving. Grandma told of taking the wash out of that iron pot steaming hot and having it freeze 'fore she got it pinned to the line. Grandpa come in walking stiff-legged and she said, 'I knows you been hanging out at the tavern, Benny Perkins, 'cause your pants froze like stove pipes.' "

Mama's eyes sparkled because she was keeping me in suspense.

"See, if they froze it meant the snow collected on them melted in front of a stove while he drank his brew, then froze up solid after he went outside again to walk home."

We didn't have to be so clever to figure out if my daddy had been drinking. I could tell as soon as I heard the latch hanging up on the back gate and Daddy cussing as he tried to force it open. Mama never went to help him. I think she was glad for it to take as long as possible for him to get in.

Across the kitchen on Mama's whatnot shelf was a plate with MYRTLE BEACH printed on it with a girl and a beach ball that had the color stamped on out of the lines. There was a dark line across it where I glued it back together after Daddy broke it when he fell over the kitchen stool. There were three cups and saucers I bought her at the dime store, made in Japan. That's all the dishes we had except the ones we ate out of.

"One night Grandpa had too much to drink and his horse throwed him. They found him at dawn, stiff as a log with his neck broke. They had some hard times and that's all we had since. Land got divvied up in so many directions, not a one of us had enough to scratch out a living. My pa never could get back on his feet, no matter how hard he tried. Mama had me right out in the field, she told me. Two days later she was back picking, pulling me along in a little box she tied to her leg, covered with a flour sack. Mama had a hard life and I reckon God will bless her for it. But if there was ever sheer unadulterated spite and gall, it was Mama. Mama shamed me to death."

Mama rolled dough balls and put them in her pan, pressed two dents in the top of each.

"I never told you, Ella Ruth, but your daddy might have been Dr. Horace Sanders."

For a second my heart dropped, thinking my mama meant she had misbehaved. But I knew better. She went on, "He come riding by our place. I saw that fine-dressed man step down from his buggy and I thought sure my pa hadn't left owing him no money. That made me certain he must be coming to ask for my hand and since my pa was gone, he was going to ask Mama if he could come courting me. And there was Mama . . ." My mama's voice cracked and she went silent.

"Horace Sanders," I said. "He don't look like no prize to me. Course neither does the daddy I got. I wouldn't give you two bits for the pair of 'em."

I looked to see if Mama was peeved at my teasing her, but her eyes hadn't changed. She sighed and put the biscuits in the oven and I waited for the blast of hot air to hit my face.

"There I saw Dr. Horace Sanders coming up the path to our place and there was Mama, her legs apart, squatting and holding her skirts out and peeing like the commonest farm animal. She went walking out to meet him wiping herself on her skirts and I saw the wet spot in the dirt. Least a cat kicks over it."

Mama's voice broke again. "And Dr. Sanders seen her and just tipped his hat and said, 'How-de-do, ma'am,' and turned tail and never come up our path again. Mama come walking back and spit a string of tobacco juice that cut through the corn stalks like a knife. I felt like a knife went in and made out with my heart. 'Peculiar fellow,' she said. 'Thought he come looking after something and all he gets me out of the field for is a how-de-do.' I heard his buggy, jingling as he went away and, at fifteen years of age, I knew for certain that Maxine Anne Akins wont never sitting up there beside him. Wont a month till he married up with Flo Cummings and her to be barren as a mule. He got shed of her and took on Amanda Carmichael whose daddy was a judge. She gave him two children though, before his hair went snow white."

Mama opened the pots on the stove and stirred the contents, filling the kitchen with good smells. She cracked the oven door and peeked at her biscuits. Every time Daddy and I found a rotten tomato in the garden, he threw it over the fence onto Dr. Horace Sanders's property. "Another tomato for Horace Sanders," Daddy would say before it sailed through the trees, splat into the leaves.

"There's two kinds of folks in this world, Ella Ruth," Mama said, "the haves and the have-nots. The Sanderses and the McKensies is the haves. The Higginses and the Akinses is the have-nots. Always have been. Always will be."

I looked at the whatnot shelf again. Mama was right. It might as well have been empty.

It is 1956, the year I will be sixteen. I put in a couple of things for my time capsule I haven't explained yet so I will now. One is a picture I got out of the newspaper of Stalin. He's near about dead in the picture and the things on his skin with the black circles around them are leeches. That's what they do in Russia where he's from to bleed a person trying to get out the sickness. My teacher said that showed you how dumb the Russians were, that they spent all their time making an H-bomb instead of making people well, and what good did an H-bomb do their number one man when he got sick, not one bit. She said they didn't have refrigerators or cars and the government won't let the people know we have them. I don't see how they could keep something like that a secret with television and all. I can sure tell a lot from television and movies about how much nicer houses people have than I do even if I'd never seen my friend Gretchen's. My family is a have-not but we don't miss meals or anything like real poor people or the ones in foreign countries.

I guess I really don't care about the government much but I did save you an I LIKE IKE button. Daddy said how could Stevenson get along with the country if he can't get along with his wife. I thought the I LIKE IKE button was cute and wore it for a while because everybody else did. Then I watched him on TV (Grandma Higgins has one, not us) and he about drove me nuts waiting for him to say what he had to say as bad as this boy at school who stutters. I heard he had them catch the squirrels on the White House lawn for chattering and messing up his golf. I figure the squirrels were there first. I don't believe in running out anything that was there first and all the animals and Indians were here before us. I can get mad as the devil at something like a cutworm that cuts down a tomato plant and doesn't even do it for something to eat, but I've got the sense to know I got no right to get mad. It's hard to feel bad about killing worms and bugs though (except pretty ones) because they kill things I like better than them. I'll let out a moth or fly before I'll kill it. I wonder if you still have them. I bet you do. They will outlive us all.

Mainly I want to tell you about our times. Mostly I just notice kids my age. I don't know any grownups but my parents and my teacher and Hazel I used to know at work. Daddy says they're talking about making us go to school with colored kids but it'll never happen, he says, no matter how hard Martin Lucifer Coon (he calls him that) tries. They got their own school and it's newer than ours. If our majorettes ever got caught strutting like theirs they'd get kicked out of school. I gotta admit I wouldn't even go to the Christmas parade if their band didn't march. I mean they *strut*, the ones playing too, and they smile and talk to their friends and laugh and march around the horse crap and our dummies are staring at the music so hard, they step right in it. Guys carry these little bags of white powder to dab on the spots on their white bucks. Guys are wearing white bucks all the time now and black pants and pink shirts. I never thought I'd see the day Al Sawyer and Stevie would be seen dead wearing a pink shirt. And they got these straps on the backs of their pants—crap straps or heinie binders—and the school is raising hell because they tear up the backs of the desks with them when they sit down.

Daddy says they're a bunch of sissies. Any boy who would wear a bracelet from a girl or some girl's ring on a chain around his neck. Daddy hates the music we like but I told him his parents hated the music he liked and he said he never could stand that sorry Snot So Hotra (which is his name for Frank Sinatra) who treated Ava Gardner who was from North Carolina so dirty and that they paid girls five dollars each to act like he was making them faint and they were doing the same things with Elvis, that no woman, decent or not, would squeal just to see a ducktailed skin shake his hips like a fairy and then tear his shirt off. He said it was enough to make you puke to hear about him wiping the sweat off his face and have women tear the handkerchief apart like dogs with a steak. He said those women with Elvis were low class enough to do it for a dollar.

But Daddy doesn't understand about Elvis. Someday when I get rich enough, I'm going to buy all his records and put them in here and hope you have a record player because I don't care a hoot about seeing him shake his hips. I just know about his singing.

Gretchen and me went to the record shop and got "Heartbreak Hotel" and went in one of those booths and neither one of us could say a word. I could listen to it a thousand times and still get this feeling down in my stomach every time I hear it. The guys all dress like him and try to act like he does, sneery and all. They wear their hair in ducktails, but they get sent home for sideburns. They don't care as much for the songs as we do. They care more about cars than anything and getting in the Road Rebels or if they have a really nice car, the High Winders, and then they can hang these plates they order from J. C. Whitney with the club on it in their back window between these two checked pillows. They make fun of our horse club. They ought to hear my daddy make fun of them for letting a girl sit all the way over on their side while they're driving.

You might be interested in how the girls dress. We wear tight belts pulled up as many notches as we can suck in. People talk about waistlines. Gretchen's is twenty-one and mine is twenty-

98

three. Scarlett O'Hara's was seventeen which is hard to believe all her insides would fit in. Mildred Peters got pregnant and didn't want anyone to know so she strapped her waist in with a big wide belt and we heard her baby was born with its legs wrapped around its neck like an acrobat. I heard talk at school that if you get pregnant, you can get a lady in colored town named Big Bertha to get rid of it for you for one hundred dollars. Gretchen and I wouldn't let those boys talk us into that but you can be sure they would try. Back to what we wear, we wear full skirts and lots of crinolines, which are starched petticoats that stand out. I see pictures of us and can't believe how floppy we used to wear our skirts. We wear long shirttails with our jeans sometimes a foot longer than our windbreakers. If you don't have a boyfriend you can wear your daddy's old shirts. We wear suede loafers and when our feet get wet, our white socks turn the color of our shoes. I hope I'm not boring you.

I have to admit it looks like to me people are too concerned with being alike. Daddy has a green truck and I said everybody has a green one, why don't you get a red one and he said because everybody has a green one. The girls at school will cut their hair just alike except for me and Gretchen. We wear pony tails just because we feel like it. I don't know a person in the world I would like to look just like except for Gretchen and Elizabeth Taylor. And you can see what I mean for yourself from the pictures of Elizabeth Taylor in here if you haven't already seen her before. The little one is me and Gretchen. As if you didn't know, I'm not the pretty one. I have to tell you this. You know the Starrie story about watching the settlers go west. Well dumb me handed it in as my special project in English class and you know what I got? *Sympathetically written—B+*. I didn't know if I didn't get an A because I left out a bunch of commas and hyphens and possessives and used to for too (which I know better), or if she thought it was no good as a story. That's the last time I do that.

When we were sixteen a big change came in our friendship. I cried about it once and Mama gave me one of her talkings to about how people grow up and friendship isn't the same anymore. I told her that she didn't understand. It wasn't that I didn't want Gretchen to become Carl Benson's girl friend.

"It was like a contest, Mama. Only we all knew that Gretchen would win because she's the prettiest and the best rider."

Mama thought I was being selfish, I guess, and jealous because Gretchen had a boyfriend and I didn't. We had seen him ride in shows, but he seemed so stuck-up and acted like he was better than us. When he decided to board his show horse, Sterling Silver, at the stables, he came out to check over the barns. I was cleaning a stable when I saw him. He stuck his face in the door and sniffed; I was scattering lime on the wet floor of the stall before I covered it with fresh straw. I wanted to tell him his precious horse crapped just as much as anybody else's. He looked different in his jeans and plaid shirt, not as scary as he had been in his riding habit. I guess I thought he was about the best looking boy my age I'd ever seen.

I heard him talking to Miss Bivens. "I will want her exercised while I'm away at school, but it must be by a seasoned rider. I'll pay for it to be done properly, you understand."

I was shocked to hear him talk. He didn't look any older than us and he talked like a grownup, a rich grownup.

I couldn't wait to tell Gretchen about him. I knew she had to be the one who would be chosen to ride Sterling Silver. I was right. At first we would all go watch her work the horse, but then we lost interest because it wasn't much fun to watch another person do something you wanted to be doing. Pretty soon Carl started coming home on weekends from school. I saw him once in a military uniform, only not like a soldier, blue with black stripes down the leg and a tight waist like a cadet from West Point. He looked as standoffish to me in that as he did in his riding habit. But not to Gretchen. She had what Mama called poise. He started taking her to shows with him. Pretty soon they were dating steady and he came home for more and more weekends. He was a junior in the Tarheel Military Academy. We all got tired of hearing what they did, partly because we were jealous, I guess. Sometimes I would daydream that he was in love with me instead of Gretchen. Then I would feel bad and imagine that she had fallen in love with another cadet and said it was OK for me to have Carl.

I had to exercise both Gretchen's horse and Maudie because Gretchen rode Lone Star only when she and Carl rode together. We had planned a long camping trip on horseback for the summer. I was afraid she had forgotten about it completely.

Things started to go wrong for Gretchen. She came to see me more often and we would sit on the window sill in my room and talk. Before, on those weekends, Carl had been coming home. He told Gretchen he couldn't leave because his grades were falling and he might not get an appointment to West Point.

"I don't think he has another girl friend, Ella. I think he is telling me the truth. I'm so afraid I won't get asked to come out in Raleigh when I'm eighteen. I know it hurt him to tell me that his parents don't think my background is good enough."

That would never have been Gretchen's word, "background." That was straight from Carl's parents, who lived in a fancy house

100

outside of town. They didn't even use Summit for their address. It was Piney Hill Acres, Route 2, Raleigh. They started dating secretly when he came home. He would meet her at the riding stables and they would go off in his car. I would arrange to be there at the same time to ride Sterling Silver in case his parents checked to see if the horse had been taken out. He had lost interest in the horse since he got a new sports car and wasn't so particular about who rode it. I felt like a queen on that horse. It walked as proud as Carl in his uniform, so I had to try to ride better to be good enough for it.

I guess that's when the trouble started, when they couldn't go anywhere public and had to just go off and park in his car on a country road. He would put the top up when he picked her up and back down again when he started back home. Gretchen looked more and more tired, more worried. Finally she told me why.

"Ella." I was grooming Sterling Silver and didn't turn to look at her until she said my name again. She was starting to cry. "Ella, I think I'm pregnant."

I don't know why I said what I did. I didn't get mad or anything. I stood there feeling my skin get cold until I couldn't stand the silence and her sniffs any longer. Finally I said, "Don't worry, Gretchen. I'll help you. We'll find a way to fix things."

I heard my voice like I was listening to a stranger I didn't know until just then. Who was that person who knew how to fix things? Gretchen looked at me like a little kid. She believed me. How could anybody believe me? She just looked so helpless and she had turned to me for help. I answered her like she was a child asking me to fix a toy.

Starrie rode Blaze, the beautiful stallion she had stolen from a rich man. She had stolen the horse after she saw a terrible thing. The rich man wanted the stallion to be the daddy of many champion horses. He had many mares that he put in a line in his corral, putting hobbles on their back legs. He made the stallion breed every mare, beating him with a whip until he did.

As she rode over the hill, she was afraid of what she would see on the other side. She had waited three days for her white friend, Madelaine, to meet her at the crossroads. Each night she would make camp, keeping a small fire in case she should arrive in the night, but sleeping fitfully, afraid that their enemies would spot the fire. After the third night, her hope diminished and she set out to find her friend, following the rocky trail back to the ranch that belonged to Madelaine's cruel rancher father. She crested the hill and her fears were realized. Not the massacre by unfriendly Indians that had filled her nightmares, not a raging fire to blacken the

101

oasis of the prosperous ranch. No. Walking alone through the weeping willow trees was Madelaine, her fingers latched over a belly that was already starting to protrude noticeably. There was only one thing to do. Go see Big Sula.

Sula Smith lived on a street as dark as she was. Everyone in town knew that girls went to Big Sula when they were in trouble. Starrie was in a dither. She had to get one hundred dollars for her friend Madelaine. Then they could go on their trip as planned, on horseback across the country, up over the Smoky Mountains and across the west where cactus stood like fingers and there were Indians wearing bright blue jewelry. One hundred dollars was a lot of money. She thought and thought but there was only one answer. She would have to sell her only possession, her horse, Blaze.

(Note to self—if she sells the horse, they can't take the trip. Maybe she can steal another one and sell it.)

One hundred dollars was a lot of money. Starrie had made a vow never to steal again even from the hated white people, but now she had to break the vow to save her friend. She knew where her mother hid her money. She would have to take it and blame it on her father. She would work and pay it back. Maybe her mother wouldn't notice it was missing, but she doubted it. She might think her father spent it on firewater.

She took the money and gave it to Madelaine, who wept with happiness over the kindness of her good friend.

"I will pay you back, Starrie. As soon as I get back, I will sell the watch that David gave me. I hate him now."

She took it off her arm. "I will hide it in my pocket so no one will steal it from me." Starrie felt a pain knowing her old friend did not trust her with her watch.

That night they walked together to colored town, hiding in shadows until they met the messenger sent by Sula Smith.

"Follow me this way," the messenger said.

Starrie told her friend goodbye.

Carl didn't act any different so Gretchen must not have told him. He didn't seem to notice how sad Gretchen was. They never even held hands in front of me. I rode in the sports car with them to the Green Light. Gretchen invited me. Carl went in after the malts, but Gretchen and I didn't talk when we were alone.

My hand dropped behind the seat. I felt a blanket, a soft nylon blanket. My fingers touched pine needles, sticks that were stuck to it. I felt a dry, crusty spot. I jerked my hand back. "You spilled something on your blanket," I heard me say. I turned my head and looked at the blanket. It was red plaid; I had thought it would be a soft color, blue or pink. Gretchen saw me looking, but didn't say anything. She looked embarrassed. I felt my eyes get hot and wet.

I tried to think of something else, but my mind wouldn't let me. I saw only a hazy picture, the plaid blanket spread in the woods, the empty sports car. I saw sun spots on the ground, the ground going dark as the sun went behind a cloud. Sometimes my mind was like a movie where they showed you enough to know what was going to happen between a man and a woman, the light going out by the bed, the couple kissing and dropping from the picture, the camera moving up a tree, over the empty car. There would be music in the movie while you imagined. But I couldn't see Gretchen and Carl on the blanket. They wouldn't come into the scene in my mind. I didn't want to see any more realness, so I didn't.

I took my scarf off so I could feel the sun on my head. My dark hair soaked up the heat like a horse's back. I didn't look at Carl when he passed me my malt. I heard myself say thanks. I waited for them to ask me why I was so angry, but neither of them did.

When I got home, I went into the kitchen because I knew Mama would be there. I was wrong. I heard her sobbing in the living room. At first I thought it might be the old TV Daddy had gotten from Grandma Higgins, but it was Mama crying.

"Mama, what's wrong?"

"Oh honey, nothing. Oh, I'm so upset."

I sat a minute because I knew Mama would tell me. She just had to wind up.

"Ella Ruth. Your sorry daddy took every penny of the money I've been saving all summer for us to have a big family Christmas. I don't know how in the world he found it."

"Oh, no! I didn't tell him where it was."

"I know you didn't, honey."

At first I felt anger at my daddy for hurting Mama so, but it didn't take long for it to hit me. I took the money. It was hidden in my billfold. And here was Mama blaming it on Daddy and I was letting her. I didn't know what to do. I left the room because I couldn't let her look at me.

"He ain't here, honey," she called. "No telling where he is, but you can be sure our hard-earned money's done found its way into another pocket."

I reached into my purse and got the money out and went to the place where Mama hid the money, in the bottom of the pecan bucket. I picked up the nut bucket and set it aside.

"I already dumped them out, Ella. It's gone, I tell you."

I walked back into the living room. I forced a smile as I opened the dollars in my hands. Mama looked at me through blurred eyes just as a blond woman on the TV screamed, "I don't know what you're talking about!"

"Ella Ruth, honey! You found it! How in the world did you find it? I looked and looked." Mama stood up so fast she got dizzy and had to grab the back of her chair.

"I saw him nosing around that pecan bucket last night looking for his bottle so I hid it under the potatoes. I'm sorry I forget to tell you, Mama."

"Oh honey," Mama was already hugging me. "That was so smart of you. We'll get to see Matthew and the children after all."

I felt a funny sting. Jealousy, maybe. Not guilt, I don't think. I didn't know.

"We'll put it back under the potatoes." Mama winked. "That'll fix his goose."

As Mama went into the pantry with the money, the phone rang. It was Gretchen.

"Ella, everything's OK. Isn't that great?"

"What?" I couldn't remember what she was talking about.

"I can't explain now. Don't you know? False alarm."

I thought a minute. "Oh, yeah. I know."

"Well, it's about time you caught on," she giggled. "I've got some more good news. I've been accepted at Winston Academy for next year."

"What's that?"

"Ella. It's a boarding school. In Winston-Salem, the same school Marcel Sanders goes to. Only twenty miles from Carl."

She kept talking. About how boarding school would give her a better chance of being a state debutante. How they had stables so she could take Lone Star with her. She sounded a long way off. Pretty soon I quit listening like I would do sometimes with Mama. I could even make conversation and not listen.

"I've got to help Mama, Gretchen," I said finally and hung up. I could tell Gretchen was peeved at me, but I didn't care. When I got on my stool in the kitchen, beside my pie tins was a lemon tart.

"A treat for you," Mama said. "For hiding our money so good from Maynard."

I ate the tart. I was hungry, but it was so sweet it made my teeth ache.

Starrie saw David first when she went into the morgue. There were many people there, including four men who had searched for the body in Dr. Horace Sanders's pond. It was no secret anymore. Madelaine had disappeared the night she went to Big Sula's. Starrie flashed back to the night she waited for Madelaine to meet her at the campfire. Madelaine would be wearing her letter jacket with a white shirt sticking out the bottom. (Check to see if they gave letters for sports back then.) The men were holding a jacket. It wasn't the right color, Starrie thought. The red was brown and the basketball letter was the same color. The letter had been white. But it had been in the same muddy pond that had made Starrie's swimsuit brown.

"There will be dental records," David stammered. (Check to see about dentists.) "But if you could make a positive identity of her clothing? The fish and snails have eaten her face away."

Starrie held the muddy jacket in her hands. "It's Madelaine's jacket. Mama sewed on the letter," she said. "I can tell by the left-hand stitches. Madelaine never wore the jacket in front of you, David, because you would have thought her childish and mannish. You told her basketball was for boys. You made fun of our girls' rules." Starrie felt proud. Her memory was suddenly crystal clear. David knew how to get a girl pregnant but he didn't know her friend Madelaine.

"Unzip the pocket," she ordered.

"What?" he replied puzzled.

"Unzip the pocket," she repeated.

David tugged on the rusted zipper and the pocket ripped open. He took out the watch he had given Madelaine and it was thick and brown as a rusty nail.

For a week that spring I heard the cries at night before I went to sleep. Until I got the sheets warm, the sound made chill bumps on my arms. I wished I had the animal right there under the covers with me so I could comfort him. Sometimes when you hear a dog, you know he isn't really hurt; he's just trying to make you feel sorry for him, a kind of whining. He's penned up and wants out. But I knew those cries were different because they were just like Mrs. Albright's dog after Maudie stepped on its foot. The foot got big and pussy and he limped for a long time, making wet prints each time he put the hurt foot on the sidewalk. Then one day he had another paw, good as new. I thought the hurt one had rotted and fallen off like a vegetable blossom.

There was a dog caught somewhere. I looked every day trying to follow his sound. I was sure I heard him near the trail so I tied up Maudie and walked past the trash pile toward the woods. My eye caught a red ball. I saw a funny-shaped dark thing tied to it, a lop-sided box the size of a cigar box. When I walked closer, I heard a humming sound coming from the box. I was scared to touch it.

I didn't find the dog that day, but I told Mama about the box with the balloon. She was in one of her fevers so I shouldn't have told her. Daddy said Mama was sick in the head, not the body. She grabbed me and held me. It embarrassed me, because I was too old and too big to be held like that. Her body was wet with fever, one arm cool, the other hot. She made my hair wet and it stuck to my face. I loved Mama, but when she felt like that I didn't want her holding me.

"Oh my baby, my poor little baby. I'm so happy you're home safe. Oh my baby."

Finally I pulled away from her and she puffed like a horse cooling down from a run.

"That was a bomb you found." Her eyes turned to slits and she looked at me like the principal at grammar school. "If you had touched it, you would have been blown in a zillion pieces."

"Mama, what a crazy thing. It was probably something they sent up to read the weather. Or to drop down advertisements. Maybe a kid made it."

"No, No. You don't understand."

Again the principal flashed in my mind. I felt like I had done something wrong. Like the day I made a handprint in rat poison in the restroom and the principal washed my hands until they bled.

"During the war," Mama went on, "there were bombs floating in the sky over this very country. Thousands of them sent from Japan. A woman hiking with five little children touched one and they were all blown to bits. Did you know a Japanese submarine got up the Cape Fear River as far as Elizabethtown?

Mama had started to talk like Daddy, and I don't think she knew she was doing it. She never had argued with him about his war stories, but at least she used to say her different thoughts. I could ignore things he said I didn't believe, but Mama had the kind of brain that he could hurt. Daddy talked about the submarine a lot when he was ranting about how Roosevelt sold out to the Japanese at Pearl Harbor because he wanted us to go to war.

Daddy wouldn't let me have this horse statue I wanted for Christmas because he turned it over and found MADE IN JAPAN in its crotch. Daddy said the coffins that came back with orders not to be opened were filled with rocks. I wondered why they would hide dead people. He said the Japs were keeping them prisoners and torturing them to find out all our secrets and making us think they were dead. Daddy made a big to-do about things that didn't matter. Like how the Japs used human manure to fertilize their gardens. What did it matter to him? He didn't have to eat the food they grew. That seemed to bother Daddy more than the bombs that hit Pearl Harbor.

"I don't think it was a bomb, Mama. The war was over a long time ago."

"It could be. It could have been there all those years, waiting for you to touch it. A child got blowed to pieces by a bomb on our very own side, playing in the woods near Fort Bragg."

Daddy told me about the balloon bombs too. I saw in my mind the death bombs going up into the sky from Japan, hundreds of colored balloons, each one released by a tiny person. The balloon people all looked alike, and they stood as tight as fruit at the market, each one sending his bomb away to hit a monster person on the other side of the water. Once I bought a raincoat, made in Japan, size small, and it was large enough to hold three people my size inside it. The balloon people didn't know every bomb was likely to land where all it would destroy was an ant hill or a cactus, or land in the snow on a mountaintop. Only one was lucky enough to find a lady and five little children in a giant forest with no one to hear the explosion. "We showed them Japs," Daddy said. Three months after the balloon bombs left Japan, we sent our bomb to them and leveled four square miles and killed 100,000 people.

"It could be one of those bombs, Mama," I kidded. "And the Japs would read about me in the paper and smile. Ah so, not one, but two out of nine thousand worked."

Mama smiled, I think because she was thinking how proud she would be if my name were in the paper. I was pretty sure her brain worked only part of the time, or only part of her brain worked at all.

When the Japs sneaked up on Pearl Harbor, it seemed like a little boy running up and slapping a sleeping lion. For a second the lion felt a small sting. Then they found the little boy's shirt and pants. The moral of the story is that smart little boys don't slap sleeping lions. I looked for the moral in every story I was told. I was sick of hearing Daddy talk about the war. The closest he got to it was working in a defense shop for two months. He brought me home airplane gears to play with. Stevie and Al thought they were cool back then because they had their uncles' sailor middies to wear. Daddy never even had a uniform.

I went looking for the balloon thing again, but it was gone. I heard the dog again, only he seemed closer. I yelled at him and he cried louder. I followed the sounds until I found him caught in the creek. A black-and-white polka-dot dog who had run away and got caught by his leash in the creek. He was so hungry I thought he might try to eat me if I untangled him, but he was too weak. When I set him free, he tried to walk and fell. I carried him to Maudie, afraid that his bones might tear through his loose flesh. He didn't even whimper when I talked to him. I rode him home to Mama, lying across my saddle. He was alive enough to make my crotch warm.

107

Mama started to cook and fix for him. Not too much water, she said, he'll get the squirts. Just wet his mouth and get bread in him first because his stomach will be raw. Then she gave him pieces of calf's liver and boiled eggs and cheese. Just when I thought Mama was losing touch, she found something to do that she was good at. Doctoring that dog perked Mama up more than anything in a long time.

I spent that whole summer with Spot and Maudie. I got like Mama, not wanting anything to change. I decided that I didn't want to be with people for a while. If we had all stayed the same age forever, I would have been happy. Maudie was starting to show her age, stumbling a lot, so I guess it was just as well that Gretchen and I didn't make our trip. Dogs are a lot smarter than horses, I found out, even though Spot couldn't figure how to get his leash untangled in the creek.

One day I heard Stevie holler, "Ella Ruth thinks she's really something with her firehouse dog."

I did feel braver. I never worried about being out after dark when Spot was with me. Then a bad thing happened. Daddy came out on the porch, yelling at Mama and me about heating up the kitchen with our cooking, always some dumb thing we couldn't help, and he tripped on my chair. I guess Spot thought he was going to hurt me. Spot bit him, right on the rear end. Daddy said it broke the skin, but he never showed us.

The next day Daddy made me go tell the newspaper about Spot because he said people would know I shouldn't have a fancy polka-dot dog and think I stole him. I did and they took my picture with Spot. The lady reporter wrinkled her nose when I told her that I had looked for him when he cried out and couldn't find him, and then I did find him when I went back looking for the bomb that I never did find again. I guess it didn't make much sense. I decided not to go into that anymore. The reporter wrote some things in the paper that I didn't say, about how my heart would be broken, but I wanted Spot to go home to his rightful owners. How I thought he was trying to tell me who they were. She didn't know Spot. All he ever told me was where a rabbit was or when he was hungry. My Mama was happy I got my picture in the paper and didn't have to get blown up by a bomb to do it. She told me I could have combed my hair first.

I will wish the rest of my life I hadn't let Daddy talk me into telling the paper about Spot. A lady carrying a baby came for him. Only she called him Freckles, which was a dumb name because he had spots, not freckles. He had jumped out of her convertible while she was visiting her mother. She was pregnant and couldn't chase him. Her mother sent her the newspaper picture to her house in

Raleigh. She gave me twenty dollars. I guess I acted polite. She snapped a leash on his collar. He didn't like that and tried to pull away. He must have remembered being caught by that damn leash before.

She handed me her baby to hold while she took him to the car. I couldn't look at him leave. I don't know why, but I started rocking the baby up and down trying to make its eyes open and shut like a doll's. It didn't work. Its eyes stayed open a long time then it started screaming until they pinched shut inside a wrinkle. I felt like I wanted to throw it on the floor. I couldn't stand its smell and its breathing sounds, even how hot it felt.

I starting yelling for Mama, who was walking with the lady to her car. Mama came hurrying back inside.

"Mama, take this thing."

"Ella Ruth!" She sounded mad at me.

"Take it. I can't stand to hold it. I hate babies."

"Ella Ruth, you're acting like a child."

The lady came back and they both acted silly over the baby. I smelled my hands. They still smelled like Spot. The baby finally shut up.

I balled up her twenty dollars and threw it on the floor. I don't know if she saw me. I guess my daddy got it. There was nothing in the world I wanted to spend that twenty dollars on.

That afternoon I went back looking for the bomb and was going to lie down on it. I couldn't find it. But if I had and if it had been a bomb, I would have killed myself. I saw Spot in a dream, in pieces, his spotted hide hanging from the trees like leaves. I never saw him whole again, just our picture in the paper when Mama would show it to her customers. I turned away every time Mama took out that newspaper picture. I knew if Mama's world had been real, I would be dead.

Right before school started, Al Sawyer bought a car, a '38 Ford. The guys rode around and yelled ugly things at girls. When we were little we used to do bad things together like knock on doors and run. I helped them drag junk out in the road to make people get out of their cars and move it. Now whatever they did, I wasn't included and didn't want to be. They talked big, said things to make me mad.

"New event at the Olympics, Ella. Skate cat. Al Sawyer holds the world record, one thousand, three hundred and eighty feet."

"Come on, Ella. How about a game of skate cat?"

Stevie dragged me over to see the cat, flattened and dry on the pavement. He picked it up and threw it. Tiger jumped over the spinning cat as it skidded down the highway.

One day they were waxing Al's car and called me over. Like a dummy, I went.

"Hey, Ella Ruth, look at the nice box of Mickey Mouse mattresses Stevie found in his Mama's closet."

They were polishing Al's car with the Kotex pads. I just turned and walked off. I never could think of anything to say back to them anymore.

They moved everywhere together like a pack of wolves. Their voices were deep and didn't match the faces I used to know. We used to be the same size; now they were much bigger. Stevie carried a pack of Lucky Strikes rolled in his T-shirt sleeve over the big muscle in his arm.

When they got in a group, I would hear them laugh so loud that it had to be fake. They wanted me to think they were laughing at something dirty about me because after they laughed all their faces turned toward me. I always felt to see if my zipper was down or my blouse unbuttoned. I looked for a reflection to see if there was a spot on the back of my skirt. I checked my nose in the image on the gold plaque on my locker door. I wish I could be like the Invisible Man. I had trouble even imagining that anymore because I had quit reading comics. The only thing I could imagine anymore was something that could happen to real people. I hated myself for letting them make me feel so bad.

The baseball team got to go to Washington after they won the conference. Partly I was sick of hearing Al brag about all the things he saw. But partly I wanted to know about it so bad, I let him talk on. Especially the zoo and Roosevelt's stamp collection and how tiny women used to be. He saw the evening dresses worn by the Presidents' wives.

"No kidding. They weren't this big around." He made a circle with his hands. Maybe Scarlett O'Hara wasn't so special with her seventeen-inch waistline. Maybe everybody had one. I didn't figure I'd ever see Washington, it was so far away.

Then Stevie ruined it all. "Did he tell you what we seen in the Smithsonian?"

I could tell by his voice he was up to something. "He told me about a lot of things there."

Stevie laughed. "He didn't tell you."

Al snapped at him: "You just said it was there. I never saw it. You waited till the bus was leaving to tell me. They don't put stuff like that out for anyone to see."

"I told you, man. Tiger saw it. Ernie saw it. I mean it was gigantic."

"You told me about the dinosaurs," I said to Al.

110

"That's not the kind of gigantic he means."

"That big, I swear it." Stevie held his hands apart like he was measuring a big fish. But not a fish so big it ought to be in the Smithsonian.

"No way," Al said.

"It was curled up in this jar, but it was that long, easy. Maybe this long." He opened his hands several more inches. "Pickle juice probably shrank it up some. He was famous. Biggest one in history."

Al shook his head. His ears were starting to get red.

I got up and started to leave.

"Where are you going?" Stevie asked.

"Off," I said.

He was really surprised. I left before he got to the punchline. But I got mad at myself for feeling bad. It was the kind of bad feeling you get when the alarm clock goes off right in the middle of a dream.

The next Sunday when I was watching a softball game at the church by myself, Stevie, Tiger and Al sat behind me.

"Terrible thing happened to me, Al."

I should have known by Stevie's voice that it was a joke they planned.

"What happened, Stevie?"

"Well, it was the first time I'd ever laid her, you know? I was really getting it on, humping her like a freight train, and her damn mother walked in."

"Jesus, Stevie. What did she say?"

"Baaaaa!"

They all started laughing after Stevie made the goat sound. Or a sheep. I didn't understand. Later I asked Mama why it was a joke and she didn't catch on either. I was afraid to ask Daddy.

"Hey, Sawyer. Ella Ruth's dying to know. She called me up yesterday and asked," Stevie said.

"I did not."

"Did you tell her it belonged to John Dillinger?"

"Fuck you, Stevie."

I knew I shouldn't have said it.

"Anytime, my li'l darling, anytime," he replied. They all began to hoot and laugh. I had made them so happy by losing my temper. Everybody was looking at me, all the women from the church. They were really shocked. Fuck them too.

Then the guys started talking about Annette on the Mickey Mouse Club, what big tits she had. I didn't even think she was pretty. Stevie tapped me on the back.

"I didn't know mosquitoes were bad this year."

I ignored him.

111

"Look, Al. Two mosquitoes bit Ella Ruth on the chest."

I got up and left. My face was stinging.

When I brushed my teeth that night, I was so mad at myself I couldn't stand to see myself in the mirror. I left the door to the medicine cabinet open so all I saw were Mama's empty medicine bottles.

My brother Matthew sent us a giant paper star.

"What kind of useless crap is that," Daddy said when he unwrapped the collection of paper points. "Matthew met up with another fast-talking salesman."

"Hush, Maynard. It's something you have to put together." Mama began to struggle with the points, only to undo the brads again and again when it failed to resemble the picture on the box. After I finished copying over my homework, I looked through the star box for instructions.

"Oh, I'm so glad you're going to do it for me, Ella Ruth. It just has to be up when Matthew comes."

"Looks like to me you could keep at it *till* he comes and still not figure it out," Daddy mocked.

"Well, let's just see you do it, Mr. Smart Guy."

"What do I care about it?"

"You ought to care. Your very own son sent it to you for Christmas."

"Mama." I had learned to interrupt their fusses. "The directions show you're supposed to do different things with the square ones than the triangular ones. You've got them mixed together."

"Two more points of intelligence and she'd be a tree," Daddy grumbled.

Mama didn't look at him. "He thinks he's so cute," she hissed.

I started to assemble the star and it went together surprisingly fast. I had a thought that maybe I should slow down so Mama wouldn't feel so stupid, but I was getting pretty eager to see what it looked like. When I saw Mama's face, my fears of embarrassing her went away.

I took it and climbed up on the kitchen table, holding it over the light bulb. "I'll cut on the light, Ella Ruth. Isn't that the prettiest thing you ever saw?" When the points filled with white light, Mama clapped her hands together and I felt like I was looking down at an enormous child. From the day the star arrived through the next two weeks, her excitement grew so large that I started to fear for her disappointment. What if Matthew broke his promise? He would go for weeks without calling or writing her. I never felt like I had a brother.

Daddy and I went to cut a tree. We snuck on the back of Horace

Sanders's property. Daddy carried his hatchet, freshly sharpened, in a leather case on his belt. I had a burlap bag in case we saw any running cedar and holly, or mistletoe we could reach. Daddy wanted to bring his shotgun to shoot it down, but Mama was afraid Dr. Sanders would come after us or call the police if he heard the noise.

"Besides, Maynard, if it's anything like that bobwhite you shot," Mama said before we left, "it'll be blown to pieces. Couldn't go two bites on that pitiful little bird 'out cracking your teeth on shot."

"You don't eat mistletoe, Maxine."

"I know you don't eat it. I don't want it unless it has berries."

"Pain in the butt," Daddy had grunted as we climbed in the pickup. Lately he complained about Mama to me, but I didn't agree or disagree with him.

We parked the pickup off the road under a clump of trees. Daddy pressed his door shut quietly so I did the same and followed him into the woods. I had to admit it was pretty exciting going to steal something with him. His step was lively. This was the best time of day for him—early afternoon—before he started drinking and after the night before had worn off. We passed through a grove of holly trees. They were covered with clusters of red berries.

"We'll get some on the way out," he said. His voice sounded different in the forest than at home, kind of nice to listen to. "If the trees are heavy with berries, you can count on a hard winter."

"How's that?" I asked. My own voice sounded strange too. Maybe it was the thick trees.

"Nature taking care of wild things so they'll have enough to eat." Maybe he saw something in my expression, that I doubted the truth of what he said, so he added, "It's in the Bible. It's just people who have to fend for theirselves."

"Why's that?"

"Because animals and birds don't ever do wrong. They just do what comes natural. People do wrong when they know better."

"You mean like stealing?"

"Yeah, like being a goddamn thief."

I giggled, but Daddy didn't even catch on. Here we were, stealing a Christmas tree.

I liked the idea of Nature being ready for winter with berries. Like the poem about the tree with Mother Nature wearing a robin's nest in her hair. Here she was wearing berries on her branches. I would add a line about that to a poem if I could make it rhyme. "Red berries clustered in her hands, To feed hungry animals in many lands. Poems are made by fools like me, But only God can make a tree."

We looked a long time for a tree. The honeysuckle had strangled most of them and made them lopsided or they had this slimy orange stuff growing on them. I saw what I thought was a pretty one and Daddy laughed. "Only trouble is, Ella Ruth, you'd have to cut a hole in the ceiling to set it up." I had to admit it was hard to tell the size of something when it didn't have a roof over it. The one Daddy picked looked much too small.

On the way back he pointed me down a side trail. "Go get some running cedar." I ran down the trail and, to my surprise, it was there, pushing up bright green under the pine straw. When I pulled it, it popped away from the ground in long vines. When I got back to the trail, Daddy was cutting holly with his pocket knife.

"Reach in my back pocket," he said.

I hesitated, then reached in. "What you got?"

"Raisins."

I looked in my hand and saw them, large and pinched, not like the ones that came in boxes at the grocery. I didn't eat them right off because I thought he might be playing a trick until he said, "Used to eat them all the time when I was a boy. Dried scuppernongs." I ate one and it was good.

"Chewy," I said and reached in his pocket again. I never knew my daddy knew so much about these woods. I never saw him go into them.

"Carry these real careful," he said, when he handed me the holly. "Don't want to knock off any of your mama's precious berries." He never called her his wife, just my mama. "Only mistletoe I seen would take a goddamn monkey to get."

I hadn't seen any. When he pointed up in a tree, I saw the round green clusters. They were too high to tell if they had berries.

"Here's your goddamn monkey," I said, and pointed at myself. I put down my stuff and started shinnying up the tree. The first part was easy, but it got hard when I started knowing if I slipped on a limb or if one broke it was a long way to the ground. The limbs were getting skimpier and skimpier and the center was starting to wobble. By the time I got to the mistletoe, my hands and knees were sore. I didn't want to look and see how far down my daddy was. I thought of his story of a bear that let go with both hands reaching for their backpacks when Matthew went fishing with him in the mountains. The bear fell all the way to the ground and knocked himself out. I started to tug at the mistletoe with one hand. A shower of white berries hit me in the face. Damn Mama and her berries.

"Should have carried up my knife, Ella Ruth." His voice sounded so far away I didn't see how he could see me that good. Just as he said that, the mistletoe popped loose and for an awful moment, I felt like I was falling. I let go of the mistletoe and grabbed the tree. My heart beat so hard it was jarring me.

114

"Dammit," I heard myself say. "Bet it ain't got a berry left."

"Naw, got a few. You better come on down, Ella Ruth. That's aplenty." I saw the top of his head as he stooped for the mistletoe, his thin hair across the top like gray ribbons. He hadn't worn his hat like Mama said. He sounded worried. I'd never seen him worried about me before. I sat a moment till my heart slowed down and my brain started working better. Then I saw if I went up one more limb, I could sit and pull it off with both hands. I was a monkey all right, like the stupid monkey who couldn't get his hand out of the jar when his fist was full of candy. I lifted myself up and braced both feet below me. I sat a minute and decided I could sit there all day, I felt so calm. I started breaking off mistletoe and dropping it for Daddy to catch. I watched it fall through the branches to his hands. His head looked overlarge from where I was, like the head on a dwarf.

"OK, that's all," I called. "Now catch me."

"No!"

I think he thought I meant it. Going down was easy. My hands were as sticky as a fly's feet on the ceiling. When I hit bottom, I felt short like when I got off Maudie.

"You went to a hell of a lot of trouble for that tub of lard mama of yours," he said.

We gathered up our stuff. Daddy pulled the tree and I carried the sack of greenery. I hadn't thought that I was doing it for Mama. I think I was doing it for me. Or just plain showing off.

How come he knew these woods better than me and I was in them all the time? All I ever saw him do was walk the path between our house and the Rebel Bar.

"How come you know so much about Dr. Sanders's woods?"

"Me and Matthew used to go down there a lot. Built him a tree house down by the big crick."

"Where?"

He looked at me and shook his head, acting like I had just asked about the stupidest question in the world. He never did anything with me. All I got for parents was an old drunk and a fat lady.

"Ain't you got better things to do? Damn near a grown woman and you're studying on tree houses."

"I'm not a grown woman."

"Oh yeah? Looks like there's something growing under that shirt there to me."

"Leave me alone."

I couldn't help it. My voice cracked.

"Oh, don't be so sensitive. I ain't meaning to pick on you, Ella Ruth. Don't go crying on me like your mama always does. Can't you take a little kidding?"

"I'm not crying," I snorted.

"I mean I'm trying to tell you what other folks is seeing."

Then he said, "You got to get over being so tomboyish, Ella Ruth. You're getting too old to act thataway. No matter how hard you try to be different, you're a girl and a girl you're going to stay."

I didn't answer him. The voice that I had liked when we first walked into the woods I now wanted to run away from and get back to the clearing. I felt like I was shut up in a closet with him and I wanted to get out. I ran out of the trees and stood beside the pickup, watching him drag the tree.

He threw the tree in the truck and looked at me. "You remember all that land we just traipsed across. Let that be a reminder. A man's got to make it. All's a woman got to do is marry it."

"I don't have to marry nobody if I don't feel like it. My first-grade teacher, Miss Mims, never got married."

"That's because nobody would have her."

"There's lots of nice things that don't cost money."

"Like what? That horse and sorry dog you used to have. Where did their food come from? From heaven? Them dungarees and boots you're wearing? From Monkey Ward's."

"Flowers and birds don't cost money."

"So why don't you take to eating flowers and birds?"

"I earn my keep."

"You're getting mightly mouthy lately."

Then he grunted a familiar grunt. For the first time I realized he sounded like Grandma Higgins.

When we got home, I saw that Daddy was right about the tree. It had looked puny in the woods, but it was fat in our living room. I had gotten so I was mad every time I had to admit he was right. I spent an hour looking through the Bible, trying to prove him wrong about what he said about nature and berries. I found it in Matthew: "Behold the fowls of the air: for they sow not, neither do they reap, nor gather into barns, yet your heavenly Father feedeth them. Consider the lilies of the field, how they grow; they toil not, neither do they spin. . . . even Solomon in all his glory was not arrayed like one of these."

But it also said God would take care of us so not to worry. To tell the truth, I didn't believe Daddy or the Bible, either one. Look what happened to the Solomon we knew, Sonavabitch Solomon, who left town and left his factory and smokestack behind. But God took care of the vines that grew up that smokestack. They didn't die in the drought like Daddy's garden. And the birds and rats that live in the building, and the cat I saw there on top of the stack of rotten cloth with her litter of kittens. I wondered what it would be like to have Matthew, my brother, instead of Matthew, the Bible, there to talk to. He might be just like Daddy.

116

I got to work on the tree lights, all the screwing and unscrewing to find the bulbs that were burnt out. Mama had bought a new string of lights, little candles that bubbled when they got hot.

"You don't reckon they'll catch the house on fire, Maynard? Ella Ruth, don't burn the lights unless you're in here watching them."

"Maxine, you probably couldn't set that green tree afire with a bucket of gasoline."

"I don't know, Maynard. Colored woman set herself afire and took off running and her little boy died from chasing her and swallowing the flames. I've read some pretty terrible things in the newspaper."

They kept going, but I quit listening. I was untangling the tinsel and deciding whether I had too many blue bulbs, which were my favorites, on one side. I liked the woods smell that all the stuff we stole from Dr. Horace Sanders brought in our house. Mama's customers would come in and say how much they liked the cooking smells, but I got pretty tired of those except mints and fudge. Mama hung some balls, but I didn't like the way she did them so I moved them after she went back to the kitchen. She would throw the icicles on in handfuls and I liked them put in place, one by one. Mama was funny. She would be real particular about decorating a cake for somebody else, but she wouldn't take pains if it was for us.

I soon found out that it was just me and Daddy who were included in the "us." The next week getting ready for my big brother, the whole house changed. The harder she worked, the more I feared he'd call like he had before and say he couldn't make it. Mama was afraid too because she made me answer the phone every time it rang.

I picked it up on Christmas Eve.

"Ella Ruth?"

"Yes, sir."

"This is Matthew."

"Hello, Uncle Matthew."

"I'm not your uncle."

"I know it."

"Well, cut it out. And don't say sir to me, either. You make me sound like an old man."

"OK, Brother Matthew."

"Is Mama there?"

"She's cooking."

"She's always cooking."

I couldn't stand it any longer. "If you say you're not coming, I'll break your neck." There was silence at the other end of the line.

"I'm going to have to leave early, is all. I have another set of in-laws, you know."

117

"Yeah, and I bet you have chicken dinner with them every Sunday."

"Every other Sunday. It's not my idea; it's Karen's."

My brother had never talked so personal to me before.

"So don't bring Karen."

"It's Christmas, Ella Ruth."

"No shit, Matthew."

"Nice little sister, I got. Boy, you're sassy."

"If you don't show up here tomorrow with bells on, you'll find out how nice I am.

I couldn't believe what I did. I hung up. I heard Mama's voice.

"Who was that, Ella Ruth?"

"It was Matthew. He's going to be a little late."

Mama appeared at the door. She was smiling. "He *is* coming."

"Yeah, he's coming. And Karen."

"And the children?"

"I guess, unless they gave them away."

"Ella Ruth, are you a little bit jealous?"

"Of what?"

"Oh, not being the whole cheese, the center of attention."

"I don't remember ever being the center of anybody's attention."

"Well, you're almost an only child."

"Almost, except for a brother."

The doorbell rang. I started to say "saved by the bell" until I looked through the window and saw a familiar Lincoln. Gretchen's. I hadn't written her in a month. I ran to the door and opened it.

"Ella."

I felt tears coming to my eyes. I didn't want to cry. She hugged me so I had time to swallow and get control of myself. Then I realized she had a present in her hands. I hadn't bought her one.

"Come on in."

"I can't stay long. Mama's waiting in the car. We have a bunch of presents to deliver."

I looked at her. "Boy, you look great."

"Do you like my haircut? It's like Audrey Hepburn's."

"Yeah, you look about eighteen."

"Oh, good." The horn blew in the Lincoln. The sound of it made me angry. "Ella, I've got to go. Call me."

"OK."

"Here." I took the present.

"Thank you," I said weakly.

"Gretchen, honey, wait up." It was Mama.

Gretchen stopped and came back to hug Mama. "Mrs. Higgins. Merry Christmas."

Mama handed her a present. It looked familiar. The tag said TO GRETCHEN FROM THE HIGGINS in Mama's block letters. Then Mama handed her a coffee can covered with Christmas paper. "Here's some mints for you and your folks. They've just creamed."

Gretchen looked sincerely happy. She ought to have been. Mama made the best mints in the world and they were so much trouble I felt guilty eating them.

The horn blew again. "Oh, my mother." I think Gretchen was embarrassed by her mother.

"Merry Christmas, Gretchen. Tell your mama for me."

"I will, Mrs. Higgins. Merry Christmas to you. And thank you."

Gretchen ran down the walk. She waved from the car but her mother didn't, driving away like a mechanical person. Snooty bitch. Mama and I went back into the house.

"Mama, where did you get that present?"

"It was the hat I crocheted for Karen."

"You gave away Karen's present?"

"I've got her another one, a slip I bought at Simon's. Gretchen will look a lot cuter in that hat than Karen would."

I hugged my mama. "Fast thinking, Kemo Sabe," I said.

"Fast writing," she laughed, "for your old mama."

Mama went back to the kitchen and I went to my room and cried. I took the paper off Gretchen's present. If it was one of those gift sets of perfume and shit like they sold at Simon's to have around in case somebody showed up with a present, I was going to bust every bottle. It wasn't. It was a stocking cap with WINSTON ACADEMY on it.

On Christmas day, I looked out the front window until I saw the car bounce in the drive, five heads inside, two grownups, two children, one dog.

"Mama, they're here!" I heard my voice. I didn't know why I was so excited except for Mama. They stayed all afternoon. Mama wore her navy blue dress which made her look a little less fat, but by the time she got dinner on the table she was covered with flour spots. Daddy looked bad as ever, not even changing his shirt he'd had on all week. He got drunk on the Jack Daniels Matthew brought and fell asleep.

"At least he's on an expensive drunk," Matthew said over his sleeping body.

Mama told stories on my brother that I'd never heard. Matthew, she said, had dumped out all her flour and sugar into mountains on the kitchen floor. She walked in and he looked up and said, "I'm awful quiet. I must be into something."

Once when the preacher came to visit, he put a thing under the

settee cushion that made a fart noise when the preacher sat down.
"Remember the expression on his face, Mama?" Matthew recalled. "He wasn't all that sure he hadn't let one slip out."

Mama was laughing with him about things she wouldn't even let me talk about. I wondered if it was because he was a boy.

"You remember Mrs. Simon?" Mama said, giggling.

"Deaf as a post," Matthew interrupted. "But there was nothing wrong with her nose."

Mama and Matthew laughed. Daddy popped and snorted. I got mad. I didn't like getting left out with Karen. The kids were outside on their new roller skates. I was too old to be outside and too young to be inside. Matthew explained the joke to Karen. "You see, I walked up behind old lady Simon when she came to get some stuff Mama cooked and farted so loud I almost blew the windows out. I wanted to find out if she really was deaf." He got tickled again and wiped the tears off on his sleeve.

"She was deaf, all right," he said. "Didn't even turn her head. But pretty soon the old nose started lifting and she said, 'I think I smell something dead, Mrs. Higgins.' Then Mama turned about ten shades of red, and said, 'Maybe it's one of the rats I set a trap for in the basement.'"

Mama said, "Basement, phooey. The rat was right there in my kitchen as alive as could be."

I had never seen Mama laugh so much. I started daydreaming. I wondered what they talked about on Christmas Day at Gretchen's. I was trying to picture the scene with the store-bought Christmas tree from Canada that is so much easier to decorate, when the kids came busting in. It had started to get cold. Everybody acted so interested in what they were saying and it was as much boring nothing as I had ever heard.

"Hello, *Aunt* Ella Ruth," Becka said to me. They all thought that was so cute since she was only a year younger than me. She already had an ass a yard wide. I thought she was a sugar-coated hunka shit. I imagined they had a car wreck on the way home and everyone of them got killed like this family I read about in the paper. Or Matthew went crazy and shot them all and then shot himself. This man did that, even the dog. I didn't like their dog, either. It was one of those little yappy dogs that Grandma Higgins called a piss dog.

After I went to bed, I thought about Gretchen some more, how grown-up she looked. I was glad Daddy didn't see her because he would have said, "See what I mean. Your best friend has outgrown you. That's why she doesn't have anything to do with you anymore." Maybe he wouldn't have said anything at all. I never called her. After New Year's, Mama got a thank-you note for the hat and candy that had Gretchen Powers McKensie printed on the front. I told Mama I wrote a thank-you note to her, but I didn't. In fact, I never wrote her again at all. I saw her once in Simon's during Easter, looking at the long white leather gloves they kept behind the counter. Hazel said you could only try them on if you were buying them because they had to be stretched and that you only bought them if you were going to be a debutante in Raleigh.

"Little Miss La-de-da wants a pair of sixteen buttons," Hazel sneered so Gretchen couldn't hear her.

I took my break so Gretchen wouldn't see me. She had on a hat like the one she had given me. I wished Mama had given the crocheted hat to Karen. Gretchen had probably worn it about as much as I wore the one she gave me.

The last time I told you things for this time capsule, I told you what everybody was wearing and doing like it was important or something. I still know what you're supposed to want to dress like, but I don't want to be with kids my age anymore or care if I look and act like them. For a while I bought the right clothes with the money I made at Simon's.

Even the girls who used to be in the horse club have started to change. They all try to sit at a certain table at lunch, where the girls with money sit. People are divided into groups and it has to do with boys and dating and how many cashmere sweaters you have. They all wear white Johnny collars with sterling silver stickpins and they collect charms that rattle against the desk top when they write. They are always taking each other's arms and going through the charms one by one, exclaiming each time they find a new one.

I started bringing my lunch and eating outside. On the days it is raining we are supposed to eat inside, but I would rather get wet than have to eat in that lunchroom. I sit up against the wall where only the water that splashes off the sidewalk hits me. Yesterday the water was starting to rush down the pavement so I lifted my feet up on the ledge. I threw my apple core into the stream and the water snatched it away downhill, bouncing it on the drain grille. The water sucked at it until the white core disappeared between the slots. I started thinking I knew what it was like where that core went. Most people didn't.

Gretchen and I used to climb down those grilles with flashlights and walk through the giant pipes to the creek. If we talked, our voices echoed. When I saw the light at the creek end of the tunnel, I cut out my flashlight because I'd rather not see the slime on the sides too clearly. The smell there was close and tight. We were walking underneath the earth where most people have never been.

121

I think I would have gone crazy if I thought I couldn't find my way out.

The first time we went I was a lot more scared than Gretchen, but I didn't let her know. I thought of a great gush of water coming through. We would have gone with the water like my apple core. I have been thinking I would like to go back down that grate, just to see if I could stand to be in there alone. Just to remember the feeling isn't enough. And when I'm by myself, I want to go in farther than Gretchen and I did together.

I am really by myself now. I'm not sure what is the matter with me. I could have made other friends. I put a picture in here that used to make me cry. I got it out and looked at it again. It is the picture of the little girl alone asking for foster parents. She is sitting on the ground crying and her belly is swollen. I reread the story about what happened to the mother and daddy and how she waited for someone to send money and say they loved her. I remember when her story made me start thinking about Mama and her veins that were clogging up and Daddy getting drunk and walking in front of a car. That picture of the little girl could worry me so much I couldn't sleep until I heard him trying to unlatch the back gate.

Now I think what good would it do to help that one little girl. And what good would it do for Michael Anthony to come visit Ella Ruth Higgins. After I bought the things that Mama needs, I could buy a nice horse like Lone Star and pay to go to Winston Academy. That's what I used to be able to think. Now I would like to go down that grate by myself and all the money in the world wouldn't be any help.

The barn cat was in heat. Usually she would be snooty and let me get just close enough to touch her with my fingertips. Then she'd run. She would grab the table scraps I took to her and growl while she ate them, pretending she was eating something she'd killed.

Today she came right up to me before I went inside the barn. She squatted and dragged her belly on the way. Then she rubbed against my legs, moving from my left foot to my right as though she were a spider winding me up with silk. I touched her back. It was soft, velvetlike. I never knew she was so soft. When I touched her, she began to belt, her voice ten times her size.

"Boy, you're loud enough to tell every tomcat in a ten-mile range."

When I spoke, she got louder as if I were competition she had to drown out. She went across the new grass in front of the barn. Her haunches were up, her tail bent to the side.

I made her sound back to her. When she got louder, I did it again.

122

I laughed out loud at her, but she didn't care. All the times I had tried to make a mockingbird answer and it never would. One even mocked the squeak of our back gate but never me. My sounds could set off the frogs and the katydids. I mocked the cat until I felt silly. She didn't tire but I did.

I did this, thinking I was alone. Then I caught movement out of the corner of my eye and turned quickly. I saw Stevie go into the packhouse. My eyes didn't focus fast enough to see his expression, but I knew he was watching me. That made me really mad, that he was there, spying on me. This was my territory. They could take their card game anywhere.

I rode away on Maudie. I decided to work on a story in my head. It was coming from a memory that I never put together when it happened. I was sick. And I was nine years old. I couldn't put it together then because I didn't have it figured out. I was when I swam out to get Oscar-Roscoe when the other ducks tried to kill him. After I got sick, he got killed anyway. He was cooked and eaten. He was the reason I got sick. I almost drowned and half froze trying to save him and in a week, he got cooked and eaten. That didn't have anything to do with being cripple. Mama tried to make it all up saying I could have another one. A baby duck. Then it could get too big and get eaten too. I couldn't keep a duck no matter what because it wouldn't stay a baby. I even gave that baby duck to Baby Ruth when I didn't feel like being a mother.

The story wouldn't go together. A branch caught across Maudie's face, then sprang loose and hit me in the face like a slingshot. I felt the ridge swelling on my cheekbone. What if that had been my eye it hit? The sun went under a cloud and when the light went dim, I imagined I was going blind. It grew dark between the trees and the darkness came at me like a moving wall. The light popped back on. The wall was never there. I felt silly. Light-headed. This wouldn't be the day the duck story would go together.

Soon the light grew duller in the woods. I missed seeing Spot run in and out of the bushes. It was the middle of March, cool enough to need a jacket, but I didn't want to go home yet. Mama's hot kitchen followed me into every room of our house and made me take my breath in short mouthfuls. It seemed Mama wanted to know what every living thing was doing as soon as it was under her roof. Some days when Maudie and I were in the woods, I would sing real loud because I knew no one was there to hear me or ask, like Mama, what show my song came from.

When I got to the field beside the barn, I got off and took the bridle off Maudie so she wouldn't have to eat with the bit in her mouth and slipped on her halter with a long lead strap. She tugged at me while I sat, tipping my body over, but I held firm, forcing her to eat the grass near me. The new spring grass popped as she bit it and made a good smell. I sang softly while she ate.

After I took the saddle off Maudie and turned her into her pen, she walked to the center, buckled her knees and began to wallow. Then she stood up and dropped to do the other side. I always thought it would have been simpler for her to roll all the way over, but that was Maudie's way. When I dragged the saddle through the door to Maudie's feed room, silt came through the cracks from the loft overhead. I thought it was because I had jarred the barn, yanking the door from its crooked socket. I rubbed my eyes, tugging at my lashes until the dirt washed out. Maudie came into her stall, bumping her wide hips against the sides. She snorted happily into her trough of sweet feed. After I said good-bye to her and she nickered from the far end of the barn, they were suddenly all around me.

One was at the door—Stevie. One was on each side—Tiger and Ernie. Al Sawyer came down the wooden steps from the loft.

"What are you guys doing here?"

I remembered they must have been playing cards when I left to go ride. I had seen Stevie then. They didn't answer me; they just stared like I hadn't said anything. I looked at Al Sawyer. I thought he was going to say something, but whatever he was thinking swept across his mind like a broom across a bare floor.

From that moment on, the stable smell went away like a wind had swept through and there was the sting in my nose of sweat and fear. I was freezing. Four of them and me, closed inside the barn. I went for the door.

Ernie pushed me back into the hay. That made me mad. I jumped up and ran at him. Stevie's arm hit me across the throat. He and Tiger grabbed me and threw me backwards again. They held my shoulders penned.

"Big brave guys. Four to one. What are you trying to prove?"

I pushed them away so hard that I thought my heart would fly out of my chest and splash in their faces and shower me with my own blood like Bluegrass the horse. I could have beat up any one of them by himself. I kicked Stevie in the chin and heard his jaw rattle.

"Fight me fair, you sonavabitch chickenshit and I'll kill you."

Tiger grabbed my hair and Stevie hit me in the mouth and I bit my lip.

"I didn't do anything."

I said nothing else. Everything I tried to do was stopped. None of them said anything to me. I got up and my legs were pulled from under me. My mind said they were going to beat me up, bloody my nose and loosen my teeth. But they were after my clothes. I held my

124

blouse together and my hands were pulled away. They tugged at my boots until my ankles hurt. I wouldn't make it easy to take them off. Stupid, Ella. Thinking it was a fight.

I rolled into a ball, but they pulled me out flat again. I saw a possum once, cornered in the shed by three dogs. He opened his jaws and hissed, a crazy smile showing all his sharp teeth. For a second he fooled the dogs. They backed up, but then they saw what was really there, a little ball of gray fur with a mouth only large enough for one dog's paw. He played dead and soon he was flying around like a ball of gray cotton. I threw water on the dogs from the rain barrel and the possum went down a hole in the floor too small for the dogs. They pawed awhile but soon they got bored and went after other things. I never saw the possum come out of the hole, but I didn't smell his rotting dead body. One night coming down the hill from the barn, lightning lit up the dark like a flashbulb, catching two possums in an embrace. The light went out and I thought of what Daddy said, that animals don't live by right or wrong. They are only right. I scratched the straw around me. I couldn't find a hole in the floor except for a knothole I poked one finger through.

I got tired. I had never felt so tired. My arms weren't strong enough to hold over myself. Stevie took off his pants on one leg and left them on the other. I saw his leg bare and white with long black hair. He didn't look like he did last summer. My legs didn't have dark hair like a boy's. Some of the hair on my arms and legs were long, but it was all golden. The hair on my head and my crotch was black. I didn't know if the sun could turn that hair golden like my arms and legs. I didn't want to see me naked there in front of them so I shut my eyes while they pulled off my jeans.

With my eyes shut, it was only a little darker than the barn. I felt for a second that I might escape, fly out the window, a bird bouncing off the walls of a room, finding the open window and being sucked away into the sky. No. I was nailed against the floor like the chicken hawk on the side of the chicken house. I couldn't use my wings; they were as good as broken. My stomach was swollen and open, turned up between my wings, spread to show my private parts. My claws were stiff. No use. Maudie squealed long after I had stopped.

They rammed me like broom handles. Soon I wanted them to find my hole so the jabbing would stop. That's all they wanted, my hole. When I was so tired and it was happening, it seemed not worth the fight I had given them. The rest of my body was just in the way. I was handled like I was not alive. They could have found another hole, one that was not alive around it. I felt a hand rubbing my breast. I opened my eyes and saw Al Sawyer, blurred. I bit his arm as fast as a snake, and he pushed my face back down.

When the hawk was nailed against the barn, I watched a sparrow bouncing around on its head, chirping, cocking its head. Then it pecked out the eyes of the hawk. After that the hawk turned to feathers and bones and fell away like paper.

When I opened my eyes, they were gone. I lay there and ran out on the straw, their juice tickling like bugs walking downhill around my hips and the backs of my legs. I scratched my leg and the juice was thick and sticky, a smell I had never smelled before. I couldn't lift my head to see. I drained there like a plant that was rained on and my drops rolled off onto the ground. If I was a plant, the storm had been hard and my leaves were torn. I dried stiff and crusty. When I moved to get up, I hurt so I lay still a while longer. I slept and did not dream.

Soon I was awake. As I awoke anew, I was afraid to move, a frozen bug, afraid the cat would crush me with its paw. Maybe I could disappear like a bug before a cat's eyes if I did not move. They would tease me, I thought, let me think I was going to get away, then slap me down again. I wondered if I had never been asleep, just paralyzed. In a bad dream you can't run and you want to wake up. You wake up and see that the reason you couldn't run was you were lying down, trapped between the bedcovers. But it's all right because the bad man has gone with the dream. I looked around me and it was true; no one was there. I felt in the straw for my clothes and put them on like a blind person. They were torn like my skin. I could see a pale square of light, the barn window. Through it, the orange square of my mama's kitchen.

They never knew, Mama and Daddy. I waited on the hillside until I saw my mama leave to feed the chickens and I could go into the house without her seeing me. I hurried to the bathroom and filled the tub. The water made me sting so bad down there that tears came to my eyes. I let the dirty water out and filled it again before Mama came back into the house. Finally, after my hair was covered with suds, the smell was gone. Mama came to the door of the bathroom.

"Ella, that you?"

"Naw, Mama. It's just an old hobo taking a bath in your tub."

I heard the voice from me, only it wasn't the new me. The new me only talked inside my head, a voice that didn't tell lies. It was the old me talking to Mama, the me who wasn't afraid. There was never any question that I wouldn't tell Mama. I couldn't stand to see something that happened to me hurt her worse than it did me. Mama never wanted to get back at people for bad things they did. She

126

wouldn't know what to do if I told her what happened. I was afraid she would want to comfort me more than I could stand.

I heard her waiting at the door and knew that I had to explain why I was taking a bath so early. Even if she didn't ask, I had to tell her or it would make two frown lines between her eyes till I did.

"I fell off, Mama. I didn't want to tell you because I was afraid you would worry."

"Oh Ella, Ella honey." She cracked the door. "Can I come in?"

"I'm not hurt, Mama. Just a little sore on my backside. And I managed to land in a pile of manure. Just let me soak."

"Oh, all right, honey. I just knew something was wrong. What in the world you want to risk your life on that animal for . . ." Her voice faded so I knew she had gone into the kitchen. She talked to herself for a while.

It didn't seem hard. To break myself in two. In the tub I thought of something funny. When I was a little girl, I found the doll clothes Mama was making for Saint Nick while I was at school, hidden in the bottom of Daddy's dirty shirt box. Every day I would sneak in when she was out feeding the chickens and try the newest outfit on Saint Nick. There was a pink crocheted hat, a blue pinafore and a yellow dotted-swiss dress with daisy buttons. On Christmas I acted like each one was a surprise. Getting away with that was more fun than really being surprised.

I saw bumps come on my legs, chilled under the hot water. I got on my knees in the dirty water and washed the ring from the tub. I touched myself where they had hurt me. It made me shiver, but their sticky juice was gone. Suddenly the water turned pink, rings of red spreading from me. I looked and saw the red running between my legs. At first I was afraid. My body was wounded and the blood poured from it like a bullet hole. But where had it come from?

Of course. I wanted to laugh I was so happy. So soon, I got to know. I felt so lucky. Now I would never have to tell because they didn't make me pregnant. I thought about Gretchen for the first time in a long while. I should call her up. Tell her I wasn't pregnant. It wasn't funny. It couldn't have happened to Gretchen. They would have seen her and run away like mice. They knew they could get away with it with me.

I hid my torn clothes under my bed. There were stiff spots on them like dried egg white. Spots like on the blanket in Carl's car. I splashed witch hazel all over me before I put on my nightshirt. The next day I would stamp my clothes in the manure in Maudie's stall before I left them in the laundry basket. Maybe the cat would sniff the spot in the straw and lock her jaws open like she did when she

127

sniffed the stain a tomcat had made on the bag of chicken mash. I walked into the kitchen and Mama shook her finger at me and smiled, then started dishing me up a plate of food.

Starrie was in the house alone washing the eggs for Mrs. Pickerell. She heard David come in and her skin prickled. He was bigger than Ricky. She was partial to thin boys. Some of the eggs had gray chicken do-do (check for right word to use in book) and she had to soap them to get it off. She wondered if the soap might soak through the shell and ruin the taste of the egg. She feared wearing a thin spot and crushing the egg in her hand. Once she had found an egg that was only skin-covered. She rolled it into her palm and took it inside. Mrs. Pickerell slid it into a saucer. She told Starrie to give the chickens broken oyster shells so they could make shells. Sometimes they put one long shell around two eggs. They couldn't sell the double yolks. Something special was no good. It didn't make sense. Mrs. Pickerell said take them out though they were a bargain. Mrs. Pickerell told of finding a triple once. She had to eat that hen because she kept making mistakes. (Maybe too much about eggs.) Someday Starrie would take a trip to the place where oyster shells came from, the ocean, and see oysters when they were alive and whole. Whole, crushed up, then made whole again around an egg. And broken again to eat the eggs, oysters and eggs. Someday she would study in school and learn how a chicken put a shell around an egg. There was so much to learn, Starrie thought.

David burst into the kitchen.

"Here alone?" he asked.

She jumped but didn't look at him for fear he would see that she was scared. Why wasn't her brother ever around when she needed him?

"I think your mother is in the hen house," she said.

How stupid of her!

He laughed. "No she isn't. I took her to town myself. I'm to get her at 4:00."

Ricky, she thought. Where is he?

She kept working but her hands had begun to shake. The worst happened. She dropped an egg splat on the floor. As soon as it left her fingers she knew it was broken. Not like a dish that might make it if it landed right.

David laughed an evil laugh.

"Why don't you take a break? You're getting clumsy."

"I'll go find the cat. She will eat the egg," she offered.

When she climbed down from the stool, he grabbed her by the shoulders and began kissing her.

"No don't. Leave me alone. I don't want to."

He tore away her dress, ripping the buckskin. One shoulder was laid bare.

"Why are you screaming? There is no one to hear you," he taunted.

As she stared at him in terror he unbuckled his pants.

"Don't be so sure of that." She turned. Ricky, his brother, was at the door. Her heart leapt.

They tried to tell me, both of them. When I went up the tree, showing off like I wasn't scared of anything, Daddy tried to tell me I couldn't stay a little kid. And Mama saw Gretchen grow up and get a boyfriend. I shouldn't have been off by myself.

Mitzi Wade's crinoline fell down in the lunchroom and about twenty girls got in a circle around her like covered wagons while she tied it back up. And nobody even likes Mitzi Wade. They wouldn't circle around me. Look how many people heard what I said to Stevie at the ballgame. I don't even know how many. If I went to court, they would all come witness and call me guilty. There is only one person in the world who would take up for me. Mama. And I would die before I'd tell her.

Daddy's words kept going through my head, "You're grown up now . . . think you're grown up now, do you?" I was in the middle of his confusion. Daddy didn't know which way he wanted to go either, awake or asleep, sober or drunk, at home or at the Rebel Bar. One day his eyes lit up as he told me of a wonderful drink he made as a boy of locust pods and wintersweet wild persimmons. I asked Mama if we could make it and her face twisted. "Pshaw. I ain't being no party to his drunkenness, not if I can help it." Mama always thinks that all you have to do is eat and everything will be OK. She covers the table with food and frets if we don't eat everything there. Then she stacks up the empty plates and acts as happy as somebody picking red apples off a tree.

There was so much I couldn't picture. My parents' bodies seemed as separate as a rock and a tree. But one goes crazy and one doesn't. Like the horse on the fence. Like them. I don't go crazy. I would give anything if I hadn't said what I did to Stevie. Then I'd know there was a different reason.

I'll never walk into an empty room and believe that it's really empty until I look in every hiding place. I sneered at Hazel and her fears. She said when she went into the ladies' room in a service station and could see every wall, the floor and the ceiling; she still checked for a small door, large enough for a man to crawl from. Then she looked for holes in the walls for them to watch her through.

129

She said her husband once caught the attendants watching her through a peephole. They wanted to see the private things that women did, the things not on the films they watched in the back of the filling station at night. Hazel told me, "What you know about men, Ella Higgins, would half fill a thimble." I didn't think those men Hazel talked about had anything to do with me. I didn't believe her. I heard men laugh at her because she thought she was beautiful and looked like a fool.

They watched me. I don't remember what I did except I threw the saddle over the barrel on the wall and hung up the bridle. I don't remember if I scratched myself, tucked in my shirttail, or touched a button to see if it was fastened. I don't think of those things if no one is watching. I smelled the good stable smell and saw the hay dust hanging in the shafts of light. I had been singing. They never noticed one way or the other about my singing. Dumb Ella, paddling along just like Oscar Roscoe without the good sense to know what they had in mind. Only there wasn't anybody there to save me from them. What good did it do Oscar Roscoe?

They talked about the stuck-up girl who rode by them every day without turning her head, acting like she wasn't interested in them anymore and pretending she didn't hear the ugly remarks they made. When my eyes did find them, they acted like I wasn't there. I know how they talked to each other too. They talked about my ass pumping in the saddle and the tits that poked at my shirt front. I knew the words they would use to name my parts. They said one day they were going to bust my cherry.

After I rode Maudie fast, my chest was sore like the two things punching up didn't have a big enough place to grow, like a seed trying to break the ground. One day I had jarred open the middle button because I wore an old, too small shirt with no darts to allow for my chest growing. I never knew whether it was open when I rode past them. When I threw Maudie's hay over, a stick hit my bare chest and I saw the open button. I dropped the fork and closed it fast. I looked around. There was just Maudie pulling at the chunk of hay I had dropped without fluffing it for her. But I still felt those eyes. The ones I had caught watching me before. I pulled the hay back up and began to break it with her impatient lips sliding over my hands. I felt like the night I fell asleep on the sofa in my clothes and woke up the next morning in my pajamas in my bed. I took that shirt and put it in the hand-me-down box.

My skin was slow to stretch. The nipples came up first, then the white skin around them. They itched so I sat drawn up and scratched them against my knees or rubbed them against Maudie when I combed her like an old cow scratching on a fence post. When it was cool enough, I wore two undershirts and kept wearing my jumpers and shirts with pockets on both sides. I found a bra in some hand-me-down clothes that Becka sent, but it didn't feel right. The girls at school talked about cramps and asked not to dress out for phys. ed., to sit on the bench while we played. My pain was in my head, a sadness because this was going to keep happening for the rest of my life. I thought about the games, running, hitting a ball, trying harder than ever to hit it over the fence so I could forget the dripping. Blood. That was supposed to mean you were hurt or dying. Every month of my life getting ready for a baby. I figured a woman could have thirty children in her lifetime. Even when Maudie was young, it hardly ever happened to her. Now, never. Maudie was lucky. I felt like girls got cheated, that boys didn't have things happen to them they didn't want.

The night after, my stomach cramped as the blood poured from me. I got up once to change my wet pad. Daddy said the reason a mosquito bites you is to get blood to feed her young. The mosquito can carry two-and-one-half times her own weight, as much blood as four hundred pounds of beefsteak. Can't blame her, he would say; she doesn't know right from wrong. Her body stretches and swells with blood like a blister. Daddy showed me a picture that made a mosquito as big as a cat. I had no young to feed. Daddy doesn't see the blood. He sees the breasts. He told me I had a tunnel, not just a hole, a tunnel to a box to make a baby in. He can't see that the door is broken.

One day on the bus, Stevie sang "Down in southwestern France, where the women wear no pants, but they do wear leaves, to protect them from the fleas."

Everyone heard him. Al would be embarrassed to do that. To do it first, anyway. Stevie always wanted everyone to hear him. He said there were places in France where naked women rode bicycles in a circle. They rode as hard as they could. Al asked why.

"Because the seats rubbed them," Stevie said. "They loved it."

"I mean why were they riding?" Al asked.

"The men made bets on when it will happen. Honest. My uncle told me. He saw it with his very eyes. I'll get him to tell you."

If I went to hell, the devil would make me ride a bicycle naked in front of them.

Now Starrie was a cripple. At first she thought it might heal completely, but she didn't get proper medical attention. The bone was crushed. She could walk, but she would always have a noticeable limp. She was a good rider and of all things it happened on a horse.

131

Ricky (he lived at the ranch where she worked) had bought a new horse. It was a beautiful and unbroken Palomino mustang. It had never had a saddle on its back. Starrie was the first to saddle it, talking to it gently and amazing even David (Ricky's older brother) with her ability to sooth the wild animal.

"Maybe the horse thinks it has met one of its own kind," he said bitterly to Ricky. Starrie didn't trust David so she was haughty to him.

Ricky didn't hear his comment. He was too busy watching Starrie as she eased her light body into the saddle, still cooing to the horse. She didn't put down her full weight, hanging by her arms from the beam over the stable door. The horse grew more uneasy, trying to see this strange object that was on its back. Her patience with the animal was outstanding. It took all afternoon, but before dinnertime she was walking it easily around the corral. That was when it happened.

Cheril Simpson, David's rich girlfriend, came galloping up on her horse, squealing and making all kinds of noise and calling David's name to come look at her. She had on a new cowgirl outfit that matched her saddle. It was too late to stop the foolish girl. She had already spooked the Palomino. What occurred next was lightning fast. It wasn't the bucking that got Starrie. She could ride a bucking bronc. It was when the horse ran its side into the fence, running in a frenzy in a circle and not allowing enough room for the Indian girl's leg. The splintering sound was horrible. Ricky would never forget it. He picked her up out of the dirt of the corral before the sharp hooves of the horse trampled her to death. He carried her limp body into the house and called the doctor.

"I don't feel sorry for her," David said. "It was a stupid risk to take, just trying to prove how tough she is. Was, I should say."

David rode off with Cheril, not even bothering to unsaddle the Palomino that was rolling in the corral, trying to rid itself of the hated saddle.

I had a dream that night that seemed real as life. I dreamed that I was going down Umstead Street Hill on my bike. Only I was naked.

Mama said, "Ella Ruth, naked as a jaybird."

I said it was OK, Mama, I didn't have any breasts yet and no hair in my crotch. But I did. I don't know why I lied to Mama. I felt my breasts like two hard mounds. They should have been covered. Covered with layers and layers of clothes so no one would know they were there.

When I slid in the leaves at the bottom, I hit the bar and blood

gushed from between my legs. Al Sawyer was waiting for me when I
ran into the woods to hide. He said to me, "Ella Ruth, I saw that.
You broke the door. Nobody will marry you now."

That night before I went to sleep, I decided I might marry Al
Sawyer someday, the only one who didn't fuck me. That is the day I
think I became a little crazy for good.

Rough Outline
Death of ~~Father~~ by Bison Herd

I. Attack of Navaho Village:

   A. Death of Mother, older sister

   B. Left with nothing but a few supplies, ten
other, and fa_____ _____ Tumbleweed an

   C. Fight for survival for brother and he

   D. Food scarce; brother gets fever, un___
in

      1. Carries him to the home of an. __)a
uple whose children had already grow

      2. He recovers; *little* Star disappears
enough, flour,
with bacon, and water to last a few u

      3. Finding dead soldiers and tak
~~the~~ Thief:

   A. Food supply becomes low - forced to

   B. Been stealing chickens - overheard
cattle rustling. When trying to well
overheard sign to run, small o
   C. ~~Star~~, chased, shot in temple, l
it hurt, recovers

The Couger:

   a. Smelled bacon, became curious

The New York Gazette, 1956:

Miss Ella Ruth Darwin, the great female scientist from Summit, North Carolina, is convinced that gray squirrels remember where they bury their nuts. Although it was formerly assumed that the winsome creature was merely responsible for planting countless oak trees with no memory of where it left its stash, the granddaughter of Charles Darwin has made many observations of squirrels retrieving buried nuts even from under a blanket of snow. What was thought to be mindless instinct is now, because of Miss Darwin's tireless research, documented as memory.

Chipmunks, on the other hand, she finds to be of lower intelligence. They hoard nuts, even expertly burying a pigeon egg once in Miss Darwin's backyard without cracking its shell. Then the nest robber promptly fell asleep for the three winter months. Sifting the soil in the spring, Miss Darwin recovered the darkened egg, still intact. Meanwhile, the chipmunk in question, carefully marked with a red ear tag, was searching for tidbits under the trees.

Does this mean that the chipmunk is of lesser intelligence than the squirrel? When interviewed, Miss Darwin said with a laugh, "How eager we are to ascribe intelligence to a creature just because it is physically attractive—i.e., cute. A hard man indeed would call a striped chipmunk a pest destined for extermination, yet I have heard more than once that a squirrel is no more than a rat with a bushy tail."

I have started a new notebook. There are going to be more pictures in it, pictures I draw. The *Annotated Notebook of Ella Ruth Darwin,* who has traveled the world over watching the habits of living things. Ella Ruth Darwin doesn't associate much with people, never attending parties or bothering to dress in the latest fashions. She prefers to stay to herself. She dresses very simply. Some people might even call her plain, but behind those glasses she always wears is an interesting face and a very active mind.

In a recent interview, Miss Darwin made this remark: "As a child I merely played in the woods with reckless abandon. Now, as a scientist, I study the woods. It is my laboratory. I can snatch up creatures quickly, bring them inside and never have to risk the discomforts of chigger bites or a sudden rainstorm."

She researches many things—for example, the carrion flower has caught her interest. It looks like a lily, but it smells so bad a bee won't have anything to do with it. It has to get pollinated by flies. Mama got an Easter lily from one of her customers. When I carried it inside, it got yellow pollen on my shirt. It smelled like Grandma Higgins's funeral.

Actually I'm doing most of my watching out my back window. Even though the weather is nice, I'm sticking pretty close to the house. My story box was getting to be a problem. I dug it up and buried it so many times and so many places, I started worrying I might forget where it was. And you never know who's watching you. Those boys or even my Daddy might see where I put it. I decided to clean it up and paint it and keep it under my bed. I felt better as soon as it was in the house with me. I even took the picture of Ricky Nelson off the ceiling over my bed. I don't like the idea of anyone watching me.

The first thing I put in my inside story box was a copy of the drawing I did of a snail—"Mollusca: invertebrate, soft unsegmented body lacking appendages enclosed by protective shell secreted by glands, creeps by forming muscular foot." I could look right at a snail and not be able to describe it that good. I went outside and got one and drew it from all directions, even waiting still enough for it to come out and not be afraid. It sure takes patience to be a scientist. I watched it make a trail that caught the light from outside, a shiny dotted line on my desk. I locked my door so Daddy couldn't come in. I'd never hear the last of letting a snail walk on my desk.

The snails divided the sidewalk and even the grass into sections like a pattern to be cut out. I have seen those same lines after a rain where they wandered out into a world too fast for them and ended up smashed like possums on the highway, stuck in place like brown eggs. A snail travels at .03 miles per hour. I wonder if it's the slowest thing alive. Protective shell. Maybe in a snail's world.

I need to do an inside drawing, slice a snail in half to see how it fills the chambers, but I can't. I'll go to the library for a picture to copy. I saw Dr. Horace Sanders's gardener pulling snails off the roses, throwing them against the stable. I couldn't look at that. I hate to even slip and step on an anthill because of all the hard work I would cause them cleaning out their hole. Stevie and Al could feel a snail crush under their shoes and think only of dirtying their soles. They salted them and watched them shrivel. I know I will never get

138

to be Ella Darwin unless I change, until I can walk out in my yard, get the first snail I see and slice him in two, just like that. I just can't do it yet.

Grandma Higgins could have done like Al and Stevie. There was a big spider on her porch. If I'd seen it first, I'd have scooted it off the edge because I knew what she'd do. She saw it and ran and stamped it without thinking twice. I thought she would lift her foot and there would be nothing but a smashed spider, but the strangest thing happened. Hundreds of tiny spiders ran in all directions. I asked my biology teacher, Miss Richmond, and she said she had never heard of such a thing. But I'm sure I saw it.

Actually, I don't want Mama to know about Ella Ruth Darwin. It might hurt her feelings to know I don't want to be Ella Higgins.

On Saturday night I was sitting in the stands with the girls from the Youth Fellowship. We went to church together on Sunday nights to get a free supper, but I was getting pretty tired of the stuff we had to listen to after we ate. It did give me somebody to go places with like to the movies and the ballgames, since I never got asked for dates. I wasn't even sure I wanted to be asked.

I heard Stevie and Ernie Langston start whistling through their teeth. I looked at the field, but our team hadn't started out yet. Then I saw what they were whistling at. The other girls in my row didn't notice what was going on because they were waiting to go crazy and start yelling when our team ran on the field. I couldn't believe it. I had heard Al Sawyer got thrown off the team for cutting practice. Now I knew why. Al Sawyer was walking in front of the bleachers and holding onto his arm was Mitzi Wade.

Mitzi Wade was head majorette, but the band didn't march at baseball games. Her face was real pretty, kind of a turned-up nose and big eyes and her hair was naturally curly with a peroxide streak in the front. She had on a pink straight skirt that was so tight you could see right where the elastic went on her underpants, and a dyed-to-match angora sweater that made her look like fur-covered cotton candy. As she bounced along, the fur rippled and jiggled over the part of her that all the boys looked at first, tits as big as grapefruits with nipples that stuck up so much they parted the angora like a dog's nose. Burrowing in the fur over her left nipple, as round as a swollen dog tick, sat Al's DeMolay pin.

"Jesus Christ, she makes Annette Funicello look like a boy," Stevie exclaimed to Ernie. Annette always pointed at her name on her shirt as if that was the reason they were staring there. Darlene was my favorite Mouseketeer because she could sing and dance and not just bounce her titties. Al and Mitzi sat right in front of Stevie and

Ernie and Tiger just as everybody started yelling when our team came out.

Every year Mitzi got mad because she never won homecoming queen. The reason was everybody got to vote, not just the boys, and there were more girls at Summit High than boys. Suzie Wade, Mitzi's own sister, didn't even vote for her. Hell would freeze over before I'd vote for Mitzi. Suzie, who was sitting with us tonight, got turned down for majorette because she was bowlegged. Suzie thought it was funny at the homecoming game when Mitzi burned her leg and a big hole in the back of her silver shorts with her fire baton. Mitzi figured with the fire and with her cheeks sliding out the back of her shorts like new moons she'd get the attention away from Shirley Sidney, who won queen. I have to admit I was real glad when Mitzi dropped her baton in the final competition for Miss Tarheel Strutter.

When Stevie started hitting the back of Al's head with peanut shells, I could see Al's ears flooding with blood. He gave Stevie the finger, but pulled it back down as Mitzi turned to smile at Stevie with her fat snow-pink lips. She drug her tits over Al's arm. Stevie made a hound-dog sound as though she had rubbed them on him instead of Al. Then the whole row of guys with Stevie started wiggling like a bunch of windup toys.

Mama called Mitzi Wade "fast." And all those guys making remarks were "skins." In Mama's book, skins had a chance to better themselves if they got a decent job, cut off their ducktails, didn't talk back to their mamas and didn't soup up their cars, put on glass pack mufflers and peel rubber down Main. But fast girls—they were ruined for life.

Al and Mitzi got up and left, right in the middle of the fifth inning. I was wishing she'd fall down the bleachers or have a wad of bubblegum stuck on her rear when she got up. She pranced out with Al and smiled back at Stevie and friends. Stevie howled again, right at the wrong time in the ballgame. Cale Jenkins was at bat and when he looked away at the noise, the pitcher got a strike past him. The kids started booing Stevie and told him to shut up. Cale was our best player. On the next pitch Cale hit the ball over the back fence so everybody got over being mad at Stevie. I started imagining having a picnic with Cale Jenkins so I wouldn't think about Al Sawyer being out in his car with Mitzi Wade. I would make fried chicken and a cherry pie. I'd need a red and white tablecloth to put the cherry pie on.

When they finally came back, it was the eighth inning. Nobody said much to Stevie for making a racket this time because by then we had Farmville eleven-to-two.

"Hey Al, I didn't know you liked rabbit."

140

Mitzi turned around again. She had put on fresh snow-pink lip-stick because a little was on one of her teeth. I was really glad I saw it on her teeth. I didn't see any on Al. Her cheeks were as pink now as his ears.

"Hey Al, you're supposed to skin a rabbit before you eat it."

Mitzi turned around again and smiled, which I figured proved she was fast. If she wasn't, she'd have ignored them. She had licked the lipstick off her tooth.

"Look at all that pink fuzz around Sawyer's mouth. Looks like somebody stuck a wad of cotton candy in his face." Stevie rubbed his hands together, I'm sure imagining they'd been under Mitzi's pink fuzzy sweater. Al gave Stevie the finger again. When Al turned around, I saw an expression on his face I'd never seen before, an expression I didn't like one bit. He was real proud of what they were teasing him about.

"One hun-dred per-cent an-go-ra rab-bit," Stevie said slowly, then squinted at Mitzi's back as though he was reading. "Hey Mitzi, what's the label on the outside of your sweater for? Did you get it on inside out?"

Al turned to look at her and I saw her snow-pink nails reach around the back of her sweater, feeling for the label that wasn't there.

"I do not," she giggled and turned around again.

"Then how come Sawyer's pin is on the inside?" Steve taunted.

"It *is not*," Mitzi whined, looking at Al as if to reassure him. "See, there's your pin on the *outside*," she tweeted, sticking them out more and pointing at the dog tick on the fur beside the dog's nose. I looked for a sign in Mitzi's round blue eyes that she realized they were implying she had her sweater *off* out in Al's car and got it back on wrong side out, but there was none. How could Al Sawyer like a girl that dumb?

I heard a cracking sound, the sound of wood splitting, and looked up to see the ball go over the back fence again. Cale Jenkins dropped the broken bat and began trotting toward first base. All the fatties and uglies in my row started humming like a beehive. I bet every girl in that row had a crush on Cale Jenkins because he could hit a baseball over the fence. Mitzi Wade wanted Al Sawyer just because he had a car.

We were down at Grandma's Lake for the Sunday School cook-out. They elected me president of all the uglies and fatties in the Girls Youth Fellowship. I felt like something Daddy had said: "In the land of the blind, the one-eyed man is king. King Ella One-Eye, that was me. Suddenly Suzie Wade appeared at the door of the bathhouse. Suzie said they asked her to hold four coins between her legs when she tried out for majorette. She laughed and said she had room for four baseballs. We started a chorus of "Miss America," bellowing the word *ideal*.

"Thirty-six-twenty-five-thirty-six," Patsy Bivens shouted back and did a cannonball into the water.

Suzie Wade walked down the pier. I looked around to make sure none of the boys were watching from the woods. The rest of us were already in the water and had been wondering why it took Suzie so long to get her swimsuit on. We climbed up on the pier and looked close at Suzie. Even her chest was flushing, her bony chest. Suzie Wade was built like a washboard, but not today.

"I borrowed Mitzi's suit," Suzie said sheepishly.

"Borrowed?"

"Took," Suzie corrected with a giggle.

"That isn't all you borrowed."

"Suzie Wade, wearing a peach one-piece swimsuit," Patsy announced, "in case you judges haven't noticed, is built like a brick shit house. For her talent she will twirl a fire baton underwater."

Suzie put her hand behind her head and began to twirl an imaginary baton. While she strutted around, all of us put together what we were really seeing, not Suzie's figure, but Mitzi's. Before we had secretly thought Mitzi was just luckier than we were. Suzie jumped in the lake and when she popped to the surface, the front of her suit had deflated. She had them in her hands. They did look like grapefruit, pink grapefruit cut in half with a big nipple on each rind. I pictured the pink angora sweater with the nipple showing through like a dog's nose. We all tried them on in our suits, but they wouldn't go in as good as in Suzie's.

That afternoon we went to Suzie's house. Mitzi was out with Al so we went in her room and found the love comic she had ordered them from. The coupon had been cut out.

"Little Lies #39 can make big romances bloom when you're suddenly buxom and sexy. Lifelike nipples and soft nude-look rubber breast pads feel natural to the touch. Only $1.95 per set, four sets for $6.95."

Suzie looked in Mitzi's chest of drawers and produced two more sets. We figured Mitzi was wearing the fourth set. "So soft and bouncy," the ad said, "only *you* will know they're not real." For sure, Mitzi's well-kept secret had the entire male population of Summit High in the dark, Al Sawyer's rabbit-eating face included.

With Suzie Wade as ringleader, one set was taken and passed to Andy Sawyer, Al's kid brother, who was in Suzie's grade. First Andy tried putting one under Al's pillow, but he slept on it and never

142

knew it was there. Andy debated whether to come in wearing them himself or to get his sister, Selma, who was ten, to do it. Then he decided to put one in Al's Wheaties bowl. According to Andy, Al sat down and said: "What is this rubber shit doing in my bowl?"

"Pink grapefruit," Andy answered.

"The hell!" Al poked at it with his spoon before he picked it up. He was definitely looking at the little lie for the first time, Andy reported.

"Congratulations. You're now the envy of Summit High," Andy said, just the way he had rehearsed it.

"What the hell are you talking about?"

"You're holding Mitzi Wade's tit in the palm of your hand," Andy said. Then he pulled the other one from behind his back and put it on his head like a beanie. Al got this horrified look, Andy figured because he thought somebody had taken a knife and cut off the precious 38D while Mitzi screamed her heart out. Al threw the tit on the floor and after it landed, nipple up, Andy stepped on it, squashed it and when it popped back up said, "Oh, 'scuse me, Mitzi. Didn't mean to plant my tootsie on your tittie."

You would think after everybody started talking about it that Mitzi wouldn't have the nerve to wear them again in a million years, but I never saw her without her Little Lies in place. Suzie told us one Sunday night supper at the church that Mitzi said she was going to kill herself. Then Mitzi told Suzie she was going to kill her instead when she was sound asleep. That sounded more like Mitzi.

The next week Daddy and I passed Al's car, sitting by the highway. Al wasn't in it, just Mitzi's blond curly head. I looked in as we drove past and saw her bottom lip was out as far as her turned up nose. She was sitting where she was supposed to sit instead of in the middle where she sat when Al was driving. A half mile later we passed Al, walking. He threw out his thumb.

"Daddy, there's Al Sawyer. He needs a ride." Daddy hit the brakes and the truck squealed and shook to a stop.

Al climbed in and said, "Thanks, Mr. Higgins. Out of gas back there."

Daddy grunted something about gauges. I hadn't been that close to Al in months. He smelled like some kind of sweet-smelling shaving lotion.

"You smell like a French whore, boy," Daddy said. Daddy looked disgusted and Al looked embarrassed, though I know neither one of them knew what a French whore smelled like.

Al's body drew up like a salted snail. Maybe he wanted to take up as little room in Daddy's truck as possible and if he got smaller, he wouldn't smell so strong.

143

"Girls wear bracelets," Daddy added. Hanging over the back of Al's hairless hand was an I.D. bracelet. On the back side, I'm sure, was "XXX Forever Your Mitzi."

I waited for a comment about Al's ducktail, his pink shirt or his black pants pegged over his white shoes. All the things that made Al hot stuff as he strutted down the hall at Summit High shriveled him up when he was stuffed into Daddy's pickup.

"Look like that white nigger."

"Daddy, why don't you lay off. Al's not your kid, you know?"

"What's old slick lips' name?" he asked, ignoring me. "The one who shakes his ass and hollers. Elvis. Elvis the Pelvis. That's who he looks like," Daddy added, thinking he was insulting Al when he was giving him the world's greatest compliment. Then he started to chuckle, which was supposed to make his teasing all in fun.

"Let me off at the Esso, Mr. Higgins." Then Al added, "Please." I couldn't imagine having to call my daddy Mr. Higgins.

When Daddy ground the truck to a halt, the brakes squealed so loud everybody working at the station looked at us. Al jumped out and slammed the door, his "Thanks" shut out from us in the middle of the word.

"Slam the goddamn door off, showing your ass. Doors ain't got safety glass, you know," Daddy said to nobody because Al was already trotting into the station. I could see Al's comb outlined in one back pocket, his wallet in the other. He pulled out the comb first and slicked back his hair, then he took out his wallet.

Daddy cackled, "That sorry little Wade girl's got his pants hotter than a hen laying fish hooks in a wool basket."

I didn't say anything. With all his strutting like a peacock, I think Al Sawyer was still a virgin.

I wanted to practice parallel parking before we went to the license bureau, but all the parking places in Summit were diagonal and anybody could do that. During that part of the test, I knocked over the posts so many times I thought sure I'd failed. I hated to face my daddy.

"I ought not pass you," the grumpy examiner said. "You go home and practice parking till you can do it decent."

"Do I fail?" I felt the tears coming in my eyes. I never failed tests at school.

"Nawp," he grunted. "In four years you have to come back."

I never even told Daddy of my trouble. I found him asleep in the waiting room. He woke up long enough to walk to the truck and rode home asleep. I don't think I could sleep with me driving. I felt like a bird on its first solo flight. I was looking for something to practice parking between, but the last place I saw was between the posts at the examiner's bureau. From the first time I practice drove until now, I had a strange feeling about being inside something that had corners I couldn't see. I wanted to do like Al and Stevie and press my foot down and peel rubber all the way down the street, only on Daddy's truck it strangled the engine like I was holding it under water. Daddy kept cardboard in the tires to keep the inner tubes from coming through in blisters.

I wasn't exactly sure how to explain it, but from the day I learned to drive my whole life changed. I looked at people like Mama differently, people who couldn't or wouldn't drive, who had to always get someone else to take them places. My life became something that my Mama could never have.

One day I was driving Mama to get her catering supplies. She was drawn up inside her coat because the heater didn't work and a cold rain was falling. I was afraid because I could barely see; the old wiper was bouncing across the glass, dragging pine needles with it. When I stopped at a stop sign, I felt the back of the truck keep moving and we sat sideways.

"What was that, Ella Ruth?"

"I don't know, Mama. I think it just slips around more when it's raining."

"Slicker than greased owl shit," Daddy talked in my head, but as usual, he didn't tell me what I could do about it.

I had never driven in the rain. I drove slower but every time I tried to stop the truck, I felt as if we were falling through space. I began to fear I couldn't stay on my side of the line, that the truck was like a wild horse that wouldn't steer where I turned it.

"I didn't like that feeling one bit, Ella Ruth."

"Me neither, Mama."

I was too nervous to be consoling. My imaginary Daddy laughed and whispered in my ear: ". . . slipperier than an eel in a bucket of snot." He never told me things that were worth a hoot.

"Don't forget about my letter, Ella Ruth."

For a moment nothing would register on my brain; everything that I had was being used to drive from stop sign to stop sign. Letter, what letter? A car passed in the other direction and dumped so much water on us I felt as though we were going down in a submarine. In the blind moment when the outside went away and the inside of the truck darkened, I saw the white letter at the end of Mama's sleeve, her hand not visible. Of course. The letter to Matthew, that I had written for her, telling him about the family reunion Mama was planning.

Finally, through the blurred windshield, Mama saw the green shape of a mailbox.

"Ella Ruth, there's one."

"I see it, Mama. I'll pull off and go put it in."

I stopped the truck about three feet from the curb, where the water ran brown and thick as a river. I took it out of gear and let it sit running a minute to see if it was going to roll. I pulled the emergency brake, but I remembered Daddy taking a large rock from the truck and wedging it against one wheel. I took Mama's letter and climbed out on the running board. I saw the rock in the back of the truck, but it was on the other side. The rain didn't seem as hard outside as inside, but it came halfway up my calf when I stepped down. I held the letter inside my jacket as I walked around the front of the truck. For a second, in the sweep of the wiper, I saw Mama's round face. My feet grew heavy as my socks filled with water and fell over my shoes. I was all the way across the gutter and onto the sidewalk, the letter out, my other hand ready to pull the mailbox handle before I realized what I had done.

The mailbox wasn't a mailbox. It was a short woman in a green coat, her chest swelling out in just the right shape, wearing just the right shade of dark green. Her face was unkind, her hair stuck to her cheeks. She had the evil look of a playing-card soldier from Alice in Wonderland. She was wet, not repelling the rain as a painted box would have done. My hand froze. Something in my brain kept me from pulling open the front of her coat and stuffing my letter inside. I turned to run back to Mama, to see her kind face, laughing at what we had done. But when I turned, I saw only the ditch full of water.

Mama was gone. Not just Mama; the whole truck. I looked up the street, my first thought being it had taken off on its own, but a dull thump turned my head the way I should have looked in the first place. The pickup was rolling backward. Already safely across the intersection, it had hit a tree on the other side where there was no curb to stop it, leaving a white slash in the wet bark, rolled back into the street, and stopped sideways in the mud. I had never driven on that street, an unpaved mud strip that emptied into Main and sent out a semicircle of mud onto the pavement.

The mailbox lady walked away from me, her eyes still on me like I was a crazy person. I ran across the street and, just like the pickup, made it without getting hit, though I had forgotten to look. The truck still chugged when I got there, its engine sputtering a little from the rain, surrounding the car with steam like a boiling pot. I climbed in beside Mama, my wet shoes and socks swollen as clubfeet from the mud.

"I'm sorry, Ella Ruth," Mama said softly. "I didn't mean to leave without you."

It was summer and we were at the beach. I thought I would be excited because Daddy let me drive most of the way, but I was afraid every car we passed might suddenly turn at us and kill us all. For a while I tried to think what Ella Ruth Darwin would be doing that day on that beach. The sand was littered with shells, bits of seaweed, hundreds of things waiting for me to pick them up and sort them out. But I couldn't get my mind to separate. All I could be was Ella Ruth Higgins, walking with her mama. And Mama was troubled. She hadn't found words for it yet, but her forehead drew up tight and her bright blue eyes looked up like pools at the bottom of dark holes.

I stopped and stuck two fingers in the sand, then watched the holes fill with water. The water had no color. The tide had gone out leaving the sand shiny as a slime slick in a riverbed. Light flickered across the puddles when the sun moved from behind fast-moving clouds. The smell was of the sea, but the sight was the earth swept over and beaten by a sudden rainstorm, a tired and barren field as far as I could see. Little silver fish were trapped in the pools that were left when the ocean pulled out, dizzying in their movements like flakes in a snow globe. My head hurt between my eyes and I pressed my fingers there, searching for a knot, something I could squeeze out like a splinter and make the hurt go away.

The waves hit hard, slapping the shallow water beside me. I watched the old shells that the ocean tossed up, worn slick and face-less, being swallowed again. I was too weak to fight. The ocean pulled away and the hill of sand I stood on stuck up as bald and round as an old man's forehead. I couldn't make any sense out of anything. That silly day moon up there, hanging on the sky from the night before like frost on glass. How could I believe that lacy sliver could suck the ocean out?

Mama dragged her big bent feet, turning up the wet sand like a human plow because she couldn't pull herself far enough above the soft ground to walk with ease. I waited for her. I don't know why, but I didn't hide my feelings from Mama.

"Mama, the world is all topsy-turvy to me today."

She panted to a stop in front of me and began to cough. "Ella, Ella Ruth, honey." she puffed. "Find some peace and don't look on things so hard. There is only peace out there." I waited for her to nod, but she didn't.

"What are you talking about, Mama? Where is there?"

"Out of our house. Heaven. Married. Anywhere away from that man I married." She gave me too many answers to my question. "Don't get to thinking you've got your fair share of life yet. I'll miss you terrible, but an old woman's got no right to keep her child."

I was sixteen.

We started walking again.

147

"How you know a man's going to treat me right, Mama?"

"Have you some babies before you get too old."

I didn't want to think of those things yet, a husband and babies. Mama was rushing me, and as I walked ahead of her, I imagined myself a horse and she was my plow. I didn't like that thought. A horse wants to be free of a plow. Mama never made me pull her. I stopped and turned around while Mama slogged to catch up. She was looking at my footprints.

"Ella Ruth, your tracks look like a child's." Then she pushed on as though her life depended on getting somewhere. We weren't going anywhere.

I looked at my footprints then; they hardly made an impression. Beside them the thin tide worked to smooth down Mama's furrow. I looked ahead and saw my mama at the head of the furrow, her stretched sweater snapped around her back. I ran and caught up to her.

The sun began to turn the world soft late-day colors, pink orange, the colors of sherbet. It seemed so feminine, so silky. The sand wasn't beaten by a rainstorm. Mama wasn't a plow. Her face was as soft as a fresh peach, her cheeks ripe spots covered with fuzz. I wondered what the pink-orange light did for me, if it gave me a prettiness that Mama could see. While everything was covered with that strange light, we saw the dark thing in the tide pool.

We walked up to it. A giant turtle. Mama's mouth opened. She looked at the ocean, then at the turtle. She said with her look what I thought, that I didn't know such a thing was under that water, so close, the water we had let our bodies sink in, Mama bobbing like a buoy inside her tractor inner tube. That turtle should have been in a foreign country, the coast of Africa, not a tide pool in North Carolina. We walked up to it cautiously. It didn't move. It wasn't alive. Its back had collected many generations of worms and barnacles. One of those worms must have drilled through the shell, curling into rock-hard circles inside the heart. I reached for the turtle's back as Mama reached for me, but I was faster. My hand touched the razor edge of a barnacle. I cut my finger. Mama said nothing. She wet her handkerchief in the salt water around the turtle and washed my finger, pressing it tight to stop the bleeding. It was good the salt made it sting, she said, because that cleaned the wound. I looked at the still face of the pink turtle, folds of skin, open dead eyes, claws. It seemed to have no smell stronger than the sea around it.

"Mama, it's so big. Doesn't it seem worse for something so big to die?" Once, when I saw a tractor-trailer on its side by the highway, I imagined the world covered with fallen, starving dinosaurs.

We had walked through the little dead that day: fiddlers, pecked out shells, a silver fish with no eye. The edge of the sea was covered with little creatures, far more it seemed than were in a cornfield or a forest. And they were so easy to find, dumped out like pennies from a jar on that blank stretch of sand.

"A big thing do seem worse," she answered, "though I don't know why it should."

"Mama, do you think it washed up and got stuck in the hot sun when the tide went out and nobody helped it back to the water? Maybe they were scared it might bite them and they just let it die." I heard my voice, thin and childlike. I felt tears coming to my eyes for the turtle I didn't even know. "Poor, clumsy old thing," I whined.

"Ella Ruth, it died because its time had come. Don't go making something out of it. It died because it got wore out. Look at that shell. Look how many years all them critters have found a place to live. Old barnacles that usually get stuck on a post, getting a free ride on the waves to see the world." She paused, "You're trying to make something out of it so you can cry."

And I cried. Tears streamed down my face and I sobbed. I sobbed all the way back to the cottage and went to my bed. Didn't she know I pictured her, her back humped with barnacles growing on her bumpy nylon dress, Mama swollen and dead in a pool of water, skin green, hair pink, turning colors that weren't the same as living colors? Soon I whimpered easily, like a child trying to get her mama to come, but Mama saw no need.

Mama was getting ready to throw me out on my own.

I never left home. Soon Mama started to get thinner, and the hot red circles left her face when she worked. Her tiny mouth, the opening that never seemed large enough to fill her body, seemed to grow. Her features got like the old photo. One morning when she came into the kitchen in a bright green dress, her hair still down, I said: "You look like Hedy Lamarr, Mama."

"Whatever happened to Hedy Lamarr?" she asked. Her voice whistled now like wind through grass.

"Don't know, Mama. The last movie I saw her in was *Samson and Delilah*."

"With Victor Manure," Daddy piped in. "He always looked like somebody took a shit on his upper lip."

"I always thought he was handsome as could be," Mama replied with her chin up. "He was so manly-looking." How could she be so beautiful and look so bad at the same time?

Daddy grunted and added, "Hedy Lamarr probably got too wide for the movie screen."

I shivered. Mama had won the word battle. For once Daddy's mean comment about a fat lady didn't include her.

After he left, she went to her room to pin up her hair.

"Horace Sanders ought to take a look at me now," she said brightly, and turned her backside to the mirror. "Skinny as a rail, skinny as you, Ella Ruth, near 'bout."

"I'll call him, Mama. Maybe he can help you," I didn't want my voice to sound so urgent it frightened her. "Maybe that doctor you go to doesn't know what he's doing."

Mama got strangled. She was shaking her head. "No," she finally gasped. "Please. Don't call him."

Tears fell on her cheeks, spattering like they were being thrown out, not falling. They must have been cold because they didn't redden her white face.

Soon she got too weak to go into the kitchen. I fixed her meals and brought them to her, but she hardly looked at food, even when I kept reminding her it was there. Her face got as pale as a drawing in a coloring book, white as the pillowcase under her head when she slept. In the newspaper I brought her, Mama saw a picture of a starving child.

"Don't it seem their sad eyes get larger," she said, "when the poor little things are starving to death. I declare, as much as we throw away. It's a sin."

As her eyes filled again with liquid, I knew what Mama was trying to tell me. Her stomach had quit working. She was starving to death.

Sometimes I thought Mama couldn't even see across the room, that all of her senses were dimming. But then she would perk up like Spot did, hearing and smelling something seconds before I knew it was coming.

"Maynard's home."

I would wait, long enough for the thought that she was imagining something to cross my mind, then I'd hear the truck door slam and him fumbling with the gate.

She patted my hand, "Ella Ruth, Ella Ruth. Lawsy. I wouldn't have willed him on the devil himself."

One day he brought her a box of chocolate-covered cherries.

"I got into them on the way home," he said when she opened the box and saw five empty papers.

She shook her finger at him and smiled, "Maynard, you're going to ruin your dinner. I'm much obliged for the sweets."

After he went into the kitchen for his bottle, she said, "That was thoughtful of him." She looked confused.

She never ate the candy. I ate all but the last one while I sat by her bed. I could tell Mama wasn't sure whether to call Daddy good or bad. She wasn't sure if I was better off with him or by myself. She

150

thought she gave me the chance to get out so I would have a choice. But it was too late now.

Mama and I had a little secret, the thousand dollars that grew in the pantry one dollar at a time until she was too sick to earn any more. Daddy didn't know we had the money; no one did. When Mama sent me for it, I told her we would use it for a doctor to make her well. She shook her head and said, "Ella Ruth, that's real thoughtful of you, but no thank you, honey."

Mama sounded like she was refusing a cookie on a tray and she was refusing her life.

"There ain't no pockets in a shroud," she added. "That's your money. That's your picking-up-and-leaving money."

"I won't leave Daddy, Mama."

"Pshaw. You wont the one who chose him. Don't stay with him on my account."

It seemed strange that Mama said that. She was always the one wanting the family to be brought together. She didn't mention the reunion again, but I was afraid she would and I would have to tell her that I found her letter to Matthew in the pocket of my windbreaker, a month after she wrote it.

I wanted her to fight, to throw her weight against this thing that was taking her away, but she was giving up. As big as she used to be, Mama became as fragile as a butterfly that shook off her cocoon and flew away. I had to believe something left that body. I couldn't believe that my mama was just a crumpled shell in the bed that hardly lifted the bed covers.

While the air still whistled in and out of her body, I tried to see the world through Mama's eyes. I listened to what she said as if I had never heard it before.

"Ella Ruth, honey, it's freezing cold in here." I put all of her bed quilts from the attic on her, stacked so high I was afraid they might crush her. She looked at me in my shorts and sleeveless blouse and said nothing.

I stayed with her through the fall, coming home from school at lunch to check on her.

"I'm like your old speckled dog, Ella Ruth."

"How's that, Mama?"

"Wet to dry, cold to warm, hungry to a full belly. That's all I need to make me happy."

If Mama had any pain, she never said so.

Each time I had to leave her room, I was afraid she might die before I got back. But I began to see that wasn't the way death came to real people, not quick as the sound of a gunshot, or falling out of a saddle, or off a building into a rain barrel. She was going away a

151

little at a time. Real death came as slow as something grew.

One Sunday Matthew was by Mama's bed, talking about how she should have a fine funeral, that people should be ". . . put away in style so you could forget they never had a nickel while they were alive." I wanted to stand up and shove him out of the room.

Her hand lifted and called me over. When I got close, she whispered, "We've made a pretty penny on pecans and potatoes, ain't we, Ella Ruth? What you reckon was our best money crop?"

A smile came on her oversized mouth.

I guess I looked confused, but when she winked I thought of the thousand dollars, hidden now under the potatoes. I squeezed her hand.

"Potatoes," I answered.

"She's talking out of her head again," Matthew said with a frown.

"No. No, she isn't," I said too loud. He looked at me, then Mama, and left us together like two crazy people. He never came in again before the end.

Mama never got to cook for her family reunion, bake all the cakes or fill the rows of covered dishes that she planned. We talked a lot about the menu, all the special things she was going to make for my brother's children. The reunion happened though, around her bed that last Sunday when everyone came at once, crowding into the tiny room. Mama looked from face to face, Matthew to his wife, Karen, Daddy asleep in the chair, the children near the window with their backs to her. I thought she would be glad to see them, but she.began to fret. She was trying to tell me something, and appeared embarrassed because everyone would hear her.

Finally she whispered loudly, "Ella Ruth, I declare I don't think I made enough biscuits. I didn't know Matthew planned to bring all his little friends."

"Mama, surely four pans will be enough. I've already baked three of them for you and the fourth one is in the oven now."

"You're a good little girl. Mama can always count on you to help her." She patted my arm with a hand that felt no more alive than a wooden spoon.

"Christ," Matthew said, "I didn't know her mind was that far gone."

I looked quickly at Mama's face to see if she had heard him.

"I snapped the beans, Mama, and put them in the pressure cooker with the fatback. All I have left to do is set the table and that won't take a minute," I said desperately, but her eyes were on Matthew. They stayed there as if his words still hung in the air in front of his face and she was rereading what he had said, moving her fingers slowly under each word. Finally she looked away and up at the ceiling. She spoke in a voice that sounded strange, a hard voice that I would not have known was Mama's if I hadn't seen her lips move. "Don't see no need for you to come anymore. There's a sight better ways to pass a Sunday afternoon."

I waited until Matthew left. On the table in the kitchen was the greasy box and crust scraps from a pizza that his kids left, so I ate them, peeling the cheese off the paper and jabbing the bits of meat on my fingertips. Daddy looked at me, appearing no more grown-up than a child in a high chair waiting for a plate of food to be set in front of him. I waited him out. One of three things always happened: He ate the food, he pushed it away, or he passed out before I finished fixing it. That day he got only the last choice. I wanted to go back in Mama's room and promise her I would have some babies. But when I looked at the stove, that seemed as big a lie as the snap beans and biscuits.

At the last, I saw her head as a melon, or a squash that got too large to eat and was left in the field to go to seed. Her smooth surface had rutted as her skin started to dry. Her arms and legs were no more than vines. I couldn't hear Mama's breath any longer. But I heard a heartbeat. I thought it was mine until I reached and touched her fallen chest. Her melon head was dead, but her heart didn't know it yet, still pumping her blood through her. It beat a long time. I felt it stop.

That night in my dreams, my mind went crazy. I thought I had a cat asleep in my lap, but when I looked, I saw Mama's heart as perfectly shaped as a box of Valentine candy. It jumped down and ran away, a cat after all with an asshole white as a pearl button. I saw a huge mound in Mama's bed. Mama had come back. I walked up to pull back the covers. But I was so small I could barely reach the bed. I tugged and tugged. When the sheet ripped away, I saw that Mama wasn't there. It was a mean trick. In her bed was a mailbox, dark green and shiny, lying on its back. I woke up. I was in my bed with my clothes on. I went to Mama's room. I met Karen, leaving the room, carrying the sheets. The bed was empty.

"I know where that mailbox came from," I told Karen.

She squinted and said, "I beg your pardon?"

I went back and got into my bed. It was a mean trick.

Daddy arrived at the graveside dangling between Matthew and Karen, his body wrecked by alcohol, not grief. I never even heard him dedicate a drink to Mama as he had to all his other troubles.

There were rich people at Mama's funeral, her customers, whose mourning clothes fit as nicely as feathers on blackbirds, their late-

153

model cars lined up behind the funeral-home car that brought us from the church. I was glad I didn't have to park the pickup there with them and put a rock behind the wheel to hold it on the hill at the cemetery. But I bought the cheapest box they had.

I saw a man I didn't expect. I had seen him the night before at the funeral home, viewing Mama alone and hurrying out as if he wanted to hide his face. Mama had on a red dress that had belonged to Karen because she was too small for her own. They must have stuffed the dress with cotton. Her lips and cheeks and nails were painted as red as cherries. Mama looked surprised, just like Saint Nick after Daddy painted her new face.

The man didn't sign the book, but I knew he was Horace Sanders. Dr. Horace Sanders. At first I thought he might have been ashamed to be seen at a have-nots' viewing. But he came to the funeral in his Cadillac. His wife was with him, a fat woman, not as fat as Mama had been, but not as pretty either. She was his second wife, Mama had told me. And the two children I had seen from a distance, their faces only white spots until today. One was about seven and one appeared my age, a girl. I couldn't take my eyes off her.

She wore a gray herringbone coat with a black velvet collar. Her hands were covered with black gloves that fit so perfectly it was like she had dipped her hands in paint. A single white pearl was on each ear lobe, hanging on her skin as delicately as a drop of milk. I knew she must have another drop on a gold chain around her neck, underneath her white silk muffler. She wore a black leather cap to match her gloves and shoes.

I had safety-pinned the lining of my coat up because it hung down below the hem and the cold pins tapped my legs. I looked down twice when I felt the pins, thinking a dog with a cold nose was rooting under my skirt. As the wind whipped open my coat and hit my legs, that might as well have been bare for all the good my nylons did, I thought how nice it would have been if I had worn black-wool knee socks like she did, dressing like a college girl. My feet were in my cheap heels from Butler's that felt as if I had blocks of ice frozen at the bottom of my legs.

I couldn't look at her face. I had to look forward when the service started. What did she think? She knew that she could never be Ella Ruth Higgins. Did the thought of such as that ever pass across her mind? But I could have been her. If her daddy, Dr. Horace Sanders, hadn't seen my grandma with her legs apart, peeing like a common farm animal, if just at that moment my grandma hadn't felt her bladder was uncomfortably full, her daddy would have come up the hill, asked my mama to marry him, and I would have been her.

When the service was over, I hurried from the family seating area.

154

I caught up to Dr. Horace Sanders before he got back to his Cadillac. My feet ached as the ice blocks closed tighter around them.

"Dr. Sanders?"

He turned and without hesitation, took my hands in his. Neither of us wore gloves, but his hands were warm and mine weren't. I didn't want him to let go. His eyes were watery. It was a windy day.

"Ella Ruth, dear. Our thoughts are with you, If there is anything at all you need, please, and I mean it, please call me."

His voice sounded like an actor. I didn't recognize it. I took my hands away and put them in my pockets.

"Your mother made the most exquisite ladyfingers."

I turned toward that other voice. It was his fat wife.

"They were always Horace's favorites. I'll never be able to replace her," she added dumbly.

I heard a woman gasp behind me. It was Karen. My daddy had slipped out of her and Matthew's grasp and hit the ground, limp as a noodle. They had him back up before I got there. While he shooed at her like she was a fly, Karen brushed the mud and leaves off the front of his coat. That was the last thing that either of them would ever do for me.

When I turned, I saw the gray herringbone coat being pulled inside before the door to Horace Sanders's Cadillac shut. I walked to the funeral car, not looking back at the men covering up the grave because I knew Mama got away long before they put her in that box.

"Daddy, it says here in my health book, before you die you'll have eaten fourteen cows. That's really something, isn't it?"

"Yeah, that's really something."

He must have been dozing because I could tell by his expression, he didn't realize what I asked until after he answered me.

"How many years I got to polish off my herd of fourteen cows?"

"Seventy years. And you get eight hundred and eighty chickens, twenty-three hogs, seven hundred-seventy pounds of fish, two calves, twelve sheep . . ."

"You know I don't like sheep," he grunted. He shook out his newspaper like a wet shirt and pinned it flat in front of him with his bony fingers. "Somebody else can have my sheep. I'll trade them all twelve for six more cows. What if I decide seventy years ain't long enough?"

"I guess you take over somebody's who dies younger than seventy. I don't know how they come by these figures."

"Maybe one of them weirdo vegetarians will let me have his cows."

"They're not so weirdo, Daddy. The man who makes graham crackers is one. And Kellogg's corn flakes."

"They're just rich, smart weirdos. Trying to sell their graham crackers and corn flakes. I bet they sneak in the icebox every night and gnaw on a neckbone and suck it dry."

"Did you know they could make a phony sunrise and setting and fool a hen into laying three times a day?"

"Hum." He moved his finger across the newspaper. I could tell he was changing his subject from me to his newspaper just like you'd turn a radio dial.

"It wears them out quicker, it says here, but they're worth more money in the long run. I don't think people ought to be allowed to do that to a living thing, do you?"

"What?"

"Never mind. You're not listening."

"I'm reading the paper. Or trying to." He put his paper down and lit a cigarette.

"What would you rather eat, Daddy, a rotten squash or a rotten steak?"

"Why? Is that for dinner, Ella Ruth? How would you rather die, huh? Boiled in hot oil or smothered in cow turds? What kinda dumb fuck question is that?"

"Fried chicken's for dinner. It says here that's one of the big things vegetarians got against meat. It can't be good for you because it putrefies too quick. What does it mean that an artificially-fed animal is full of excretory substances?"

"Putrefies? Excretory? It means it's full of shit. You're old enough to know that word. What kind of garbage are you reading? Why don't you read the other half of the paper? Read the funnies. Here. You getting ready to feed me some of that soybean shit?"

"If you didn't eat meat, you probably wouldn't die of a heart attack."

"Yeah, and if I didn't smoke," he inhaled, then exhaled an exaggerated cloud against his paper, "I probably wouldn't die of lung cancer. And if I didn't drive a car, I wouldn't die in a wreck. But we all got to go some way, Ella Ruth."

"Why do you reckon we call it sausage or baloney? And hamburger's not ham. We don't go around saying we're eating pig meat, or cow meat."

Daddy was silent.

"I know," I said. I knew I sounded like a first-grader with the answer. Daddy snorted at my imaginary classroom. "So we won't think of it as pigs and cows. So we won't see those nice little animals eating their grass and slops and making sweet sounds. Sweet live sounds." I was making him mad, but I couldn't help myself. I was doing what he called talking to hear myself talk. But when I got him going, he talked back to me more than Mama used to. "And what does the cow say? Moo-moo, we said in the first grade and the pink piggie, oink-oink. And they put a pig cartoon on the weenie package smiling like he's proud as punch getting made into a weenie. So we won't see some big colored man with an ax slitting their throats with all the blood and guts on him . . . ."

My outside voice ran down and a picture I had seen before came into my head: Under his nails was dried flesh and blood that he picked out with his pocket knife. A person not knowing better might have thought it was red clay from suckering corn. He wiped the blade clean on his overalls, swish–swish, and snapped it shut. Blood soaked in his boots, dye that wouldn't polish.

My wool hunting hat blew off my head when me and Maudie were galloping. The ear flaps were turned up and it wasn't tied under my chin. I let Maudie reach the end of her gallop before I went back for it. I passed the slaughterhouse man coming at me with my hat on his head. I saw him walking home every night, wearing my hat, cutting through on the white street. He used to ride in his wagon until his mule dropped dead in its traces. The glue factory truck came to get the mule and the big man got in the harness and pulled his wagon home himself. I saw the wagon by a wet-looking house, filled with stove wood, split sections from logs bigger than I could reach around, shattered by an ax blade.

Maudie snorted when she smelled the animal death that I couldn't smell unless I got real close to him. I saw him on a nail barrel, cleaning his fingernails in front of the feed store, and I stood in his air then, near enough to grab my hat.

Mama said, "You don't want that hat back, Ella Ruth. Don't know what could be on a man's mind who could do a thing like that all day long."

After that my hat became as alive with him as the knife blade that cleaned his fingernails, as his boots that made a wet, sticky sound that caused Maudie to stop eating and stiffen her ears. After he was past us, she rolled her eyes and I could see the whites. She ducked her head, grabbing at the green grass shoots and I heard them popping like little bones breaking as if she was trying to make a sound that would scare the big man away.

"Do you think we give jobs to colored people we can't stand to do ourselves, Daddy?"

"I think a nigger's damn lucky we don't make him pay us to let

157

him work. Why don't you read murder mysteries or something? You're worse than a goddamn preacher, Ella Ruth. With you a little learning is dangerous."

"What right do we have to raise an animal just to kill it? Treat them good as gold getting them fat, then we kill them. Animals don't do anything mean," I said lamely.

"Right. Perfect in every way. Ever seen a weasel kill a chicken?"

"Just to get something to eat."

"Horseshit. I saw a weasel kill three chickens, one to eat, two for the fun of it."

I'm not smart enough to argue with Daddy.

Once he told me how they did chickens at the farmers' exchange, tying them up by their feet to a wheel that turned them one by one to a pair of scissors that snipped off their heads. I told him he was making that up, but I wouldn't go with him to see him prove it.

"OK," he had said, "be an ignoramus the rest of your life and see if I care. Easy enough to do without ever leaving the house," he added, throwing off on Mama.

"Weenies. Frankfurters. Footlongers. They're dead animals, Daddy, that's all. No matter what you call them."

His finger on his newspaper stopped, marking the spot where I interrupted him.

"I don't call them nothing. I just eat what's put in front of me like everybody else. Will you shut the fuck up and let it drop? I've had enough people on my ass today without coming home for a little peace and quiet and getting a frigging sermon like I committed a cardinal sin for eating a hamburger. Your mama didn't have much sense, but she did know when to shut up."

I stared at his finger pressed on words too far away for me to read. The words were between pictures of tangled football players. What's the point of those pictures, to see if one team falls down in a pile on top of a pointed ball differently from the other team?

"You know, Ella Ruth, I'm not the only person who ever mentioned that sometimes you act like you don't have good sense. Matthew says you've been mighty funny-acting since your mama passed on."

"Meat eaters are more likely to hurt people. It means they don't care if something alive has to suffer pain. I don't ever want to eat meat again." My voice had gotten too shrill and I wanted to bring it down, but I couldn't.

"So who cares what you eat. I said shut up."

But I had shut up, before I heard him say it, before he heard how

158

stupid I was. Just that minute as I said meat eaters were more likely to hurt people, I read that Hitler and Mussolini were vegetarians.

Hitler and Mussolini. Two of the meanest men in the world. They couldn't get the smell of dead people out of their noses so they went into their offices and peeled an orange. Best smell I can think of. Wish I had some orange juice, the real squeezed kind with pulp in it. Hitler couldn't stand the thought of putting a live lobster into a pot to boil, it says. Like all those rich women customers who came to Mama, and had to have their food just so. They were the kind who'd say, "I can't stand to eat a lobster that was cooked dead," acting like they're so fancy they know the difference. Mrs. Simon said, "Ella Ruth, I thought you were a smart little girl. Didn't they teach you in school that lobsters were cold-blooded. It doesn't hurt them." She talked real loud because she was deaf.

"Then how come it goes in alive and comes out dead?" I asked her, talking to the floor so she couldn't read my lips. I looked to make sure Mama was in the basement before I walked behind Mrs. Simon and said, "and when it hits that scalding water, it kicks like a sonavabitch."

Perish the thought she should have to eat margarine instead of real butter. She can eat beans or caviar, they all go to the same place just as quick. I couldn't stand Mrs. Simon. She had been one of Mama's best customers. At first I tried to do the cooking, make the cookies and tarts I had helped with all those years, but they didn't turn out like Mama's, even when Mama brought her chair into the kitchen and instructed me. After Mama was gone, as soon as I got one complaint—Mrs. Simon who said my pecan tarts were a little gummier than Mama's—I took the customer book and phoned every one of them to say there would be no more tarts, no cookies, no more catering from the Higginses' house. Then I refused to give them any of Mama's recipes.

I felt like the old colored man Daddy told me about. The court-house records room caught fire and all the maps of Summit's sewer system were lost. Eli Whitney Waters, who lived in an unpainted shack all his life beside the railroad track, was the only living man who remembered where all the veins of the network went under the city. He had dug the trenches with his own hands for ten cents an hour. And he died, refusing to draw another plan. Eli must have laughed his head off, sitting on his cloud, while the city looked for the lost pipes by flushing colored dye down toilets, and waiting for red or blue or green to run out into the Yellow River. I hope he and Mama are up there, laughing together. I could really make Daddy mad saying that, saying colored people went to the same heaven.

159

When I was a little girl, I watched my mama pick a chicken. I smelled it go into the boiling water and saw the feathers come out in handfuls. Nothing smelled like that. I saw the skin blue and pink under the white feathers like an old woman's arm, no pigment or sunburn on the blue swelling veins. After the wet feathers were out, Mama slung them off her fingers and threw the chicken into the sink and cut it to pieces. I saw that and said to myself I could never do something like that. I thought my mama must be a tough person. I never thought she might be a mean person.

I have a lot of pieces in my head, floating around. Why have I saved certain ones and let the others go? I didn't cry when Mama cut up the chicken, but did when I saw her pinning a pattern to a piece of cloth. I thought she might suck in accidentally and all the pins she held between her lips would go down her throat.

Mama, how could you wring a chicken's neck and turn around and think hard of the man who kills the ones you buy?

Don't you miss Mama, Daddy? Just to talk to? There used to be three of us here, my way of seeing things, Mama's way and your way. I can't say I miss her out loud because I'll cry in front of you. I don't like pretending I'm a grownup, keeping house and cooking. There are times I pretend she's still here. There were times when I thought having two parents was almost more than I could bear. Now that Mama's gone, the only talking I can seem to do is inside my head. You won't talk to me. I can't make sense outside and I don't know if I do in my notebook because nobody reads it.

"Daddy, do you ever worry when you see me washing the dishes, that I might reach in the soapy water and close my hand by accident on the blade of the butcher knife?"

He doesn't answer. His paper is sagging. Maybe he is asleep. Maybe I didn't say it. My voice doesn't hang in the air a moment, like bubbles from a wand.

I melted the fat in the frying pan and rolled the two pieces of chicken in flour. Once they were white, I couldn't see the pinpricks where their feathers used to be.

Daddy thinks I am so stupid.

One day after we had gotten out of school for Christmas, I got a phone call from Dr. Horace Sanders. He sounded very business-like.

"Ella Ruth, Horace Sanders here."

"Hello, Dr. Sanders," I replied, trying to sound like him. I hadn't talked to him since Mama's funeral.

"Mrs. Sanders and I were in the process of planning our holiday calendar and your name came up as a possible sitter for Nancy."

160

It took me a moment to realize he had asked me a question. I tried to picture Nancy, the little girl I hadn't really looked at. I had seen a blond child playing on a swing set when I went to feed Maudie. I was also having trouble with the word "sitter."

"Ella Ruth, are you still there?"

"Oh, yes sir. I'm here."

"Then do you sit?"

My mind wasn't helping me. Of course I sit. I sit, walk, run, stand. "Yes sir," I said, just to say something.

"Good, very good, I hoped we could count on you. I've always told Mrs. Sanders how responsible you are about remembering to feed that old horse even though she's gotten too lame to ride. We pay the other girls fifty cents an hour and seven dollars if you stay overnight."

I had lied to him. What if he found out? I had never been a babysitter. Why didn't he just say baby-sitter? Probably because Nancy was beside him saying: "I'm a big girl, not a baby." Big-girl-sitter.

As soon as I agreed to come the next day, he dumped a ton of information on me about living in the big house on the hill. They were going for the whole weekend, after Christmas leaving Friday at noon. Marcel was in New York with a friend from boarding school. The cook would fix a ham and a chicken. We could charge meals to him at Agnes Brown's Café if we liked. The gardener and his wife were in their house if we needed them. Don't let her play too hard because she just had her polio vaccination. Horace Sanders said he was sure I would have no problems, but if I did I could phone them long distance.

After I hung up, I felt a panic. I had completely forgotten about Daddy. I hadn't left him alone at night since Mama died in November. Even when Simon's asked me to clerk during the Christmas rush and offered to up my pay to sixty-five cents an hour, I turned them down because I'd have to work until nine. By the time I could get home, Daddy would be so drunk he would hurt himself falling and break things in the house. One night while I was washing dishes, he fell and broke the globe and tore the shade on the floor lamp, knocked off a full ashtray and shattered it, and flattened the blue dogwood wastebasket, all in one fall. Every weekday morning I left for school with him still asleep. Yet during the day he got up, ate the breakfast I left on the stove, and went to work. He was painting the inside of the courthouse. Because Officer Ellis had taken his license, he rode the bus home at 5:00 P.M, his skin and clothes speckled with green paint, carrying a bottle in a twisted sack.

"Why don't you go to the Rebel anymore?" I asked him.

161

"Why don't you mind your own business?" he answered.

Nancy Sanders and I were mixing flour glue on the table in her kitchen. I don't know why I had to do it that way when this little rich girl had produced three different store-bought bottles of glue. Except that is the way Mama would have done it. We were making a jigsaw puzzle, taking the placemat I saved from Agnes Brown's Café—a pair of cardinals in the center with ABCs around the edges—and backing it with a cardboard we had slipped out of one of Horace Sanders's white shirts. I couldn't buy glue or a jigsaw puzzle either, knowing I could make it.

"Which you think is the prettiest, Ella Ruth, the boy or the girl?"

For a moment I didn't answer, wondering what prompted the question and afraid I would give a wrong answer she wouldn't forget. Then I noticed her finger pointing at the birds. She answered her own question, which was what she meant to do anyway.

"The girl is the prettiest. I bet a lot of people would say the boy because he's all red. I think he's tacky."

Tacky. Did the mother, who left for her holiday weekend in a dress made of sequins, looking like the picture in our history book of Hannibal's elephant in a suit of armor, give her that word?

I read off the placemat: " 'Did you know that a red bird is the only bird with a solid red feather?' " The bird sat on a dogwood branch, the state bird posing with the state flower. " 'The dogwood,' it says, 'was once a big tree, but God made it small and twisted after its wood was used for the cross to crucify Christ. Look closely at the flower. See the blood stains on the tip of the petals where the nails went through His hands and feet, and the crown of thorns in the middle? The flower is a symbol of the cross.' " Please don't ask me what a symbol is.

"I go to Sunday school."

"When I was a little girl like you, I heard there were more different wild flowers in the Smoky Mountains than anywhere in the world. I wanted to pick one of each and preserve it. I tried dipping a black-eyed Susan in hot wax. What a mess. So I pressed one, but that just made it look dead. Then one day in Simon's I saw a puffball in a clear plastic cube. It was perfect. I don't know how in the world they did that. I didn't have the money to buy it. I wish I could show it to you, Nancy."

She looked at me dully. I was babbling. Why couldn't I make things real to her like they were to me? I knew I'd never have those flowers preserved to keep. A thing like that made me sad all out of proportion. Mama would never have told me such a stupid story. Nancy still stared at the birds. "Do you think he's tacky?" she asked. She liked the sound of that word. She said "tacky, tacky, tacky" just to hear it.

"I don't think tacky is the word I'd use. Flashy maybe. Gaudy," I said, picturing her sequin-covered mother. I was letting her influence my opinion. I decided to be honest. "No. Actually, I think he's a real pretty red. I like to see his bright body in a tree, especially on a dreary day. I would like to have a dress the color of his feathers and let somebody try to call me tacky."

Nancy's lip went out. Was I teasing her? Did I really care if this little girl understood anything I was saying? Mama would never have done that to me.

"The reason the mama is greenish," I explained to Nancy, trying to redeem myself, "is to be safe when she's sitting on her eggs, hiding in a green tree."

"Does the daddy look after the babies?"

"I don't think so. Maybe he gets worms for them."

"My daddy doesn't look after me."

"Well, he does in a way. He goes off to make money to buy your food and clothes."

"He went off to a party and to go hunting."

"The mother was meant to look after the babies," I pushed on.

"How do you know she was meant to look after the babies?"

"Because God made the mama so she could hide." I thought of her sparkling mother, hiding in the scrap metal pile at Greenberg's Salvage Company. "All creatures, big and small, know the mama is supposed to look after the babies. Do you remember the fat possum we saw waddling across the yard today when we got back from downtown?"

Nancy's face lighted up. "She ate the hamburger I threw out. She ate everything but the onion and the pickle. I thought they ruined it too."

"Why didn't you take the onion and the pickle out if you didn't like them?"

"You mean open the lid?" she asked. I laughed so she giggled. "I made a funny," she said.

"You made a funny. Now, pay attention. I am going to tell you some more mama–baby stories. That possum has a pouch on her stomach to carry her babies in. You ever heard of a kangaroo?"

"There's one on Miss Mims's wall."

Same one. It was there when Miss Mims was my teacher. I was surprised Nancy went to public school. "That's right. It has a pouch and so does a plain old possum. Do you remember what was in the kangaroo pouch?"

"A baby," Nancy said. "Only not anymore because it got lost."

"How did it get lost?"

"It fell out and the janitor swept it up."

"How come the janitor didn't put it back in the kangaroo? "

"Don't know. Miss Mims looked in the garbage can. She said it was twenty-five years old."

I thought a minute, feeling frustrated. I could never be a teacher like Miss Mims. I never could seem to tell Nancy a story the way I wanted to.

"Real babies don't fall out," I offered. "The reason that one fell out was because it was made out of cardboard. You could pick up that possum and shake her and her babies wouldn't fall out. She has a dozen of them no bigger than bumblebees, each one stuck on one of her titties and you can't make them let go." I had her attention. She was watching my face instead of the razor blade that I was using to trim the cardboard around the puzzle picture. "Another strange animal is the bat. Blind as a bat, you've heard that? Can't see, but they can hear a wall in front of them by making a noise and listening for the echo." Don't ask me about the echo, not now, let me finish. "The mama bat," I said too loud, trying to drown out the question that didn't come, "carries the babies while she flies until they get too heavy, then she hangs them on the ceiling of her cave, all together so they'll stay warm."

"Do they ever fall down?"

"Sometimes they do and they cry just like little people babies. Down at my Grandma Higgins's farm I saw them when I was a little girl, some of them crying on the floor with their brothers and sisters stuck on the ceiling."

"Why didn't you hang them back up?"

"I didn't know how. I was afraid I would hurt them. I might make their mama mad."

I remembered looking at the ugly screaming babies and thinking how they made my skin crawl, that there was something living that my brain wouldn't let me touch. A bat came in Grandma Higgins's house and stuck over the door and wouldn't let go until my daddy yanked it away, then it stuck to his hand. He went outside and slung his hand till the bat flew away. It bounced on the grass twice before it flew up. Mama said, "Poor little thing don't know which way is up." It looked like a rat with cartoon wings.

Nancy began to hum. Her eyes were wandering around the room, her gaze between sleepiness and boredom. She looked as though she might cry. I recalled an embarrassed mother in Mama's kitchen who had to carry her screaming, kicking child away, saying, "She's missed her nap. She's just tired." I was amazed that tired could

164

create such a monster. I didn't know what to do if Nancy started crying.

"Do you want to go to bed now?" I asked. "It's eight o'clock."

I was supposed to be in charge, but couldn't imagine telling this little rich girl what to do. "Our puzzle won't be dry enough to cut up until tomorrow." She stared at me, her eyes half open. I thought she looked angry now, not sad, that she might say if we'd used her glue, we wouldn't have to wait. But she just nodded and said, "OK," then she suddenly sprang to life, "I know which pajamas to wear," and she ran up the steps. I followed her into her room and watched her go to the right drawer, expertly removing a pair of pajamas with road-runners on them. She began to undress so I turned away.

"You can sleep in Marcel's room instead of the guest room."

"I better sleep where your parents told me to."

"It's OK. I let the other sitters sleep there."

I felt a little sting; I thought she had flattered me, then she took it away. Sometimes this child made me feel that she was more adult than I was, more in charge, as she told me where to find things in the big house.

"Marcel's bed has a cloud over the top. Mommy says I picked the wrong kind of bed to have one and I can't have one until this bed is worn out."

I began to feel very tired. I was glad when Nancy finished brushing her teeth, went beep-beep zoom, and shot like a roadrunner into her bed.

"Good night."

"Good night, Nancy."

"Do I have to say my prayers?"

I hesitated. "If you want to."

I left the room with her mumbling. When I cut off the overhead light, I saw little lights pop on around the wall like white Christmas bulbs, lighting her path in the dark. That was nice, I thought. Daddy left things on the floor, paint cans, bottles, chairs out of place. I stubbed my big toe so hard on the footstool he left in the hall that I saw stars. Mama called them his booby traps.

I went to the guest room. I didn't even open the door to Marcel's room. When I went to the window to see if I could see lights on down the hill in my house, I felt a little sad. I had always imagined this view, looking out of the big house, and now that I could look to my heart's desire, I felt disappointed. Maybe that was because I had imagined the big house was mine, not the little box at the bottom of the hill with my daddy in it. I wondered if he had found his pajamas and gotten in bed yet. When I reached the window and pulled open the curtain, I saw a strange sight. No, I couldn't be mistaken. It *had* to be my house. When I had asked Daddy if we could have a Christmas tree, he said: "Too goddamn much trouble. You shoulda outgrown that foolishness by now."

But in our living room window, I could see lights: blue, green, red and white. Three days after Christmas, Daddy had put up a tree.

The next evening after we fed Maudie, Nancy and I walked down the hill to my house to check on Daddy. I saw that the tree lights were burning again. When we walked inside, Daddy jumped up from the couch and told me proudly: "Got it at Simon's half-price yesterday. See, you can put it away"—he demonstrated, folding one side of the artificial tree inward—"without even having to take the balls and lights off." I watched half the tree collapse, its branches too green, its needles too evenly spaced and too perfect in length. It had looked better from the hilltop.

"Great, Daddy. That should save you two hours of valuable time every year of your life."

He didn't seem to notice I was making fun of him.

Suddenly a strange voice boomed from behind me: "The whole thing is frippery."

I turned and saw the speaker, a large woman, using a word my Grandma Higgins would have used, but with a foreign accent. When I heard the shrill voice and looked at her, I got a chill. I hadn't even noticed her; if she'd been a snake she would have bitten me. She sat in Mama's old chair like a ghost, filling it almost as full as Mama had, yet with a bulk that seemed ready to stand and butt down anything in its way. When she gripped the sides of the chair and leaned forward, her bare arms bulged with lumpy muscles like a sack filled with potatoes.

"Hanging balls on a tree. *Scheinheilig*," she sneered.

I looked at Daddy. "Daddy?"

"This here's my daughter, Ella Ruth. This here's Gertrude Schmidthelm. She's the cleaning woman down at the courthouse."

"This is Nancy Sanders," I said. "My daddy and Mrs. Schmidthelm."

"Miss," Gertrude snapped.

I noticed the needlepoint she was working, flat flowers for a sofa pillow that her buttocks would swallow like a hen over a chick. When Nancy and I sat on the couch, Nancy asked where the bathroom was. Gertrude glared at us as if Nancy's whispers were a plot against her. I showed Nancy the bathroom. She stopped in the doorway.

"Ella Ruth, why do you have your hot-water bottle hanging up there?"

I looked in and saw a hot-water bottle with a long hose.

"It isn't mine," I told Nancy.

There was a strange toothbrush on the sink. My daddy hadn't had teeth to brush for thirty years. Stockings, thick heavy tubes of cotton, were draped and drying on every rack. The bathroom had the odor of dirty feet as though the stockings had not been washed. My towel and washcloth were gone. I lifted the lid on the dirty clothes hamper and they were on top. They weren't even dirty yet.

This woman had moved into my house.

"Hurry up," I said to Nancy, as I closed the door. My voice sounded mean. I knew I shouldn't be ugly to Nancy. What right did Gertrude Schmidthelm have to move into my house?

"*Ich sage dir, Ich sage dir,* I tell you, Maynard Higgins. They run you over," she was saying when we went back into the living room. She continued to talk as though Nancy and I weren't there. "When I come here eight year ago, they had laws in this country kept them out of places. You watch what I say. If Southern Pines, North Carolina, give in and sell them one inch of land, I tell you, it will be Miama Beach. New York City. They run you over."

A woman after his black heart, I thought, yet Daddy seemed to be listening glumly. Maybe because she did all the talking. Nancy trotted over and sat in front of the TV, staring intently at the Western in progress as if she already knew what had gone on before she got there. The picture on Grandma Higgins's old set jumped and gave all the cowboys and horses four eyes.

"*Um Himmels willen.* That child will ruin her eyes," Gertrude said accusingly at me. Her eyes rolled around like marbles in a jar behind her thick glasses. When I ignored her, she shouted at Nancy, "Your eyes will catch on fire and burn out of your head!" Her voice was muted by a gunfight and Nancy never turned away.

"It is a crime what they teach them. What little they teach them."

Nancy had the best teacher in the world, Miss Mims.

"We studied it in school," Gertrude went on, "the science of race. We cared about things. We could turn in our parents, if they behaved improper. I made a report on my father. He gave a Jew a extra week to pay for his shoes. A Jew saying he had no money. Ha!" she snorted. "The Jew wore a button, *Ich bin ein Jude.* Ha, I could tell you. Show me his hands, the way he fingers a cloth." Gertrude's thick fingers rubbed her needlepoint. "I show you a Jew. They had all of our property. We had a right to take it back. We were starving.

167

I saw my Führer. *Das war der gluecklichste Tag meines Lebens.* It was a beautiful day. Me with Julius down by the river in the crowd. My Führer stood on the deck of a white boat, rocking in the sun. He spoke to us in the Nazi Youth. He was a angel on a cloud. I would have died for him. Alas, he died for us, our father."

She began to mutter a kind of prayer, her eyes filling with fluid. Bubbles popped in the corners of her mouth and clear drops hung on her lips as though she had stray tear ducts. I thought I should take Nancy and run from this wet-faced monster, but Nancy was safely absorbed by cowboys that were now gathering around a ranch house Christmas tree and singing "White Christmas." I thought it was a newer song than cowboys.

Just as I started to say something about the song, Daddy grunted. "He made a stupid mistake. He farted around and let the English slip away and then he turns around and goes after Russia and his troops, they freeze their fool butts off. Even a good rabbit dog knows to stick with one rabbit. . . ."

"*Hund!* You call him a dog. The Russians had to be stopped. Stalin was a pig!" she shouted. *"Schwein! Schwein!"*

I bet the neighbors could hear her three houses down. My daddy leaned back in his chair, stunned by the heat from her voice. I read a story once about a catamount that jumped a cow. The cow fell on the attacking cat and crushed it, the king of beasts bit the dust. My daddy, the catamount, had jumped the wrong cow.

"You are an American, you know, Daddy?" I said, trying to stir up a little patriotism before he went completely down to defeat in front of this bully.

"American," Gertrude said, the hate in her voice only slightly muted from the way she said "Russian." "The hospital I work in, I tell you about your precious Americans. Two prisoners, Italians, just young boys. The Americans took them out in the courtyard, yank them up out of their beds with one of them so bent over he could just walk. They shot them, bang, bang, showing off for their girl friends."

Gertrude made a gun with her finger and pointed at the back of Nancy's head. That gesture bothered me far more than her story.

"No need to put the young boys back in their beds this time," she went on. "Put them in their graves. Myself and another nurse package them to be taken away, just like they die in their beds. The next day, I hear, they attempted escape from the Americans. *Versuchter Ausbruch.* The German prisoners who worked in the hospital?" I cringed waiting for more horror stories from Gertrude, stories I had a feeling she wasn't making up. "The Americans would give them no food. They had to eat the scraps left on the plates filled with the

168

filthy germs of the sick. Little babies died in Dresden. What did little babies have to do with war?"

I forced myself to shut her voice out as the lecture droned on. I tried to pick up on Nancy's Western so Gertrude would see I was not interested. I imagined looking her squarely in the eye and saying, "The Germans, Gertrude, did *start* the war," but I decided I might as well throw gasoline on a fire to put it out.

"Women should not wear trousers," Gertrude said suddenly, poking me as if she were trying to press a tack in my shoulder.

"I beg your pardon?" I asked, knowing exactly what she meant to say. I was sent home from school for wearing britches in the seventh grade.

"Trousers. Britches. I will never wear pants like a man."

She nodded at my blue jeans and her face froze as stiff as the portrait of Hitler on the stamps I took out of my book. Maybe she was right. Except for the skirt over her cardboard-colored legs, nothing about Gertrude Schmidthelm told you she was a woman. I turned to Daddy. I could see old words darting across his eyes: "They don't make pup tents in your size . . . ass a country-mile wide . . . your ass jiggles, woman, like a sack of kittens going to the creek," but he never said them. He didn't make a peep. I remembered all the hurt I used to see in Mama's eyes when he ridiculed her fat. It was as if Gertrude Schmidthelm had succeeded where Mama couldn't in cutting out his tongue.

"I recall Clara Petacci, Mussolini's mistress," Gertrude reminisced, "hung upside down. In those days someone in the crowd had the human decency to tie her skirt about her legs so her *Unterhosen* would not show. Now, *Mir ist alles egal.*" She waved her hand.

Gertrude and I shared a memory. I remembered that picture too, out of Daddy's clipping box, three people hanging up like sides of beef. Mussolini was cut down, five more bullets shot into his dead body for a woman's five sons, then the townswomen gracefully lifted their skirts, stepped daintily on his chest and one by one, peed on him.

Still Daddy listened without speaking, his lips quivering only from his breathing. I don't know why I hadn't noticed it before. His limp wrist over the arm of his chair, the stained fingers I used to remove a lighted cigarette from when he fell asleep on the couch, holding an ashtray to catch the long ash when I jarred it. No glass. Daddy wasn't drinking.

As if my stare had reminded him of something, Daddy began to pat his chest, his empty hand feeling for the pocket that held his cigarettes. When he dragged a match across his sole, Gertrude snapped at him before the flame touched the end of his cigarette.

169

"Filthy habit. Ashtray not ten feet away and they stamp them out on the floor at the courthouse. Burned brown spots all around the toilet tank that *nothing* will wash off. I like to go in their fancy houses and stamp one out on their fancy carpets, see how that makes them feel."

Daddy touched the match to his cigarette and defiance glinted, for an instant, in his eyes.

Gertrude looked at me, I thought for sympathy. Maybe she was waiting for me to light a cigarette. Daddy inhaled deeply, and more smoke than his skinny chest looked like it could hold poured from his nose and mouth. As a little girl, I drew a picture of him blowing rings from his ears.

"I want to show you something," Gertrude said suddenly.

I thought she was talking to me, but when I glanced up I saw she was looking at the back of Nancy's head, the same little blond head she had put two imaginary bullets into earlier. Without waiting for a response, Gertrude left the room and after popping open a catch in the bedroom and rustling through some papers, she returned with two battered books. They appeared to have been wet then dried out, the pages swollen open like fans. "When the bombs came, we kept our bathtub filled with water to save our things," she explained. She tapped Nancy on the shoulder, handed her the books, and the child, ever polite, said "Thank you," then looked at me for her next instruction. When there was none, she began thumbing through the pages. I felt guilty, as if I had deserted her.

"There, that one," Gertrude said sternly. Nancy held the book open and stared at the page.

"I don't know the words, Ella Ruth."

I stooped beside Nancy to read it to her. It appeared to be a child's book, but I saw immediately what she meant. The text was in German.

"Neither do I, Nancy. It's not in English. I think Miss Schmidthelm just meant for you to enjoy the pictures."

I looked at the picture in question. It was a little girl. She played with matches on one page and her cats tried to stop her. When I turned the page, I found out she had caught on fire and become a cinder. Her cats put out the fire with their tears.

Gertrude began coughing in Daddy's smoke and rose from her seat again. She marched toward the door, opened it and swung it back and forth like a giant fan. The cold December air blasted across the room. Daddy used to do that as a joke when Mama farted. I looked at Daddy, thinking surely he'll tell her to shut the door, saying, "What's the matter with you, you born in a barn?"

His eyes dropped and he shook his head, maybe reading my

thoughts. "Too weak to bust a bird egg with a ball peen hammer," he muttered.

I couldn't bring myself to look at his tired old face. I think I didn't want to feel as though he was confiding in me; that gave me some obligation to help him out of this mess. Somehow Gertrude Schmidt-helm, the loser in the war, had defeated him. Now she was occupying our house. Daddy got up and went to the bathroom.

I turned more pages in Gertrude's books, trying to picture her as a little girl. I thought of my books, Miss Muffet being scared by a spider, Bo Peep losing her sheep, Jill spilling her water, all children facing problems that I might face. In one of Gertrude's books, a boy was sucking his thumb. That was solved by cutting it off on the next page. One boy wiggled at the table and got buried by food. Kaspar wouldn't eat. He grew thinner and thinner. Soon we see his grave with his soup bowl on it. There are three bad kids, Kaspar, Ludwig and Wilhelm. They laugh at a colored boy so they get dipped in an inkwell and come out much blacker than the colored boy.

The other book is about Helmut and Otto. They keep doing bad deeds, but somehow they get away from their punishment. Finally they are truly punished. Looking at the last page, I see how the German writer made certain we wouldn't believe Helmut and Otto would return to do more evil deeds. They got run through a meat grinder and their bits and pieces are eaten by ducks. I had never seen such a final ending to a story.

Daddy came back from the bathroom with a faint smile on his face. It was getting dark out so I got up to take Nancy home.

"If we hurry, Nancy, we can finish dinner in time to see *Have Gun, Will Travel* before you go to bed."

Nancy had a color television, the first one I'd ever seen.

"You ever seen 'Matt Bastardson'?" Daddy giggled.

I looked at him. How could he be drunk with no glass?

"How about 'Wyatt Urp'?" He belched loudly on the "Urp."

The bathroom. Gertrude didn't know about his bottle under the sink. No telling what she would do to him if she found it.

I hurried Nancy out the door. It felt strange, running away from my own house. As soon as we were outside, the colored lights on the tree went out. I could picture Gertrude holding the plug and glaring at Daddy. A dictator. We studied it in history: "The nature of a dictatorship," my teacher, Coach Beale said, "is never to ask questions and to see things the way you are told." We had to memorize that, all he taught us about Nazi Germany, before he diagrammed the plan for Friday night's football game on the blackboard. In my mind I substituted marriage for dictatorship so I could remember it: The nature of a marriage is never to ask questions and see things as

171

you're told. Only I thought of the weak person as the woman, my mama. Daddy had said Mama was the one too weak to bust a bird egg with a ball peen hammer, every time he made her cry.

After we left I thought about him, how I had been worried about leaving him alone because of what he might do to himself. I think I wanted to feel sorry for him, but I couldn't and I wasn't sure why. Gertrude Schmidthelm sitting in my Mama's chair, ordering me around. He quit going to the Rebel for that woman and he wouldn't for Mama. By the time we reached the big house on the hill, I was mad. Why did he think he had any right to let that woman in Mama's house?

"Tell me a story." Nancy crawled up on her bed.

"You mean make one up?"

She nodded.

"How about an animal story?"

"OK."

"Let's see, a raccoon story or a shrew story?"

"A shrew story. Then a raccoon story."

I felt flattered. Nancy's eyes were still wide open, the pupils opening and closing as my head crossed the light from the lamp. I noticed her cat, Snowball, could spread his eyes into fat black circles, just before he jumped on something he had stalked. But Nancy's eyes couldn't be controlled from within. She knew her way around the big house, but there was something helpless about her. When we had walked back up the hill to her house, I jumped from one footprint to the next in the trail left by the gardener, while Nancy walked in the grass as though she was afraid to make an impression or to get her shoes dirty. I made a row of prints up the footpath, half slue-footed, half pigeon-toed. When I was little, I used to press out giant prints in the mud to make like a monster had come through. Right before we went into the house, Nancy made one print, so carefully it seemed she thought the ground might squeal and grab her foot. She squatted and touched her print, then ran into the house to the TV set.

"Once upon a time," I began, "there were three little shrews: Sally Shrew, Sam Shrew and Shirley Shrew. Sam Shrew said to Sally and Shirley, 'I'm starved,' but they only laughed a shrewish laugh because everybody knew that shrews are always starved. So the three tiny shrews, no bigger than June bugs and with no further to-do, all went trotting off in search of food. And what should they see?"

I paused.

"What?" Nancy asked on cue.

"A rat. A big, nasty rat eating a farmer's corn. So the three

172

shrews crept stealthily up and pounced on the rat, *kabom!* and cut his throat with their razorlike teeth."

Nancy trembled and I saw goosebumps come on her arms.

"The rat died quickly because they had a poisonous juice in their mouths that enabled them to kill bad animals much bigger than they were. Then a strange thing happened. After their big meal, the three little shrews curled up and went to sleep. Now, everybody who knows about shrews knows that shrews don't have time to hibernate—hibernate is like a bear does when he goes to sleep for the winter—because a shrew has such a mighty appetite it would wake up in the middle of the winter starved to death and have to go and rob nature's refrigerator.

"While they were sound asleep, a little boy on a picnic happened by. When he saw the three sleeping shrews, he slipped up on them, trapped them in a jar and put them in his picnic basket.

" 'Oh, Mother,' said the little boy when he got home. 'Look at the three cute little mice I found.'

" 'Andrew,' she replied, 'they are mighty cute little mice. Don't you figure they must be getting hungry?'

"His mother gave him some cheese and sesame seeds and a scrap of bread to feed his new pets, thinking just like the little boy did, that they were mice he had found. He dropped the food into a basket where the three sleeping shrews, Shirley, Sally and Sam, were just waking up.

" 'Here, mousies,' said the little boy. 'Eat your supper.'

"Shirley took her paw and knocked the cheese off her head, sniffing it. Sam, who was still drowsy, picked up the bread scrap, fluffed it up and made a pillow. Sally, the most wide awake of the three, held the sesame seeds in her paws and stared angrily through the cracks in the basket at the little boy, thinking in shrew language, 'Now, who in the world does he think we are?' Before long the little boy, Andrew, grew bored waiting for his captured shrews to eat their dinner and he fell asleep.

"But the shrews didn't go back to sleep. They were wide awake. The little boy didn't wake until dawn when the sunlight peeked in his room, lighting up his shrew basket. And what do you think he saw when he crawled from his bed and lifted the lid?"

I paused for Nancy to respond, but she was silent. Her eyes were closed and her upper lip was puffed out. She was asleep.

"Andrew saw one big fat shrew, Sally Shrew, sitting on a pile of cheese, sesame seeds and bread. Sally Shrew belched loudly and said to the little boy—though unfortunately he didn't understand shrew language—'The moral of this story is, don't put all your shrews in one basket.' "

Snowball walked up my chest, pressed one foot down heavily on my tit and sweetly nudged my face. His purr was a steady hum as I carried him to Nancy's bed to put him down.

"Did you know," I whispered to Snowball, "that lions and tigers can't purr steady like you? They have to stop for breath." He jumped down, running out of the room. He liked to choose his own sleeping spot and he had my chest in mind, not Nancy's bed. I ought to have known people can't decide what animals will do.

I sat down beside Nancy's bed and picked up my notebook and began to write the raccoon story that I didn't get to tell.

Once upon a time in the deep forest of Battle Creek, Michigan, there lived a beautiful raccoon named Rema. Her tail was bushier than the other raccoons and her mask was as perfectly edged as if it had been plucked. No, painted.

It was harder to write a story than to tell it.

Rema was also a very brave raccoon, famous in raccoon land for luring a pack of coon hounds into the lake and sitting on their heads, holding them under, one by one, until they were all drowned but one, a wise old dog named Jimbo.

I am afraid, thought Rema, that Jimbo knows where my house is and he will come seeking revenge. So Rema picked up her babies in her mouth and, one by one, carried them to a safer place.

I was getting frustrated with how slow I could write and how fast my story was coming to me.

I know my children are safe so I can hunt for dinner now. I like to eat a lot of different things. I steal honey from the bees and if I am clever, I can get away without a single sting on my tender nose. I cleverly watch the turtle when she buries her eggs so I can dig them up and have a feast for me and my babies. Sometimes I am teased by human beings. They give me sodie crackers and laugh at me as I wash their flimsy, dirty food before eating it. But my favorite food of all is the frog, tender delicate frog legs, a treat for my palate. I even wash my frogs.

Suddenly the phone rang. Nancy's face twitched, but she didn't wake up. I rushed into the hall as it rang again, screaming at me from extensions all over the house. I picked up the hall phone, but before I said all of "Hello," the person hung up. Wrong number and not polite enough to say so. Made me mad because it messed up my story.

I reread: *I even wash my frogs,* and started writing again.

A coon can't be too careful about germs, you know.
And then after a dinner of one frog leg for each of my sleeping babies, three for me . . .

It was no use. I was going to think of an adventure where Jimbo tried to get Rema's babies, but she outsmarted him. The phone call had messed up my thoughts.

I will amuse myself by watching the legless frogs go by, sitting on platforms with wheels like the man who sells pencils at the bus station, pushing along the bumpy shore.

My story was ruined. I couldn't see Rema in my mind anymore or picture her babies.

The phone rang again. I grabbed it quickly, ready to tell the person to use his phone book, but it started buzzing before I could speak. When I put back the receiver, I heard Nancy call my name. I took it off the hook and laid it on the table.

"Ella Ruth." Nancy sat up when I looked in her door. "If Helmut and Otto were in little pieces and the ducks ate them, do they just become duck do-do or is there some way the man who wrote the story can make them little boys again?"

She fell back on her pillow. I listened and heard her regular breathing start. She was asleep. I would never have to make an answer. I would just know the question was there behind those eyes that told me no more than two bachelor buttons floating in milk. I unbuckled her shoes and took them off. Her feet felt cold so I left on her socks and clothes. I held her legs up and pulled the covers from under her and tucked her in. She didn't make any noise. She was so little. A bad person could scoop her up and run away with her. How do you know what they will remember?

I could get chills just looking at her shoes. I couldn't remember when my foot was small enough to wear those shoes.

I went into the living room and picked up our puzzle. Nancy had put it together three times, getting faster each time. I sat on the rug in front of the fireplace and put it together again. The gardener had built a fire and his wife had washed the dishes and put the food away. It felt strange being waited on. I was at a job, but I was working a lot less than I did at home.

Scattered on the rug around the tree were enough toys for ten children. Everything was store-bought, already put together. I remembered the doll clothes with tabs that bent and hung over my Polly Paper Doll's shoulders. Polly stood, leaning on another card-

175

board tab. So unreal now, they seem, awkward prop-up people. Nancy had dolls as real as flesh.

My mama played paper dolls with me like another child. She cut out the dresses in Polly's book so carefully, so afraid she would snip off a tab. She said she never had such fancy toys as a little girl. She would fix the broken-up toys I got from Daddy's idiot sister Grandma Higgins had had by accident, a late-in-life baby that was messed up. Her eyes were slits in a round face. Her body grew up, but her mind didn't. She would take her Kotex off and throw it on the floor, crying the whole time she had her period because it couldn't be explained to her why she felt bad. Once she got in my paper dolls when we were visiting and started tearing them up. She bent my cardboard Polly in two and tore her evening dress. When I jerked them away from her, Grandma Higgins switched me and called me selfish. Michelle Higgins. She had a prettier name than me. She died of pneumonia when Grandma Higgins thought she had a cold. Mama called it a blessing in disguise.

Not only could Mama make paper-doll clothes by hand, she could make a dress for me without a pattern. Once a year we went in to pick out the cloth for my Sunday dress. Mama knew when Claude James was getting a new shipment of chicken mash because his wife told Mama she could have second choice after her. Mama felt real privileged.

"Second choice after the lady what owns the store," Mama said proudly. No picked-over mash sacks for my mama.

Mrs. James and Mama joked: "I have a dress from sacks."

"Fifth Avenue?"

"No, Main Street Poultry Supply."

I didn't know why it was funny and forgot what Mama told me after I asked. I ran up and down the rows of bulging bags, looking for my material. There were flowers and stripes and checks; it was hard to decide, but exciting to know that all I had to do was point and say, "That one," and Mr. James would roll it out to Daddy's pickup. I was still little enough for one bag to do, so if we got two bags of mash, I got two dresses.

"Now, Ella Ruth, pick them with washing in mind," Mama cautioned. I looked at the dusty colors, knowing that Daddy would lift it up, unravel the opening string and let the mash run out into a barrel. My fat bag would lose its insides like a person turning to an angel, leaving its shell and becoming a spirit. When the mash was in the barrel, Daddy had no more use for the sack. This wasn't like when I got hand-me-downs from my cousins with worn cuffs that had to be turned up to hide the loose strings, with stains under the arms, holes and lost sashes. This was new, brand new. I didn't have to wait while

176

it sat on the feedroom floor to be emptied, because once Daddy left one like that and a mouse ate in and the feed spilled. I cried for my ruined dress and Daddy cussed about his feed, my fat bag lady spilling out like a sawdust-filled teddy bear. Because the mice had peed on it, the chickens threw it out of their dishes, and we had to get a new bag.

I picked one with trains, doll trains with faces and wooden wheels, and one with a town made of candy, lollipop trees and candy canes holding up gingerbread porches. Mama had hopes I would get one with flowers. She was partial to buttercups.

Mama pulled my cloth through the soapy water in her sink to wash out the mash. She slid away the soap bubbles on the water; the water was red as blood.

"I'd just as soon you picked yellow," she said. "Red ain't never made to hold."

After the cloth was dried and pressed, she spread it against my body and studied it. Then it went on her table, where she cut it with the big scissors she used for nothing else so they would stay sharp. No pattern, no dotted lines to follow, just the crunch of the blades. She pedaled at her machine, stopping, going; snipped the thread. Soon she held it up to me again and smiled. A dress.

I picked up my notebook and began to write:

People are mixed up in my mind now: Ella Darwin, Michelle Higgins, Al Sawyer, Polly Paper Doll, Pandy, my no-eyed pandy bear; the day I got the note from my teacher and my mama made certain Ella Ruth Higgins was a girl. When I was little, I liked dresses and being a girl. Then one day I didn't. Then I did again. I don't know now. I don't know Ella Ruth Higgins now.

I am in the big house by the Christmas tree with all blue lights. On the table in front of the couch is a silver box filled with cigarettes. In the cabinet under the Chinese dishes, are fourteen glass birds. From here it's hard to see them, but their glass catches the blue light. The fireplace has tools with gold handles. Over the mantel is a painting of a woman ironing. She looks tired. Those poor people at the bottom of the hill do that: iron. So does the gardener's wife. I just have a picture of it in my big house. There is a container of rusty colored whiskey surrounded by little glasses. I pour some for me and drink it. It tastes strong like cough medicine, but it made me cough. I poured one more and looked at it through the cut glass. I drank that one more slowly. It makes me too dizzy to write.

I went upstairs. My feet seemed to be a long way from my head and I stumbled on the carpeted stairs. I opened the door and saw the bed, the bed that Nancy said had a cloud over the top. I sat on it and looked up through the eyelets of white lace. The holes moved a little, trying to go in a circle. Then I got up and opened the closet and looked at the long rack of clothes, as many as were in the Simon's teen department. I started taking things down and looking at them. It felt like being in Simon's, looking, waiting for the Can-I-help-you-No-thank-you-I'm-just-looking. I decided to put on a prom dress, strapless, light blue net over taffeta. I took off my clothes and pulled it on. The net material felt scratchy and it smelled of perfume. After the first dress, it got easier. There was a tight-waisted black velvet coat with tortoiseshell buttons to wear over the prom dress. I found shoes. Inside was a label: ESPECIALLY HANDMADE FOR MARCEL SANDERS. They fit my feet tight but didn't hurt. I kept looking. It was there, the herringbone coat with the velvet collar. I put it on. On a rack above the clothes was the leather cap. In the pocket of the coat were the gloves. I walked into the hall to look at myself in the big mirror. I laughed because the herringbone coat rocked like it was hanging on Polly Paper Doll. I realized something. I didn't know what Marcel Sanders's face looked like. If I saw her on the street without her herringbone coat and black hat, I wouldn't know who she was.

The phone rang again, screaming in the quiet house. I snatched it off the hook and said hello, too loud. There was silence at the other end, but except for the faint sound of music, a song I had heard but couldn't recognize. While I was trying to think of the name of the song, a muffled voice said something.

"What?" I asked. My heart started to beat hard before my brain said I was afraid.

"You are going to die," the voice said, clearly now.

My body felt as cold as a frog's, though I had on the herringbone coat in the warm house. I saw my back in one of the side mirrors. I looked at my reflection and replied, "This is Marcel Sanders. What do you want?"

The voice at the other end answered, "Oh," and added stupidly, "thanks," and hung up. I held the buzzing phone while I thought. "Oh . . . thanks." I knew that voice. I had heard the "thanks" as he slammed the door of my daddy's truck.

I ran to the doors and checked the locks, front and back. I peeked through the curtain in the living room. The lights were out in the gardener's house. I went back to the room with the cloud over the bed. I opened the bathroom door that led to Nancy's room, opening her door at the other end so I could see her in the bed. I cut off all the lights but the one at my desk before I sat down. I would wait out the night. How did Al Sawyer think he could scare Marcel Sanders?

Nancy rolled over and said a few words in her sleep. Snowball jumped from her bed and ran through the bathroom into my lap. I rubbed the purring cat and watched my little sister sleep. The phone never rang again. I knew he wasn't outside in the bushes at Horace Sanders's house. Don't be silly. Snowball climbed up my chest and put his legs around my neck like a baby. I just can't stay awake. Once you have a baby you should keep your eyes on it every second. My mama never went off to parties and left me by myself. Mama said to have some babies before I get too old. That damn Al Sawyer isn't one bit sorry boys can't have babies.

I ran Al, Stevie, Ernie and Tiger through a meat grinder in my mind. Then I put in Gertrude. Oscar Roscoe ate them. It gave Oscar Roscoe a terrible stomach because they wiggled inside him like worms.

I woke up at dawn, still sitting in the chair with Snowball in my lap. The cat had made a sore spot on my leg and I had a sorer place between my eyes as though a wedge was driven into my skull. I looked straight in front of me and saw Nancy, still asleep. I jumped up and shut the door and began to quickly take off Marcel's clothes and put on my own. There was white cat hair on the coat that I picked off before I put it back in the closet. My head was splitting. I rechecked the closet over and over to make sure everything was back in place. Then I went downstairs and straightened up, washing the fancy glass I had used and putting it back on the tray with the rust colored liquid. If Daddy felt like I did every day, I don't know why he touched the stuff.

As I walked down the hill to my house that afternoon, I saw that not only were the Christmas tree lights out, the whole tree was gone. Horace Sanders's wife had counted out the money they owed me as carefully as the old colored women who came into Simon's with their money knotted in their handkerchiefs. Only I figured it wasn't that she was careful with money; she just wanted to spend it on herself instead of me. I could tell Dr. Sanders felt uncomfortable, maybe because it was Christmas. Though he was polite, he seemed like a little kid whose mama told him how to act. He reached under the tree and quickly got two boxes: one was an assortment of jelly and cheese and one a box of glasses.

"We'll never use all the presents my patients give me," he said without looking at me. "Maybe you can find some use for these things."

"Yes, sir," I said. "Thank you."

He nodded and started lighting his pipe, acting more like a person who had answered a question instead of giving a present.

When I walked into my house, I looked first in Mama's chair but it was empty. I could hear Daddy snoring and found him face up across his bed. I looked in the bathroom, but the stockings and hot-water bottle were gone. Could Gertrude Schmidthelm have been just a bad dream?

I took my presents to the kitchen table and took them out of their boxes. Eight glasses with the letters H S S cut into them. I threw the limburger cheese out the back door for the squirrels and spread me a marmalade and garlic-cheese sandwich, pouring milk into one of my new glasses. The milk seemed a little sour. Daddy hadn't been to the grocery. I opened the cabinet and put up my glasses.

After I went to my room, Daddy woke up and went to the kitchen.

"Where's that little old girl gone?" His words were slurred.

I went to the kitchen door.

"Nancy?" He couldn't have meant Gertrude.

"Yeah. Horace Sanders's youngun."

"She's at home. Her parents are back."

"Right cute little youngun. Didn't have much to say."

"She was just shy in front of you. And your friend."

He grunted and looked at the door. "You wont shy at that age."

"I don't remember me as ever being that little."

"Shoot. I can remember when ever square inch of you would go in a shoebox."

That bothered me, that I was in his memory before I was in mine. I thought of a shoebox as something to bury a dead animal in.

Daddy reached into the cabinet and took out one of my glasses. I felt my cheeks get hot.

"What's this hiss?" he asked.

"Daddy, you put that glass back. It's mine."

"Hiss?"

"H S S. Horace Something Sanders. He gave them to me."

"Humph. You stole them."

"I did not." Mama would never have accused me of stealing. "Put it back. It's mine. I've got a right to have some things that are just mine. And where's that woman?"

"Like a monkey fucking a football," he began to snicker, his drunk not slept off. "Gone like moth piss on a sixty-watt bulb."

I took the glass out of his hand and put it back, closing the cabinet.

"You want a glass, use a jelly glass."

No sooner than I got back to my room, I heard glass break. When I ran back to the kitchen, I saw Daddy in his stocking feet, glass shattered all around him. I saw H S on one of the fragments.

180

"Goddamn you. I told you not to use them."

"I wasn't using it. I wasn't. I was trying to reach a glass in the back," he whined like a child, "and it just fell out. It didn't used to be so full of glasses in there."

"You're nothing but a goddamn drunk."

"I'll buy you another one."

"With what?"

"I got money." He reached into his pocket and pulled out some wadded bills. "Here, take all I got." He dropped half of it.

"Yeah, you'd hand out your money to any damn body. Let any damn body in this house."

"I said I was sorry. I didn't mean to."

"Shit." I turned to go back to my room.

"Ella Ruth!"

"What?"

"Aren't you going to sweep up the glass?"

I looked at him, wobbling in the center of the broken glass like a scarecrow in the wind. "You sweep it up. You broke it. Get your German whore cleaning woman to clean it up."

He lifted his hand, still cupped around the glass that wasn't there. "I can't," he trembled.

I went to my room and slammed the door and waited. My legs were frozen. I wouldn't go back into that kitchen. Finally the screams I expected broke the silence, but still I didn't move. I looked out the window and watched it get dark. It was too overcast for the sun to set with colors. A gray squirrel ran across the yard with my limburger cheese in its mouth. I heard the squirrels up a tree fussing over the cheese as bits of the foil wrapper fell to the ground. I got out my thousand dollars and counted it twice before I hid it again and added the money I just earned, $25.00. I zipped it in the white Bible Grandma Higgins gave me.

When it was dark, I left my room. I saw Daddy on his stomach on his bed. He wasn't snoring, but he never did when he was face down. It was too dark to see the bottoms of his feet, but when I went into the kitchen, I saw what I expected, blood splotches on the linoleum like red flowers stamped over the ivy pattern, wads of green money, red and green, Christmas colors. I swept up the glass and picked the money out, putting it in my pocket. Then I counted my glasses— seven—and put them back in their box. I mixed some suds in the mop bucket. The floor was due for a scrubbing anyway.

Starrie thought she had ~~ne~~
many ~~people~~. The girls w
around; nothing but g
frilly dresses. Starrie
over at the table cove
foods of all kinds. ~~
tiny cookies~~ and ,
all decorated to the ~~utm~~
Everything was galyly d
~~tugged~~ at Johnny's ~~dre~~
"When do we eat?" Joh
at her and said, "No
won't be too long. ~~T~~
speak to everybody."
began introducing Starrie
Some of the people see
friendly; but the others
a snobbish "to please d
And S. knew they weren
began to quiet down and th
"Do you want to dance ~~
Starrie was glad her dre

"Hey, Ella Ruth. Come on out here, quick. You gotta see what I got."

Daddy hadn't been there when I got home from school. He had a painting job. When I heard his voice over the sound of the pressure cooker tweeting, I pretended I didn't hear him, the way he did me.

Then he came in, looking like a little boy who had been standing on his head waiting for his mama to come look. "I thought you were going to come look."

I cut the heat down under the pressure cooker and set the timer buzzer. When I went to the door and looked out in the driveway, I saw it in the back of the pickup, standing tall and black—a piano.

"Look at that. Can you believe she give it to me just for hauling it off?"

"Yeah, I can believe it." Then I laughed and added deceitfully, "Hard to believe somebody would just give that away."

"I mean that thing is worth a bunch of money. Where are we going to put it?"

"Just like that. Where are we going to put it? It isn't like I knew, when you went over to paint a garage, that you were coming back with a piano. I'll have to do some serious rearranging."

"I've got to get it inside. It looks like rain. I can't keep this outside with my other stuff."

I looked over his shoulder at his "other stuff" that had been piling up in the two years since Mama died. He had quit gardening, probably because she wasn't there to remind him when to start his tomato seeds and to tell him to plant straight-neck, not crook-neck squash. I couldn't pay attention to food like Mama did. Through the dead pokeberry bushes, I could see the mustard yellow of two junked school buses. Then there were the seven barrels filled with parachute-release mechanisms, bought at a surplus sale at Fort Bragg because a typist put one too many zeros on the requisition form. Beside them leaned the back half of a Harley-Davidson motorcycle.

"Where's the other half of the motorcycle?" I had asked him when he rolled it out of the pickup bed.

"It went with the guy riding it," he replied. "Stuck to the front of the 7:30 from Raleigh."

I had shivered as I looked through the row of cotton-stocking machines from Solomon's Hosiery that formed a framework for a community of hedge spider webs. The spiders worked away, weaving zigzagging letters in the air, carving the cycle rider's tombstone.

Already tumbling over was the tire wall that he built after the town accused him of running an unfenced-in junkyard. But he won that one. Junkyard operators made money. All Daddy ever did was keep things until they rotted into the ground, or else he glowed when someone went through his junk patch, plucking just the piece of iron they had been looking for.

"Now, I'm glad I kept that," he would say proudly. "I almost throwed it away, but I said to myself, that might be just what somebody needs someday."

I hadn't been over there since he found a nest of copperheads in the English car he could never get running because they quit making parts for it.

"We can just sort of sit my piano in the middle of the floor until we find the right place. I'm concerned about that rain."

I heard my buzzer going and went to the stove to shut it off. The cooker still perked and spewed. For a moment I thought I should turn it up full blast until it blew its top. Every kitchen I knew as a child had a stain over the stove where the pressure cooker had gone off, my mama's included.

Daddy picked up the phone and dialed O. "Operator, give me Raleigh, 781-5121. I gotta get Matthew to help me with this. It's too heavy for you. I sure hope to hell he's not out hunting or something. My number?—476-0382. Get his ass rained on if he is. I wasn't talking to you, Operator."

"Daddy, it's against the law to cuss on the phone."

"Hello, Karen? Maynard here. Matthew home?" A frown. "Oh yeah? Well, I need him. Tell him to call me as soon as he gets in. Late, huh? Shit. Excuse me. Oh well, no, it's nothing you can do. I got a piano to move. Never mind. Ella Ruth can give me a hand."

I could hear Karen's voice beeping out like Morse code. I could easily guess what the words were.

"What do you mean? Men get hernias, Karen. Oh, her womb. Ella Ruth's pretty tough, Karen. She ain't delicate like you. See you, Karen, OK? This ain't getting my piano moved." He hung up. "Jesus, that woman can be a pain in the ass. Especially on my dime. I don't see how Matthew can stand her. No Matthew, by the way."

"I gathered that."

186

He grabbed my arm and felt my biceps. "Shit. You're man enough to haul it in by yourself."

The next thirty minutes was a comedy of errors—struggle, strain, tug, push. Daddy treating this piece of junk that nobody wanted like it was a rare antique. We slid it down two planks out of the truck bed, me with visions of a movie scene that still haunted me, two natives in *King Solomon's Mines* crushed by a fallen elephant. We inched it toward the door. When we got to the porch steps, he said, "Damn, I should have thought to back the truck up to the door. Would have been a lot easier. We could have slid it straight off into the house."

He waited for my comeback comment, but I panted like a dog, speechless.

Overhead the sky darkened and I heard thunder rumbling. The shine left Daddy's face as the light went away. He became frantic, like a child afraid of the dark. As expected, this piano had become the most important thing in the world to him. And he couldn't play a note.

Once, when they sent him to repair one of the windows in the church, he stayed all afternoon, playing notes on the organ. Finally one of the neighbors came in, thinking it was vandals, and there was Daddy at the giant Wurlitzer, looking up at the silver pipes that howled out the notes he hit. He had been in ecstasy. I asked him if what he was doing had sounded like music to him and he said, "Yeah, kinda. Yeah. I guess it did."

Just after we stopped at the door stoop and Daddy had placed his ramps for us to slide the monstrosity up, Al Sawyer and Stevie turned into the driveway.

"Need some help, Mr. Higgins? Hey, Ella Ruth," Al said.

Daddy straightened up slowly. We were both puffing too hard to answer. Al laughed uncomfortably until Daddy finally said, "Sure could use a hand."

When Al and Stevie lifted the bottom end of the piano, it suddenly felt hollow.

"Wait," Al called. "Hold it. The door."

The ornate back wasn't clearing the door frame. "Ella Ruth, go get me a Phillips screwdriver out of the box on my back seat," he ordered.

When I looked on the back seat, beside the tool box I saw a pink lipstick melting and running out on the slipcovers. There was a small and a large Phillips; I took the small one and decided not to tell Al that Mitzi's lipstick was messing up his car.

As I handed the tool to Daddy, Al's eyes twinkled when he said,

"Damn, she got the right one on the first try. Most girls wouldn't know a Phillips screwdriver from a monkey wrench."

Daddy rolled the screwdriver in his hand. "Craftsman screwdriver, eh, boys? You know what they say about Sears tools?" I could tell by his tone that he was telling a dirty joke.

"What do they say, Mr. Higgins?" Stevie led him on.

"They're like a short dick," he answered. "All right to use around the house."

While they laughed, I slipped through the door before it was filled with piano and watched it edge into our living room, appearing even larger now. The piano's keys, as stained as a smoker's teeth, fit the décor in a room my daddy occupied. Not even the refrigerator or a porcelain doorknob could stay white in his cloud of sixty cigarettes a day. The living room darkened from the storm with the black piano wall cutting out what little light was left, shadows falling over the oranges and yellows of the curtains and furniture, dulling them like a cloud over the sun. That living room had always cheered me up on a dark day.

When the piano was finally inside far enough for them to shut the door and walk around it, they went to the kitchen. Rain hit the front window as suddenly as if it was tossed from a bucket. I heard the opener cut into three beers before they came back.

"Got a new movie down at the station, Mr. Higgins," I heard Stevie say. One night they had called me to get Daddy, who had passed out at Owen's Esso. I had to wait till one of their dirty movies was done to get them to help me carry him to the truck. I saw it reflecting in the mirror behind the counter.

Stevie sat down beside me and pretended to pat my knee, one finger sliding under my skirt and briefly fingering the flesh on my knee, making me want to brush him away like a caterpillar. He had snagged the knee in his black pants. I got up and crossed the room.

"You should have burnt that piece of shit on the lawn, Mr. Higgins," Stevie said. "What you want a player piano for?"

Player piano.

I watched Daddy's eyes open wide as he looked at the piano and then at me. Why didn't he look at the damn piano before he brought it home? It *was* a player piano. Now was I supposed to make it all well for him? He had gotten so he would do that, a flat tire on the truck, leak in the plumbing, as though I was some kind of fairy with a magic wand. Daddy walked across the room to the piano, looking at the keyboard and then at the glass box that held the player paper. I heard Al gulping down his beer.

188

"Them player pianos are real cheap shit," Stevie said with authority. "The blind guy down at the bus station, you know him, the wino? They hired him to tune the one at the roller rink where my old man works and he stuck up his nose and told them to shove it off in the Yellow River. Shit, that might be the same one. I bet it is."

Sadly, Daddy lifted the front of his piano. I felt the tightening in my chest I got when I knew someone felt hurt. For a moment my mind didn't function and I didn't realize what was happening. Tiny white pieces were floating out in all directions. It seemed that the paper had broken up and wind from inside was puffing it out, snowflakes tumbling through an open door. But the white flakes moved up and around the room on their own steam, heading through the doors into the kitchen, the bedroom, toward the closet where I kept our winter clothes, pouring out as uncontrollably as the brooms in the *Sorcerer's Apprentice.*

Moths. Hundreds of moths crawling out of the piano and flapping through my house, looking for a mouthful of wool.

I got up and threw open the front door, a stupid, useless gesture. I watched the rain splatter on the porch, running over out of the gutter that was clogged. A moth flew over my shoulder, then whipped back in as fast as it could go.

Hurry back into the house, you little bastard, back into Ella Ruth's house where it is nice and dry. Behind me I heard Daddy start to play a tuneless song.

The next day after school I paid Al and Stevie two dollars apiece to haul the piano back outside to the vacant lot. The ground was soft from the rain and when they let it down, the two front legs with claw feet sank into the mud. An occasional moth still fluttered out. Stevie played "Shave and a haircut, two bits" and they left. I put mothballs everywhere until our house smelled like Grandma Higgins's used to. I swept the dead moths out like confetti.

While I was fixing dinner, I heard the piano again. My first thought was that a raccoon or a cat was walking on the keys. I went to the living room window and saw Daddy, dressed in his baggy painting clothes and sitting on a rolled over barrel of parachute-release mechanisms, playing his piano. The piano sat at a dangerous angle, looking as though it could tip over and crush him. He lifted his hands elegantly, running them up and down the keyboard like he had seen Liberace do on TV.

"That guy is queer as a football bat," he had said, "but he sure can play a piano."

I went out on the back porch, shutting the screen silently. The notes were clear in the evening air, a few strains of "Chopsticks," a

189

slow, one-hand rendition of "Whispering Hope," and then like a child, he began shamelessly smashing down on the keys with both hands, on occasion accidentally hitting a pleasant chord.

Around him a squealing sound rose and fell—peepers, cicadas, crickets. I couldn't tell if they were offended and were trying to drown him out, or if he was accepted as part of their chorus.

Finally he reached the end of his nocturne and with a trill of two flat notes, lifted his hands and placed them in his lap. I don't know why—I did it without thinking—but I applauded. He stood up, wobbly, as if he expected it, and took a sweeping bow. He stumbled toward the house, then stopped, remembering something. Back at the piano, he picked up a flat sack and headed back for the house.

"Daddy, take off your muddy shoes. I just waxed the floor," I called before I went inside. I heard him fumbling, then he came inside in his sock feet, and sat down to eat.

After dinner, when he had fallen asleep on the couch, I looked in the sack. It was a thin red book, filled with music with large notes: *Teaching Little Fingers to Play.*

That night in my notebook I imagined I was a lady showing a visitor the sights in Summit, in the year 2020:

Over on the left is the house where Ella Ruth Higgins grew up. Hard to believe she came from such a humble beginning. That house is no different from any other lower-class house in town. Paint peeling off, a disgraceful junkpile beside it. Is that a piano? Yes, it is. You can see the mentality she rose above—imagine the kind of family that would discard a piano as if it were no more than a broken-down washing machine, just something to throw out after the novelty wears off. Or imagine a young Ella Ruth, trying to learn to play and her angry, drunken father saying to her: "Get that noisy piece of junk out of the house." Then a brokenhearted Ella Ruth turned to a silent expression of her feelings—writing about the world around her.

Look at the house on the hill, see it up there? Beautiful. That must have looked like heaven up there to her, down here hanging her wash and feeding her chickens. That was the home of Horace Sanders. His daughter, Marcel, the problem child, married a gangster and disgraced the family.

But I still can't get over that piano, rotting and grown over with vines. A piano.

"Daddy, look at this funny-looking Christ child."

The Byzantine madonna in my history book had the Christ child

190

on her lap. Only he looked like a little man instead of a baby.

"What do you think, Daddy? Maybe the artist couldn't draw babies. He looks like a midget."

I spread the book across his knees. He looked at the picture a second, then said, "Looks like a Jew to me. Looks like that Jew Greenberg that runs the junkyard next to the Rebel."

I took the book back and looked at it again. The baby did look like Mr. Greenberg.

"Ella Ruth," Daddy said, when I went back to my chair. "Did you know Christ was a Jew?"

"Yeah, Daddy. I knew that."

He cackled like he had gotten away with something. Then his laughing faded to the snorting sound of his breathing. I left him in front of the TV and went to bed. When I fell asleep, I had a funny dream: Daddy was on the piano bench in his junkyard, playing. I watched him play and he made beautiful music, hymns that filled the air like organ music. Then he played "The Star-Spangled Banner" and got off the stool to come into the house. When he walked by me in the kitchen, I realized he was a little man, not even up to my waist. A few seconds later, he walked past me again, carrying his Christmas tree over his shoulder. I held the back door open for the little man to pass on the way to the junkyard with his tree. When he tossed it on the pile of junk, a loud buzzing sound started and he went running. Before I could let him back into the house, I woke up.

I got out of bed and went into the living room. The TV buzzed loudly with a test pattern and my full-sized daddy was snoring, his sound drowned out by the TV. Yet he did seem smaller. It must have been happening gradually, like a gourd drying up. Lately he preferred Mama's chair where he was lost in a giant lap. Mama's, the madonna, Gertrude Schmidthelm, who never came back. I didn't know why she left except maybe he didn't need a woman when I was there.

When I cut off his TV, he sat up suddenly as if I had made noise instead of stopping it.

"I was watching that," he whined.

"Bedtime, Daddy."

He grunted and got up slowly, walking toward his room. I heard him sit on the bed and then there was silence.

"Kick off your shoes."

Clunk. Clunk.

"Good night, Daddy."

"Night," he answered like a frog.

I saw the bunch of wires he had been working on, still in the

191

middle of the floor like toys. That afternoon I had gone out to his junkyard to pull the cover over the piano keys. I didn't know why but it bothered me to see them curl up. I jumped because I felt something move beside me, but then I saw what it was, a frog in the old bathtub. The water burped out the overflow as he swam happily in his private pool, eating the baby mosquitoes as they lifted from the water. When I saw him, I thought of one of Daddy's sayings. I couldn't wait till he got home. I met him at the truck and took him toward the tub.

"What the hell are you doing?" He was grumpy, tired. I thought, Oh no, what if the frog's gone? But just as we approached, the frog jumped into the water and swam across, then looked up at us, its legs extended.

"Lonely as a frog in a bathtub," Daddy chuckled.

That was it. The totally expected. It made me feel good, as if I had watched a diver go off the high dive, a perfect dive, a 10 from all the judges. Then Daddy stumbled over to one of his parachute-release mechanism barrels and got a handful of the gadgets.

"Ought to be something these are good for." He took them inside. I knew they'd be there a few days, then I could throw them back in the junkyard. He sat in the middle of the living room floor that night with his tools, trying to make something out of the mechanisms.

"What are you making?" I asked.

"A thingamahoochi," he said and held up a bunch of twisted wires.

"What does it do?"

"It picks the food out of a crocodile's teeth."

"Whatever you say."

He pulled on the wires and laughed. I heard him mumble: "Happier than a nigger with a three-inch navel." Then he climbed back into his chair in front of the TV and left the thingamahoochi on the floor.

I thought about another woman from his life, Grandma Higgins, dead now. She would look at him and say, "When you become a man, Maynard, you put away childish things." That's what she would have said, as always missing the point. He is just like me writing things for my story box. Except I know where my daddy went wrong.

He's more like Al Sawyer. One day Al was feeding the fruit flies in biology class, when he left the lids off the jars too long. They went flying out in all directions. Al reached for them, grabbing at the air, jumping in and out of the desks. I covered the jars to at least save the ones we had left while Al ran around trying to catch the tiny insects. Stevie and most of the class were laughing. Mrs. Warner opened the window and slammed her ruler on top of her desk.

192

"Hey, Mrs. Warner. You're letting them get away," Al pleaded.

"Al Sawyer," she said angrily, "Go to your seat."

"But Mrs. Warner."

"Don't you 'but' me. To your seat. I wasn't hired to teach kindergarten."

If Daddy and Al Sawyer really were little kids, they'd get away with things. Daddy's junkyard is like my story box. Only he never figures out what to do with anything he saves.

Ella Ruth Darwin, the great female scientist, spent years studying the natural camouflage of animal life, the wonder of how a delicate creature can live safely in a hostile environment.

"The fawn and the fish must protect themselves without bombs and guns," she states. "Note the speckled fawn in the woods, curled up as still as a rock, blending into the leaves because it is not only leaf-brown, but sun-spotted. And the little fish with an imitation eye on his opposite end; his enemies don't know if he is coming or going. It is surely true that a fawn or a fish born without the proper spots would not be long for this world."

The scientific community, ever eager to believe that man can change to meet a new environment, suffered another setback when Miss Darwin exposed the fraud of Paul Kammerer. The following statement was issued to the press:

"It is with great regret that I expose the shame of my grandfather's successor, Paul Kammerer, who so much wanted to breed salamanders whose telltale yellow spots got smaller when placed in a black environment that he painted the spots away with India ink. And his further claim that nuptial pads suddenly appeared on the forelimbs of male midwife toads when forced to breed in a slippery environment? Rubbish. I regret to inform you those pads were man-made.

"After reading my grandfather's books, Mr. Kammerer wrote in despair: 'If what he says is true, man lives and suffers in vain. . . . His children and his children's children must ever and again start from the bottom.'

"What will we give our offspring, Mr. Kammerer? Will Frank Sinatra's son sing 'The Lady Is a Tramp' from the crib, Jesse Owens's run like Mercury at the age of seven, or Einstein's formulate the theory of relativity at nine? No, alas. We can only entertain the possibility of blue eyes, brown skin and unruly curly hair, in that order, for the children of those accomplished men.

"Yes, Mr. Kammerer, sad, but true. Would it not be nice if we could change because we wanted to or needed to? I might add that, if you have a son, may he be blessed with his mother's last name."

Miss Darwin, herself, one critic wrote, lends credence to her grandfather's hypothesis that what man learns in his lifetime is, unfortunately, not passed on to his offspring. She has been criticized recently by her colleagues for collecting wood-turtle eggs, trying to hatch them in the safety of her laboratory. "Sadly, the raccoons are too smart for the turtles," she explains. "They lie in wait while the female turtle lays her eggs, carefully burying them and leaving them unguarded as her instincts tell her to do. As soon as she is gone, the masked bandit gobbles up every one."

Further damaging her credibility, a critic wrote today that: "A basic truth that appears to have escaped Miss Darwin's superficial analysis of the wood-turtle situation is that man is the only creature who has been responsible for the extinction of another creature. But that misjudgment surely occurs because Miss Darwin is poaching in a man's area herself—science—and her female instincts have gotten the best of her attempts at rational thought. Surely mothering a wood-turtle defies all known scientific reasoning."

When asked to defend her position, Miss Darwin displayed an uncharacteristic loss of self control: "Fools! I am my father's daughter, but he gave me nothing but my body, an empty house that I had to furnish. I studied to be both a doctor and a minister in your male-dominated institutions of higher learning. Yet until I left alone on my voyage into nature, I had not spent my first day of real training or education. I saw enough to fill a thousand books and I knew enough to know there was more to learn.

"I ask you, the men in my profession, have you ever noticed how most female birds are more modestly colored than their mates to protect them while on their nests? Well, take a hard look at the blue jay. Can't tell one from the other, can you, and do you know why? Because she's so tough, she doesn't need to be feminine and delicate and go off hiding in the bushes. No imitation eye and sun spots to camouflage her. She's tough enough to be as pretty as a male. And don't think for a minute that females can't be tough when need be. The harpy eagle abandons her unhatched eggs when the first chick arrives and a female ostrich will feed hers to the first born.

"Charles Darwin, my grandfather, once said: 'The mystery of the beginning of all things is insoluable by us, and I for one must be content to remain an Agnostic.' He was a very smart man, but he knew humility. His granddaughter, I remind you, is not so humble."

"Well, let's have Mendelssohn's 'Wedding March'!" was my cue line.

194

Just as I lifted the record needle off "Blessed Be the Tie that Binds" and set it down on the "Wedding March" section, there was this terrible noise. I jerked the needle back up, thinking for an awful moment that I had used the wrong record, but the roar—it wasn't music—didn't stop. Out on the stage I saw Mitzi Wade, who was playing the part of Emily Webb in our senior play, *Our Town.* Her chest was swelling and falling under her wedding dress like a wind-filled sheet on a clothesline. All the people on stage were frozen except their heads, which twisted around trying to figure where the noise was coming from.

I dropped the needle back on the "Wedding March" and turned the sound up full blast, hoping to drown out the roar that was getting louder. Mitzi still didn't move so George Gibbs yanked her arm and dragged her down the imaginary aisle. The girl playing Mrs. Soames shouted her lines:

> Aren't they a lovely couple? Oh, I've never been to such a nice wedding. I'm sure they'll be happy. I always say: *happiness,* that's the great thing! The important thing is to be happy.

A horrible squealing filled the air. Then there was a gigantic explosion. When the auditorium shook, dirt fell from the rafters onto my record and in the silence after the explosion, the record arm began to skip. I lifted it quickly, blew off the record and started the music again. At this moment Mitzi and George were supposed to run down the aisle in the auditorium with people onstage throwing imaginary rice so the janitor wouldn't have to sweep it up. They were also supposed to wait for a spotlight, but Mitzi took off before her cue with her skirts up, leaving a confused George in the dark. Then suddenly he was bathed in light, all alone.

The guy playing the Stage Manager shouted: "That's all the second act, folks. Ten minutes' intermission."

His words came out abnormally loud because after the explosion, the roar had quit. I turned down the "Wedding March" and dropped the curtain, since the guy who was meant to do it was looking out the back door of the auditorium. The smell of burning rubber and oil drifted inside through the open door. I climbed up on a ladder to look out the back window and saw Mitzi Wade darting between the parked cars, squealing and fluttering like a wounded white bird on a dark beach. Suddenly she went to the center of the lot and began to beat on a car.

"What's going on?" Patsy called from the foot of the ladder.

"Mitzi is out there hitting on a car with her fists, having some kind of fit."

After Patsy climbed up beside me, the lot began to fill with people from the audience. Our English teacher, Miss Sammons, was coming toward the back door, guiding a sobbing Mitzi inside and to the makeup room. Mitzi had torn her wedding dress away from the waistband; it had a black stain across the front.

"Don't you worry, dear," Miss Sammons was saying, "that's the last time you have to wear that dress anyway."

"She looks like she got left standing at the altar," Patsy kidded.

I didn't have much to do in Act III but some crickets and some bacon frying. After the audience began to come back into the auditorium and the cast got back in place, I went out and looked at the car that Mitzi had attacked in the parking lot. It wasn't left in a parking slot but was in the center of the lot. Then I got the picture.

Oil oozed out on the pavement and shone under the street lights like the gooey guts of a stepped-on cockroach. It was Al Sawyer's new '55 Chevy on the staging line for a drag race.

When rehearsals had started for *Our Town* a month ago, Al had come to watch Mitzi every night. He and Stevie sat in the back and made fun of Freddie Bivens, who was George Gibbs, because his voice was high and squeaky. I couldn't stand Freddie either. He was the only guy at school who ever called me for dates and Daddy thought he was a girl. Miss Sammons, who was directing the play, was usually really nice but got pretty irritated with Al and Stevie. She had wanted Cale Jenkins to play George, but he wouldn't do it. I had a daydream of being Emily Webb myself if Cale played the part. I knew he wouldn't and no way would I want to be Emily if that jerk Freddie was George. I never went out with him even when it was a movie I wanted to see.

Nobody but sissy boys and teacher's pets tried out for parts, except for one: Walton Abbot, who was playing Mitzi's father. He was president of the debating club and real good-looking, kind of like Tab Hunter. That's when the trouble started with Al Sawyer, when they were rehearsing the scene where Emily gets cold feet about marrying George:

> I never felt so alone in my whole life. And George over there, looking so . . . ! I *hate* him. I wish I were dead. Papa! Papa!

It wasn't hard to sound convincing when you said you hated Freddie Bivens, but one night when Mr. Webb went running to comfort her, Mitzi decided to toss in a little something that wasn't in the stage directions—she threw her arms around Walton Abbot and buried her face in his chest:

196

MR. WEBB: Emily! Emily! Now don't get upset.

EMILY: But, Papa,—I don't want to get married. . . .

MR. WEBB: Sh-sh—Emily. Everything's all right.

EMILY: Why can't I stay for a while just as I am? Let's go away—

MR. WEBB: No, no, Emily. Now stop and think a minute.

EMILY: Don't you remember that you used to say—all the time you used to say—all the time: that I was *your* girl! There must be lots of places we can go to. I'll work for you. I could keep house.

Walton stroked her blond head as Mitzi delivered her lines, tear-filled and muffled into his chest. Right after she said ". . . I was *your* girl!" the back door slammed and Al Sawyer was gone. Everybody else watching the rehearsal clapped for the scene and Miss Sammons was so pleased with Mitzi's performance that the embrace became a permanent part of the show. After that, Al Sawyer was permanently missing, and Walton Abbot left with Mitzi every night after rehearsal.

Two nights after Al stormed out, Patsy and I and the two girls doing costumes and makeup stopped by the Green Light for a Coke. We pulled Daddy's truck up beside Al's car before I realized he was with Stevie in his new Chevy. He was usually with Mitzi, parked over in the dark corner. When Al saw us he got out and sat on his fender on our side, lighting a cigarette. Stevie walked over to talk to some girls that I didn't know in another car. Patsy was in the back of the truck.

"You still working on that stupid play?" I heard him say to Patsy. I was surprised he'd bother talking to us.

"Yeah. What's stupid about it?" she asked.

"A bunch of talking dead people, that's what's stupid. Only good thing in there is where the guys on the baseball team make fun of the wedding."

"It's not about a bunch of talking dead people."

"How come they start out in high school and then everybody gets old too fast and dies and she dies having a baby and that dumb queer Freddie cries on her grave? Don't make any sense. Things don't happen like that."

"It takes place a long time ago. And it was in Grover's Corners, New Hampshire."

"Well, things don't happen like that in Summit, North Carolina, then."

I couldn't stand to stay quiet any longer. I opened the door and put my feet on the running board.

"It's about the future, Al. If we knew what was coming, we couldn't stand to live today."

"I sure as hell could."

"What if you knew when your mama was going to die? Could you stand knowing it the day before and not being able to tell her or to stop it? And that your wife was going to die having a baby or of cancer? Or even who your wife was going to be?"

"I don't like that creepy shit. I like stories about real things."

"Like what?"

"Like war movies. Like *The Fly*." Everybody laughed, but I knew Al well enough to know he was being serious. He was quiet for a minute, thinking. "You know that stupid part where Mitzi asks if she's pretty?" he asked.

"Yeah, we know the whole thing by heart now," Patsy replied.

"Well, you know damn good and well Mitzi knows she's pretty."

"That's not Mitzi, Al. It's *Emily Webb*," Patsy answered.

"It's bullshit." Al began to kick his tire with his heel. "You know the place where Mitzi and Walton start making out?"

"He's her *father*, Al," Patsy insisted.

"Yeah, don't you know it. Tell me that's not Mitzi getting her paws on that asshole hotshot. I seen the script. Mitzi left a copy in my car and it don't say nothing about doing that shit. She's supposed to go after that queer Freddie Bivens and you ain't seen her touching him unless she has to." Then Al got quiet and looked over at Stevie. Maybe he had talked about Mitzi with Stevie, but with us it was more embarrassing.

"Hey, Sawyer, did you find out yet?" Stevie called. Al didn't answer so Stevie walked over. "Did Mitzi leave with Walton Abbot?" Stevie asked bluntly, looking at Patsy. Patsy looked at me, but neither of us said anything.

"She did, didn't she?" Al blurted, then got in his car and started up the engine without waiting for an answer. After Stevie jumped in, he peeled rubber all the way out of the parking lot and disappeared into the night.

After the third act had ended the night of the last performance of *Our Town* and the audience had gone home, all the cast and stage help walked out to the parking lot. Only our cars and the carcass of Al's Chevy were still there. I stepped on a piece of something metal on the ground and had to pull it out of the sole of my loafer. There were scraps all around the car.

"Don't puncture a tire getting out of here, Miss Sammons," one of the guys said. He waved her around the scraps of metal with a flashlight.

After she was gone, Patsy asked him, "What happened?"

198

"Blowed the clutch. The bell housing exploded."

"I seen a guy do that at Hillsborough Dragstrip," one of the guys said, "and cut half his foot off."

"Shit, yeah. Like stepping on a land mine."

"I don't believe you," Mitzi said with a trembling voice, not acting now.

"You look." He took his flashlight and we all crowded around the car as he shined it toward the pedals. I couldn't see anything, but Mitzi screamed and buried her face in Walton's chest again. When I finally got close enough, I saw that the floorboard was blown out under the steering wheel. Jagged metal was where the pedals used to be. The guy held the flashlight steady a moment on one spot, then reached in and touched his fingers to the torn place.

"Gear oil?" one of the others asked as he sniffed the dark liquid on his fingertips.

"No." He shook his head and started to wipe his hand on his pants, then decided to use Al's slipcovers. "It's blood."

Mitzi fainted—or pretended to. Anyway, she messed up because Walton missed catching her and she landed on the pavement. She cut her elbow on one of the pieces of metal and had to have five stitches. After that, every time she dropped her baton, she rubbed her elbow and looked brave.

Al Sawyer got expelled the month before our graduation. He was on crutches with bandaged feet for the whole month. Lucky for him, he said, he had been wearing his iron-toed engineer's boots. Everybody knew that Stevie, Tiger and Ernie had to be in on the drag race too, because there were tire marks from the other car, but Al wouldn't say. It was just as well he got expelled because he wouldn't have graduated anyway.

When we voted on class superlatives, Walton Abbot got Most Likely to Succeed Boy, I got Most Intelligent Girl—which at Summit High was an insult, but Mitzi didn't get Best Looking Girl. She tried right at the last to win by eating lunch at the tables where the girls sat, but it was too late. She also tried to get Miss Sammons to introduce a new superlative: Best Actress, but the principal didn't think that had much to do with Summit High. We all got together and voted Cale Jenkins Best Looking Boy and Best Athlete, but he didn't even show up to get his certificates.

I saw Al Sawyer's mother in Simon's and she looked embarrassed when I spoke to her. In a town the size of Summit, everybody knows everybody else's business. I heard that what really bothered Mrs. Sawyer, who is real religious, more than Al's not graduating was the motto he put under his picture in the annual:

Get Thee Behind Me Satan For Behold . . .
On the Seventh Day,
God Created the Chevrolet.

The day I graduated from Summit High, I was meant to be part
of a pattern, one of thirty-six squares all the same size like checks on
a tablecloth. The band played the same song that was played when
every other person graduated. We wore the same robes. Mine might
have been worn twenty-five times before.

Gretchen McKensie and Marcel Sanders graduated from Winston Academy. I saw their pictures in the paper in white dresses
holding a chain of ox-eye daisies. They're both going to Converse
next year. They're in a pattern too, just a different one.

Like fried chicken and mashed potatoes for Sunday dinner. And
deviled eggs and watermelon-rind pickles at family reunions. That's
what Mama wanted. For people to come together on schedule: Sunday, Christmas, a reunion to see the new babies and the old people in
a chair in the shade one last time. At the funerals there are always
the folding chairs lined up for the family, the tent, the dirt covered
with the same green cloth. One graduation or family reunion or funeral isn't supposed to be different from any of the other ones.

When I was a little girl, the whole Akins clan would gather under
the locust tree at their home place. Grandma Higgins brought her
people together down by the lake so we could see the baptizing of
each grandchild.

The day of my graduation I dressed Daddy in his coat and tie,
jerking and yanking at him to straighten his clothes. I might as well
have been trying to dress a doll, for all the help he gave me.

"Next time you put me in this goddamn thing will be the day you
put me in a box," he fussed.

Neither one of my parents ever got a diploma. Mama got a cer-
tificate for a sweet potato pie at the county fair. I drove with my robe
pulled up so it wouldn't tangle around the pedals. I guess they picked
those square hats so there'd be no mistake what people were doing
when they wore them.

I figured that the rituals people went through on special days did
one of two things. The ritual took care of everyday decisions: what to
wear—a black robe with a square hat, or a white dress with a veil;
what to say—good luck, congratulations, I do. That meant you had
time left to think about what it all meant. The other way of looking
at it was the opposite. You could keep your mind on what you were
expected to do next and not think about what was really happening
to you.

I took Daddy to the school auditorium and put him in a seat. I

200

gave a speech that Miss Sammons wrote for me about how the class of '58 was going to change the world in the '60s. I tried to write it, but kept thinking about *Our Town* and how today would be unbearable if we knew the future. She said that was OK for a play, but not cheerful enough for a graduation. After the ceremony was over, all the parents got up to go out on the lawn for the reception. Miss Sammons came up and hugged me with tears in her eyes. I didn't feel like crying. She had Cale Jenkins's robe over her arm. I saw him take it off when the service was over and hand it to her and walk out. He had his jeans and a T-shirt on underneath.

Daddy was still slumped over in his seat like a ventriloquist's dummy left behind. I thought of going out to the reception, pulling up a chair and sitting his bony frame on my knee and reaching inside his back: "Hello, folks. I'm Maynard R. Higgins, Ella Ruth's father. Oh yes sirree, I'm proud. She's pretty as a speckled pup and a brand new red wagon. Smart too. Smartest kid in her class. Smart as a whip. Sharp as a tack. My little girl's going places in this world. Chip off the old block."

I couldn't reach inside the dummy's arms to hug myself. They would be as boneless as Daddy's arms felt when I threw them over my shoulders and pulled him to his feet. I pointed him toward the car, guiding him with my hand against his back. I opened the door for him and he climbed in on his own. I drove away from the reception. When I looked back, I saw all the graduates standing around in their robes, looking like an island covered with penguins.

When we reached the center of town, as suddenly as a dog scents a rabbit, Daddy's head popped up, turning toward the window and back at me. He said, "Let me off here." I saw my dummy come to life. He threw off his necktie and coat and pranced toward the Rebel Bar.

I had a funny thought. I saw a greeting card once that said, "Thank you for caring." I wanted one to give my daddy with a small change: "Thank you for *not* caring." Right then I figured that was the best graduation present he could give me.

The week after graduation, I got a phone call from Dr. Horace Sanders. I thought he was calling for a baby sitter, but he had a different job for me. They needed a girl to work at the hospital in food services and to do light cleaning. The job paid twenty-five cents an hour more than my job at Simon's. I told him I would take it. After I worked the first weekend, I got a note from Dr. Sanders that the supervisor was pleased with me and wanted me to be measured for a uniform. The next Saturday I went to pick up my uniforms, all white like a nurse with a gray apron to wear over it. When I got home, I put one on and went out in the yard to show Daddy. He was trying to start the lawnmower.

"Hey, what do you think?" I asked.

He glanced up, continuing to wind the rope around the pulley. "Goddamn sonavabitch piece of shit. If I had a decent push mower, I wouldn't fuck with it."

"Do you think I look like Florence Nightingale, or a waitress at Agnes's Café?"

On the next pull, the motor started, filling the air with blue smoke. I followed him around for a while, trying to tell him about my new job, then decided how silly that looked. He couldn't hear me anyway. When he stopped to poke the gumballs out of the blade, I could have continued but decided to sit on the steps. My first day at work, a man had come in the hospital with his big toe in a sack after pulling his power mower over his foot. I decided not to tell Daddy that either, but he made me nervous jabbing in the blade with a stick.

I noticed he had started chopping the wildgrass away from the walk, something he hadn't bothered doing for years. Although the paint was peeling off the house and squirrels had broken one of the attic windows, he decided to chop the walk. I just didn't understand him. When I tried to move a picture in the living room, the wall was so badly stained from his cigarettes that I had to put it back in place over the white square.

I said, only half joking: "Guess I'll have to hire me a house painter."

If Mama were alive, she would have taken the hoe out of his hands and pointed at the house with the handle, saying, "Maynard, first things first." But I let him go. He had gotten dizzy on his last painting job and had fallen off the ladder. And Officer Ellis told me he didn't want him driving anymore. It was just as well he didn't try to work for other people.

After I started my new job and I wasn't there to wait on him at night, I found that Daddy did things in any order he wanted to. Since he had slowed down in the last year, it meant he lost things in a smaller area and usually could find his cigarettes himself. He washed dishes when he ran out of plates, or ate the first thing in a can he saw on the shelf. Sometimes he walked to the store and bought strange combinations: canned peaches and Vienna sausages, canned meatballs and dill pickles. Sometimes he ate straight from the can or off a used plate, or if he warmed his food it was in a used pan. He changed his clothes when he felt like it. Mama used to say that when you smelled yourself, other folks had been smelling you for three days. On the rare nights he got into his pajamas before he fell asleep, I would go get his clothes, carrying them to the washer as far away from my body as I could reach.

On my Saturday off, after I returned from shopping for groceries, I looked through the window at the white glow of the TV and the bristly back of his head in his chair. The screen flickered and crawled with life while the white head in front of it was still as death. I rushed inside and before I saw his face, he belched loudly. I stopped and watched him pick up his Pall Malls and waited for the smoke to rise over his head. It did make me think, what would I do if I came home and found him dead?

Since I was valedictorian of my class, the Rotary Club offered me a scholarship. Miss Sammons tried to talk me into taking it, to commute to Raleigh every day. I decided to see what it was like in the old pickup on Highway 70. I went about five miles with trucks roaring around me before I turned around and came back. I had to go downtown and tell the president I couldn't take it.

"I've come to tell you I can't accept the scholarship," I told him after I sat in the leather chair he'd pointed to. I felt silly sitting down since that was all I had to say.

"Soon as I saw it was a girl come up with the best average this year," he told me, "I told the membership, she'll wanna get married. It's a man's club. Oughta be a man's scholarship. Girls are bookworms. Make good grades, but that don't make them smart. . . ."

"I'm not planning to marry. I do want to go to college," I interrupted. He was making me mad, but I was afraid I might start crying. "I would like to be able to use it later."

"Later? What do you mean later?"

"I mean after my daddy dies."

His eyes jerked in their sockets when I said that.

"I have to stay home to care for him," I added.

"Your father is an invalid?"

"No. He can walk just fine when he's sober."

The feeling that I was going to cry went away. What made him think that men were so great? The man's eyes began to wink from side to side like he couldn't get them together to blink.

"I'll have to read the guidelines," he started to stutter. "I think it goes to the salutatorian now."

"Freddie Bivens," I said. "He doesn't need it. He's rich." I suddenly felt the need to leave, as if I was so hot I had to run outside. I didn't say anything else to the man.

My mind snapped back to the present: Daddy, grinding his cigarette out in the ashtray. If he had really been dead in the chair, what would I have done? Switched off the TV and called the funeral home.

People at the hospital got hysterical when their daddies were sick or dying. At the hospital I saw a little boy whose daddy had broken

203

his arm. One little girl was covered with burns on her stomach where her mother's boyfriend had mashed out his cigarettes. My daddy had never done anything to abuse me. Maybe he only had bad feelings toward the people we were different from: rich people, Jews, colored people. He figured I was like him.

He had nothing to disrupt his evening boredom in front of the TV except getting up to go to the bathroom or to fix something to eat. No friends, no visitors. I couldn't stay that interested in the TV. I remember when I saw my first TV, in the show window at Simon's. Tiger and Al and I snuck through the crowd to look. I saw the face of Perry Como singing in a snowstorm of interference. Al said he didn't see why that was so great, watching something that small. He'd rather see a movie in Technicolor. I told him it was great because that picture came through the air from somewhere else. If Daddy had been born a hundred years ago, I wonder if he would be staring at the wall.

On the table beside him was a combination of sardines and smelly cheese on old bread with blue-green fur around the edges. Although it looked like a sandwich he had made days ago and forgotten, he picked it up and bit into it, his beard stubble piercing the crumbs. He squeezed his nostrils shut as he picked at a little of the mold, dropping it in and around his butt-filled ashtray. He looked as though someone had stood over him and crumbled his snack over his face, half of it missing his mouth. I didn't attempt to stop him; I just watched the rest of the furry green growth roll into his mouth. I knew his mouth, churning like a meat grinder, could suck in that horrible food and reduce it to something to stay alive on. Spindly, pale and sickly looking, he was probably going to outlive us all.

The TV was so loud I got up to turn it down. He started shaking his head and grunting when I did, so I left it as it was. I couldn't imagine what there was to interest him in watching giant athletes galloping up and down with a basketball, their wet muscles aglow.

"Our niggers are better than their niggers," he muttered.

Then he grunted at me. "You look, that one right there," he pointed. "There, the one who got that basket. He is from West End, *North Carolina.*"

Daddy slapped his leg. I watched one of their niggers go to the free throw line.

"He'll miss it. Shaking like a dog shitting peach pits," Daddy giggled.

The shaking dog made the shot.

I watched his face, but his expression didn't change. I had learned it didn't matter if my daddy found he was right or wrong. He never admitted it, one way or the other. Mistakes went through his system with as little effect as the moldy bread.

I asked Daddy what he would like for dinner, pork chops or chicken. He waved his hand for me to be quiet. When Mama and I used to talk while he listened to ballgames on the radio, he would get mad and shout, "You two having a talking contest?" I went back to the kitchen. His eyes never left the TV.

I looked at the bright vegetables on the table, the colored cans, all my careful picking and meal planning. After I packed the stuff away, I walked back to the living room. The game was over and the news was on. His head was slumped forward. I cut off the TV, went back to the kitchen and took down a can of tomato soup for me. I saw the stack of winter clothes I'd laid out to patch where Daddy's player-piano moths had enjoyed their dinner. His wool vest sweater looked like it had been hit with a shotgun blast. He would wear it anyway, maybe looking down and saying, "I'm as holy as the Pope on Sunday morning."

I guess I would never understand how Mama kept trying. I was the one who had decided not to leave. It wasn't fair to blame it on him. He never told me to stay. He really didn't need either one of us.

Though one of our patients, Katherine Hinshaw, looked old enough to be someone's grandmother and be sitting in a rocker, she still tended bar at the Rebel. An intern convinced her to come to the hospital and get the goiter on her neck removed. She hadn't had any visitors, not even the intern, and was taking her anger out on the people in the TV commercials. While I was setting out fresh pitchers of ice water, Katherine pointed at the TV and said, "That one oughtn't have any desire to have a baby, if she's ever looked in a mirror." Katherine sat up straight in her stiff hospital gown; the goiter moved in her throat when she talked like a mole looking for the way out. Her thin white hair, as sparse as seeds on a thistle, clung to her head in tufts. She cocked her head so she could watch Elisa Simpson's TV. Elisa was on top of the sheet in the next bed.

Although she was past her prime, Elisa Simpson was still a pretty woman, carefully made up with her hair fixed and nails polished, wearing a lacy gown and robe. She had put in curlers the night before as if she were at home. Dr. Sanders brought her in for tests, breast lumps, she said. It ran in her family, she told me, to have harmless cysts.

Elisa, who didn't offer to turn the set at a better angle for Mrs. Hinshaw, didn't respond to Katherine, so she babbled on alone.

"Have to be a glamour gal to peddle scents and paint up your nails, but it takes a plain one to dust a baby's ass. She shoulda stuck to radio work."

A baby's bright eyes filled the screen, surrounded by soap bubbles that didn't sting. Both Elisa and Katherine stared quietly at the baby. Katherine smiled a little. Another homely TV mother arrived and they compared babies before the ad ended.

"I've always hated the way people make over babies," Elisa put in finally. Katherine brightened and turned her head; the mole inside her neck stayed put.

"My mother told me," Elisa continued, " 'Wait till you get your own.' Well, I had my own and Mother wasn't alive for me to tell her how wrong she was. She had me believing my baby would love me better than its next breath, see me, her mother, and reach for me, making cooing sounds. Not so. They go inside themselves, squealing and squirming when they're wet and hungry. I try to make things all right and they turn right around and fight me. Having babies wasn't the way my mother made me believe."

I wasn't sure if Elisa was saying this for my benefit. I glanced at the girl three beds down who had had a child. She couldn't hear them, sleeping curled up like a child herself. She was two years younger than me. Elisa saw me looking.

"Like that girl down there." Now I was sure Elisa was directing her remarks at me as I changed the empty bed beside her. "If you saw her waiting on a bus, without her baby in a bundle, who'd ever look at her? Just a chubby girl with thin mousy hair and no rings on her left hand. But now, everybody who comes by her bed has to see what's in that pink blanket, ooh and aah, and poke at it. 'What's the baby's name? How old is she?' " Elisa mocked. "It isn't that she loves that baby. It's that she loves what that baby made her."

Katherine Hinshaw glared at her. "That ain't what I meant. What has that girl getting knocked up got to do with who gets put on baby commercials? She can't help she got the face that broke the mold. Poor child's the granddaughter of Homer Crutchfield. I *mean* them TV people figuring if they hire 'em ugly as homemade sin like the most of us, then we'll listen to them."

"What *I* mean," Elisa insisted, "is she doesn't have a husband. She has no right to have a family."

"Happens to the best of us," Katherine said dryly.

Elisa shushed her as the soap opera resumed.

After I washed the sinks and came out for my mop bucket, Katherine and Elisa were back at the commercials.

"I hope that before I die," Elisa was saying, "one thing in my life stays the same. That one day I polish my stove and never find another drop of grease on it. Never see another circle of hair in the tub. Like that handprint she just took off around the light switch, gone with one sweep of the sponge." Elisa waved her tiny hand in a sweeping motion and the diamonds sparkled. "Put a meal down and have it freeze like it was varnished, and while I'm at it, I'll take the dozen

206

red roses that Albert gave me on Valentine's Day when I was eighteen, right there, permanent as stone."

Mrs. Hinshaw grunted and went back to babies, "I used to wish my little girl would stay a little baby forever in that bassinet beside me and I'd never have to fret she might be hurting or that some old man had made off with her on the way to school, because she was right there. But then I got this awful fear. I seen me old and sickly and so feeble I couldn't look after myself, much less her. What if I had a baby like that girl down yonder? In my grave 'fore she cut her teeth."

Elisa smiled at the old lady and said, "It's a good thing that things are the way they are, because if people like you and me were doing the deciding, we'd make a mess of things. It scared the stuffings out of me when my Nadine became a little person on her own, walking, saying things that had to come out of her own brain because I never heard them till she said them." She pointed at Mrs. Hinshaw, "What's this grave talk anyway, Mrs. Hinshaw? My grandmother lived to be ninety-two. How old are you?"

"Two hundred," Katherine grunted.

I started to change Mrs. Hinshaw's sheets, moving her and doing half at a time. I never thought of how much trouble a bed was to change with the person still in it.

"You know, I could get my behind out of your way," she said.

"No ma'am. Dr. Sanders said to keep you quiet. I don't mind doing it this way."

"If Dr. Sanders wants me quiet, he better knock me in the head."

"Now's when I usually do my ironing," Elisa went on, "watching other people's lives, dressed up in their houses like I'd go to a party, in their kitchens on high heels. Their lives are always in such a mess, it's a wonder they ever get anything done anyway. That lady right there," she pointed, "the one who talks all the time, her daughter has run away. She's mean so I'm glad that she is hurting for a change. And that other woman, she thinks it might be with her son so she is itching for her to leave so she can find out."

The woman on the screen talked slowly and paced about on her high heels, leaving long silences for Elisa's commentary.

Elisa snapped when another commercial came on, "But she won't find out today because they have to drag it out. Makes me so mad how they do it."

I tucked in Mrs. Hinshaw's top sheet and she smiled at me as I spread it over her legs.

"I like the cartoons," she said to me. "But, you see, it ain't my TV. You ever see Tom and Jerry swimming with Esther Williams?"

I nodded. "When I was little," I told her, "I thought of cartoons as real, that Tom and Jerry were really swimming with Esther Williams. And Peter Pan was coming to my window to take me away to Never-Never Land."

"How about Popeye? Who you reckon come up with that Olive Oyl?"

I laughed and said, "I never have been able to figure that out, why they'd fight for her."

She pinched my arm and whispered loudly, "Maybe he was one of them queers. Like the one who come up with them new hairdos that mat your hair out like a punkin on a stick and them spike-heeled shoes women wobble along on. A queer loves to see us girls stumbling with our hair stuck up with spray net so no man on earth wants to put his hands on it, laughing at women catching them spike heels in the escalator. . . ."

"My friend, Agnes, did that at Simon's," Elisa interrupted, "and embarrassed her prissy self to death. I hear those women are just asking to go bald."

Elisa's hair was as perfectly in place as hen feathers, but Katherine's thistle hair looked as if one gust of air from a spray-net can would scatter the puffball and leave her head slick as a shiny knob. But Elisa and Katherine had finally found something to agree on.

"Look at that!" Elisa pointed at a woman in the next soap opera pulling off her blouse to reveal the top of a frilly slip. "She oughta know some men watch these things too. I wouldn't wear a slip in front of a camera for any amount of money. Those girls in Albert's *Playboy* magazine with their bare rears on a rug, turned just so the wrong hairs won't show. You know that every single man there sees those hairs. Just not the camera. I can't even stand to sleep naked. I thought maybe the reason was if the house caught on fire. But the worst thing is being asleep and anybody can look at you not fixed up. Lying in my casket after some undertaker fixed my hair and face and somebody else picked my dress."

Katherine pinched my arm again and shared a secret snicker. Then suddenly she looked at the TV and shouted: "Kill all household bugs! You make me sick. One little bug and you have to go buy some shit to kill it." Katherine's Rebel Bar voice echoed in the quiet room. "Raid. Air raid. Such a big to-do. Get a can of poison and be a killer. Why don't you catch the damn bug and put it outside? I'm sick of commercials."

I went into the toilet and filled the paper machines. When I went out, she was still ranting, but the young girl slept on. No one told Katherine to shut up. I went to the other side of the ward and started putting fresh sheets on the empty beds. Sometimes I felt like I worked in a crazy ward, not where they kept the normal people.

"Now show us that snooty lady seeing a bug *again*. Jesus Christ, I've only seen this commercial three times today," Katherine said loudly. "She ought to come in my house and I'd show her I didn't give a happy damn if a cockroach ran up her leg and bit her twat."

Elisa responded, I thought in a self-consciously soft voice, hoping Katherine would turn down her volume too. "They work on making you feel ashamed. Ashamed your breath is knocking somebody over, but your best friend won't tell you. They don't know my friend Agnes. She'd tell me and love doing it. Those people who make commercials must think we're dumb as posts. And who else would be watching them now but some woman whose child is asleep and her husband's at work and she wants some noise to keep her company while she does the ironing. Or somebody stuck in a hospital bed."

"That snooty lady ought to have been in my house the night of the disappearing biscuits." Katherine was not to be stopped. "I leave the room three times, once the phone, once my little girl busting a glass in a million pieces and her barefooted, and once the door collecting for the paper, and every time I come back, one more biscuit is gone from the plate. That night I open my trash can and he's in there, damn sight big as a cat. A rat. So my first husband, the big hero, put out this damn poison and it died in the plumbing and I tell him I'll live in the yard till he finds him and gets the smell out. Finds him under the sink where the poor old thing tried to get water to cool off that rotten poison," Katherine was out of control, "and Alvin tries to pull him out by the tail and the tail is all he gets. Sure-fire you're getting that stain out with Tide. Bullshit, lady. Anything strong enough to get that grease out takes the cloth with it. And that's all it takes to make you happy, right? Your darling husband patting you on the butt and saying, 'Beautiful clean wash, honey.' Give us a shit-eating grin now. Who the hell are these commercials for? I never got outta high school and they're too dumb for me." I stuffed the dirty sheets into my hamper. I wondered how Dr. Sanders expected me to keep her quiet. "All a real-life husband does," she went on, "is reach in his sock drawer and his underwear drawer where clean clothes have sprouted like rabbits. Nobody has to wash them with Tide, lady. Any husband knows that. That's why he got married. The only way he notices a clean waxed floor is if he busts his ass coming through."

Elisa picked up a magazine and pretended not to hear her.

I finished all the beds but the one where the young mother slept. She had probably never had clean sheets so often in her life anyway. Her hands, large and callused from farm work, were sunburned so much darker than her upper arms they could have come from a man,

209

stitched to her wrists by a doctor. Last night an old woman came to see her, talking like the ghost of Grandma Higgins, and read the Bible to her:

" 'I will greatly multiply thy sorrow . . . in sorrow thou shall bring forth children.' "

The girl had a breach baby so they gave her a Caesarean. She had listened to the old woman without speaking, her face turned away from her visitors.

I decided to let her sleep. If I had had a baby, I would like to be asleep because then I wouldn't know I had it unless it was in my dreams. I'd be free of worrying about taking care of it. But I could tell from that girl's face when they brought her baby that she wouldn't see my thinking at all. She looked at the baby and touched it as if she couldn't believe she had made it, as if it had popped up out of the ground, all fresh and new, and was the first pleasant surprise of her life.

Today when I walked around Horace Sanders's barn, I found a strange thing: a stiff snake hanging down from the knothole like a tiny elephant's trunk. The knothole was filled with a bulge in the snake's body where he had trapped himself. Inside the barn was its head, filled with fangs and poison. . . .

Did you hear the story about the snake, Ella Ruth? He swallowed a biddie whole and crawled off through a knothole and got himself stuck good. Then a rabbit come hippedy-hopping by on the other side, right under his nose, so he gobbled him up whole too. But lo and behold, the snake found he couldn't go backward or forward. So he starved to death with a full belly. One bad deed got him in a heap of trouble, but two was the ruin of him. The moral of the story is get out of the first mess before you get into another one.

The snake was dead. I had heard of possums dead on the highway, their pouches full of living babies if you would go rescue them. Mama told me of a dead doe, shot in the head, but when the hunter cut her open, he found a living fawn.

"Did it die, Mama?"

"It died, honey. But it stood and walked and looked a minute until it found its mama's tit, then it lay down against her bleeding belly and closed its eyes."

That story made me so sad I couldn't stand it. I wished she'd never told it. I decided I would write it over and the fawn would live. A little girl would feed it with a baby bottle until it was old enough to be free.

210

Though I hated to touch it, I pried the dead snake out of the knothole and cut it open with my pocket knife, so afraid I would harm the frog or mouse or biddie that was trapped in there, all wet and sticky with the snake's insides, waiting for me to rescue it. When I slit through the scales and the snake opened up, I saw feathers, brown and wet, unfolding like a bird from an egg. There was a loud chirp as the wings began to flutter and the barn swallow flew into the air. It dove twice through the barn then spotted the light through the knothole where the snake had been. The bird shot through the hole like an arrow and was gone. I looked at the dead snake and it seemed no more than a ruptured garden hose.

Though I hated to touch it, I took the snake out of the knothole and cut it open with my pocket knife. When the gray skin pulled apart, a shiny white oval broke through. It is an egg, I thought, but a closer look revealed it was solid. The snake had swallowed an oval-shaped white porcelain doorknob.

Ella Darwin cut into the snake as her students looked on. "Scales are a bit tougher than human flesh," she noted as she worked with the skill of a surgeon. "A snake," she went on, "has a special jaw structure that enables it to swallow food much larger than the circumference of its body." She wrenched the dead snake's jaw open in her strong hands so they could observe the hinge structure. When one of the girls squealed and stepped back, Miss Darwin frowned slightly. "This specimen probably swallowed an egg and intended to break it for digestion by passing through the knothole."
While she worked on the dissection, she continued to lecture the students, not wasting a second: "All vertebrates start from a similar embryo and, because of a different combination of genes, emerge as completely different creatures. A three-ounce mouse comes from the same size egg as a two hundred pound whale. Eureka!" she exclaimed. "This snake made a fatal mistake." She extracted the snake's mistaken prey: a white porcelain doorknob.
"The decoy placed in a setting hen's nest to fool a representative of the Aves class has in turn made a dead fool of Reptilia."

So many thoughts rushed through my brain as I cut open the chicken snake I had found dead in a knothole in Maudie's stall. Then I took out what it had swallowed and none of those thoughts came together: Mama's doorknob that she used to fool a setting hen.
"That egg-thieving snake," Mama would have said with a laugh. "Serves him right. Let's go tell your daddy."

I didn't tell Daddy. And Mama's dead.

"Mama, did you know that everything that has a heart is given the same number of heartbeats, a hen, a snake and a person? Some beat fast and some slow, which is why some things live longer. But they all use up the same number and then they die."

"Who in the world would spend his life counting heartbeats, Ella Ruth?"

"A scientist, Mama. That's the sort of thing they do, then they write up their experiments and share them with mankind."

"I like you telling me about the heartbeats, honey, but I ain't one meant to do the counting. Lord, I can't count a dozen cookies 'out starting over a half dozen times. Are you right sure that Ella Ruth Higgins could sit still for all that counting? Did Maxine Higgins's heart beat too fast and waste its beats?"

Before I could answer her, a slurred voice said, " 'Why Chicken Snakes Swallow Porcelain Doorknobs,' an essay by the phony scientist, Ella Ruth Higgins."

Mama and I looked up and Daddy had been watching us, wobbling in the doorway. Then he fell over asleep.

"Mama," I said, "I wish he'd never found out," but when I turned, Mama wasn't there. Daddy was gone too. All I had was the doorknob and the split snake. I wanted to tell somebody and nobody was there. It had to mean something.

The next morning I noticed where Daddy had chopped the wildgrass back from the walk. He had uncovered cement that I didn't know existed. At first I thought he had been continuing his yard work outburst of late until I realized that most of the walk was still covered with grass. All of his chopping had been concentrated in one area.

Up close I found the impressions of three tiny feet in the cement with names and dates roughly scratched beneath them. One of the footprints, Matthew's, was in the main part of the walk. One marked Ruth and one marked Ella Ruth were in an add-on patch. Ruth was dated one year before I was born.

I asked Daddy about the third foot.

"Took two tries to have a little girl," he answered.

My name is Ella Ruth Higgins. I am poor and very religious. I had planned to marry very young and have lots of children. Today my life took a different course. I got a sign.

My Grandma Higgins taught me that the answer to every question could be found in the Bible. Mama told me to have babies, but

212

she never told me that one of her babies died. I discovered that today. She never told me that it hurt to have babies either, but I learned that in my Bible:

> And I will put enmity between thee and the woman, and between thy seed and her seed; it shall bruise thy head, and thou shalt bruise his heel. Unto the woman he said, I will greatly multiply thy sorrow and thy conception; in sorrow thou shalt bring forth children; and thy desire shall be to thy husband, and he shall rule over thee

said the snake in the garden. Enmity is hatred between husband and wife. My parents had that because God was punishing them. But today my mama, who is in heaven, gave me a sign. The snake in the garden is dead and my mama put him to death. When she was on earth, she couldn't kill one living thing. My mama was telling me not to have children.

I will put my snake and doorknob to rest. They're like a dress I used to like that I've had to wear too many times. There was no one to tell about the snake and no one to ask, so I wrote. In my notebook, it is easier to be who I am not. Sometimes I feel I am struggling to find the answer to a question, but I'm not even sure the question was asked. I wonder why I can't let a stupid chicken snake swallow Mama's doorknob and die in peace.

One day in July when I stopped at Owen's Esso to get gas for the pickup, I watched a black hand with a white wrist unscrew the cap in front of my windshield.

"Don't fill it too full, please," I asked. "It leaks on curves."

In the oval on the boy's blue shirt was the name "Al." Al Sawyer. I watched one hand press the trigger on the pump and the other start wiping the windshield. The ID bracelet was gone.

"I didn't know you worked here, Al."

"Yeah." He didn't sound enthusiastic. "Might as well." His hair was greasy and hung limp on his forehead.

"Are you getting your diploma in summer school?"

"Naw. I been to school long enough. Don't need a diploma to drive race cars, which is what I wanna do soon as I get the money. What you doing?"

"I've got a job over at the hospital."

"You a nurse?"

"No." I almost laughed. "You have to study to be a nurse. I'm doing a little of everything. Part of the time I keep the snack bar, then I take meals to the patients. Haven't performed any operations yet," I said, trying to make a joke.

"I thought you might be a nurse because you got on that white dress," he explained, I guess so I wouldn't think he was stupid. "I couldn't stand being around sick people all the time."

"I know what you mean. But I want to go into science. Maybe biology. Or maybe be a vet." I didn't know why I was telling Al Sawyer this.

"Shit, and I flunked biology. Shoulda got you to cheat me through. I guess you always were kinda brainy."

"Don't fill it too full," I interrupted him. "The fumes come in . . ." Too late. The gas burped around the hole and ran down the side of the car.

"Ah shit. I'll get it up." He began mopping up the gas with his windshield rag. "After you told me too, huh? Got shit for brains."

"That's OK, Al."

"I won't charge you for what I spilled. Five cents off, OK?"

"It doesn't matter. You don't have to do that."

After I paid, getting an extra nickel in my change, I figured out the answer to a question I didn't have to ask. Al Sawyer and Mitzi Wade had busted up for good.

"Aw, come on, Ella Ruth," Tiger begged. "Patsy said she'd go if you would. Al and Stevie are going to be there."

Tiger had driven up beside Patsy and me at the Green Light. We were still dressed up from the Y-Teen party at the Rec Center.

I asked Patsy, "Did you?" I knew she had a crush on Tiger.

"Yeah. I told him at the party. I thought he'd forgotten about it."

I leaned back in the seat so he couldn't hear me. "I don't trust him, Patsy. You never know what he's up to."

"We don't have anywhere else to go. If we don't like it, we can leave."

I didn't like the idea, but since I had the truck I figured we could leave. Tiger wanted us to go to the colored night club on the other side of town to hear the Hot Nuts. We drove out of the Green Light with Tiger leading the way. As we got to the dark end of Gaut near the old deserted hosiery factory, Tiger turned into the parking lot. Before I realized where he was going, I had turned in behind him. He stopped his car and came running back, whispering as I rolled down the window.

"Look, there's Sawyer's car. Come on. Let's see what he's up to."

"Not me," I said, but Patsy was already out before I could stop her. They went in the door and for a second everything was quiet. Then I heard Patsy laughing. I heard a man's deep voice then Patsy screamed and suddenly there was an explosion, a firecracker or a gunshot. I started the motor and she came running out the door and jumped in. The truck had never seemed so slow as I backed up and headed out of the lot.

"Hurry, hurry, hurry," Patsy pleaded.

I looked in the mirror. No one was following us. We went back to the Green Light and Patsy didn't calm down until she realized there were other people around us. She had gone through the door and bumped into Tiger in the dark, but he grabbed her before she fell down and started tickling her. Then when she thought he was lighting a match so she could see, Tiger lit a cherry bomb. She saw Stevie at the top of the stairs as the match flared and Tiger yelled out in a phony deep voice: "So you're the goddamn little prick who's been fucking my wife!" and threw the bomb on the steps.

A few minutes after we got to the Green Light, Tiger and Stevie drove up beside us laughing.

"Hey, want to go to the Stallion Club and hear the Hot Nuts?" Stevie called.

"Eat shit and bark at the moon," Patsy answered as I backed out to go home. It was a week later before I found out what had really happened.

Al Sawyer called and asked me to go to the Y-Teen retreat at Crystal Lake. I had planned to go anyway, but not with a date because I figured no one would ask me but Freddie Bivens. After I told Al I would go, I got nervous. I didn't think I knew him anymore. I hadn't thought about him when he had been Mitzi's steady. When he came to pick me up, he was a mess. He had tincture of violet all over the side of his face and arms. It was strange, but because he was so beat up, he seemed harmless.

"Don't ask me, OK?"

"Sure, Geronimo. I'll just pretend I don't notice it."

But as soon as I got in the car with Al, something happened to me. I couldn't talk. At first I thought it was because I was uncomfortable in such close quarters with him. When we left the Summit city limits, he started driving faster. I slid over against the door and held the handle. Then I knew what my problem was. I wasn't in control of the car and I had never driven so fast before. All those times I had seen the guys go past or heard their wheels squeal, I never knew what it felt like, inside.

"Ever heard of Fireball Roberts?" Al asked.

"No," my voice sounded braver than I felt. "Am I riding with him?"

"How about Little Joe Weatherly?"

I shook my head.

"If you're gonna lean on the door, you better lock it."

I pushed down the button and stared outside. We passed a highway patrol car in front of a roadhouse. Al let off the gas and the car rumbled and popped as he slowed to fifty-five. I looked at his feet and wondered what the scars looked like from the explosion the night of the play. The car had been patched with bright new metal, shiny as scar tissue. Al nervously watched his mirror. I would never have believed Mitzi was braver than me. I was halfway hoping the cop would come after us so he'd slow down.

The side of the road was lined with fresh-vegetable stands with signs that appeared to be painted with a broom. Everyone we passed was colored. The closer to the lake we got, where the black dirt turned to white sand like patches of unmelted snow under the pine trees, the fewer houses were painted. They had cardboard windows and walls as dark as a wooden tub, as though they held water, not people. On the porches were women, small, medium and large, all holding babies, and in the yard were more babies in different sizes.

Al started to speed back up so I said, "I think I saw a cop down that dirt road."

"Where?"

"About a half mile back. And there was one behind the Ku Klux Klan billboard outside of Smithfield," I lied.

"Shit, they're everywhere. You keep watching, OK?"

"Sure."

"They're like cats," he said.

"Who? Cops?"

"Naw, those nigger women out there. Having one litter after the other."

We started down the narrow blacktop that passed through the swampland where pools of water flashed at us and white birds stood as still as plaster statues. Redwing blackbirds caught bugs and went to their nests that hung in sacks among the cattails. There were no farms here and the land was as uneasy as the tides. A black loop passed under the car.

"Dead snake?" I asked.

"Naw, fan belt. Probably some New York asshole up the road with his motor fried."

Suddenly I saw a huge house. It was brown, like the others, but of giant proportions. When we passed, I saw through it like a hollow log, to the river. Then I saw another, only pink as a conch shell, old brick pink, more elegant than the last, but it was a skeleton too.

"Dead houses." Al's voice made me jump. I didn't know he was looking at them too.

I didn't say anything but nodded my head. We passed another. I

216

saw two chimneys, tall and fat, facing each other like bookends, the books burned away long ago.

"Rich people houses," Al spoke again. "Rich people who owned a bunch of niggers to do the work for them. If the goddamn Yankees had just let the South be a country all by itself, there would still be windows in them houses, and fancy people coming in and out. Now they got the niggers thinking they can act like white people."

I figured I was hearing the general opinion from Owen's Esso.

"So what do you figure would have happened to the colored people, if there hadn't been a war, Al?" I wasn't sure it was a good idea to try to talk seriously with Al Sawyer. Just as I asked him, we passed another shack, a wringer washing machine on the porch and a stove rusting in the water-filled ditch by the road. A little boy watched our car go by. I waved at him and he waved back slowly like a person in a trance, then ran and hid in the bushes.

"Right where they are now. Except that little pickaninny would be dressed in a fancy suit."

"Where do you think you would be, Al, if the war hadn't happened?"

"Flat busted, changing tires at Owen's Esso."

I laughed and so did Al. When he asked "How about you?" I was sorry I had started the discussion, but it wasn't fair not to try to give him an answer. I liked to imagine in private.

"I think I would be wearing a hoop skirt and sitting in a swing with ten guys waiting to see which one I would dance with."

"Yeah, Miss Scarlett. And I'd be the one who got in your bloomers."

"That wasn't funny."

"Don't get so hot. I was just kidding."

"You think that's something to kid about?"

"Why are you acting so high and mighty? You're so damn snooty, no wonder you don't have any dates."

"I could have dates if I wanted them."

"Yeah, who with, then? Freddie Bivens?"

"You've got no right to talk dirty to me."

He was quiet for a minute, then he said, "You asked for it."

"Asked for what?"

"For what happened to you that day in the barn."

"You stop this goddamn car."

"What for?"

"So I can talk."

"Why can't you talk riding? You're not talking anyway, you're yelling. I don't wanna miss the fishing boat. Forget I said it, OK? Can't take a damn joke."

"No, I won't forget you said it. You tell me how I asked for it."

"I'm sorry, OK? Jesus." Al was quiet a minute. When he stopped talking I could still hear our angry voices. After I got mad fast, my hands shook so I clasped them together. I wanted to aim my fist right at the scab on his cheek.

"You remember that cat?" he said finally. I looked at him. "Don't look at me like you don't know what I'm talking about, Ella Ruth. That cat in heat over at Sanders's barn."

I thought a moment. A cat in heat. I remembered the cat. She moaned and dragged her belly along the ground, her haunches sticking up.

"You mocked her," he said before I asked. "You mocked her, remember? You made fun of her noise and made her moan louder."

I had. I made the same noise she did. "What the hell does that have to do with anything, Al Sawyer?"

"Stevie said you were dying for it, he could tell," he blurted. He turned his face so far away from me, he had to watch through the windshield out the corner of his right eye.

I couldn't help it. I started crying. "I want to go home. I never should have said I'd come with you today."

"Ella Ruth, I'm sorry. Don't cry, please. I didn't mean to make you cry. Damn, I don't understand girls at all."

"You can say that again." I sat back and tried to calm down. I took out my compact and dried my tears with a Kleenex. My eyelashes were stuck together in points and I could see most of the mascara I had put on was on the Kleenex.

"I don't believe you thought that for one minute, Al Sawyer."

"I don't know," he said weakly.

"I think you went back and figured that out afterward, so you'd have an excuse."

"I wish Stevie was here. He'd tell you. It didn't seem to bother you none. You just went on acting like nothing happened. Stevie said I shot you with a gun even and you didn't tell the police or nobody."

"You know what I wished for a long time?" I said. He shook his head. "That all four of you would be in a car and drive right in front of a pulpwood truck. But I hoped nothing would happen to the man driving the truck because I'd never wish something bad on an innocent person. Once I imagined you killing your motor on the tracks when you were trying to beat the train and all of you got smashed like pancakes."

Al shivered. "Tiger said if you got us put in jail you'd have to tell and everybody would call you names. I told him I didn't do nothing. I didn't do what they did. It wasn't my idea. Stevie talked us into it.

218

That was all he could talk about, fucking girls. He ordered a bunch of pictures he kept in the packhouse."

I saw it all clearly again, them coming from all directions, afterward me thinking Al was innocent. At times I had imagined that day with Al not even there. "Why didn't you?" I asked.

"Because it didn't seem right, I guess. It seemed like you could do the deciding on what you wanted to do."

I thought a minute, looking at him. I thought of the day I got his rifle and his Phantom ring. I had always thought of Al as different from the others. I was right. He was. But he didn't want to be.

"You don't know, Ella Ruth. How hard it is. That's all they talk about, doing it with girls. You've got a right to walk around with your nose stuck up saying no. That's OK for a girl. You don't know how hard . . ."

"Why did you call me that night at Horace Sanders's?"

"Then it *was* you. I thought it was Marcel Sanders."

"Why did you do it?"

"Me and Stevie was trying to scare you. We did, huh?"

"No."

He seemed really disappointed. "Don't nothing scare you?"

"Some things do."

After a while he said, "I got the hell scared out of me last Saturday. I'll tell you how I got messed up if you promise not to tell anybody. OK to change the subject, huh?"

I shrugged. I didn't know of anything else I wanted to hear from him. I guess I could have known what he had just said all along if I had asked.

"Dying to know, right?"

"OK. Who beat you up?"

"I did this to myself, trying to keep *from* getting beat up. Or killed, one. Shit, was I scared? You know that empty building near the warehouse, the one that was part of Solomon's hosiery?"

I nodded. I saw it as it looked the week before, with Al's car parked in front and Patsy running out the door. Then Al gave me the other side of the story.

"I tried to climb down from the fifth floor window and I made it three floors before I fell." He hit his fist on the steering wheel. "See, me and Stevie had this, uh, meeting set up, you know, with a couple of real nice-looking women."

I felt my anger coming back. Then it was a trap for Patsy and me.

Al went on. "Stevie knew them and he'd gotten it on with one of them a bunch of times before and she had this pretty girl friend who wanted to meet me. Only trouble was they was married and played

219

around while their old men worked the night shift at the mill. So me and Stevie were where we was to meet them, up on the fifth floor. Stevie had these two blankets he spread out on some piles of old rags." Al began to squeeze the steering wheel with his battered hands. "We hear these cars drive up and the doors slam, then these high heel shoes come in the door and a woman giggles. Wow, I mean I was ready for it."

I couldn't stand to look at him now.

"Stevie goes to the door of the room and walks out. Then all of a sudden this guy yells, 'So you're the goddamn little prick who's been fucking my wife!' and a gun goes off and I'm so goddamn scared I don't know where to go. I hear a thumping down the steps and I know it's Stevie's dead body so I went out the window. I figured it was all over for me. I hear a car start and I try to hurry up and slip off the ledge about halfway down. I hit the ground hard, but this bush broke my fall. I had almost crawled to the railroad tracks on my belly, when I heard another car start and leave and it got real quiet. I waited a while before I snuck back and looked for Stevie's body. I couldn't find him so I got in my car and started looking. I found him two hours later at the Green Light."

"I hope you broke his neck."

"Shit, he's lucky they didn't kill him. Tiger found him walking by the highway where those guys threw him out. They held a gun on him the whole time, but he was in a hell of a lot better shape than me. Stevie said they would have shot him, but the chick who liked him talked her husband out of it. He'd already done time for assault. Some story, huh?"

I didn't know what to say. For a moment I could only think how dumb Al was. But I decided that wasn't fair. It was like a crossword puzzle and I had the answer page. Or a movie where I had already seen the ending. We drove through a long pine grove in silence. I thought back through the night, all the pieces going together for me like the end of a mystery. But Al had lived through a completely different story. I decided not to tell him what really happened. In a way, Al was their victim now instead of me.

That afternoon after he got back from fishing, we took a walk. We didn't have much to talk about. He picked some flowers for me that I put under the rubberband on my ponytail.

"That's an ox-eye daisy, a sundrop and a blue-eyed grass," I said before I put them in my hair, trying to make conversation and showing off.

"No shit. I thought they were flowers. I bet you can name every tree too."

220

"Most of them. Some of the bushes I don't know, but I can take the leaves and look them up."

"You're weird." A bumblebee droned by and landed in a Rose of Sharon bush. "Look out, low flyer. You're so smart," he said, "tell me, how come the bumblebee can fly? And don't say 'cause nobody told him he couldn't."

"That's not entirely wrong. You really want to know?"

"Sure. Don't tell me you really know?"

"Well, I know some of the theories. He's a cold-blooded insect so if he is going to fly at all, he has to warm up his engine. He does that by trembling. That takes a lot of gas so he makes sure he goes to flowers that are close together and that have more honey." We stopped by the bush "Watch him. He'll walk to flowers that are real close to save his energy." The dusty bee walked out of the pink bloom and into the next one.

Al laughed out loud. "Sonavabitch, he did."

"When he's flying, his stomach is in front like a radiator to keep his motor from overheating. The reason he can fly is he's smart enough to know it isn't going to be easy."

Al looked at me in disbelief.

"Told you all you ever wanted to know and more about bumble-bees, huh?" I said.

"I don't know how to act around smart girls."

"I'm not so smart, Al. I'm just interested in things."

"My ma calls them humble bees."

"Humble bees?"

"Yeah."

"That seems like a better name."

We walked a little farther and then he said, "I know all the parts of an engine."

I didn't know what to say. "I don't know the first thing about cars. They must be interesting." I wondered if he was going to recite all the parts, the one test he could have passed in high school.

"My new car's a V-8."

"That's nice."

"Yeah. Let's go look at the monkeys."

We walked over to the monkey cages. Stevie and Tiger were laughing and teasing a monkey with a stick. "Hey, Sawyer. They got your brother in a cage," Stevie called. The monkey chattered at them and jumped on the front bars of its cage. When it stopped moving, I realized it was looking at me. "Uh-oh. I think the monkey just fell in love," Stevie kidded. "Guess it's all over for you, Sawyer, with competition like that." The monkey was staring at me with a

221

funny look in its eyes. Then suddenly, so fast I didn't have time to jump, it reached through the bars and grabbed my ponytail. I pulled away, and saw what it had been after. It was eating the flowers I had been wearing in my hair.

"Damn rotten manners. Hey, Al, remember that monkey my old man bought?"

They all laughed the dirty laugh, Al included.

"So do you want to know, Ella Ruth?" Stevie asked.

"Know what?"

"About the monkey."

"I guess."

"It would go crazy, swinging on things in our house and one night it got real pissed off at my old man for picking at it." They all laughed again. "It's the truth. Sawyer was there. It jumped on this fancy light my ma had put over the dining-room table and wouldn't get down. She was cussing at him, so Daddy got in a chair and reached for it and this monkey put . . . put,"—he was so tickled he could hardly talk—"put one hand under its ass and shit in it and threw it all over my old man."

"I knew I shouldn't have asked," I said.

"My ma had already told him it had to go because one night when my grandma was there—his mother—and she talks in this raspy voice, and I guess the monkey didn't like it because he got up on the china cabinet and pissed a stream right over her head into her dinner plate."

Tiger was really tickled. "Tell her what your old lady did."

"She got Pa's shotgun outa the closet and come in saying, 'Which one gets it first, you or the monkey?' He talked her outa it because she was going to hit her fancy chandelier and blow the roof off the house to boot. We give the monkey to a zoo. Might be him right there."

When the monkey got to the ox-eye daisy, he decided he didn't like flowers anymore and threw it at Stevie.

"Nasty-tempered little bastard."

"Maybe he doesn't like being in jail for no reason," I said, "where a bunch of guys can tease him."

"He's not in jail. He's in a cage," Stevie said seriously.

"You're a real wizard, Stevie," Tiger put in. "What's the difference?"

Stevie's eyes went blank.

I looked at the cage one last time. The monkey hated me as much as he did them. There was a padlock on the door.

We walked back to the pier, where the chaperones were starting to spear hot dogs on coat hangers. After supper, before we went to our cottages, Ernie played his guitar and sang folk songs. Stevie and Tiger sang dirty verses until the chaperones called them down. Al didn't sing, but he laughed at them. I figured the guys were going to be the same the rest of their lives. Going to Crystal Lake was the farthest away they could see beyond the city limits of Summit, North Carolina. In a few years they would all be married, going fishing at Crystal Lake, drinking beer and getting pot bellies.

All the pieces of the hosiery mill mystery were there, a simple plot devised by Stevie and Tiger to fool Al. Someday they might tell him what really happened, maybe after too many drinks on a fishing trip, and he wouldn't believe them. I watched their plot, but I wasn't part of it. But the other mystery, what they did to me, was not so simple.

When Tiger and Stevie weren't looking, Al reached over and held my hand, but I didn't feel like I was inside it. I didn't want him to do that. Before I went to bed, I walked over by myself to the monkey's cage and gave him three marshmallows. They glowed in my hand like white nuggets until he snatched them. I couldn't see his face in the dark while he ate them, but I could hear him chewing and smacking. He probably still hated me.

I think when Al and Mitzi were going steady, Al was in a deep freeze. He hadn't changed. He watched that day in the barn and now, three years and Mitzi Wade later, they made a fool of him again. Because he was a boy, he had to have sex or act like he did. All I had to do was say no when he called and do it until he quit calling. I realized that in my fantasies with Al Sawyer, he never touched me. And I didn't want him to in real life. In my fantasies we talked and we were interested in the same things. Nothing real that could happen with Al would ever be as good as I could imagine.

Coming home from the lake the next day, Al and I stopped in a rest area. No one else was there. The trees, heavy with Spanish moss, drooped gray and gloomy like the canopy for a graveyard. The semicircle of kudzu behind the picnic table was cut with paths where people went into the woods. I looked at the word LADIES neatly lettered on a metal sign. Spider webs bound the door shut like ropes. We had stopped in a country store and I had packed a lunch, banana sandwiches for me and bologna for Al.

I was unpacking the sandwiches when he came back from going to the bathroom in the woods. He jerked his foot from a kudzu vine.

"Goddamn vines. No wonder the fucking Russians sold it to us. Cover the country and smother us a lot cheaper than the atom bomb."

"Chinese."

As Al frowned at me, I jumped. Something had moved behind him.

"Al, be careful," I yelled. "I think I just saw a snake in there."

He leaped forward and looked back at the vines. He saw it before I did.

"Don't scare the shit out of me like that. It's just that old cat."

"What old cat?"

"The mangy old cat I almost pissed on that I hoped you wouldn't see."

"Why did you hope that?"

"So I wouldn't have to hear you say 'poor old cat' all the way home and give it half my lunch."

I walked over to the cat. It didn't run. When I stooped to pet it, I saw it was mangy with clumps of hair missing all over its back. I could see giant fleas moving like ants across its snakelike skin.

"Here," Al was behind me. He handed me half a piece of bologna out of his sandwich. I held it out to the cat. It snatched the meat, eating it like a dog and leaving traces of mustard and mayonnaise around its mouth.

"You want my handkerchief to wipe his mouth?" Al laughed. "Slob."

Now the cat was friendlier. It began to rub against my hand, moving toward my knee. I had on my best white polyester slacks. When it got close, I could smell something foul. I saw sores across the back of its neck. Something rose in my throat as I saw white worms moving in the sores. Maggots. I could hear Mama's voice, "They'll eat out the infection, Ella Ruth. Maggots are good." Suddenly I felt like vomiting.

When I stood up and turned my head away, I saw Al drop another piece of bologna in the dirt in front of the cat. It gulped it down, dirt and all. Then it came toward me again, rubbing against my leg. I stepped back, but not soon enough. The oozing wound on the cat's back wiped on the cuff of my pants.

"Oh shit, get away from me. Goddammit. Ruined my new pants." The cat didn't move. Al looked shocked. I walked to the picnic table, I had to breathe the air away from the foul-smelling cat. I took a Kleenex and tried to clean my pants. I felt confused. I was supposed to act a certain way, but I'd acted mean without thinking. And I talked out loud like Daddy. Or Al. I picked up my two banana sandwiches and took them to the edge of the woods. The cat dove for them.

"Cats don't like bananas," Al said.

"Well, they will just have to do." My voice sounded high and whiney. I felt hurt about my pants and a little angry. I didn't know at what. I sat on the bench. Al was eating an apple and watching the cat. "See, I told you cats don't like bananas," he said. The cat had eaten the bread and around it on the ground were the white banana slices. "Got a little self-respect left. Monkey food."

I didn't see how Al could eat with the cat still there. He packed up the basket and put it in the trunk.

"You didn't eat a thing, Ella."

"I lost my appetite."

We got into the car. I saw the cat from the window, licking the mayonnaise off the banana slices. Maybe after we left it would lose its last shred of self-respect and eat the bananas.

"You sure fooled me, Ella Ruth," he said as he started the car.

"How's that?"

"I thought sure we were going to have a scene and it was going to be me telling you that you couldn't put that mangy thing in my car. I ought to put it out of its misery."

I felt overcome. "Oh no. But it was so pitiful. Poor old thing."

"Uh-oh, spoke too soon." He drove back onto the highway.

"Well, you ought to have some feelings for it."

"Don't give me that shit. I gave that sorry bastard half my sandwich trying to please you." Then he paused and said with a grin, "I don't see it riding back to Summit right now, curled up asleep in the lap of those fancy white pants, either."

I felt tears come in my eyes, but not for that cat. It would stay alive until people quit coming to the rest stop. Then it would probably go somewhere else and find a way to stay alive. I didn't see how something could want to live that bad. Maybe it would be nice someday to have a kitten. A pretty one with long hair like Snowball. One that I went and picked out, the prettiest and healthiest in the litter. I rubbed my arms, the hair bleached blond from the sun. If my body were as battered as that cat's, I think I would give up and die.

"I'm sorry, Al," I said finally. "I got no cause to be mad at you."

"That's OK."

"Especially since you were right."

"About what?"

"That cat. It didn't need me. And I don't need another beat-up creature to look after."

"Careful."

"What?"

"We beat-up creatures are pretty sensitive."

Al reached over to hold my hand again. His hand was so covered with scabs I felt like I was holding a wart toad. This time I didn't

225

leave my hand there. As we passed back by the dead houses, the sun setting behind them made jack-o'-lanterns. A lightning bug caught in the windshield wiper, its light still flashing on and off, then it blew off into the darkness.

I think I got mad because Al saw something about me before I did. He didn't have any right to see something unless I told him it was there. He didn't know me that well. I didn't want that cat sitting on these fancy white pants, Al Sawyer, but I don't want you there either.

I learned something today. We can all see the same thing and have it come out different. You can put something in front of people as careful as a painting in a frame or a play on a stage, and when they see what's there, they see it using what is in each different head. I went out in front of them, moaning and crying for them like a cat. All these years I thought it was because I showed my woman things, my dirty talk that I kept inside and the body that I covered. It came out of my shirt, pulling apart the button like a monster splitting its skin. How silly to keep it all covered up. How can that keep it safe? They already knew. Like a moth coming out of its shell. The warm air comes through and touches it. It isn't ready until the summer. What if a hot, sweaty hand squeezed it in the winter? Would it break out and die in the cold? Ella Ruth Darwin would know. Why didn't she tell me I acted like a cat?

Suddenly Al interrupted my thoughts. "Why do you pretend you're an old maid schoolteacher or something? You don't look like one."

"What do you mean?"

"I mean you dress like a normal person, a girl. You don't paint your nails or nothing, but you fix up like a girl. You fix up your hair. I know it don't just grow like that."

"I rolled it up. But I'd rather not. I like to leave things just like they grow. I can't stand to see my fingernails shaped all just alike and painted a color."

"Huh?"

"Never mind."

The road began to feel narrower. At first I thought it was because it was dark, but I realized it was different from the one we came on when Al began to stop at stop signs and make turns. I had no idea where we were.

"Al, where are you going?"

"I'll show you in a minute."

He turned down a narrow dirt road. Other cars had been there recently, because as the lights bounced in front of us I could see tire tracks through the mud. Suddenly he swung the car sideways and stopped, cutting off the motor. For an instant it seemed silent. I could hear the sounds of the night bugs around us. But I could also hear someone singing, a song on the radio. I heard a car motor idling outside, then it quit and the radio was louder. I looked through the windshield. The road was no longer there. It was as if we had stopped just before we went off a cliff. Out in front of us were lights, some colored, some white.

"Raleigh," he said. He pointed out the windshield and dropped his hand on my shoulder.

I didn't say anything.

"Nice view, huh? Ever been up here?"

"No. Have you?" I asked stupidly.

"Sure. Lots of times."

I heard a girl laugh in the car next to us.

"Want to listen to the radio?"

"No. I can hear theirs."

"Want to move somewhere more private?"

"No!" He jerked his hand off my shoulder as if he'd been burned. I was starting to shake. "Al, please take me home."

"What for? It's early."

"Please. I don't like it here."

"We can go somewhere else."

"I want to go home."

"Jesus, you are really fucked up."

He started the motor and slammed the car in gear. It bolted backward and turned down the road. He was driving so fast down the rutted road that the bottom of the car was banging the ground. When we got back to the smooth highway, he slowed down. After we were moving again on the blacktop, I felt better. I was thinking, trying to come up with an excuse. I needed to get home because I was worried about my daddy. I had to be at work early the next day. I didn't say anything. I knew the whole reason was that I was scared to death.

He didn't say anything to me until we turned into my driveway. I reached in the back seat for my things. He was staring straight ahead.

"Good night, Al. Thanks for taking me."

He still didn't say anything. I thought I ought to apologize but I didn't know what to say. I wanted to get out and run for the door of my house. When I stepped out, I heard him say, "Bye," before the door slammed. As I walked up the sidewalk, he spun his wheels in the driveway, kicking gravel across the grass.

I looked at my house. It seemed to be darker on one side. A shadow. No, the street light was on the dark side. I walked closer. Daddy's ladder was across the walkway. When I saw Daddy lying on the steps, I heard Al's car squealing its tires down my street.

I turned and screamed Al's name, but I could hear him already turning onto Main. He was gone.

I didn't look at Daddy again. I ran up the hill to Dr. Sanders's house, up the path that I could find my way on with my eyes closed. When I reached his door and knocked, a floodlight came on around me. I could see Mrs. Sanders peeping through the curtain. When she opened the door and said my name, I could smell alcohol in the cool air.

"Mrs. Sanders? Is Dr. Sanders home? My daddy is hurt."

Why didn't I think to use our phone? For an instant I had a terrible fear that Dr. Sanders wasn't there, that I had wasted valuable time running to their house. Then he appeared behind her.

"Ella. Does he need an ambulance?"

"I think so."

He phoned the hospital and then picked up his black bag, going out the door. "Don't leave, dear," he said to his wife. "Stay right here until I get back."

"He fell off a ladder, Dr. Sanders. He's outside, in front of the door."

We rode in his car down his driveway and around the block to my house. When we stopped at our house, for a terrible moment I thought, What if he isn't there? This is one of his jokes. He will be standing in the door like a bad dream, laughing at me.

But when we got to the door of the house, I knew it wasn't a joke. Dr. Sanders bent down and lifted away the ladder. I should have done that. He picked up his hand.

"Is he alive?" I couldn't stand to touch him for myself.

"Yes."

The woman on duty at the hospital gave me a form to fill out.

"Hey, it's me, Alice. Ella Ruth. I don't have to do this."

"I think you have to anyway."

I filled out the form in the waiting room. My mind felt crazy.

Name: Maynard Higgins
Occupation: Alcoholic
Spouse's name: Maxine Higgins
Occupation: Eating
Deceased: Yes. At 56 years 60 pounds
Cause: Starvation
Children: One son, Matthew, early thirties,
　　　　　married while in high school,
　　　　　2 children, mildly successful in real estate,
　　　　　extremely boring
　　　　　Deceased: Unknown

228

One daughter, Ella Ruth Higgins
Ruth's OK but Ella's crazy

I sat in the waiting room by myself with words marching like a little army through my mind and out on my notebook. I couldn't stop writing and I couldn't let myself stop writing. I played a game with myself. If I stop, then Daddy stops living. I saw him go through that door on a stretcher, but it wasn't like Lavonia Pitts. Now I knew what was on the other side.

When I saw Lavonia Pitts die, I found out how easy it would be for my Mama to die and leave me as alone as I was in that waiting room. Mama never would have left me by myself if it had been her choice. She wrapped her big body around me when Mrs. Albright hit me and I was safe. I stayed there safe while her tomatoes were smashed on the pavement. After the day in the barn, something was inside me that Mama never saw. I learned to use the outside voice and keep the inside. I thought I could stay a child outside and be a grownup inside. I misheard the two voices. They were both me. I was right about that. But I thought I was hiding what I was, not what I was going to be. I thought they let it out that day, something wicked, something that had to hide from good people. Mama died and she never knew what happened. Mama never thought for a minute that she would die before I grew up.

"Ella Ruth, you don't mean to hurt your mama. You can try to be as good as you can be. But there isn't a child on this earth didn't hurt her mama coming in. Little as you were, Ella Ruth, you hurt me awful. More than Matthew, more than Ruth, rest her little soul."

Once upon a time this house was too small. It had a mama and a papa and a little girl. Now it is too large. It just has a papa and a daughter. The mama went away. Before she left she said to fill it up with babies, lots of babies in every room. Then, she said, I guess you should have a husband too to be a daddy to all those babies that Jesus brings to the hospital at night.

And every time you are sad, eat something. A banana split will dry your tears. And when you're afraid, blueberry pie will help. If someone hurts you, try a sandwich. You got cheated out of a dime at the grocery store? A cherry tart will do wonders for that.

Then one day, the little girl who did everything her mama told her to do tried to leave her house. That's when she found out she wasn't a little girl anymore. She couldn't get out the front door. So she put her arms and legs out of the windows and lumbered down the streets of Summit like a giant turtle.

Daddy: See, it's a device for picking a crocodile's teeth. It works like this.

Ella Darwin: Mr. Higgins, the crocodile has a far more efficient system. It's called the plover bird. It flies into the croc's mouth and pecks the bits of food from its teeth.

Daddy: You mean somebody beat me to it? Sonavabitch.

I don't know what I'm going to do. But I know what I'm not going to do: 1) get fat 2) have babies 3) marry Al Sawyer.

What makes me think I won't get fat like Mama?

I got mean like Daddy.

When Maynard Higgins was a little boy, he worked at the egg house. He held the eggs up to a lightbulb to see if they were fertilized. If they were dark and rotten, he took them down and broke them on the side of the railroad station. He waited till the bossman left and he put the roosters together and watched them fight. Animals never have taken a liking to my daddy. Spot and Maudie turned on him. Mama would say that animals were good judges of character.

I made like I loved Oscar Roscoe so much and as soon as he got to be trouble, I gave him away to Baby Ruth. Mama did the same thing to me. She gave me to Daddy.

Al Sawyer: I could have done it, same as those other guys, if I'd wanted to. I just got me some wild oats to sow first. If I'd of poked it to you, with the way my luck is running, your old man would have me at the altar with a shotgun in my ribs.

Al Sawyer stood over the fallen Ella with his smoking gun. He saw her twitch. There was still a little life left. He pointed the gun at her head and squeezed the trigger.

OK, Miss High and Mighty. You stood and watched your daddy walk on glass. Don't blame me.

Being raped and making love don't have anything to do with each other. You can use the same hand for stroking a chicken as for wringing its neck. Who said that? I don't know.

An average hen lays 240 eggs a year.

Mama was scared of her bad dreams. Daddy was scared of being in the outhouse with his pants down. Nancy Sanders was scared of the blank eyes in Little Orphan Annie and every day she took her crayons and filled them in in the newspaper.

I'm scared of Homer Crutchfield's daughter: I heard of a woman what wanted her a baby so bad, she got swole up and come due and give birth to a bag of air. It's the truth. Grandma says my sin is wished on my baby and the Lord could have turned her to stone if He pleased.

Did that bag of air start on a hillside overlooking Raleigh?

Katherine: What do you mean I couldn't chop up a snail and I could cut my own father's feet up without batting an eyelash? What did a snail ever do to me?

Daddy: Ella Ruth, what did you think of the color? Remember the

230

night last fall I got mistaken and went up fumbling with the door at Ed Albright's and almost got my fool head shot off? Even a stumbling old drunk ought to be able to find a robin's egg blue house.

When you're upset and try to write, things come out fast, but they don't make enough sense. Soon my brain was tired of writing, but Daddy still hadn't come out through that door. I couldn't let myself stop. I'd never forgive myself if he died. I believed he was like the cat at the rest area, that he would make it, with or without me. My hand was shaking. I was slowing down. I tapped my pencil on the paper until Alice at the desk looked at me and cleared her throat. I hadn't given her the form yet. I finally thought of something else to write in my notebook, like in grade school when you were bad. I wrote over and over: *I will not speak out of turn, I will not speak out of turn, I will not speak out of turn . . .*

When Daddy came back through the door, he was sitting in a wheelchair. He had patches on his head and his right arm was in a sling. He was smoking a cigarette that was different from what he usually smoked. Must have bummed it off Alvin, the orderly who pushed him out. Yes, I could see the Lucky Strike circle through the white pocket of Alvin's jacket.
"Miss Ella. This here your papa?"
I nodded. I felt ashamed. Maybe someday I could explain him to Alvin.
"Ella Ruth," Daddy asked, "what did you think of the color?"
I handed the form to Alice and she put it in the file under H without looking at it.
"I'll give you my opinion in the daylight."
I didn't work on the writings I did that night. The only thing I could find that held it all together was that I was afraid. Once I wasn't afraid, what I wrote didn't mean much to me. It was different to take an object and turn it in my hand. A feeling could slip away when the reason was gone. What was in my notebook was all I had left of that night in the waiting room.
I had to take my next three Saturdays off to finish Daddy's paint job. Before I started, our house looked like a giant had picked it up and dipped one side in blue paint. Maybe time would tone it down a little. I couldn't help but think our house was like Hazel at work with her bleached hair. If it wasn't so gaudy, people wouldn't look at it when they drove past. If it was still white, they wouldn't see all the bad things they'd never paid any attention to before.
"Ella Ruth, if I didn't have this broke arm, I'd be up there helping you. I'm much obliged."
Since Daddy got hurt, he had been nicer, more appreciative. I

231

think something might have slipped in his head before his foot slipped on the ladder. I liked him better the old way because I knew what to expect.

"Ella Ruth."

"Yeah."

"You missed a little spot over there by the window."

Prologue to the Last Notebook of Ella Ruth Darwin:
The great scientist, Ella Ruth Darwin, in the woods one day collecting specimens—wood-turtle eggs—was struck by a terrible misfortune. She stepped into a bear trap, concealed under the leaves, and its powerful jaws snapped shut on her ankle. The extent of the tragedy will never be known, because of the immeasurable loss of such a great mind to future generations. We mourn that she fell prey to a trap set by her fellow man.

The following notes—unedited and unchanged—were found beside her skeleton and will be known to the world as The Last Notebook of E. R. Darwin:

Day 1: I am still alive, goodness, but what a fix I'm in. I cannot move. The pain in my leg is severe because a trap has closed on it. What a silly place for a bear trap. I could have told those trappers myself there hasn't been a bear in these woods in twenty years. I am so irritated at myself for leaving my lunch in my car. A banana sandwich would taste superb right now, if I'm allowed such a mundane speculation. Surely someone will miss me soon at my laboratory and come looking.

Day 2: I hope someone thought to feed my hamsters. And not cabbage leaves. There is enough insecticide on a commercial cabbage to poison their tiny systems. Honestly, at this point I would leave my foot behind if I could get out of this trap. I could take a knife and cut it right off. Oh, but I don't have a knife. There is a coral snake in the sandhills to be the subject of my future research. It hangs on your body, chewing through your flesh in a disgusting manner. Once its poison has penetrated, you have seven minutes to live. If you are lucky and it chews on your hand or your foot, you can slice it off and live.

I can certainly find unpleasant comparisons in situations.

But how would you know how much to cut? Looking at my ankle, here maybe, up two inches? Surely would be nice to have enough left to attach an artificial limb to. What a time to have a thought like that. How far has the poison gone? you'd have to ask. The snake poison is not like a rotten spot in a good old Irish potato that I can slice and slice again until all the black is cut away and not have to waste the whole thing. How can I bear to cut away part of my pretty young body?

Day 3: In my madness I think that I am running. I am running down a hill as fast as I can go and suddenly up in front of me pops a wall. But I am going too fast to stop. That means I did it to myself. If I had been walking I could have walked right by the wall or around or climbed over it or gone in another direction. Multiple choices. But E.

232

R. Darwin always has to go running right at things. Never was she accused of timidity. Running at the ocean that's waiting with a wave to choke her, stinging the top of her head with salt water, slapping her down again before she gets up. But sometimes that wall is like the invisible shield that the man taps in the toothpaste commercial. It keeps the ball from hitting him. It would keep the wave from slapping her down. Is the reason it doesn't hit her now that she never goes into the water, never has the nerve to get out in the smooth water beyond the breakers? Or is the wall as visible as the black and white clothes that nuns wear? No, it is invisible and as close as the tips of my fingers, at the end of my reach. These colleagues of mine teased me and called me the flycatcher because I caught insects for my laboratory. They bit me until I was delirious. I can't touch the world and it can't touch me. A mosquito floated past me in the sunlight, her blood sack glowing like a ruby. The mosquitoes are draining me. I never claimed the insects were my friends.

Day 4: One minute I was a happy little animal, bouncing through a meadow; the next I was caught. Like a rabbit, running is my only defense. I have no natural weapons. Now I am at the mercy of anything that passes. I can scratch and squeal. What a pathetic fight I put up. A freak of nature. I have no business being alive, I'm the first to admit it. They can just take their turns on me. What can I do to stop them now? They are on me like wolves, smelling my blood. A thousand hands couldn't stop the holes where I spill my blood. For a second I had a silly thought, that maybe I was wrong about the blood. Well, just to prove how wrong I can be, I smeared it off my fingers on everything white I touched. I had a perfectly decent pair of white slacks and what do I get caught in but my raggedy khaki pants and an old shrunken blouse. I don't even have a pin to clasp it shut. It doesn't need to be shut anymore. I'm shrinking fast.

Day 5: There is no reason to hope my dog will save me from them. His crying stopped weeks ago. What a silly dream I had last night, that I found him and he became my loving pet. I think I called him Freckles in the dream. Later in my sleep I saw him in a nightmare. A polka-dot dog and the stench was awful. The stench went away when the wind blew over me. I walked around and picked up polka-dot scraps of him. Blown apart in a million pieces. Poor dog never knew what hit him. I stack the pieces and they are smooth as cloth. They hang on all the brambles in the river, a pretty sight. The rest of him is gone, except for his shadow, burned in the moss on the creek bank like a dog in Hiroshima. I'll sew the fur scraps together, first chance I get, and have a fur lap robe to warm me when I sit in my rocker in my old age. Beats an old dog I will have to get up and feed, any old day.

Goodness, do you think the stench could be me?

Day 6: When the time comes, how do I get rid of me? That's going to be something of a problem. There is a chemical vat at the factory. Before I was born they say a man fell in and nothing was left. That is out of my field. I would like to walk across the earth and have the ground open with a quake and seal me up tight inside, flat like in an

233

envelope, snug as a bug. Did you know the earth moves with tides just like the sea? Earth Tide. Another theory I planned to write about. Now, I don't see me floating bloated on the bubbling chemicals like a dead fish in bad water. That just isn't the way I like to do things. I will go into the ground like a shadow too.

Day 7: I dream I can walk over the hills, going home. The path is worn deep as a ditch where the cows have come home before me. Their manure is in the ditch and it is slick from the rains. I fall in it and it coats my body, but I don't mind the smell. There is something good about the smell of a stable, the sting in my nose and throat. Spot found three dead dogs that the train had run down and he rolled in them until he smelled like one of them. And he wallowed in excrement left in the woods by the men who work on the roads. I'll have to beg to differ with you there, old Spot. Unless maybe they were vegetarians like horses. A stable smells different. Don't make me afraid to go back to the stable. I loved it outdoors so much. How many more days can I hope to be rescued?

Day 8: At last. Today I put my hand on my bound leg, a sanitary bandage. I lifted my hand. Nothing. Nothing there but a soreness as far away as a knee skinned on the sidewalk. When they found me, I have to tell you they treated me like a stuck hog, rolling me, tossing me, jabbing me. A hundred and fifteen pounds of flesh and bone, I used to be. I couldn't fight and I didn't help. I was lifted from a stationary bed to one with wheels. Has she purged herself, a voice asked? Goddamn right, she has shit and puked and sneezed and squirted out every drop of precious body fluid she had in her. Purged. Just like they won't say cancer. It's malignancy, growth, mass. Piss in a jar, shit in a pan, right Daddy? People like me have to be mad to cuss. Angry, I mean. I don't do it for the fun of it. Like the time I said cocksucker, right in front of Grandfather Charles when I was passing a car and it decided to make a left turn. I ran down a mailbox. Maybe doctors are like me. They think one way and say it another.

I'm not angry this time. Not like before. I don't make a noise. Not a peep, Grandfather would say. No reason to be a fighter. Too many of them. The fat anesthetist laughed and jiggled. I wanted to cut off her fat like trimming a steak. I saw a purple USDA stamp on her arm. She let me wake up so I must not have called her a steak.

Day 9: As soon as I'm able to get up and about, you know what is the first thing I'm going to do? I'm going back into Paul Kammerer's laboratory and set all the animals free. And I'll tell you why. One hundred duck eggs he had, to do an experiment on the hatching of eggs. So they hatched. End experiment. What about the hundred ducks? You can guess as good as I. A man like that is surely not worth a hundred ducks.

I told the steak the reason I didn't remain a doctor was I couldn't stand the blood and gore of her profession. Before I went to sleep I told her to enjoy my show. She thought it was to be no more than a marble she was digging out to thump around the lab. That's what she told us all, me included. I knew it all went wrong when I saw the clock. It took

234

too long, even for amateurs. I was shifted again from the bed with wheels, the sheets hot with me. Two orderlies threw me on a haystack. When I landed, a stick stuck in my left buttock. I knew when I felt the hay beneath my back, they were done with me. I could rest and my body could dry.

Day 10: I want to leave you with some heretofore unpublished scientific data from my grandfather, Charles Darwin. He put his snuff in the basement, and the key to his snuff box in the attic. Like my grandfather, I think all stories should have a happy ending. So I'll simply repeat what he said: "I am not in the least afraid to die."

Postscript: A female psychiatrist was quick to object to the publication of the final notebook of Ella Darwin: "It is hardly fair for our last memory of one of the great female minds of our century to be of totally nonscientific data [a remedy to curb the dipping of snuff?] compiled in a state of intense physical pain. On the other hand, she has documented most accurately the despair of a free spirit—naturally selected not to survive—that has run out of choices.

"When you were a little baby, I touched your pecker when I changed your diaper and, I tell you the truth, it got hard as a little stob."

Mrs. Hinshaw was babbling face down in the bed while I bathed her backside. I was using warm water, though I heard one of the nurses say it didn't matter while they were too groggy from the anesthetic to know the difference. The old woman had been shivering when I opened the curtains around her bed and now the warm cloth seemed to be soothing her.

As I rubbed the back of her thighs, her skin as white and hairless as the sheets, she went on: "You don't have a lot of hair like Alvin. Now, mind you, I'm not complaining. Hard as a rock. No bad spots from eating too many gravy biscuits. Drinking too much beer. I never went for the gorilla type myself. Kind with hair coming out the neck of their shirts. How 'bout me 'membering changing your diaper? Heh, heh. Didn't tell you that before, did I? A girl don't need to tell all."

She thought I was a man, but she wasn't ashamed to be naked in front of me.

"Who am I, Katherine?" I asked.

She moaned. "I love the way you say my name. Katherine. I know which side of the bed you're on, Andy, even though the lights are out."

It was bright daylight in the room. "Which side, Katherine?"

"My left." She snorted with laughter into her pillow. She was right. "I can feel you hot as a two-dollar pistol without laying a finger on you."

I dipped my cloth back in the pan and wrung it out, spreading it on her back. It smoked in the cool room. She moaned with pleasure.

"Do you know who I am, Katherine?" I asked again.

"Andy, Alvin will never know. Don't you worry for a minute. Off in the woods drunk and scaring the deer. He can't hit the broadside of a barn sober." She began to open and close her fist, her veins dark blue knots. "You know what you're like, Andy? Like sticking your foot in a hot tub. Too hot at first, then just right, m-m-m-m-m. Don't your stob even go down when you sleep?"

She had her head turned enough now that her voice wasn't muffled by the pillow. Her glazed eyes were open, but they saw only what was inside her head. I began to wash her more rapidly, starting to fear what she might say, ashamed in the cubicle with only a curtain to shut out the sound. She started laughing as though I was tickling her.

"Piss proud," she blurted. "Look at your pecker, up and ready all night long. Alvin's falls over before the job is done."

"Shhhhh, Katherine. Alvin will hear you." I used the name of the hairy man, her husband, I guessed. When she heard it, her face twisted in anger. I felt bad, taking her good memory away, but she was embarrassing me. When her memory of her good times left, the pain of her bed sores came to her and she twitched each time I touched them.

"And whose pecker tracks are these, Alvin'll say," she snorted. "None of your goddamn business, you S.O.B."

I dipped the rag back in the pan and rushed to finish. Her loose skin moved around like dough. Her puckered buttocks were like two dough mounds, waiting to be rolled into pie crusts.

Her face relaxed a little as she said, "In the morning, Alvin had to turn on the spigot so he could piss."

That was familiar to me. My daddy stood in front of the toilet with his penis out, clearing his throat and wobbling, while I brushed my teeth. Finally he would reach over and turn on the spigot full blast. Then the piss would pour out and around the toilet bowl. I thought it was because he drank too much.

"Alvin took me out to see them castrate the hogs. Threw their bloody balls on the ground and they ate them up like slops. You women think you have it so rough, Alvin tells me. So that's how you keep a boar at home, I say, and he laughs. Then I say, look how big and healthy they get after their oysters are gone, Alvin. Kat, oh please, Kat, don't serve mine up to me. And I played him for all it was worth."

"All through, Katherine," I interrupted and pulled her hospital gown back down. Her skin that folded over her bones was looser than the cloth.

"Yes, Lord, through. Come back, Andy." A tear fell out of her eye and I mopped it away from the groove beside her nose. "I hate you had to die. War takes the best and leaves the trash behind," she said with a trembling voice, then was silent.

I pulled the sheet over her and picked up the pan. When I walked through the curtain, Elisa Simpson glared at me. "Decent people shouldn't have to stay in the room with the likes of her."

"The gas hasn't worn off yet. She doesn't know what she's saying," I defended.

"What makes you think that nasty old woman is any different when she's sober? All that dirty talk about sex. Worse than a filthy-mouthed man. White trash."

"I'm sorry she bothers you, Mrs. Simpson. She's asleep now."

"Did you hear what she was saying?" she insisted. "I bet you're too young to know what she meant. You are, aren't you?"

"She thought I was . . ." I hesitated, knowing if I said husband, I'd sound foolish. ". . . her boyfriend."

"Her cuckold! I wouldn't go within fifty yards of that sorry place where she works. And I get put in a bed ten feet away."

"Do you want me to see if I can have you switched to the other end of the ward? I don't know if I can, but I will ask if you want me to. There is nothing I can do to stop her from talking."

She looked taken aback by my suggestion. "No, never mind."

The rest of the day, I couldn't get Katherine Hinshaw off my mind. It was as if I was told a love story, like George and Emily. I was in her audience and so was Elisa. Only Elisa made like she wanted to get up and walk out, and I wanted to hear every word of it. But her story was in her head, in a dark place I couldn't see, someone else's dream that came only in words. I had to imagine the picture, see Andy with his strong body, see Katherine like she was for that moment, still someone a man would want to touch, her white skin tight and smooth. When the gas wears off, her lover will be dead, but for a moment under the anesthetic, she was free of being old. I'm glad I don't have to act fancy like Elisa and pretend I didn't want to listen. Katherine Hinshaw gave her story to me. If she hadn't, it would have been like the stories I write in my notebook—stories with no one to hear them.

The day before, Elisa Simpson had sat in the middle of her bed, her legs crossed, Indian-style. She had painted her toenails to match her fingernails and her feet pointed prettily from under her lace robe. She talked in an animated way to her husband, Albert.

"Remember the game we used to play when we were kids? Big brown bear?"

237

Albert grunted.

"Oh, you remember, Albert. When you had to sit in the corner for fifteen minutes and not think of a big brown bear. When the time was up, you were supposed to be honest."

"I guess I remember." Elisa told me that she had lived in the same neighborhood with Albert all her life.

"I have to confess to you," she said gleefully, "that I used to fib and say no, even when I did think of a big brown bear. Once I saw the bear, dressed in a suit like Papa Bear in Goldilocks, and once he galloped up a mountainside like the one I saw in a movie. I even said no once when I saw it written behind a skywriter in brown letters: Big Brown Bear." She wrote the words in the air with her finger.

"I don't reckon that was the first or last time you ever lied to me," Albert said, with no expression in his voice. She giggled and winked at him. I could tell that Albert wasn't too concerned about her confession.

"If you were weather, Albert, and not a person, what would you be?"

"Shit."

"Aw, come on. Play. It gets boring here."

"Sounds like you been watching them kids' shows. *Captain Kangaroo.*"

"I have. Play."

He was silent for a few minutes. I could tell that Albert knew better than not to play with Elisa. He was trying hard to come up with something. Elisa had her answer ready before she asked. She decided to tell him what kind of weather she was first:

"I think I'd be like rain in the spring, real hard for a while, then stop real quick and the sun would come out and things would glisten, then start growing and have flowers.

He nodded, "That's you, all right," and relaxed as if he was off the hook.

"Why do you say that?" she asked suspiciously.

"Hot and cold."

"Moody would be a nicer way of putting it, Albert."

"Yeah, hot and cold."

He was getting braver. She was the big brown bear and he was rattling her cage.

"You know what you are, Albert?" The edge was on her voice now. "You're one of those cold winter rains that doesn't know when to quit. The kind that starts out doing some good, but ends up *mud.*"

"Aw, I thought you were gonna say I was a sunshiny day with birds singing. Shoot."

238

Albert leaned back and smiled while Elisa pouted. I think he was pleased that he didn't have to come up with a weather. Although Elisa talked about how great marriage was, mud seemed like a good description of Albert.

But today the child in Elisa had gone away. Her outside told how she felt inside. Each day she fixed her hair and face very carefully, primping again before Albert arrived, but today she took the curlers out, leaving her hair in unbrushed coils. Dark smudges were under her eyes where her tears had washed the mascara off. The two top buttons of her silk pajamas, that usually were left open like a movie star's, were done up. This morning Dr. Sanders had told her that her lump was malignant and her breast would have to be removed.

"Can I get you anything, Mrs. Simpson?" I asked. "How about a doughnut and some coffee?"

She shook her head and reached for my hand. At first when she tried to speak, she got only a cracking sound. But, just like Mama at the last, she found her voice and started talking, trying to keep me at her side.

"Albert will be here soon. He likes to do those little things for me. He had to fix a stove today." When I tried lightly to get my hand out of her grasp, she asked, "Do you like movies?"

"Very much," I told her.

"I do too. Albert doesn't care for them. Maybe you can go with me when I get out of here. Did you see *The Living Desert?*"

"Yes, the one with the flowers opening."

Her eyes began to brighten a little and she tipped her head sideways, as if to see this new thing she had put her mind on better. "It gave me chills all over," she said, "to see something happening that you can't really see. Except I did have a grandma who claimed if she sat on the porch all day she could watch the plants grow."

"Mine said the same thing," I told her.

She smiled and patted my hand, but grabbed it again when I tried to pull away. "You're a nice little girl. We really see things eye to eye, me and you. Must be something that happens to people who sit still a long time."

I must have looked confused because she added, "Seeing things grow, I mean."

I had a bad memory of *The Living Desert*. I watched it three times and when I came out, found it was as dark outside as in the theater. I had been scared walking home from the bus stop, and as soon as I walked in the door of my house, thinking I was safe, Daddy grabbed me and spanked me. He threw me against the door and I bruised my side on the doorknob. Mama said it was because he was frightened that some bad man had gotten me. She put a washcloth with an ice

239

cube inside on my swollen place. I couldn't share my thoughts with Mrs. Simpson because I was afraid I'd say the wrong thing and make her cry again.

"Remember the spiders who walked in time with the music?" she asked and sniffed loudly, trying to hold back her tears.

I nodded. I think something happened to women who got sick, to the way their minds worked. That was like something Mama would have said, thinking the spiders walked with the music instead of the music with the spiders. But that wasn't like Mrs. Simpson. If she hadn't mentioned the spiders, what I would have remembered was the roadrunner killing the rattlesnake. I wondered why she thought we saw eye to eye. I couldn't reach inside her mind because I was afraid to. I felt afraid of her sickness even though I knew it wasn't catching.

"Those flowers sitting on the TV are opening right now. By tomorrow, they'll be past their prime." I looked at the pink roses that Albert brought from their garden. Home-grown flowers seemed to die faster in the hospital than the florist variety. Why couldn't I answer her with something, anything? She shouldn't be alone now. Katherine was asleep and snoring. I wished one of the nurses would come in. Or Dr. Sanders.

"You know how they come on at the end of those animal shows and tell you that some of it is simulated," she went on. "There was this pair of animals on today, I don't remember their names. Pretty little furry, catlike animals. It was real. I know it was." She was remembering something that upset her because her hand was shaking my arm. "I can still hear the sound of that little animal moaning. Its mouth moved with the noise and it shook its head, so I know it wasn't simulated like they said. They were a pair and they had babies. The people doing the movie spent a lot of time showing you their daily lives, how they caught mice and nursed their babies. Then suddenly this big cat came up out of the bushes and snatched up the mama, just like that." She clutched the covers with her loose hand. "I couldn't believe they would show that on TV. Just like when they let Bambi's mama die in the fire. I couldn't believe it." Mrs. Simpson was starting to cry again. She was crying slowly, like the sedative had slowed her tears down too.

"They were so happy taking care of their babies and this damn big cat that could have eaten anything comes and takes the mama. It was just a meal for it. You don't think, that when those things go out hunting, they might catch something in a pair, do you? Maybe the man with the camera didn't know that was going to happen. Why didn't he go running out and scare the big cat? Scared for his own hide, that's why. Wanted to be the only person in the world who took

240

a picture of this awful thing. The little man cat keeps running up and trying to fight the big cat and doesn't get the time of day." She was banging her hand on the covers with my hand still in her grasp. "He's willing to fight and die for his little mate and that bitch of a cat brushes him off like he's no more than a horsefly. And he has to sit there and moan and pace the ground and watch that cat tear his mate into pieces and eat her. And him with no way to nurse his little babies." I thought of stitches in her body pulling apart as she flailed her arms, but she hadn't been cut yet. "People think they have it so rough. Watch those soap operas all day long and you don't get anything like that."

"Honey, what's wrong with you? I could hear your mouth halfway up the hall."

I turned and saw Albert. When she released my hand and grabbed his, I moved away from her. She looked at Albert, puzzled, as if the subject she had been ranting about had flown away like a bird. She pulled his hand over to touch a picture in the open magazine in her lap. It was of a woman in a fur coat. "She's got one of those looks I can't stand."

"What kind of stuff they got you on?" Albert asked. As I picked up her water pitcher, I looked around Albert at the snooty model in the magazine, wearing a coat it said was made of fifty seal pelts. Then I hurried out, afraid I wouldn't get out before she told Albert about the cancer. Instead, I heard Elisa say, "That woman isn't worth one baby seal."

By the next morning Katherine Hinshaw appeared wide awake, but her loose white skin had taken on a gray tint that wouldn't wash away, falling in place on her cheeks like feathers. I noticed her head bobbed as though suspended, a ball floating on a pool of water inside her neck bandage. She ignored me while I changed her sheets. Her eyes were fixed on something outside her window. When I looked over her shoulder, I saw the pigeons, marching single file on the ledge outside. A large pigeon followed a small pigeon, making tender noises. The small pigeon appeared to be hurrying away from the larger one, yet the distance between them stayed the same. I realized that Katherine Hinshaw's head was bobbing in time with the pigeons' heads as she followed the rhythm of their dance. Suddenly the little one stopped and the big one instantly jumped on her back.

Katherine Hinshaw hollered, "Yahoo!" and clapped her hands together as though the home-team hero had just hit a ball over the back fence.

Day in and day out, I have to concern myself with what goes in and out of women's bodies, cleaning up the mess of grown women.

241

All of these women used to look after other people. Now, just like my mama in her last days, they have to be cared for like they are babies. Some days I think this can't be what I was meant to do, scrubbing out toilets, spreading sandwiches, making up dozens of beds. Anybody can do those things. But then I find myself listening to the patients, all the crazy things they say when they're under gas. Or when they're hurting or afraid. It is part of my job to comfort, but that isn't what I am listening for.

I think when somebody hurts, their mind turns up like the volume on a radio, almost too loud to make sense of but demanding to be heard. They're afraid because what they had is slipping away. Do you have to hurt or fear to say what you feel? When I worked in Simon's the women complained about the job, the money, their families. But it wasn't the same. Here it's like someone twisting your arm behind your back until you have to scream uncle to get them to stop. Pain forces you to show what you feel.

When I wash my hands before I leave the hospital, I hold them in the hot water as long as I can stand it. I leave my jacket off when I get outside so I can feel the air hit the wet cloth that touches me. Sometimes I want to forget their agonies and have my own feelings. But then I think that studying their feelings is looking after my own. I feel like a soldier walking a battlefield after a war. I know I could be on the ground bleeding, but I feel the privilege of being able to stand. None of these women around me are me and yet I move in and out of their bodies like ghosts.

ELISA RUTH: I watched my little Nadine bury her goldfish like it was a special occasion. Made it a casket out of a watchbox, velvet-lined. Put a violet on the grave. It was the cutest thing. Just like a grownup.

KATELLA: Just like a grownup. Doll it up so you'll forget what really happened. Spare the child. She's got the rest of her sad life to be a grownup.

ELISA RUTH: Well, I happen to think she is cute as can be stumbling around the house in my spike-heeled shoes. All little girls do that. That's what they're supposed to do. Pretend they're grown women.

KATELLA: Now you tell me what's the rush? Forced to stumble on them shoes soon enough. They teach you at Sunday School that God created man. Ain't a man on this earth didn't come out of a woman with it being another man's fault. My pretty boy got sent off to Korea. Left on his feet. Come home on his back in a pine box. Sent off to fight a bunch of slopes in a country clean on the other side of the world. Girls don't have to be soldiers, you see. But it ain't us girls who start the wars. I would have fought in his place. I was young

242

and healthy then. Strong as an ox. I might have been harder to kill. He was a gentle soul. Protect the home front, he said. What from? Indians? The British? Remember Pearl Harbor, he said. What did that have to do with getting up crusty-eyed to a factory whistle in Summit, North Carolina? Little girls play mama. Little boys play soldier. Little girls get to die close to home.

ELISA RUTH: I'm too young to die. You don't know what it's like, old woman, something inside you eating you up that you can't reach in and grab. They had no right to it. It's got no right being in there. Dr. Sanders tells me it's in there, I don't know it. And I'm supposed to ask him to help me fight something I can't even see attacking me. Let him see my naked body? Remind him that I was once the pretty little girl he thought of making his wife? Please don't look at me now. I'll tell you the truth, Dr. Sanders. I'd rather die than let you see me now.

KATELLA: Pretty little girl. Honey, it ain't your womanhood they was after. Hell, they figure they give you that. After they pulled that stunt in the barn, you were a woman whether you liked it or not. It was your childhood that they made off with.

ELISA RUTH: The first time for me was in a beautiful canopy bed with white eyelet lace ruffles. The light came through the eyelets like the sun through a cloud and danced on our bed the next morning.

KATELLA: Bull hockey.

ELISA RUTH: Well, he thought it was the first time. I left a drop of blood on the sheets.

KATELLA: In the olden days, they broke it with a rag on their finger. They showed the blood to their family and boasted.

ELISA RUTH: I cried and pretended it hurt.

KATELLA: The bull struts out in the ring and the crowd cheers as he puts up a fight. So what? Still makes hamburger.

What's the difference between a canopy bed and the back seat of a '38 Ford?

After my morning shift, I got into the truck and decided to take a drive before I went home. The truck made so much noise it was hard to think and drive at the same time. I would like to have gone beyond the tobacco farms to the place where the empty mansions stood by the river, but I was afraid to go far with the truck, "No further than you feel up to walking back," as Daddy would say. I drove down by the Yellow River, where the red clay and eroded topsoil made the water anything but yellow. I stopped a moment, then realized everybody picked that place because the vines were spotted with beer cans and food wrappers.

Someone was on the riverbank, an old man. Homer Crutchfield. His granddaughter was in the hospital with her baby. At first I thought he was fishing, but then I saw a yellow arch of piss in front of him, breaking apart in the wind and blowing back at him. I started the motor and left, hoping he wouldn't know I saw him. It was hard to get away from people in Summit.

As I drove off down the road, the nervousness I felt when I first saw Homer began to go away. I didn't want him to be there, but he was. Yet when you have a car, all you have to do is drive away and he is gone. It was like a getaway car, like I was getting away with something. That wasn't exactly it. Homer could have been my daddy, or Al Sawyer, anybody. All I had to do was drive away. Just like the old days when I rode off on Maudie. When I was little, I thought the freest thing in the world would be Starrie galloping across the plains on a stallion. Not now. It'd be Ella Ruth Higgins going down Highway 70 in a '55 Chevrolet.

When I drove back toward home, I saw a row of cars under a string of lightbulbs: $900, $800, $750, written on the windshields in white shoe polish. It didn't seem right for no one to be using all those cars, when I had nothing to drive but the old truck. But it didn't seem right either to spend Mama's hard-earned money on a car when she didn't even know how to drive.

I turned into our driveway. Daddy was on the steps. Before I was halfway up the walk, he hollered, "You got five bucks?"

"Yeah, what for?"

"A shave and a haircut."

I gave him the money. He frowned and said, "Five bucks is what I get."

"That's what you asked for."

"Gimme the keys to the truck."

"No."

"It's my truck."

"Officer Ellis says no."

He grunted and walked away. Before I got inside, he called my name.

"Yeah." I answered. "Do you need more money to buy a new suit at the Rebel to go with your shave and haircut?"

He turned his head and spat. "Where you hoarding that money you make?"

"None of your business." My voice trembled a little. He stared at me a moment and shuffled off. I waited until he was out of sight, then ran and looked in my Bible. I relaxed when I saw it was still there, but as soon as I zipped it up, I felt uneasy again. Every cent I had in the world was in the house with him all day.

When I reached the first floor of the hospital, I heard a familiar voice behind me.

"Ella, Hi!"

I turned and saw Dr. Sanders coming down the hall.

"Hi, Dr. Sanders. I didn't know you worked tonight."

"I came over to check on Mrs. Simpson. She's having a hard time coping with her operation emotionally. She should be thankful to be alive."

It seemed strange that a man smart enough to be a doctor would say that. Elisa was already alive and she couldn't see the thing that would kill her. I didn't think she thought of the operation as saving her life. She thought of it as the ugliest thing she had ever seen happen to her body.

"I thought Dr. Bivens did her surgery," I said.

"He did. But I have known Elisa and Albert for years. He does all our electrical work. I talked her into the operation, but there was no question. It was malignant." He put his hand on my shoulder. "Have you got time for a Coke? I'd like to see a cheerful face for a while."

"OK, thanks."

As we walked in and sat down, he said, "I heard one for you today, for your strange animal-fact collection."

"What's that?" I took out my small notebook that I carried while I worked.

"If you could unravel a hedge spider's web, the silk would reach three hundred miles."

I jotted down "hedge spider web 300 miles." "I've never even been three hundred miles from Summit."

"I haven't had a minute to talk to you lately. Do you still like your work here?" he asked.

"Oh, yes. I do like it. I have never met so many different kinds of people." I wasn't saying what was in my head at all. I meant I got to see all kinds of pain without having to suffer it myself.

"Except they have one thing in common," he said. "They're all in need of repairs. I bet you've never had a sick day."

"Not many. Once, after I rescued my cripple duck from drowning. I jumped in your pond in the wintertime."

"A crippled duck. It's a strange thing. An afflicted animal always dies. Yet an afflicted human often goes on to greatness in the seemingly impossible endeavor. A deaf Beethoven, a blind Milton. Our strongest president was confined to a wheelchair."

"Actually, to be honest, Dr. Sanders, my crippled duck died because Daddy gave it to a lady to cook." He lifted his eyebrows and chuckled. Then he asked me, "What do you have your sights set on, Ella? Summit's first lady doctor?"

I was shocked when he said that. He suggested it seriously, that Ella Ruth Higgins was even allowed to dream of being a doctor.

"Actually, I'd like to be a scientist."

I couldn't believe I said that to him.

"Of course. I should have guessed. Biology. Zoology. You've made applications?"

"Applications?"

The door swung open behind us. It was Alvin.

"Evening, Doc Sanders. Miss Ella."

"Did you finally get Mitchell Mann tucked in?" I asked him, relieved I didn't have to answer Dr. Sanders. Mitchell was a colored boy.

"Ain't he the cat's meow? He says, 'Alvin, you ever hear of Jesse Owens?' I says, 'Don't know the man.' He says, 'Alvin, Doc Sanders says he got four gold medals in the Olympics and he was a colored.' That true, Doc Sanders?"

"Absolutely. In 1936, Hitler intended for the Olympics to prove white supremacy and Jesse Owens broke his bubble."

"Beg pardon? Anyhow, this Mitchell, he asks me, 'Does that Jesse Owens have an appendage?' And I says, 'He's most likely got four, far as I know.' And that Mitchell's bottom lip go out and he says, 'Doc Sanders took out the onliest one I got.' " Alvin began to laugh loudly and said, "That's what took me so long down there. Talking about appendages. Lawsy, when I was Mitchell's age, I didn't know an appendage from an apple tree. You know what he figured give him appendicitis, Doc Sanders? String beans. His mama made him eat them for supper the night he went to hurting." Alvin went into the kitchen.

Dr. Sanders didn't let the interruption change the subject. "If you would like to talk seriously about going to college or some sort of professional training, please feel free to ask me anytime. I know your father is a problem, but I'm sure some arrangement could be made."

"Yes. He's a problem. I had to give up my scholarship and I don't have but one thousand, three hundred twenty-two dollars of my own saved up."

"Ella!" He was surprised. "That is quite a bit of money to have saved. Most grown men, I assure you, can't lay claim to that sum."

"Most of it was Mama's."

"And do you have it in savings?"

"No, sir, I have it in my pocket."

246

"In your pocket?" he whispered.

I nodded.

"Ella, honey. That is *much* too dangerous. You're afraid your father would find it?"

I nodded again.

"Ella, this is a dangerous part of town. The Good Humor man was murdered out there for less than fifty dollars cash. Nobody should carry that much cash. You should have a savings account."

"I had it with me because I thought I might buy a car during my lunch hour today," I said stupidly. I had done that, dreamed of trying out each of the cars in the row and picking one to take home.

"I see. Well, I guess that's what all you young folks want." He seemed a little disappointed.

When I left that night, my uniform was damp from sweat. The night air felt cool as I went through the automatic door into the little park beside the hospital. The curbs were sloped for wheelchairs and the ground was punctured with cane holes. Once I had asked Dr. Sanders about the holes, feeling silly because I thought they were made by an animal. Nothing was in the park but a stray dog tugging at a hamburger wrapper in the wire trash can. I sat down on one of the benches and listened to the dog, his paw holding down the wrapper and his rough tongue rasping at a stuck bit of cheese. After a while he left, probably going to the back of the hospital to push open the lids on the waste food containers. We scraped the patients' trays and the food was picked up by farmers to be recooked and fed to their hogs.

I wasn't sure if I was afraid, or if I was testing to see if I would be afraid, knowing Ella Ruth Higgins had something a person would want. That dog didn't even know me. He wouldn't come to my rescue. Someone could jump out from behind a tree with a knife or gun and take my money from me. Then I wouldn't have to decide between a car and going to school.

Maybe tomorrow I'll go to the Fidelity Bank and open a savings account. They will give me a book with my name on it. As I walk out the door of the bank with my savings book, an old colored woman will come up to me. She will point her finger at me and say: "You white bitch. I *knew* you took Lavonia's savings book."

Was what I told Dr. Sanders about my daddy the truth? If it was, then none of the things I was writing in my notebook were.

Dr. Sanders. I want you to know that my daddy isn't as bad as I made him out to be. He has never stolen my money or tried to even. All he asks for is enough to go to the Rebel or to buy a pint when he feels like staying at home. I've thought about it a lot and he's the

247

only right father for me to have. If I'd had all those clothes with my name tags in them, I would never have known about feed-sack dresses or had a fat mama who made me a wardrobe fit for a princess when my teacher said I had to dress like a lady. I bet Marcel's never painted a gingerbread man. Or baked a chicken even. Surely never plucked one. I know you know what it's like, living with a drunk. Don't you see the difference? You made your own choice. You turned down the best woman in the world because people from your class always use toilets. Our drunks are different anyway. Yours rides a Cadillac and mine rides a crocodile and picks its teeth at the same time. I'll take mine any day. My mama tried her whole life to bring this family of ours together with a reunion, so I guess it's up to me to do it for her. I haven't decided whether to cut down a fresh cedar or to get Daddy's folding tree out of the attic. I want to invite them all to something, every one of them.

On second thought, Dr. Sanders, it's best I don't tell you this. It's just as well I wasn't quick enough to say it at the time. The only people who say just the right thing at the right time are on soap operas or in books.

I have a confession to make. Just a few weeks ago, I decided to kill Ella Ruth Darwin. If I had told you, you wouldn't have asked me about being a scientist. Maybe I can find another use for your spider with the three-hundred mile web. I'm into something new now. Two women, not one. What would Elisa Ruth do? What would Katella do? That's the question. I have to admit, Dr. Sanders, I'm more interested in the survival of these two human animals than I am in the possible extinction of the southwestern dung beetle.

On the days I got to keep the snack bar, I imagined what it would be like to be Katherine Hinshaw at the Rebel, mopping the counter and waiting for my customers to come through the door. Outside the door, doctors and orderlies rushed to save injured people, brought in the ambulance. They ran past old people in walkers who moved so slow that it seemed while you started and finished a chore, they had been caged in the hall. Inside the snack bar, the movement stopped completely and, like a bartender, I heard bits of everyone's stories. Each day was a living soap opera. I soon found that around the patients the hospital employees acted the way they were supposed to act, but the snack bar was where everyone came to be themselves.

When Dr. Bivens came in for a rushed cup of coffee, I heard of the problem in the broken bones ward where legs and arms hung from straps with people sprawled like puppets with tangled threads.

"Nice, huh?" he said to me. "Supposed to be the most sanitary place in the world." I didn't understand. "You haven't heard? The patients have lice."

He explained that all of the broken limbs had to have their casts removed, no matter what their state of repair. And it had to be done fast before anyone outside the hospital found out, especially the newspaper.

"I came in this morning and it sounded like a party, cussing, giggling." The tiny bugs had slipped around the edges of the casts and wiggled underneath. "You think it drives you nuts to have an itching foot inside a laced shoe. Then imagine those poor devils."

An intern stuck his head in the door. "Barnacles, Mr. Darwin? Write about pigeons. Everyone is interested in pigeons."

"We should be so fortunate to have a hospital covered with barnacles," Dr. Bivens replied. "Inside joke, Ella. Charles Darwin chose barnacles . . ."

"They need you upstairs in a hurry," the intern interrupted. Dr. Bivens paid for his coffee and left.

I found that the pigeons who cooed on the outside ledges and spattered the marble steps were the culprits, setting loose the lice who marched like a miniature army from the window sills into the hospital rooms.

Next the supervisor came in, Mrs. Floyd, an expensively dressed middle-aged woman whose office was beside the lobby. She ordered an untoasted egg salad on wheat to go, impatiently tapping her heel while I spread it. She told one of the older doctors who hovered over a cup of tea in the corner, "I can't believe what they've done. Those poor birds. Just because they're a little noisy and make a spot or two on a car is no call to shoot them. I can't believe one of our people would be responsible for that. It's enough to make you nauseated, birds bloody and dead all over the steps. Just disgusting."

As her high heels clicked away, an older doctor turned to Red, who was in charge of maintenance. "She's really on top of things, eh Red? How about stopping what you're doing and get somebody to get that mess up out front."

Red nodded and the doctor left. Red turned back to the man helping him work on the light switch. "How in the hell could I shoot them? Just blow their goddamn guts out all over the side of the hospital, windows, patients be damned? Sure. Stupid old bitch . . ."

A shhhh and a mumble.

"Well, Christ, they asked me to get rid of them. What'd they think I was gonna do, say boo, catch them in a sack and take them to the pound? Yeah, I poisoned the fuckers." Red added, "Nigger birds. Rats with fucking feathers. Feathers don't make 'em a bird. Plastering up my windshield. You see how it feels, like all over you, you high-toned old bitch, itching where you can't reach. Them busted boners could all end up on the nut ward."

I heard the clatter of Alvin's wooden handles behind me in the

249

kitchen. Mumble. A colored female voice: Roberta. She walked to the door and yelled at Red, "Well, I ain't washing *that* up, I tell you! Ain't my doing and ain't my job."

I wondered if she heard "nigger birds."

"Look, Roberta, tell old lady Floyd the reason for the blood is that the sons of bitches *fell* about fifty yards, *after* they died, OK? They never felt no pain. Dead birds fall head first. If they're dead, they don't set down on their little footsies like they're flying in for a landing."

"You want Mrs. Floyd told something, you tell her." The door swung shut. I had never heard Roberta talk that way to a white person.

"I know about birds," Red went on. "I've shot a few birds out of the sky and the sons of bitches come down head first like a kamikaze, *splat!*" He turned and looked around. No one else was there but me and his helper. Red looked at me as if I were invisible. "Like to give that old bitch a few lice up her ass. She'd send me out to blow apart every pigeon, here to Georgia, *oooeeee!*" He laughed and they walked out.

After he left, one of the nuns walked in for a cup of black coffee. I wondered if Red would have talked that way with her there. The nuns didn't have to pay for their food. Little Sisters of the Lakes. Their names were like romantic novels, Angela Faith, Maria Camilla, but when they moved through the corridor, I thought of witches and brooms, blackbirds. They were old movies, black and white, from another time.

Maria Camilla had left Katherine Hinshaw in the lobby, her wheelchair in a pool of sunlight. Katherine, whose neck had looked as though she swallowed an egg whole and it got stuck, now had a strange scar. I pictured somebody taking a hammer and trying to beat an egg, no, a porcelain doorknob into her throat and all it left was a dent like a giant bellybutton.

When the nuns pushed the patients down the halls, shoving their chairs over the doorsills, their treatment was rough as the skin on their faces that flaked and hung like peelings. I looked at their faces puffed out of their black and white shells like blisters and wanted to take lotion and rub them until they were slick, take scissors and snip the tufts of hair away from their chins. Men must see them and think all women would look like that if they didn't use cosmetics, their eyebrows thick and heavy. I thought Maria Camilla looked like an ugly man.

One day I had asked her, "Do you work for nothing, Sister?"

Her expression didn't change, "We work for the Lord."

That wasn't the answer I wanted, as sure as rows of sardines in a

250

can. She talked softly as though she was telling me a secret, every word as cautious as talking in church.

"I mean, do they pay you?"

"Not as regular people are paid. But of course money is not necessary for me since all my needs are taken care of."

It was nice to hear Sister Maria Camilla talk so much and say "me."

"Not even spending money, if you want a Coke or something outside the hospital?"

Then she smiled at me as if I were a child. One of the lady patients told me a nice thing about being around the nuns; they made you feel young after your sickness had made you feel old.

"We get five dollars a week," she whispered.

"What about college? Did you get to go to nursing school for nothing?"

"Yes, dear. But remember, I have given all the fruits of my labor to the church."

I figured that would be a way to go to college, become a nun. But I wasn't even Catholic. I had asked Daddy, "Daddy, what do you know about nuns?"

He was starting to get senile because his head would bob and his lips would move long before he could make any noise. Then he couldn't control the volume of his voice. I figured the cigarettes and alcohol had burned out his vocal cords.

"They don't never get none!" he blurted.

While Maria Camilla sipped her coffee, I looked over the top of her head. Suddenly I gasped and she sat her coffee down with a clunk.

"Dear, what is the matter?"

I looked around the room. No one else was there so I had to tell the nun.

"Sister, I just saw a naked behind go out the revolving door."

That evening after the orderlies brought Katherine Hinshaw back and strapped her in her bed, one of the nurses' aides put makeup on her and held a mirror in front of her face: "Don't Mrs. Hinshaw look pretty?" the girl said.

"Don't she look like a goddamn old fool," Mrs. Hinshaw replied.

"Are you Catholic, Mrs. Hinshaw?" I asked when I picked up her dinner tray.

"Baptist," she answered and crossed her pillow, pulling at the strap around her bed.

My Grandma Higgins, who was Baptist, would figure she had

reserved a place in hell for using the Lord's name in vain. Mrs. Hinshaw put the side of her face against the pillow and white circles of light through the Venetian blinds danced on her face.

"Then why do you cross your pillow?"

"So I'll wake up live tomorrow," she cackled. Another bunch of tiny white ghosts poured across her face as a car went by outside. Her eyes were closed.

Katherine had had no visitors since she checked in. She called the nurses different names: Eunice, Bertha, Nancy. I figured those were the names of her children that she thought were coming to visit her. Yesterday she called me Wilma and I said my name was Ella. Before she had gotten on regular food, she had taken down all the plastic bags and bottles that were hooked to her from their racks and put them into a large plastic purse. That must have been part of her escape plan before she was unhooked. Then during the confusion over the pigeons, she walked out the front door with her puckered butt shining out the back of her split hospital gown.

Elisa Simpson, recovering from her mastectomy, saw Katherine go so she left too, but she left fully clothed and undetected.

I talked to Mrs. Simpson after she came back to the hospital on her own. The orderlies had tied her into a bed beside Mrs. Hinshaw's.

"Albert brought me my button-up nightgown that looks like a regular dress so I wouldn't have to wear the scratchy hospital gown. Actually I wanted it so I could make my escape. I followed old lady Hinshaw out the door. You caught her, but I walked right on out," she said proudly.

Albert came to visit at dinnertime. He left the children in the lobby. The day before when he brought them up, she chewed him out because the little boy had on mismatched clothes.

"Really, Albert, a plaid shirt *and* plaid pants."

"What's wrong with that? They're both plaids," Albert defended. Tonight he still had on his blue work clothes and his hands were dirty. "Elisa, honey, please stay put. I can't stand to see you strapped down like this. Try to stay in bed even when you feel a little out of your head."

"I'm not out of my head, Albert. I'm in my head." She became incoherent as soon as she started talking to him. "All of me was right there in my left breast and now it's gone. If you were a real man, you'd have stopped him."

"Who, honey?"

"Horace Sanders," she said in a hateful voice.

"Horace Sanders is the man of my dreams." That was Katherine Hinshaw, awake now.

252

"I hope you can come home real soon, honey," Albert said.

"Elisa Simpson is at home with her family where she's supposed to be. You ought to know she's at home with you, never missed feeding you three hot meals a day since you got married. She's in bed with you every night."

"Nobody is in bed with me at night," he said sadly. Poor Albert was not equipped to handle a sick Elisa.

"*She's* in bed with you at night."

I looked and Elisa was pointing at me. My hands went cold. Albert dropped his face in his hands and started crying. Elisa turned to me as if she had never accused me of sleeping with her husband and said, "He's so silly. He's such a big baby. You didn't cry when you shot three little birds, Albert," she scolded.

He looked at me, confused. I didn't know what to tell him. She walked through the dead pigeons on the steps maybe.

"Then don't cry now," she snapped.

Mrs. Hinshaw beckoned me over to her bed. I figured she might split my skull with her bedpan for stopping her escape, but she appeared to have forgotten about that. Maybe she blamed it on the nun.

"Where's that handsome devil, Horace Sanders?"

"He should be in tomorrow morning."

"I'd like to get my hair done," she cackled, "I have a feeling he's going to propose marriage."

"He's quite a catch," I said.

Her lip curled as Sister Maria Camilla walked by.

"Sister Maria Camilla," she whispered. "walks like she's got a broomstick up her ass."

I laughed and bent over her bed. "Did you hear about the lice getting in?"

"Yeah, hey yeah?" she said like someone eager for the rest of a joke.

"Maybe a few of them got under the old bird's feathers," I told her.

Mrs. Hinshaw began to whoop with laughter. She hung to my arm like a child when I tried to leave. I thought of Nancy when I swung her in a circle, "Do it again, do it again."

"You know why a nun is called a nun?" Mrs. Hinshaw asked me.

I said no.

"They don't get none."

"Daddy, did you ever know a woman named Katherine Barber Hinshaw?"

253

He wrinkled his forehead a minute and then his eyes brightened. I recognized the look; it was the one he got when a dirty joke was on the tip of his tongue.

"Kat Hinshaw? Is she still alive?"

"Very much. She came in to have a goiter removed."

"Kat Hinshaw could burn off a sailor's ears," he chuckled. "Worked at the Rebel until right recently. Gertrude Schmidthelm, you remember her?"

"She would be hard to forget."

"Gertrude was so jealous of me and Kat carrying on she said she'd wring my neck if I ever downed another drop at the Rebel."

"How would you like to make a little visit tomorrow night?"

He grunted and shook his head, wiggling back in his chair.

"Let me rephrase that. You take those clothes off tonight before I burn them while you're still wearing them and you take a bath. You're going to visit an old friend tomorrow."

I ran his tub water and shoved him into the bathroom.

"It's too goddamn hot."

"You know which spigot the cold water comes out of."

After I shut the door, I heard the water running, but I stayed at the door until I also heard the water start splashing.

"If you're just reaching over the edge splashing that water with your hand, I'm coming in there and throwing your ass in."

"I'm in, I'm in." I heard the squeak as his foot hit the bottom for the first time.

"And use soap."

After he went to bed, I scrubbed the ring out of the tub and picked his clothes up from the bathroom floor. As usual, burning seemed to make more sense than washing. I put them in the washer and started the cycle. Then I washed my hands in scouring powder to get rid of the smell.

The next evening I left Daddy in front of the TV in the patients' lounge until visiting hours, then I led him into the ward.

"Got me up right in the middle of *Cheyenne*."

"They'll rerun it this summer. This is more important."

I led him to Kat Hinshaw's bed. She recognized him immediately.

"Maynard Higgins. You old son of a bitch," she shouted. "You oughta be in this bed. You look a sight worse than me."

"You move your ass over a little, Kat, and I'll get right in there with you."

She laughed so loud all the other patients and visitors looked at them.

"Daddy, keep it down, OK? Sit down here and visit with Kat."

254

I moved a chair behind him, and when he felt it jab the backs of his legs, he sat down, trustingly. I stopped at the door and looked at the two of them talking. Kat threw back her head and laughed, then cupped her hand over the side of her mouth. Daddy began to bounce at her answer. Kat might curl a sailor's ears, but my daddy's ears, sticking out like tree mushrooms, loved every word of it.

The Family Reunion

My audience is starting to arrive. There are my parents going to the front row. They have reserved seats. Mama has on her navy blue suit that has the shiny iron marks on the back. I see a little flour on her sleeve, but I'm not going to be picky tonight. I'm proud that she came.

She made Daddy come. I didn't. He has on his funeral suit. I'm not sure how I feel about her forcing him to come. One side of me says, If he isn't going to enjoy my play, then I don't want him to feel forced to watch it. But my other side says, I've put up with enough from him over the years, it won't hurt him to do one little thing for me. Funny all those years I hid my journal, afraid he would read it, and tonight I want him to hear every word.

I'm not afraid anymore. Elisa Ruth and Katella don't always do and say what I want them to, but my feelings are safe inside them. I do have to ask myself, wouldn't my feelings be safer if I said nothing at all? But I can't help it. I could no more seal these two women in my memory than I can pass by the snake that swallowed Mama's doorknob.

I don't think I can explain to Mama that I write things to make sense of them. Words on paper came too hard to her. That's the way things come to me. They go into words so I can deal with them. And then I feel better. But I know it's more than that. I know it's something I want to share.

You wouldn't remember, Mama, actually had no way of knowing, but I couldn't share. I didn't want you to be the one who comforted Daddy when Maudie hurt him and I didn't want Matthew to share the past with you at Christmas. I guess it comes as a surprise to find out how selfish your daughter really was.

I may not have to worry about Daddy's reaction to my play because I think he's already asleep. There's Grandma Higgins beside him to jab him in the ribs every time he snores, just like she does at church. I don't have to guess what her reaction will be. Just one word—sassy, Ella Ruth, sassy. I have to be honest with you, Grandma Higgins; if I think a dirty joke is funny, I laugh.

So Mitzi Wade brought Al Sawyer. Or maybe it was the other

way around. At least that keeps him from staging a drag race in the parking lot during my play. I know what his comment about my play will be too: I don't know how to act around smart girls. Like Daddy would say, trying to give Al Sawyer a little culture is like sprinkling Evening in Paris behind the ears of a billy goat.

There's Matthew and Karen and Becka and Arnold. Becka and Karen's faces are as blank as the back of the program. Tonight, when Matthew was talking to one of his clients who had come to the play, I heard something for the first time in my life. I heard Matthew tell someone that Ella Ruth Higgins was his sister. He'll probably change his tune after he sees it.

There's Gretchen. I think that's Carl with her; he looks so much older. I guess she had two reasons for coming. She used to know me and it is the social event of the season in Summit. I'm a little glad Dr. Sanders was on call at the hospital tonight. He expects me to be a scientist. I'd like to slip out and wave at Patsy and all the girls from the Youth Fellowship, but I suppose that would look tacky.

Poor Mama. I can't keep my eyes off her. She is smiling as though she is looking through the gates of heaven when the curtain isn't even open yet. This probably makes her happier than the time my picture was in the newspaper for finding the polka-dot dog. Finally I've found a way to bring the whole family together for her. I know this isn't exactly what she had in mind for me, but I wonder if she can understand. Any girl can have a baby, Mama. I have all the things inside me to make one and they probably would work if I used them. I might have a smart child or a pretty child or an idiot like Grandma Higgins did. But I have to make my life into something it wasn't going to be naturally. It's important for me to fool people. When I pull the curtain, and they see Katella and Elisa Ruth, not a person in the audience will think they're not real.

Curtain

The stage is bare except for two hospital beds. In one is an old woman, Katella. In the other, an attractive middle-aged woman, Elisa Ruth. Both women are strapped in their beds.

KATELLA: This silly freckle-faced nurse who comes to do my hair pokes a mirror in my face like I should be thrilled to death with what I see. She hasn't the slightest idea how I wear my hair. Horace Sanders won't look twice at that. Puts circles on my cheeks so I won't look sick. Look like I'm ready for Ringling Bros. Katella Higgins Hinshaw never painted her nails that tacky hot pink either. Fuzzy as Mitzi Wade's angora sweater where I got my cotton on them before they were dry. Mitzi Wade. I declare she's so fat now

256

she couldn't hang those rubber titties on the ends of her real ones. Don't times change?

"Don't Mrs. Hinshaw look pretty?" that birdbrain nurse said.

Don't she look like a goddamn old fool? Like an old whore making one last try to drum up some business, my thing stretched out and flopping like the top of Grandpa's socks. Ain't I something? Filthy-minded as a sailor on leave and I act like I'm shocked to death if a nurse says "damn" out loud, make her feel guilty as homemade sin.

I asked that high-toned nun, Maria Camilla, I said, "Do they pay you a salary for putting up with me? Can a nun have a pet? Say you want a monkey," and I get a lecture on working for the Lord and earthly possessions. At my age, she gives me a lecture. I closed my eyes and let my head tip over. She patted me on my hand. Old people get good at pretending. Act like you're asleep and people say what they really think about you.

When Maria Camilla talks, I swear her breath is as rotten as a stump and I can see her teeth leaning in her mouth like tombstones. Nuns don't get braces. I wonder if they get dentures. She would never get away with that breath blasting in a man's face, woman to man. That gold band marries her to an invisible pecker. What good times is there in that? I wonder if she has seen a pecker. She has a furry thing underneath there like the rest of us. 'Cept mine has gotten near 'bout as slick as Maynard Higgins's head. I'll put on being crazy and ask her if she shaves her head and her beaver. She's got two boobies too. If she didn't, she'd be a monk.

ELISA RUTH: It isn't kind of you to talk about having two breasts when you know I don't have but one. You get to die all at once. I'm going one piece at a time.

KATELLA: You're going to hear a lot of talk about two boobies, dearie, the rest of your days, so get accustomed to it. Besides, I'm just a senile old biddie. We always say tasteless things and get away with it. So they've got you strapped down like a lunatic too?

ELISA RUTH: They caught you, leaving with your hospital gown on. I had better sense than that. I didn't even have to come back. I just wanted to. This hospital is in a bad part of town. There was blood all over the steps. I watched my feet, step on a crack, break my mother's back, down the basement stairs, the slits between buildings, they lurked there, their flat heads like snakes, picking the one to strike. I came back because I don't belong there—I live in the new development in Trotter Ridge—coloreds live out there. At Christmas I carried an old lady a basket from the church. I waited while she unbolted her door. I didn't carry my purse out there

257

today, but it wasn't because I was afraid. They took it away to put in the hospital safe. When I got tired, I would want to drop it anyway. I sweated and I wanted to throw away my clothes, leaving a trail like I used to down to the pond when I was a little girl. The thick bandage around my chest that should hold me straight bent me over like an old woman.

KATELLA: Now you're throwing off on an old woman. Nowadays when I walk I carry my body and it used to be that my body carried me.

ELISA RUTH: I walked slowly around the corner where the Good Humor man got stabbed and fell on top his coin holder. The murderer tried to turn his heavy body over to get his money, tugging at him like a crow at a possum stuck to the highway. Children came from everywhere, plucking his truck clean. It was like a dream, Christmas morning, sugarplum fairies and ice cream for all. The ice cream melted before they could eat it all and the Good Humor man melted red on the pavement like a strawberry-filled sundae.

As they watched me from alleys and doorways, I talked to myself. They were scared of me because they thought I was crazy. "You can't kill me. I'm already dead," I snapped, and they ran deeper into their hiding places like scared mice.

KATELLA: You talk big, but I believe you were the scared one out there. You wouldn't know what in the world to do without Albert to look after you. Otherwise, why did you come back?

ELISA RUTH: I hate this place. I want to go home. Yesterday Maria Camilla rolled my chair through the nuns' section. She banged me over the doorsill and my sore chest hit my bandages, but she didn't care. How can a nun understand? There's nobody who cares about me here. In the chapel were old nuns in wheelchairs, saying their rosaries. They didn't smile at me when we entered. Not even Sister Maria Camilla. In the lounge was a nun Sister Camilla told me once made beautiful lace. Her fingers moved in her lap, making imaginary lace, but her sad face told me she knew nothing was at her fingertips but air. I saw a German nun, and in her hands were playing cards. She was playing Solitaire, cheating someone and having great pleasure doing it. Sister Camilla did seem to be ashamed. She said, "She has been in her own world for a long time." There was no peace as they waited for their deaths. Those old women were unsure they had lived their lives the right way. They were going to die and would die alone except for other old nuns who were waiting too. Once I saw a woman drop dead on the sidewalk. But she had a purse with her kinfolks in it. A nun doesn't have a purse. A nun doesn't make anyone and those who made her are long gone. Except the Lord, they say. Your Lord lets you die slowly like every-

258

one else, shriveling until your black robes look like suits on a scarecrow. No family. No kin people to stand around their beds and wait for the end to come.

KATELLA: You tell me not to talk about two boobies and there you go talking about being an old buzzard and having no family. Pot calling the kettle black. Not one visitor this week except that sotty old sonavabitch, Maynard Higgins, who ain't got no friends hisself. I tell you a secret about that German nun. She don't work for the Lord. She is playing cards with the Devil. She's beating him because she is cheating. No ladies of the church here. No, just like me. Nasty old women waiting to die.

I got a set pattern. Old people get like that. I believe it is the year 2020. I wake up at the same time every day. As soon as I have my coffee, it's time to sit on the toilet. The same amount goes in and out of me every day. I don't like to change my pattern. When my daughter, Nancy, asked me to stay with them, her children woke me up too soon. I didn't like that coffee she used and I got bound up. I get sleepy at ten o'clock every night and their TV is blaring away. I want to be here, in my house. You see, if I don't change my pattern, then there won't be a time in the day set aside for my heart to use up its last beat, no strange staircase to break my hip that is too soft to heal, no time for the blood to rush to my brain and clot and black out my sight. My eye is like the hole in a label, telling you the jar is full. But jars empty out. Never mind, never mind. I won't die because there is no time in my busy day set aside for dying.

People phone and stop by, but I declare I never hear them and I bet they go off saying poor old lady Katella Hinshaw, deaf as a post. I could hear them, if I wanted to. There are days I hold the phone like Granny Higgins used to, and can't make a word come from my dry throat. "Hello, hello, hello," and they hang up. Used to keep a house full of pets, but they all died or run off. All them little deaths. You get an animal and the day you bring it home, might as well tell yourself, there's a death you'll have to endure, or put it off on somebody else. I remember Mrs. Simon's old dog that bit everybody. Gummed them; his teeth were gone. She died and nobody wanted the sorry thing, so her son got Alvin, my first husband, to shoot it. Granny Higgins used to say all them dying pets and flowers got you used to taking it in small doses. Maybe I'll end up like Granny Higgins. Now that I'm old, I'm not so hard on her. She lost her husband to a wasp and her idiot child to a bad cold. The world didn't deal her a fair hand.

If it was just me and my dog left and I died first, wonder if he would starve by my body like in the movies? Hell no, he would pull my carcass apart and eat it, sorry that his owner didn't have more meat on her bones. Not a thing has ever cared enough about me to starve on my grave.

When I was just a young thing, in the flower of my youth, I got gangbanged. My second husband, Alfred, God rest him, stood right there and watched them. I never forgave him. I think he thought he was noble not to participate. Standing there in his nobility with his pecker about to pop his zipper, telling himself she loves it, she's just screaming and scratching and fighting so we won't call her a whore. He turned around and beat off, he told me that in those very words, watching his spew spatter my horse's hay. When the cat smelled the hay with her mouth locked open, I thought it was what ran out of me.

I told him I was a baby chick in a room full of cats. Alfred said they did what come naturally because I was not a little yellow biddie a'tall. I was a cat. It was spring and they figured I was in heat, all the toms in my neighborhood.

Me and Alvin had a tomcat, Snowball, but he was young and afraid of the big, wild toms from the woods.

"Bullshit, you'll get him castrated," Alvin tells me.

I tell him the vet told me that housecats never get any anyway, that he was miserable for no good reason.

Alvin says, "You let him decide how miserable he is and leave his balls alone."

I took him right down to the vet and told him, "Make it look like he still has balls." Alvin never knew. Snowball still watched the females in heat, his pupils big as pennies. The dumb fuck just didn't know why.

ELISA RUTH: I hate to see a female cat humiliating herself, squatting and backing up so the tom can get in easier. I remember a cat. She was crying like she was dying. I thought when I had my period and cramps, I would like to walk like that, come up to every person under my roof and howl in their faces. The boys lined up at the window and pointed and laughed at her. When she turned her back to the toms, I told myself it was so she didn't have to look at them, didn't have to see the scars on their faces in patches where hair didn't grow.

KATELLA: Now ain't that what a woman would like to think? Animals don't notice a pretty face. I'll admit you don't see a cardinal nesting with a blue jay or a goldfish fucking a guppy. Did you know guppies are fucked for life? Long after my male guppy went to the great fishbowl in the sky, my female floated around like a submarine, squirting out babies coiled up like worms. Unless they hid from her in the rocks, she ate them up.

ELISA RUTH: Animals do remember faces. Canada geese mate for life. And if a goose mate dies, they grow old and die alone, even if the sky is full of geese.

KATELLA: Honey, it ain't their faces. How long you seen a cat stay interested in sniffing a face? I won't sell them geese short, though. I heard they won't fuck their brothers and sisters. People stoop to that, for sure. When they planted Alvin, I gotta admit I started checking out the ganders in the sky. Alfred, I regret, wasn't the pick of the gaggle.

ELISA RUTH: Albert says men are like honeybees. They were meant to go from flower to flower to flower.

KATELLA: Tell your precious Albert that tiger beetles smell like roses. They eat a lot of bees.

ELISA RUTH: But orchids smell sweet like female bees and male bees fall in love with them. A hundred million years ago, wasps ate each other. Then they decided to become bees when flowers to love came to the earth.

KATELLA: Don't you forget, dearie, flowers or no flowers, everything changed when men arrived.

ELISA RUTH: Men. I looked at those men laughing at that cat. I hated the sparkle that came on Albert when he heard a dirty story. Why couldn't he sparkle like that at something good so I could love him for it? If I told the dirty story instead of one of his friends, he would act shocked at me, like I got no right to it. They mocked the cat's noise, calling back at her in her voice and she cried louder as though their sounds were raking an open wound. I wished she had pretended not to hear the sons of bitches. She rolled on the ground, flipping like she was having fits. Albert said she was afraid she wasn't going to get any.

I didn't do like the cat. I never asked for it.

KATELLA: Now what difference does it make? They beat you to take something away or they take it sweetly. Don't it go just the same? I woke up from my sick bed and said, "Daddy, where is my duck?" and he said, "Nigger ate it a week ago." You don't keep nothing in this world. Your smooth skin, your pretty hair. I didn't say nothing about a boobie, so shut up.

I caught my second husband, Alfred, and his friends watching this movie on the wall over my couch. Alvin and I did it a time or two on that couch. I stood at the door and said if one of you fellers had a pecker like that, maybe a woman would go to that much trouble. The man in the movie was as phony as those wrestlers acting hurt. When he came, the camera was on her hand and he foamed like beer running over a glass. Then we saw his eyes rattling in their sockets. Maybe it was a beer or something fake. All my years at the Rebel, I oughta know a beer when I see one.

261

All their dirty talk of cunts and getting in a girl's bloomers, then they get you between the sheets and you're supposed to believe they think it is as pretty as little pink petals. Might as well be honest and go crashing in like the swinging doors to the bar saying, "Gimme, fast, I'm horny as a four-peckered goat."

That day in the barn when I was in the flower of my girlhood, when one got wore out, another took the pump handle. There was a pump in Granny's yard with a rusty handle that squeaked up and down, until it belched out water and rust and lumps of mud. I had to empty my bucket, but by the time the water was clear, Alvin would be done and fall out and I would trip like missing one last step in the dark. Making ice cream that didn't make it. Alvin wasn't worth a cunt full of cold water.

ELISA RUTH: You aren't making a lick of sense.

KATELLA: I seen dogs locked up once, the boy dog with a lump in his pecker like a golf ball in a sock. The pack waiting their turn ripped open the back of his neck while he tried to yank it out. Oh, me, I was hurting for her. Mama ran them off with a hose, knocking the dogs over with a blast of water, spreading pink blood over the grass. If my mama had known, she'd have taken her hose and run them goddamn boys off me.

ELISA RUTH: I saw two dogs hooked too, the female was tired and ready to wait for her pups, getting a longer stay with their daddy when she wanted. When he finally came out, they slept like two creatures who didn't know each other. I thought they might be dying. The female got up and walked away, leaving bloody spots behind her, looking forward to six warm pups, wet and slick, pushing into her belly. She would die to protect those pups with the daddy long gone.

KATELLA: On TV I saw these two insects, praying mantises. They were hooked together and rubbing like two sticks. Did you know insects did it like people? Then all of a sudden, she chomped his head off, then his shoulders, his top legs, and still the bottom half of his body pumped away. I got so tickled. I said that was one of the funniest things I ever saw. Alvin said he didn't think it was one bit funny.

ELISA RUTH: The cat in heat turned her vagina toward me and I could see it blinking like an eye.

KATELLA: Don't think you got it hard, dearie. A bedbug's got a spike on his pecker and he pokes a hole in the female's back and the sperm swim around in her blood to her ovaries. Well, I told you how I lost mine. Ain't you gonna tell me how you lost yours?

ELISA RUTH: I don't want to talk about it. It's not something I can ever laugh about. How can you be so insensitive?

KATELLA: Elephants can hear the footsteps of a mouse.

ELISA RUTH: You're a crazy old woman. I'd as soon be in jail as strapped down in a bed next to you.

KATELLA: It's hard for you young ones to take it. Love me true. I will love you forever. I will love you forever until tomorrow. I understand the young ones, though. That happens when you live a long time. At my age I've seen a lot of dying. I've lost my husbands, two of my children, a grandchild in a car wreck, plus the ones to be expected before me: my mama and then Daddy, at a ripe old age. I'll tell you a secret. I had a young lover. Reason I'm telling is he's dead now too. Nobody left to give a damn. At my age you don't feel the jolt so hard even when it comes unexpected. The hardest are the children. A woman's greatest pain is to outlive her children. My little girl, Nancy. She did the cutest thing once. She stood by the railroad tracks and when the passenger train came by she yelled, "I'm going to be great. You hear me? I'm going to be great!" They didn't hear her and she couldn't hear herself for the noise. But I heard her. I wish she would come see her old mama.

We go a complete circle in this life. Come out a little baby, messing in our britches, got to be toted from place to place, fed by another's hand. Leave us by ourselves and we'd die like an uprooted plant. My mama's mama tugged her in a cardboard box, a string tied to her leg, dragging her down the rows while she picked tobacco. When she cried, she stopped and nursed her, sitting in the shade of the fat plants. My mama, good as she was, clean forgot about me one day. See, I was a late-in-life child. She was shopping and left me on a shelf and walked right out and had to get Mr. McKenny to open up the store so she could go back and get me. Lord, she suffered over that. My mama was a woman with simple ways. Her and her mama before her figured with their last breaths they was counted on for a pan of biscuits. That was a damn sight simpler than it is for me. Mama could heal things without doctors, everything but herself. Having babies is supposed to make the bad things OK.

But Lord, old folks is just like babies. We know we should use the toilet; we just wait for the urge, forgetting it takes us longer to get there than it used to. We fall and we know good and well how to get up; we just can't make our old bodies do it. That's a day I'm dreading. Ought to chop my head off like a hen that's quit laying and put me on the table for Sunday dinner while I've still got enough meat on my bones to pick.

I get cravings for things, creamed yellow corn in a can or Vienna sausages. I walk down to Parson's and come home and eat as much as I thought I wanted in my mind. That craving I got for canned creamed corn took care of my wanting that for good. I could go to my grave satisfied if I never ate creamed yellow corn again. That mama of mine, good woman, through and through, mind you, but she had one big fault. She tried to eat her problems away and ate herself into a bigger one.

My basement shelves are full up. I took after her worriment over going hungry. Just don't have her appetite. Need to date them, eat the oldest first. There might come a season so bad a summer gets wasted, but I got enough right now to live through two such summers. All my saving. Nothing passes in my house don't get studied to be saved. I take my daughter Nancy's coffee grounds and spread them in tin pans in the sun. Every envelope I get, I open and flatten. I write notes around the plastic window on the phone bill envelope. I got a bucket of rubber bands come off the newspaper, like red and blue worms. I save the papers too, of course, but it's my civic duty to give them to the Jaycees every year for their paper drive. Crawling with silverfish. Jars and cans and paper oatmeal boxes. Egg cartons. Used to save them for Elsie Parsons to sell her home-raised eggs in but she's dead now and they'll arrest you for reusing a carton. Wasteful world. Lord, when they go to my house to haul me out that last time, they'll have to send three wagons to cart off my worthless collecting to the dump. I take after my daddy there, God rest his soul. If he had one.

ELISA RUTH: My husband, Albert, caught me doing the silliest thing. One day I had this thought: If I die over this breast thing, Albert won't know which eggs in the icebox are boiled and which are regular. So I marked a B on the boiled ones with an ink pen. "B for what?" he asked when he went in for a beer. "Busted, broken?" "Boiled, stupid," I answered.

KATELLA: I used to put Xs on the boiled ones. Then I fixed that lazy sonavabitch second husband of mine and put an X on a fresh one. I can still see Alfred with the slime on his fingers and the yoke on top his shoe.

ELISA RUTH: They make fun of you, say anybody in the world can keep house and the day I left to come in the hospital, Albert tells me, "Some of your canning's missing, honey. Arnold got up on the shelf and busted about ten jars. Made a hell of a mess," he tells me. "I didn't know how spoiled rotten he was until you left. I'll put some locks on your new cabinets I'm making to keep him out. I heated up one jar of snaps and they tasted like they was made of rubber. Me and the kids squeaked like three little mice eating them, honey. Nancy looked at me and said just as serious, 'I think you musta forgot to do something to these, Daddy,' " he tells me.

KATELLA: My living child, Nancy—my youngest, Arnold, got

killed in the China war—she accuses me of not eating proper, but that's not so. I eat when I want to. She says I go hungry because I'm too tight to buy food. I eat. I just get littler and littler. Thinner than a fart skin. I read where old people quit making cells and they shrink. I used to stand five-foot-six and, though for my age I hold myself pretty straight in the shoulders, the mark I make now on my kitchen door comes out a sight under five foot. Lost the ruler, but I look to be eight inches shy. Gone from a tall woman to a short. I felt my body quit making cells. Just stopped. I'll get too short to reach the doorknob and they'll come in looking and squash me like a bug: "Wonder where old lady Hinshaw's gone?" Like that movie The Fly; when the man's head was on the fly, a little voice said, "Help me. Help me." Did you hear something, Joe? Nope, he'll say, and scrape me off his foot on the door stoop like a dog turd.

ELISA RUTH: Lord, you're lucky. I wish my cells would quit growing.

KATELLA: Lucky? Lucky to be twice your age?

ELISA RUTH: Lucky that you're so old it doesn't matter if you have a woman's body or a man's body because you don't use it.

KATELLA: If I didn't want to use it, honey, I'd of been a nun.

ELISA RUTH: It's so easy for them. They act like it's such a hard thing, taking vows. They are denying the hardest thing of all. I didn't deny it. I was a woman. Now part of it is gone. My cells are eating me up from inside. If my cells are growing, why don't I get so big I burst out of the house? Big. Little. What does it matter? I won't grow old. Like that movie, I'll step into a spacecraft and fly away and time will stop for me while the others grow old.

KATELLA: You know what I think, dearie? The truth is you're scared that Albert will go out looking now.

ELISA RUTH: Mitzi, Albert's pretty young girlfriend he thinks I'm not wise to, she'll wish she didn't squint so much back when she was young. And eat all those candy bars. She'll get to thirty-seven and see my picture in that album, leaning on Albert's car in my pink wool suit and say Mrs. Sawyer was a real good-looking woman. How old was she when that picture was taken? Thirty-five, Albert would say.

KATELLA: Rats double in number every hundred years, but it only takes a human thirty-five.

ELISA RUTH: Two years before she died, he tells her. That cancer was in her tit then, about pea-sized. Look how flat her stomach was. And this one at Myrtle Beach. How many women her age could wear a bikini? Her legs were tight as a girl's. Elisa Ruth hated to see women get lump-legged, mashed-potato thighs, she called them.

She said there was no excuse for not forming back up after the babies. She was a fine figure of a woman, till the day she died before her time.

KATELLA: Ain't you got a better subject?

ELISA RUTH: Fat Mitzi. You'll learn how easy it was to take him away when you had youth on your side. How do you feel now, waddling around in your marvelous molder figure holder? People always say she'd be the prettiest thing if she wasn't fat as a hog. You know, dear, fat women always seem to have pretty faces.

But Lord, he'll get old too. After I'm long gone, him and her together will get to that age when he'll stay home because he's too old to do anything else. And a young girl won't do a thing for him without pay. My picture won't be out on the table anymore, the one of me that Mama had made when I graduated that she framed in a golden circle. But it'll be somewhere, maybe in Nancy's things. Take it out and look at it, fat Mitzi. Elisa Ruth Sawyer never got fat and old. Albert acts like it doesn't matter, that he'll love me just the same with one of my woman parts gone. The only person in the world who'd love me the same would be my mama.

He says to me, "Honey, show your operation to me later. I don't want all these women around, you know what I mean? I mean it's kind of embarrassing, like you're pulling out your tit in public and you're my wife. All these women don't have to see it. You'll never see them again."

"I don't have a breast to pull out, Albert. Why can't you understand? Why don't you admit you're ashamed of me now? I'm not one of those nuns who keeps everything they got covered. I'm a woman and if I didn't have breasts, I wouldn't be dying."

I am like the people in the war news. I get up and put on my clothes. My red polyester dress. Brush my teeth. Eat my egg and today it will be sausage. Tomorrow it was to be bacon. Tonight something will break my routine. When I close my eyes to go into my dreams, suddenly the screen will go black. The bulb in the projector burns out. The reel stops turning. Only difference is the people in the news didn't know it was coming.

"You're not dying, Elisa Ruth. Your dead part is gone. You're safe now. Dr. Sanders is sure of it."

Safe. Dr. Sanders made me safe, all right. What does a man know about that?

KATELLA: Dr. Horace Sanders knows. And you'd be a wise woman to listen.

ELISA RUTH: And what did he do for you? Cut a cancer out of your neck and told you it was a doorknob and you believed him?

KATELLA: You've got to believe in something. I believe in that silver-haired man in the black suit. I don't care to hear anything bad about him, that he cheats his taxes, that he beats his drunk wife, that his children hate him. I don't want to hear it. And I won't.

ELISA RUTH: That's because he took something you didn't want. Look at me.

KATELLA: I don't hear you.

ELISA RUTH; I'll be glad to get away from you. At least I have someplace to go.

"Mommy?"

Which one said that, girl or boy? I couldn't tell.

They're at the door. Nancy and Arnold. Albert dressed them up. Arnold has on his everyday socks with his Sunday suit. Men just don't know any better.

"This is my husband, Albert. Albert, this is Katella Hinshaw."

"You have a handsome family," Katella says.

"Honestly, you say that because you just don't have any idea of how much trouble they can be."

Albert did bring me the right dress to wear home, my red polyester. It was the only red dress in the closet.

"Can I give you a lift home, Mrs. Hinshaw?" Albert asks.

"No, son. Thanks anyway. I'm waiting for Horace. God bless him. He's the one thing in the world I can count on."

Curtain

After the many nights of putting my play together, I feel tired. But it's a different kind of tired than usual. Not like after work at the hospital or when I was done painting the house. Or even like the old days when I rode Maudie so long I felt short when I got off and as if my legs would buckle under me. I just feel like I'm done thinking about those two women. There are new women in their beds at the hospital. Right now, no matter where they might be or what might happen, I know what Katella and Elisa Ruth would do or say. I've put things together that were in a thousand pieces. I have made something that won't go away, something as real as Mama's bed quilts. I just had to find the pattern.

Tonight I went all the way to the bottom of my story box and I found a bunch of old stories about an Indian named Starrie who was cripple. They were in pencil and most of them weren't finished. One was about Starrie's mother dying. I can't believe I wrote that. But I did.

Ella Ruth Higgins thought she was pretty big stuff in those days, that it was up to her to tell future mankind what the world had been like. She wasn't smart enough to know she didn't count. Ella Darwin saw that, when all is said and done, nothing will be left but pigeons, rats, coyotes, every insect that ever crawled on the earth, and my daddy.

I can go in and out of my worlds now much easier, walk on the different levels, those I make up and those I find in my memory. When I leave my quiet house and go to the hospital, I go easily, not thinking of the change. Mama couldn't stand for things to change. When we went to town, she never tried to adjust, only looked to the day we'd go back home. An animal can change. Not just the fittest. If a dog loses a leg, it learns to walk on three. It doesn't lie down and mope over its lost leg. Only people have to endure the sadness of remembering the way it used to be. I fell down, shot by Al Sawyer. He took my leg from under me. Yet the sharpest fears last only a few seconds.

When I think of Al Sawyer scaring me the night Daddy was hurt, I get mad. But only at Al now, not as a little boy. As a little boy, he was like the time I fell on my pencil. It hurt when it stuck in my hand, but I don't feel the pain again when I see the black spot healed under my skin. Mama said, "It'll get well before you get married." Thinking of Al scaring me that night in his car is like knocking off a scab too soon. I wonder if the day will come when I can see the world through a man's eyes.

Going to work this morning, I had a funny memory. Grandma Higgins once said to Mama: "Honestly, it's hard to raise a boy. It was a happy day for me when you took him over," she added, meaning Daddy.

Then Daddy pointed at me and teased: "Little Audrey, as mad as hell, pushed her sister in the well, said her mother drawing water, 'Damn, it's hard to raise a daughter.' "

Grandma Higgins had a look on her face, as if she doubted whether she had raised him yet. But she made a mistake with all her religion. The Bible tells us to put away childish things, she says. That's not right. You shouldn't cut the child in you off like a leg and learn to walk without it. No matter what I never get, I always had Mama and always was a little girl. There's not much pleasure left for Daddy but being a child.

On the way down the walk, I picked up a jay feather. I took it with me and held it in my left hand as I drove to work. All the precise areas of color; every one of its feathers is like that. Every bird. Every part is so carefully made. Yet they are so predictable. Each new jaybird is just like the last one. This morning after I threw out the scrap bread to the mockingbirds and jays, their quarreling filled our house.

268

Daddy called from his bed, "Damn it, Ella Ruth. Why can't you put the butt-end-skis in the trash?"

Butt-end-ski. He knew what they were fussing over. When Grandma Higgins got down to the heels of a loaf of bread, she'd say: "Nothing left but an old butt-end-ski to make a sandwich." That word came to Daddy from her. When he was a little boy, she made him butt-end-ski sandwiches, butter and jam. There were no pictures of him then, during the years he burned off his warts with a magnifying glass, making those holes in his arm like a pancake ready to be turned, and when he painted his neighbor's dog green. All in all, it seems I've been stuck with a lot more of his raising than Grandma Higgins.

"The birds are hungry too," I told him.

"You sound just like your mama."

"Daddy, don't you want to eat your breakfast hot? Sure would taste a lot better."

"I'll get it. I'll get it in a minute."

My voice and the voices of the birds screamed through the house. Then his snoring started again before I got out the door. I stopped for a second and listened to Daddy's sound as steady as the ticking of a clock, like Oscar Roscoe, asleep in Baby Ruth's belly, listening to Mama's Baby Ben.

When I passed the hospital kitchen, I smelled something. I had to stop because it was one of Mama's smells. Lemon. Lemon was sour, but Mama could make it so sweet my teeth hurt. I have her recipe for lemon chess pie, but not one for making kites. She never thought to write that down. The last kite she made rattled up high, caught in the chinaberry tree until winter washed and blew it away. I've never tried to make one without her. She gave me a lemon pie for a reward after I stole her money.

I saw Alvin, going out the back door with the food the patients wasted.

Maybe it made Daddy feel good to throw away the heel of the loaf, because he could now and they couldn't then. We don't have to boil bones and save drippings. Dirt poor was what his family was. I'm like my mama who never wasted a scrap. Not if there was some living thing somewhere could eat it. Carrot tops and peels for the rabbits, meat scraps on newspaper by the trash can for the stray dogs, her flopped angel-food cake for the birds.

"That thing's so darn heavy, I don't see how they fly over the house. I ought to shoot myself for the sugar and flour I wasted."

The starlings tore into her angel-food flop, tugging war over a large scrap. We laughed together at that. We cried, me and Mama,

269

when we read about a twelve-year-old boy who hanged himself. He left a note: "I killed myself on account of me shooting a red bird." He must have aimed and meant to miss. Mrs. Albright's tomatoes died on the pavement, one by one, like red birds who couldn't fly. And all I did was watch because I was safe in my mama's lap.

Mama hid a part of her pain from me. There were things we never laughed or cried about. Ruth, dead so soon after they pressed her tiny foot in the concrete. I don't know how Mama stood to keep it from me. I'll never find all her secrets. I kept things from Mama; what the boys did to me that day in the barn, how I stole her money for Gretchen. I should never have told her I wanted to give away my eyes. "Mama, what's the difference? I give away clothes I've outgrown. We feed stale food to the birds and squirrels. Shouldn't feed my eyes to the worms if some blind person could use them to see."

"Ella Ruth, what an awful thing to think about!" she exclaimed. "You most certainly will not do that and I don't care if Miss North Carolina did do it. She just did it to get attention. Them cutting up your pretty skin and taking out your eyes. What if they found out you weren't dead? What if you need your eyes to see heaven?"

Poor Mama, her body went away before her heart finished its count and left nothing fit to hand-me-down to anybody.

Today I found a tiny fear that stuck in my memory like a splinter. I can pull it out, but it hurts like it's still there. I walked out of the house just as the sun went behind a cloud and the world suddenly went dark. Spot had been running between the trees, his black and white hide the wrong colors to camouflage him in the green and brown woods. I thought I was going blind because I had just been hit by a branch across my eyes. I had put things together wrong. When I found I was fooled and could still see, blindness seemed realer than sight. I will think of the day in the woods on Maudie the next time the sun does that. But I'll forget the darkness today, walking out of the house.

I don't fear the dark. I always liked to close my eyes and feel Mama's kites tug on the string like something alive that I couldn't see, a mouse flying a tiny airplane. I can see my no-eyed Pandy, trying to look at me and Saint Nick with her scared look.

I am a blind woman going down my walk, listening to the mockingbirds and jays start up at dawn and screaming into the morning. They make sounds so ugly it is hard to call them songbirds.

You used to say how pretty the jay was, Mama, till it opened its mouth. But you said it wasn't right you couldn't tell the boy from the girl. Remember when the mockingbirds had eggs, how they'd fly down and pull your hair while you hung out the wash? They fussed at me all the way down the walk after I was the one nice enough to feed them. But I don't even hear the fussing at me at home now, Mama. You ought to be here to see it. I'm the one in charge. I take that ornery old man of yours and order him around, and he either minds me or does without.

Before I started my first chore of the day, cleaning the toilets on the ladies' ward, I put the jay feather in my notebook. Its pattern was prettier than any piece of cloth. When I was a little girl, I saw a huge Luna moth stuck on the screen, pale green with swallowtails on its wings trimmed with feathers as fine as hairs. There was a hole on each wing I could see through, encircled with rainbow colors. And pink rosebuds like decals on a teacup. I imagined a miniature dancing girl, rosebuds and feathers and green silk. Up close it was the most perfect living thing I'd ever seen.

I looked at it by myself until I could stand it no longer. I had to show someone. I showed it to Al Sawyer.

"Wow, can I have it?" he asked. I didn't answer because it wasn't mine to give. He ran to get alcohol to preserve it.

While he was gone, I watched the moth's delicate movements, its feelers rubbing its head. I tried to scare it away, poking at it gently with a straw, afraid to jab hard; but it kept on rubbing its head, basking in the porch light. I couldn't touch it with my fingers that surely should have been strong enough to pry loose an insect. I thought, What if I pressed my fingers around its wing and I tore that soft tissuelike green? It stuck to the screen as if it were sealed over something it didn't want me to see.

I turned and saw I was being watched, a face as round and lumpy in the porch light as the full moon above the pines.

"Ella Ruth," Mama said gently, "all you have to do is cut off the light." She clicked the switch. "That's a moon moth."

As soon as there was darkness, I watched the moon moth's soft shape lift away. I felt a moment of terrible sadness that it was gone, flapping silently into the night. When Al got back, he was so mad he broke his alcohol bottle on a tree. I had to clean up the glass. I wonder if he remembers. The moth would be long dead. Maybe he would still have it if I'd let him kill it.

The moth sat there with both of us thinking about what was to become of it. It was long in the making but could be destroyed so easily. It was like a child with nothing in its head to tell of its danger. But if I hadn't been free then, there would be nothing inside for me to reach for. If I was covered with a hard beetle shell, nothing either good or bad could have gone through. I think I have made me a new shell. Nature didn't give it to me. I have to fold it back a little at a time. When I'm as sure as I can be that I'm safe.

271

I'm more complicated than that moth. No one would look at me and my daddy and wonder which was the female. I have no pretty marks like the blue, black and white of the jaybird feather. No pink rosebuds and transparent spots with colored circles. On the back of my hands are spots. Liver spots, freckles, plain brown spots. But if I could catch a jaybird, I could hold in my hand the whole creature that pumps out its big noise from the gutter. I see and hear him up there and can catch and feel him as his wings swell under my grip and his claws dig into my skin.

Mama could make things so simple. In the darkness the moon moth fluttered away, up high where it was safe. Mama knew it would do that. Daddy is at home, snoring in his bed, but Mama goes with me.

"Ella Ruth, all you have to do is cut off the light."